TORN 2:

PASSION, PAIN & PROMISE

Will Melissa's Pain Gain Her Anything?

Ella Johnson

Order this book online at www.trafford.com
or email orders@trafford.com

Most Trafford titles are also available at major online book retailers.

Print information available on the last page.

ISBN: 978-1-4907-6151-0 (sc)
ISBN: 978-1-4907-6153-4 (hc)
ISBN: 978-1-4907-6152-7 (e)

Library of Congress Control Number: 2015910221

Trafford rev. 02/17/2021

Trafford
PUBLISHING®   www.trafford.com
North America & international
toll-free: 844-688-6899 (USA & Canada)
fax: 812 355 4082

This Book is Dedicated

To my children and grandchildren - *Chenaya, Jonathan, Devion, Stefani, Brianna, Justice, Isaiah, Sarah'ya, and Josiah.* My will to live is because of each of you. You are my greatest inspirations for all that I do. What I admire the most about you are that it never really mattered how bad things were during those bad times, you never stopped believing in me. When most people had walked away, you stood up for me, which always gave me the strength to go on another day. For the rest of your lives, I want you to never give up, never give in, and never give out. You can do all things through Christ who strengthens you.

To my mother Cora Johnson – Without your sacrifices, I wouldn't be here. Watching you sacrifice your life for your family inspires me to be a better mother. I watched you go to work day after day to make sure that all of our needs were met and what really inspires me is that I don't ever remember hearing you complain about having to make those sacrifices. I am eternally grateful for you. Thank you for being the woman I needed to see so that I can be the best woman that I need to be.

To Michael Hale, the man I love - After 30 years, most things pass away, but who would have thought that after all of this time we would look into each other's eyes and feel something real? I dedicate this book to you because you walked into my life when I was deep in the belly of hell and you kept me from focusing on the fire. You held my hand through it, you made me laugh through it and you walked out of it with me. What we share is special. Thank you for believing in me, supporting me, and loving me. You are truly the love of my life. Let's see where the rest of our life takes us.

To my sisters, brothers, nieces, nephews, cousins, aunts, uncles, and special friends – Thank you for your love and support.

*E*lla's bestselling work, The Torn Series, is a collection of books about the life of Melissa Williams. Throughout the series, you'll feel as if you're walking right alongside Melissa through her life's journey. You'll need to buckle up because the Torn Series takes you on an emotional roller coaster ride. Not only will you cry through her struggles, but you'll also celebrate in her triumphs. Throughout the Torn Series, you'll see Melissa make some good and not-so-good decisions in her life. Despite all that the hardship she's experienced, it seems as if Melissa is constantly caught in the middle of one crisis after the next.

Torn 2: Passion, Pain & Promise is Ella's recollection of events that take place years after Melissa and Kalin's day in court. Over the years, Patrick has struggled with his feelings for Melissa, but after all this time, something surprisingly happens that forces him to turn up the heat in Miami. Melissa's faith continues to be tested to the extent that she has to make some critical decisions that could possibly end in destruction for her and her entire family. Although some of the children are away from home and seemingly doing well, Sharelle, Amber, Princess, and Justice are still at home, but will they be able to adjust to the new changes?

In Torn 2: Passion, Pain & Promise, you'll be scratching your head until you find out who sends Melissa over the edge. Will she recover this time? Unfortunately, there may not ever be a next time. Across town, Stevie returns to Miami for his first time sold-out comedy event, but what was meant to be an enjoyable event turns out to be a nightmare when Melissa's darkest secret is revealed. What is it that sends him back to California with a broken heart?

It's always been said that where there's no pain, there's no gain, but does Melissa's pain gain her anything?

CONTENTS

Melissa Remembers It All
Torn 2: Passion, Pain & Promise.

CHAPTER 1

"Our Day in Court"

"*I* want to remind all of the spectators that there are to be no outburst after the verdict is read. Will both the prosecution and defense please stand?" he instructs.

"I don't know what I feel at this moment. I always knew that I felt like the State of Florida should pay for all of the hurt that was caused to us, but this is the final moment. Whatever happens, I am very proud of Stuart. Look at him. He was once a man on crack and now he is standing in this very courtroom standing toe to toe in a lawsuit against the State of Florida. He is excited to have such a big case. He knows that after this win, he will be able to open up his own firm, and perhaps, give Johnny Cochran a run for his money. And who knows, maybe Amy will leave Johnny and follow Stuart.

After all of the celebrating, we finally leave the courtroom. I look to Heaven and say, "It is finished. Thank you Jesus!"

"In the case #2007-CFS3587441, Kalin A. Thomas versus the State of Florida, we find that the State of Florida is guilty of malicious intent to cause harm to Mr. Thomas. As a result of this guilty verdict, we find that Mr.Thomas should be awarded punitive damages of $3 million", he says, before being interrupted by the Judge.

"Order in the court! Order in the court!"

Did I just hear $3 million dollars? Oh God, did I just hear $3 million dollars? Tears begin to flow down my face uncontrollably. I finally lose it! I can no longer hide what has been in my heart for these last 8 years. Each of my children rushes up to me and kiss me. Christy walks up to Kalin and gives him a big hug and says, "Congratulations, daddy!" This is the moment I have dreamt of for so many years and it is finally here! Seeing her grow into a beautiful young woman throughout this entire process and making her very own mark in this world is all I ever wanted. "Honey, we did it! We did it! All the crying, all the waiting, all the stress, all the late nights of sitting in that jail without seeing my wife and children - it is all worth it right now! The sufferings of this present time are not worthy to be compared to the glory that we shall receive! In Jesus name!"

Kalin raises his arms to heaven and gives God praise right there. I am crying. Stuart is crying. Amy is crying. The people who know us best are crying with us. Cynthia knows more than anyone what this whole ordeal did to me. She never gave up on me. She never stopped believing in me. I am glad that she took the time off to be here, but she is family to me. She is my sister and my dearest friend.

"Melissa, it's over, sweetheart! It's finally over! We talked about this day and look at you. Cry, baby! Get it all out! It is over!" Everyone is congratulating us, when all of a sudden, my cell phone vibrates. The phone reads, "New Text Message". Before clicking on "View", I get this feeling in my stomach that this is Patrick. Even though we have had no communication over the last 5 years, I feel that he is with me. Snap out of it, Melissa! He is not here. This is probably from someone else. As curious as I am about who this text message is from, I don't want to alarm Kalin, especially if this is Patrick. Kalin is distracted with talking with Stuart and I decide to click on "View" to see who it is that is sending me a text message.

> *"Melissa, I love you. For me, the kiss was not innocent. From the moment I first laid eyes upon you, I have wanted nothing more than to kiss you. I have tried to forget about you. But I can't. And now, I want you. I don't want to live without you. And if you give me this opportunity to love you, you will grow to love me, too. Congratulations on your win. Love, Patrick."*

I can't believe this! He must be here! How will he know the verdict if he's not in the courtroom? I look around to see if I can find him, but I don't see him anywhere. I can't believe this!

"Melissa, are you okay?" Kalin asks. He can tell that something is wrong. "Did you get a call?"

"Everything is fine." *What an awkward position to be in right now.* I'm here with my husband celebrating our victory, and mind you, a victory that everyone said would never happen because, according to them, nobody can win against the State. My three older children are doing well in their careers and the four left at home are doing well and are all college bound. My son is playing in the Super Bowl this weekend. Everything is going just great in my life. After all these years, I finally think about Wendy, who was also in the courtroom today, without her husband. Was she here for *Kalin*? Are they seeing each other? I can't seem to forget what Kayla said to me before she died. It seems like, perhaps, Kalin has some type of connection with Wendy. Why else would she be here? To think about it, she never really says anything to me. I'm a little confused right now, but I really need to stay focused. I know that it's because of this text from Patrick. As happy and excited as I am about this win, I have to admit that I'm glad that Patrick is here. I miss him and I, too, can't stop thinking about that night we kissed. After all of the celebrating, we finally leave the courtroom. I look to Heaven and say, "It is finished. Thank you Jesus."

Once we make it through the courtroom doors, I look up and right into Patrick's beautiful eyes that have always made me weak. He's standing there and crying, with his cell phone in his hand. Kalin sees this connection and looks at me and I look back at him. We both look at Patrick. Patrick looks into my eyes and senses my confusion. Neither of us can say a word. The way I feel right at this moment makes me wonder if maybe I feel something a little stronger for him. God knows I didn't mean for it to happen. Because he is the gentleman that he is, he says, "Chao for now!" He winks at me and walks away.....

CHAPTER 2

"I Just Want to Know."

"What's wrong with the car? Why won't it start?" I ask Kalin, while he's under the hood of my car. "I have to get to work. What am I going to do if you're not able to fix it?"

"I don't know. I'm not quite sure how to make this piece stay on", he says, holding a part that's dangling from the car.

"I'm going to have to find another way to get downtown. I can't miss this appointment. I just can't."

"Well, why don't you call Cynthia? Maybe she can give you a ride", Kalin suggests.

"I already tried that. She has to take her grandson to his first doctor's appointment today. Don't worry about me. I'm sure I'll get a ride. I know who I can call", I say, walking back into the house.

Dialing my *friend's* number when I'm in trouble has become too easy. The truth is that I'm actually tired of having to call him to bail me out just because my husband isn't providing as a husband should. Unbeknownst to Kalin, my friends have been doing it for a few months now already. Kalin thinks we're getting by because of these so called "bonuses" that I receive from work. At least my Photoshop skills didn't all go to waste.

"What did you come up with?" Kalin asks. He notices that I'm getting my things out of the car.

"Cynthia called in a rental car for me. I told her that I'd pay her back when we get paid."

"It's funny how you and Cynthia work at the same place, but it seems that she always has money, but you don't", Kalin complains.

"Please don't start with me today. I'm doing the best that I can. It's not my fault that your company went out of business. It is not my fault that the Lawsuit didn't come through like we thought. Our lives have been turned upside down and all we have are each other", I say, starting to get frustrated and annoyed with this conversation.

"I'm sorry, honey. I didn't mean to snap at you. It's just that with things the way they are, I'm just a little stressed", he explains. *Why is he so stressed? I'm the one getting up every day to go to work, while my husband stays at home, complaining that nobody wants to give him a break.*

"Me and the kids are right here going through it also. So, I understand."

Within 30 minutes or so, Enterprise is pulling into my driveway to pick me up. Ever since I saw their commercial about how they'll pick you up when you rent their car, I haven't used anyone else. It isn't until this very moment that I realize how easy it is for me to leave home without kissing Kalin goodbye. I remember a time when I would never do that.

"Excuse me, Mrs. Thomas. You trying to leave here without giving me some love?" he asks. With only two steps away from him, I reach over and kiss my husband goodbye.

As we are driving away, he waves one final time, drops the hood on the car and heads back into the house. "So, is your car still giving you trouble?" the Enterprise driver asks after turning onto the next street.

"Yeah. I think it's time to just get another car, but, unfortunately, we can't afford it right now. So, until I can, I'll just have to keep renting yours." We both laugh.

In what seems like just a few minutes, we finally arrive at Enterprise and the paperwork is at the front desk awaiting my signature. After getting the vehicle of my choice, I'm finally driving off in a Ford Escape and on my way downtown to my pre-scheduled appointment. Christy must be calling. My cell phone is beeping at me. It's always a rule that they call me after a long trip just to let me know they have arrived. Before I call her back, I also notice that Kalin called a few minutes ago, but he didn't leave a message. Something could be wrong, so I have to call him back. I dial our home number.

"Hello, baby", Kalin says when he picks up the phone.

"Is everything okay?" I ask right away.

"Yes, Mrs. Thomas. Everything is okay. Is there something wrong with me calling my beautiful wife just to tell her how much I love her and miss her?"

"I guess there isn't. Kalin, you scared me half to death calling me like this. Are you sure everything is okay? Did the girls all get off to school okay?"

"Yes, they did. Justice almost forgot her book report", he says, jokingly.

"Now you know I'm not surprised about that at all", I tell him.

Our conversation goes on and on until I make it to the parking garage of the building downtown. I'm surprised that Kalin hasn't asked me about my appointment. I'm sure he assumes that it has something to do with my job. He'd be somewhat surprised if he knew that my appointment is actually with a divorce attorney. I'm not sure if a divorce is what I want or if counseling will be just what Kalin and I need, but, things have to change between us. For almost two years now, he hasn't had a job and I'm struggling to pay all the bills. When the Judge announced his overturning of the court judgment due to new evidence, we were both dumbfounded and things haven't been the same since that day. I admit that getting that lawsuit would have put our family in a more solid financial status, but life must go on.

Making my way through the 10 ft. solid glass doors suddenly sends chills up my spine. I begin to have flashbacks of my life with Kalin. My thoughts run quickly to the first time that our eyes met, the first time we kissed, the first time we made love and the births of our two children together. My life with Kalin has not been all bad. But then, I also start to remember what his ex-wife, Kayla, said to me on her death bed about his connection with Wendy. The most hurtful thing, that Kalin doesn't even know that I know, is the fact that Wendy was actually pregnant with his child, until she aborted the baby. This child was conceived during my marriage to my husband. I don't think that counseling can help me deal with that betrayal. Only God can. I believe the only reason I never questioned him about this betrayal is because of my secret one-night kiss to Patrick and the guilt I felt for having feelings for him.

"Good morning, Mrs. Thomas", the receptionist says, as I approach the reception area.

"Good morning, Lisa. How are you this morning?" I say to her while signing my name.

"I'm wonderful. That's such a beautiful dress you're wearing today", she compliments me.

"Thank you so much. My girls bought this dress for my birthday", I say, walking to the seating area.

"I'll let Mr. Abney know that you're here. So, have a seat and he'll be with you shortly."

"Thanks."

I hope that this divorce attorney is just as good as Stuart says that he is. All I know is that he despises adultery in the marriage and usually goes after everything on those grounds. I wonder if he will call what I did adultery. I mean I didn't sleep with Patrick, but I have definitely spent many nights wishing I had. Should I tell Mr. Abney the truth about that?

"Mrs. Thomas, the attorney is ready for you", she announces, pointing in the direction of the hallway that leads to his office. From the looks of this building, it appears that this Firm is quite successful. All I know about this guy is that he knows his way around the courtroom. Stuart speaks highly of him. I've made it to his office door and he invites me in. I'm sure that his wife took part in putting the decor together. When I walk in, Mr. Abney stands to greet me and invites me to sit in the chair across from his desk.

"Good morning, Mrs. Thomas. How are you this morning?" he asks.

"Doing just fine and good morning to you. How are you this morning?"

"I'm blessed. Thanks for asking. So, let's get down to business, shall we? What brings you here today?"

"I'm here because I need to get more information about how divorces work and just to see what my options are if I decide to go down that road", I explain.

"Sure. Divorces can range from being simple and quick to disorganized and messy. It depends on where the two of you are with the decision. If he does not want to be divorced from you, he could fight you all the way for everything that you have both acquired during the marriage, including the children that you have together. If you share property together, he *is* entitled to half. I tell all of my clients and potential clients that you have to be willing to walk away from everything if you're ready to walk", he says.

"I see. Honestly, I'm not quite so sure if I'm ready to walk away from a 15-year marriage with this man. But, he has really hurt me and the hammer that nailed the coffin was the day I found out that he got his best friend's wife pregnant. She aborted the baby, but he slept with her and he hasn't been truthful with me about their relationship", I say.

"Oh, wow. That's a lot to deal with. I'm not here to make the decisions for you. I'm not a counselor and my position is to simply give you the information and guide you in your decisions. It sounds like you still have quite a bit of thinking to do", he responds.

"Is it possible for him to gain full custody of our children?" I ask.

"Yes. It's possible", he responds. "Anything's possible. Has he been in their lives since birth?"

"Yes", I tell him.

"Has he supported them?" he asks.

"Yes."

"Ok. So, there you are. He could be as good a parent as you are to the children."

"What about the fact that he had an affair with another woman? Can I use this against him to gain benefit in this divorce?" I ask, trying to gain more knowledge about divorces.

"It's certainly frowned upon with any Judge. Why don't you think about this? Pray about it. If you still love your husband, talk to him about your concerns and how you feel about where the both of you are. Don't be afraid to let him know that you feel as if your marriage is in trouble. Do you think you can do that?" he asks me.

"Yes. I know I can. I appreciate you for taking time to explain things to me more clearly", I say, as I stand up to leave his office.

I'm not sure how I feel about my conversation with Mr. Abney. Still thinking about all that he just said, I'm not sure if I can even talk to Kalin about what I'm feeling as it relates to our marriage. He's already under a lot of pressure to find employment and to do it with have a criminal history. I just feel bad for him and I can't hurt him with this or at least not now.

CHAPTER 3

"The Prince that Turns into a Frog."

"*A*nother one came today", Cynthia tells me after walking into the office.

"Wow! This is like the 10th letter that has come here, right?" I ask, looking at the envelope Cynthia just handed me. Since we received full custody through the courts in Alabama and after Brittney's betrayal was revealed, she has sent letter after letter of apology for what she did to me and my family. Although I have forgiven her for what she did, I refuse to speak with her or to see her.

"That girl just doesn't quit, does she?" Cynthia asks.

"I guess not. Anything else come?" I ask.

"I've been holding onto a piece of mail that came in here yesterday. The truth is that I've been trying to decide whether I want you to have it or not", Cynthia tells me.

"Really? What piece of mail?"

"Here it is. It's not mine. It's yours. I can't keep this from you." She reaches inside her top drawer and hands me an envelope and as bright as day, I see his name across the front of the envelope, "From Patrick". Now I see why she withheld me from this. Cynthia is the one person who knows about my kiss with Patrick and how I truly feel about him. She's been a true friend about it and hasn't tried to steer me one way or the other.

"A letter from Patrick? This is odd. *Why would he send me a letter here on the job when he could have easily picked up the phone and called me?*"

"Well, aren't you going to open it?" Cynthia asks.

"I don't know if I should or not. You know I'm weak for him. It's almost as if I'm under a spell or something. I'm not sure if I want to know what's in this letter. What do you think?"

"MeMe, open the letter. It's not going to kill you to at least know what the man has to say", she tells me.

I open up the letter as if it's a piece of fine china that I don't want to break. As soon as I open the envelope, I realize that it's a greeting card, titled "The First Time I Met You". I begin to read the card and can't seem to tear myself away from the words. It's obvious that I'm starting to melt. I feel so special that he remembered again that this is the day that we met years ago.

"What is it? What does it say, Melissa?" she asks.

Tears begin to form in the corners of my eyes. Patrick is so thoughtful and knows just the right buttons to push to make me want to run into his arms. But, I owe it to my husband to give our marriage a try. We've been together for 15 years and I believe in the institution of marriage and Patrick will have to understand that we can only be friends right now. I hate to admit it, but I'm enjoying watching Patrick try to win my heart.

"It's a card from Patrick. Once again, he remembered that today is the day that we first met years ago."

"How thoughtful, Melissa", Cynthia comments.

"Yeah, I know. He's very thoughtful. He knows just the right things to say and when to say it", I say, as I put the card in my drawer.

"So, how did your appointment go this morning?" Cynthia asks.

"It was fine. I just wanted to speak with the attorney and gain some knowledge about divorces and how it all works and to simply explore my options", I respond.

"Well, if you're trying to make the marriage work, why would you even agree to speak with an attorney?" she asks me.

"Knowledge is power. I just wanted some information."

"Do you love him, MeMe? Do you still want to be his wife? Do you still want to be a wife? Are you falling for Patrick or what's really going on?" Cynthia asks.

"Yes, I do still love my husband. But things need to change. I'm tired of being the sole provider for the family. It's just as much his responsibility as it is mine when it comes to taking care of the children. I didn't mind it at first because I felt like I was being a supportive wife, but he's taking this too far. He sits at home every day, using up all the electricity. I have to put gas in his car. It's bad enough that I had to buy the car for him, but I have to pay for the upkeep also. I love him and I know that he wants to do better, but that's just not enough for me. I need him to figure it out", I say, starting to cry.

"Melissa, things will get better. Just pray to God about your marriage. God can fix anything. Talk to Kalin and tell him how you feel. Seek counseling if you really want to fix the marriage. I know you love your husband and I ...", she says before I interrupt her.

"Yeah, but does he love me? Does he love me enough to take care of me and our family? Did he love me when he had sex with Wendy and got her pregnant?" I say, starting to get angry.

"What!!!!! Wendy got pregnant for Kalin? You never told me about this."

"I didn't tell you because I couldn't talk about it. I was so embarrassed about it", I admit. "Remember on the day of the trial when we had brought out the videotape and how Ms. Rita revealed her betrayal?"

"Yes I remember. I won't ever forget that day", she says.

"Before court began, the State Attorney summoned me to his office to speak with me. I had no idea what that could be about, considering the fact that I was a witness for the Defense. When I got to his office, he showed me a videotape of Wendy visiting Kalin in Jail", I begin to explain.

"What? She visited him in Jail? Oh my goodness! Why? Why would she visit him there?" Cynthia asks, shocked at Kalin's behavior.

"She went there to tell him that she was pregnant with his child. I guess she thought that by getting pregnant for him, it would make him drop me and run to her or something. He didn't give her the response she wanted, so she aborted the baby."

"Oh my God! Are you serious? How in the world could Kalin have let this happen?"

"I don't know the answer to that. He gambled at our marriage, our friendship, and everything. He doesn't know that I know about it. After all this time, I never told him that I knew about this", I confess.

"So, you've been holding onto this all this time? Are you going to speak to him about this?" Cynthia asks, with a very concerned look on her face.

"I believe so. Just not sure when", I tell her.

"I'm here for you, MeMe. Just know that, okay?" she says.

"I don't know what I would do without you", I say, giving Cynthia a big hug.

"Perish, that's what!" We both laugh.

The phone rings. Cynthia answers it and I can hear her say, "let me see if she's in, please hold". She calls out to me, "MeMe, it's Brittney. She says that it's urgent that she speaks with you. Do you want to speak with her?"

"Put her through. Let me get this out of the way once and for all", I say. I pick up the call. "Brittney, what's wrong?" I say to her, almost sounding annoyed.

"Thanks for taking my call, Melissa. I'm so ashamed of what I did to you. You and I have been friends for so many years and I can't believe that I allowed money to get the best of me. I just want….", she says before I interrupt her.

"What do you want? What is so urgent that you need to speak with me?" I ask her.

"I simply want to ask for your forgiveness. I'm not doing well right now. I'm sick and I need to know that you forgive me. I hurt you and I can't blame you for hating me, but I need you to forgive me. So, I am asking. Will you? Do you?"

I don't know what to say. I'm completely blank for words. She's practically begging me to forgive her. What would Jesus expect of me right now? What would I want someone to do for me if the shoe were on the other foot and I needed forgiveness? How hard can this really be?

"Melissa, are you there?" Brittney calls out when she doesn't hear an immediate response.

"I'm here, Brittney. I'm here. I forgive you. I know that you didn't mean to hurt me. We've been friends for so many years", I tell her. "I understand how tempting money can be. I love you and I forgive you, B."

Brittney begins to cry and so do I. We sit on the phone and cry for several minutes. Forgiveness can be so therapeutic because at this very moment, it feels as though a weight has been lifted. So, this is what it feels like to let go and let God.

"So, how have things been with you? You mentioned that you're not feeling well. What's wrong?" I ask.

"I was in a really bad car accident and it caused some serious damage to my lungs. I get treatments, but it's just buying me some time. And I just need to make sure that things are right with everyone before …….. ", she answers.

"Oh no! I'm so sorry to hear that. What about your children? What will happen to them?" I ask.

"I'm not sure. My mother is getting up there and she definitely can't take the children. And of course, I don't have any siblings, so I'm still trying to figure that out", she tells me.

"What about their father? Will he be able to take the children if anything happens to you?" I ask her.

"Afraid that's not possible either. He died last year. His family is not that supportive. But don't worry, my friend, you know I'll figure this out."

"I hope so, B. I really do hope so and I'm so sorry that you're going through this. But, you just gotta hang in there and I know you'll be just fine. Just trust God and He'll work it out for you", I encourage her.

"I appreciate you so much for saying that, MeMe. I really do appreciate it. I hope that we can get together for a family vacation one day. My kids would really like to travel to Miami", she says.

"Of course, we will", I assure her.

Brittney and I go so deep into our conversation that I forget that I'm still at work. After talking with her, it actually feels like things can be okay between me and Brittney. She made a mistake and I truly forgive her.

But what's even more unbelievable to me is that I finally said the truth out loud to someone about Kalin and what's *really* going on. People really think he's this prince charming, but sometimes I think he's the devil. The pain he causes me sometimes feels more like someone who hates me more than someone who loves me. Now that the cat's out the bag, so to speak, I wonder what it sounds like to other people. *Do I look stupid? Am I stupid for staying with a man who got another woman pregnant? Should I walk away from my marriage or should I stick it out?* Deep in thought, there's a knock at my door and Kalin is walking through my office grinning from ear to ear.

"Hi honey, how's my wife?" Kalin asks. He takes the seat right in front of my desk and picks up our family portrait and mumbles, "these were the good ol' days".

"I'm fine. What are you doing here?" I ask, sounding surprised.

"Just wanted to stop by and see you. I was in the neighborhood. Would you like to have lunch with your husband?" he asks.

"I'm really busy, Kalin. I have ….", I begin to say before he interrupts me.

"Yes, you have lots of work that will be here when you return. Please, sweetheart", he says with the puppy dog face. "I need to talk to you about something", he admits.

"Ok. Fine. Let me tell Cynthia I'm going out for lunch", I say, leaving him standing in my office.

Cynthia is in the middle of moving someone in, so I decide to just leave a note on her desk that says, *Going out to lunch with Kalin*. She acknowledges my note with a nod.

Kalin and I leave in his car and head downtown. Kalin has no idea about Patrick's restaurant so there's no way we'll end up there. I have to admit that the more we drive, the more it feels like this is exactly where we are going. Lo and behold, we end up at Patrick's restaurant, *"Enchanted"*. Kalin has no idea that I've already been here and with Patrick on top of that. We finally arrive and it appears that we've missed the busy lunch crowd. *It won't be good if I run into Patrick in this restaurant. My eyes won't lie if I see him.* The service is impeccable. We're greeted by the friendliest hostess. She leads us to our table. It's interesting to see how Patrick has added the jazz band for lunch. What a nice touch!

"Hello, my name is Ethan and I'm your waiter for today and I look forward to serving you. Please let me know what drinks you'd like while you look over the menu", he says, looking from me to Kalin.

"Raspberry sweet tea for me and the same for him", I say, confirming first with Kalin.

"Here are your menus. Look them over and pay special attention to the specialized lunches, arranged by our owner. I'll get your drinks first, but please, look over the menus and I'll be back shortly."

"Thanks, Ethan", I say, as he walks away.

Are my eyes deceiving me? Did he actually label one of his lunches, Ella Enchanted? That is too funny! This man is full of surprises. I'm so glad that Kalin won't get it.

"I don't know what's good. Everything looks so good", Kalin announces.

"Yeah, I know what you mean. I'm going to try the *Ella Enchanted*."

"I think I'll have the same. Isn't this a beautiful restaurant?"

"It's lovely. Melissa, I brought you here today so that we can talk, but the only way this conversation will benefit us both is if you're honest with me", he begins.

"That's not a problem. What is it?"

"I'm just gonna come right out and ask you. Are you happy? Are you happy with me, with us, with this relationship?" he asks.

Without hesitation, I respond, "Happy is *not* how I would describe how I've been feeling these days. Are *you* happy?" I ask him, looking away to keep from crying.

"I'm going to be honest with you, MeMe. I feel that there's a very strong disconnect with us. I can't put my finger on it, but there's something missing in our marriage. I've been....", he says, before I interrupt.

"..absent from our marriage? Yes, the truth has been absent, Kalin. I guess this is the best time for me to ask you why it is that you have a secret email account that your wife doesn't know about? Why do you have naked pictures of another woman in those emails? Yes, you're right! Something *is* definitely missing. I want the truth. Why don't we bring that back into our marriage? I would love to know the answers to these questions. So, why don't we start by bringing the truth into *this* conversation?"

"What are you talking about, Melissa?" he asks, sounding surprised.

"Please don't sit there and act like you don't know what I'm talking about. The email account with Hotmail that's identical to your email address with Yahoo." Kalin looks puzzled and angry all at the same time, which lets me know that I've obviously stepped on his toes. "Yes, I broke into the account and I've been following your conversations with this mystery friend of yours, Diandra. Who is she? Don't lie to me or I'll walk out of this place right now and leave you sitting here by yourself and embarrass both of us! I'm not playing with you right now, Kalin!"

"Melissa, it's nothing. This email account has nothing to do with me. This is an account that was set up for my brother to communicate with this woman. I can't believe you broke into the email account. Are you crazy?"

"Listen. If you think I believe that bull, you have another thing coming. I know that this communication with this woman is yours, Kalin. I've read all of the e-cards she's sent you. I have read all of your responses to her advances. I tracked your cell phone and I know when you've spoken with her. So, please don't insult my intelligence right now. I want the truth!"

"Ok! Ok! I met her when I visited Alabama once. You and I were on rocky times, of which we both acknowledged that I needed to get away. You sent me away, Melissa, and I met this woman and we became friends. I never slept with her if that's what you're thinking. We would....", he begins, before I interrupt.

"You're a piece of work, aren't you? You make me sick right now, Kalin. When we're done with this lunch, I'm leaving here and going back to work, but don't expect me home tonight because I won't be there.

Looking away, I can see that the waiter is walking this way with our food. "I don't want to discuss this anymore", I say, as Kalin turns to see that the waiter is really heading our way.

"But, Melissa, I love you. Please don't do this. I want to make....", he says, as the waiter puts our food on the table.

"Two *Ella Enchanteds*. Please enjoy your meal. Is there anything else that I can get for either of you?"

"No. This is quite lovely, Ethan. Thanks so much", I say, looking away quickly.

Ethan walks away and Kalin and I sit and eat our food in silence. I have to wipe a tear away from my face before it falls on the table and into my plate. Kalin isn't touching his food for staring at me. He tries to say something, but I throw my hand up to indicate that I'm not really concerned with what he has to say. Kalin and I finish our lunch and head to the car. You can hear a pen drop in this car right now. We aren't talking to one another. He tries to break the silence to explain his side of the story.

"MeMe, why are you doing this? Why can't we talk about this like two adults? We have been married for almost 16 years. Is this the best we can do?" he asks, trying to grab my hand.

"Don't say anything to me right now. You make me sick and I really don't want to listen to your bull anymore! I have put up with all of your stuff long enough. I need my space right now. Don't try to stop me. Just let me go right now. You have issues of your own that you need to work out and until you can be totally honest with all of your infidelity, we don't have anything to talk about. I'm going back into my office now. Do not call me. When I'm ready to deal with you, I'll call you", I say, as I step out of the car. Kalin reaches for my arm, but I snatch it away.

"Melissa, I love you and I'll do anything to make our marriage work. I don't want to be without you. Please, don't walk away from me. I need you", he says, as tears begin to fall from his face.

"Kalin, I've loved you from the moment I met you. You have hurt me and I don't know if I can recover from it. I've done nothing but support you since we've been together and I need someone to love me and support me for once."

"So, this is about money? You're upset because you feel as though I can't support you? You are such a bitch, you know that?" he says, as his voice begins to elevate.

"I'm going now because you will not speak to me like that, you jerk!" I get out of the car and head into my office.

"So, how was lunch?" Cynthia says, as I quickly walk past her desk and into my office, shutting the door behind me. Cynthia follows me into my office. I've already begun to cry. "What happened, Melissa, and why are you crying?"

"I can't talk right now. I hate him, Cynthia!"

"Who? Kalin? What happened at lunch? Please talk to me, Melissa. I'm worried about you", she tells me.

"I confronted him about this secret email account that I discovered that he has. But as much as I wanted to be wrong about it, this man admitted to me that this Diandra woman is someone he met in Alabama when he went there to visit his brother. He was so clever to remind me that I pushed him out of the house and that's why he started talking with this woman. I didn't want to hear anything else he had to say."

"Why didn't you hear him out? That's the only way you'll know the truth. It sounds like he was about to tell you the truth. Don't you want to know what really happened?" Cynthia asks.

"Listen, it's obvious that he has a "thing" for the woman. I don't need him to tell me that. I can see that from his emails with her. He's such a jerk! I sit here day after day and work my butt off to support our family and this is how he repays me, by having a secret email affair with another woman? Forget him and the mule he rode in on. I am so over this marriage, Cynthia. I don't want it anymore!" I say, shaking my head.

"Are you sure about that MeMe or are you just hurt right now? I happen to know that you love this man very much. You can fool other people, but you can't fool me. Remember that I'm the woman who watched you stand by this man's side and even after an accusation was leveled against him by your very own child. I've watched you visit him in jail and I was also there to wipe your snotty nose when you didn't have the strength to do it for yourself. So, don't sit there and tell me that you're ready to walk away from this marriage. I'm not buying it!" she says.

"You know what I'm gonna do? I'm leaving here and going to see Patrick. I need to be held right now, Cynthia", I tell her, with a smirk on my face.

"Melissa, don't do it. Don't run to this man because Kalin has hurt you. It's not fair to Patrick, especially if you're going to end up in Kalin's arms at the end of all of this mess. Don't do it for the wrong reasons. You'll regret it, sweetheart", I advise her.

"You're right. I should do it for another reason. I'll just simply do it because I want him to make love to me right now. How about that?" I say, as I wipe the tears away from my face and begin to laugh.

"You know what, girl? You're a mess!" Cynthia says, as she jokingly pats me on the back and walks back to her desk.

CHAPTER 4

"Not Here...Not Now!"

---

*I*t's just past midnight and my cell phone has rung at least twenty times already. Kalin doesn't get it that I'm just not going to answer his call. I don't know why he's ringing my phone off the hook. What he should do now is call Diandra, or better yet, Wendy. I'm sure that either of them would love to talk to him right now.

Why did he have to go and completely mess up our marriage? After all these years, I never thought that Kalin would betray me the way that he has. And he still hasn't come clean with me about Wendy. My husband got another woman pregnant. My husband has a secret email account with another woman. And I really thought I married the most perfect man that existed. I should have known that it was too good to be true.

I finally make it to my hideaway spot and this glass of wine has been staring at me for the last half hour. I need to devour it and move on to the next one. I know I shouldn't be thinking about him, but I wonder what Patrick is doing. I would love to see him right now, but maybe Cynthia is right. I don't want to involve Patrick if I'm not ready to let Kalin go. *Can I still love him after all he has put me through? Maybe I should just go home and work things out with my husband? Who is knocking at my door at this hour? And who knows that I'm here? Did I ever tell anyone about this place?*

I walk slowly to the door and look through the peep hole. Are my eyes deceiving me? It's Patrick! How did he know to find me here? *Cynthia couldn't have told him I was here because she doesn't even know about this place. Now that he's here and I was just saying I wanted to see him, should I answer the door or what?*

"Who is it?" I yell, already knowing who it is.

"It's me, Melissa. It's Patrick. Please open the door. I need to talk to you. Please let me in", he pleads.

"What are you doing here, Patrick?" I ask, with a slurred voice.

"Talked to Cynthia and she was worried about you. She said she didn't know where you had gone, but that you weren't home. Said the children were even worried about you. Are you going to make me stand out here all night or will you answer the door?"

Hesitantly, I twist the lock and within seconds, Patrick is standing before me. He must have rushed right over from work because he still has on his work greens. He's even more handsome than I remember. I hope he doesn't notice me staring at his lips. I can't help it. They look so inviting.

"Melissa, are you okay? Cynthia was worried sick about you, so she called me to see if I had heard from you and I figured you would come here. Did you drink the whole bottle of wine or what?" he asks, as he grabs the empty bottle.

"Why do you care, Doctor? Why are you here? Don't you have a hospital to run or something?" I ask him.

"Melissa, I care about what happens to you. Now, why don't you tell me what this pity party that you are throwing is all about? What happened?" Patrick asks me.

"There you go again, acting like you care or something. You don't love me, so please just leave. Okay?" I say to him.

"I'm not leaving here until you talk to me, Melissa. Tell me what happened", he insists.

"Ok. You wanna know? I'll tell you, good doctor! My sorry behind husband has been cheating on me. He got another woman pregnant, but she aborted the baby. And check this out! Now, he has an email set up for him and his little girlfriend. He admitted to me that this woman was a friend he met when I put him out of the house awhile back. Ain't that something? How can I be so stupid?" I tell him.

"Melissa, nothing *he* did is *your* fault. Stop blaming yourself for *his* poor choices. This is not your fault. You hear me?" he asks. "It just isn't your fault! Stop doing this to yourself and pull it together."

I tear away from Patrick and fall face first into the king size bed. I'm starting to feel sick to my stomach. *Oh no! Am I going to throw up right here and right now? Oh, please, no! Not in front of Patrick! Too late!* Hoping to make it to the restroom before I spill my guts in the bed, I jump up and end up with my head over the porcelain bowl throwing it all back up.

Patrick is right there patting on my back to encourage me to get it all out and telling me that everything is going to be just fine.

Hours later, the phone is ringing and it's the front desk making their wake up call that I pre-scheduled. My head is splitting. Much to my surprise, Patrick never left me. He stayed with me all night. He looks so cute over there curled up on the couch. *What a friend?* The wakeup call wakes him up and he catches me staring at him.

"Are you okay, Melissa?" he asks.

"I have a splitting headache, but other than that, I'm doing just fine. I can't believe you stayed here all night", I tell him, squinting my eyes.

"Why wouldn't I? My friend was in trouble and I couldn't bail out on her. I had to stay here to make sure that you were okay", he explains.

"That was so nice of you, Patrick. I won't ever forget it. I mean it", I tell him.

"Think nothing of it. Well, if you're okay, I need to rush home and get a shower and change clothes and make it to work, as I'm sure you have to do, as well", he says.

"Why rush home? There's a shower here and I can take your work greens downstairs to the laundry facilities. It's the least I can do to thank you for being here for me."

"Are you sure?" he asks.

"Of course, I'm sure. Now, no more talk. Jump in the shower while I take your clothes downstairs to wash. I'll grab you a toothbrush while I'm down there. Ok?" I insist.

"Sounds like you have it all figured out", he tells me.

Patrick turns to go to the bathroom, but throws his clothes outside the door for me to grab them. *Would I be wrong to take a peek inside knowing that he's naked on the other side of this door? I'm curious about what he looks like in the nude? Am I crazy or what? I need to stop thinking this way. He has been a gentleman to me and why can't I show him the same respect?*

He yells from the bathroom, "Melissa, are you still there? Did you leave yet?"

"Walking out the door now", I say, as I make it outside the door and rush downstairs to the laundry facilities.

When I return, I walk in to find Patrick standing in the bathroom with the door open, with the towel wrapped around him. He's standing in front of the mirror and is about to shave.

"Oh, you're back! Great! Hand me my clothes and I'll be out of your hair shortly", he tells me.

"Here you go, doctor. Fresh, clean, and ready to go!" I say, handing over his clothes.

Patrick grabs the clothes out of my hands, but right before he turns around to walk away, our eyes meet and immediately, my body tingles. This is something new for me and Patrick. *Could it be that I am just craving a man to hold me right now? Would I feel this same tingle if Patrick were someone else? How can I be sure that Patrick has the effect on me or would I feel this if he were just anybody?*

"Melissa, you okay? Seems like you have something on your mind", he comments.

"No, I'm fine. Just thinking about work", I tell him.

"I see. *Work?* That's understandable." Patrick walks back into the bathroom, but the door is slightly open. I almost feel as though he did it on purpose. Whatever the reason, I have to take advantage and get a look at him. The towel drops and I can only see him from behind. I can feel myself getting so turned on by standing here watching him get dressed. Patrick slides on his briefs and his greens and quickly heads towards the bathroom door to step outside.

"So, looks like I'm off to work now. Are you okay now? Do you feel better?" he asks.

"Yes, Patrick. I do feel better. Thanks for everything. I really appreciate you for being here. It means a lot", I tell him.

"That's what friends are for, right?" he asks as he grabs my face in his hand and kisses me on the cheek like he would kiss his little sister.

"Yeah."

Without telling him how I really feel about him, he leaves the condo and is already half way to his car by now. *What a gentleman! He never tried anything funny with me. Most men would have taken advantage of my being drunk. But Patrick didn't.*

CHAPTER 5

"He's Back!"

"*M*elissa, you have a call on line 2. And if I'm not mistaken, I think she said she's Carole Ginnis from Miami-Dade High School", Cynthia announces from the intercom.

"Thanks, Cynthia. I got it!"

"Yes, this is Melissa Thomas. How may I help you?" I say to the person on the other end of the phone.

"Mrs. Thomas, my name is Carole Ginnis and I'm the guidance counselor from Miami-Dade High and I need to speak with you about your daughter, Sharelle", she says.

"Oh, no, what did she do *this* time?" I ask.

"Your daughter left the school without our permission. From what her teacher tells me, Sharelle asked to go to the restroom and never returned. And then shortly afterwards, she was seen jumping into a white car and leaving the property, so you might want to contact the police department to report it", she suggests.

"Unbelievable! What's going on with this child?!!!" I exclaim, without giving Ms. Ginnis an opportunity to respond to me. "Fine. Thanks for calling me." I don't mean to be rude, but I'm extremely upset with my child. *What is this girl thinking? Why can't she just do like she's told to do? Why must she experience everything the hard way?* Immediately, I hang up the phone and dial 911. After giving the operator all the information she asks for, she informs me that the Officer will be out soon for me to fill out the report.

"Is everything alright, Melissa?" Cynthia asks, walking into my office.

"Sharelle ran away from school. I don't know what's going on with this child these days", I tell her.

"Teenagers, honey. They don't need a reason. Believe me. This'll pass. I'm sure of it; but, in the meantime, you have quite a few things that you have to deal with right now. Don't worry about Sharelle. She's just going through that phase that all teenagers go through and she'll snap out of it. I promise!" she tells me.

"I sure hope you're right. Just buzz me when the officer arrives", I say.

"I will", Cynthia promises.

Cynthia knows how important the reports that I need are so she gets back to work. But, back at my desk, my computer is beeping at me letting me know that there's a message waiting for me to open. *Who could this be from? I'm not particularly waiting on anything right now.*

The message is from Patrick. *"Good morning, Princess. I hope that your day is off to a great start and I really hope you don't have too much of a hang-over. Take it easy and allow yourself to just relax. Things will get better if you just hang in there and never give up. Love, Patrick."* I read his email over and over again because it's so sweet and his timing couldn't be any better, so I decide to respond to him right away, typing, *"Thanks so much, Patrick, for your support. It really means a lot to me. You, too, have a great day!"*

Before I can get too deep in thought, Cynthia interrupts my sweet moment when she buzzes me to tell me, "The officer is here, Melissa."

"Send him in." The Officer comes in, takes a seat, pulls out a pen and begins to take notes.

"I know this may be difficult, but I don't want you to worry too much. Believe it or not but we see this all the time. Tell me. What was your daughter wearing this morning when she left the house?"

"I'm a little embarrassed to say this, but I'm just not sure, Officer. I didn't stay home last night, so I wasn't there when she left this morning", I respond.

"I see. Was she left home alone?" he asks, raising an eyebrow.

"No, sir. Absolutely not! My husband was there with the children. You see, we are not doing great these days and I didn't stay home last night", I explain.

"Oh, I see", he says.

"Let me make a quick call to my husband to find out", I tell him.

"Ok. That would be helpful", the Officer tells me.

Kalin answers the phone right away. "Honey, are you okay? I've been worried sick about you. I called you several times last night. What's wrong?" he asks, sounding very concerned.

"Not now, Kalin. I'm actually calling on a different matter right now. I'm here with a police officer because Sharelle ran away from school and I need to know what she was wearing this morning when she left the house", I explain, without showing any emotion whatsoever, even though my heart is bleeding.

"Oh my God! Is she okay? Melissa, what happened?"

"We don't know much right now other than she left the school and was seen getting into a car with someone. I'll call you back when I'm done with the officer. What was she wearing this morning?" I ask again.

"She had on blue jeans and a red shirt. What can I do? Do you need me to come to your office?" he says.

"No. That won't be necessary. That's all I needed to know. Let me finish talking with the Officer and I'll call you back to fill you in on what's going on with Sharelle", I tell him.

"Ok, but please call me, sweetheart", he says, sounding desperate.

At this moment, it feels like it's me against the world. Not even my concerns for my marriage matter to me right now. Honestly, I could care less about what it is that Kalin wants to say to me. He has had more than enough chances to show me how he feels about me and it's come to this. My daughter is missing and to think that it has *anything* to do with this messed up marriage makes me sick to my stomach. I'm sure that Kalin is probably not too happy when I hang up the phone without acknowledging his comment.

"Sir, my husband said that she was wearing blue jeans and a red shirt."

"Ok. Got it. Ma'am, do you have any idea of who could have picked up your daughter from school? Which friend of hers would have done this?" he asks.

"I have no idea. I'm shocked that she has a friend who drives. For crying out loud, Sharelle is only 12 years old. What do we do now?" I ask him.

"Let me get back to my office, write up this report and put it in the system. Don't worry, Mrs. Thomas. We'll find her. We see this sort of thing all the time. My guess is that she'll be home by dinnertime", he tells me, sounding quite confident.

"You think so? But, I'm worried about her. I mean, is she safe? Is she scared? This is just horrible", I say to him.

"I know. Teenagers are rebellious and sometimes we never figure out why. But, let me ask you. Is everything okay at home? I mean this definitely sounds like what we're typically used to dealing with when it comes to these runaways", he tells me.

"Honestly, her stepfather and I will most likely separate. Money has been a big issue at our home. The arguments. The stress. So, no, it hasn't been all that good at home with my husband not earning a paycheck and putting everything on me", I admit to him.

"Sorry to hear that, but we've seen many young ladies have difficulty coping with what's going on at the house and they cope by running away for a little while until they realize that being out on the streets is not the way to handle their frustrations", he explains.

"Okay. So what now? Do I just sit and wait?" I ask the Detective.

"Here's my card and the the report# is on it. Whenever you want, you can call me or you can call this number here to get an update on this report and it'll let you know whenever there's any new information on your daughter's whereabouts", he explains, handing me his business card.

"Thanks so much, Detective", I say, wiping away a tear from my eye.

The Detective leaves my office and Cynthia walks into my office with a very concerned look on her face.

"What do we do now, Melissa?" Cynthia asks.

"The Detective seems to think that she'll be home by dinnertime and that she's just being rebellious. I'm so mad with her right now for making us worry like this."

"Kalin called while you were speaking with the Detective. He's extremely concerned. Give him a call, MeMe", she tells me.

As much as I don't feel like talking to Kalin, I decide to call him because of the look Cynthia is giving me right now. After calling, I'm totally convinced that Kalin must be sitting right by the phone because he answers right away.

"What's going on, sweetheart? Where's Sharelle? What happened?" he asks, not stopping between questions.

"She ran away from school and I had to file a missing persons report. The Detective seems to think that she'll be home by dinnertime and that she's just being a rebellious teenager", I tell him.

"All I know is that she needs to be punished for this. I'm serious, Melissa. You have to stop letting these kids get away with everything", Kalin suggests.

"And who gave you the authority on raising children, Kalin? I guess you want another shot at it, right? I guess that's why you...", I begin.

"That's *why I what*, Melissa? Tell me. That's *why I what*?" Kalin demands.

"Forget it. I'm just upset right now because of Sharelle. I'm just a little upset right now. That's all", I tell him.

"And where were you last night? You had me worried sick about you. You didn't answer any of my calls. How could you do this, Melissa?" he asks, sounding disappointed.

"Kalin, I was fine. I just needed some time to myself. That's all. Another call is coming through for me right now. We'll have to talk later, Kalin. Ok?"

I feel horrible having to lie to my husband about last night. I'm confused, angry, and hurt and Kalin is not my favorite person right now. Honestly, I don't know if I can continue to be with the man I've considered my best friend for over a decade. I'm just not sure if we'll be able to get past this.

"Melissa, can we talk when you get home? I love you. Ok? I love you very much and I don't want to lose my wife. You know I love you."

"Kalin, I can't do this anymore. I'm very unhappy in this marriage. I'm tired of struggling to pay bills. I'm tired of arguing with you. I'm just tired. You and I both deserve better than this. So, why don't we just call it quits so that we can at least walk away from this marriage with a friendship?"

"You telling me you want a divorce?!!" Kalin yells.

Fighting back the tears, I say, "Yes. I do. I think it's the best thing for us right now."

Being the crybaby that he is, Kalin starts to cry and pleads with me. "Baby, please don't leave me. Let's take some time apart and then we can discuss things. Is that what you want? I'm willing to do that if it will keep us together. I can't lose you. I just can't", Kalin says.

"Ok! Let's try a separation and see where that takes us. Where will you go?" I ask.

"Maybe I can bunk with Carl and Wendy", Kalin suggests.

"Of course you'd say that. You'd just love that, wouldn't you? Look, I have to go now", I tell him.

"What was that for? Did I say something wrong?" he asks.

"Our marriage is over if you move into their home. Now, what's it going to be?"

"Where am I going to go, MeMe? You tell me where", Kalin demands.

"Figure it out, Kalin. I can't tell you where to go or what to do. You have to figure some things out on your own. We're trying to save a marriage and I guess you want to…", I begin.

"What? What are you trying to say to me, Melissa? Just say what's on your mind. It's the only way we're going to save this marriage. We have to be honest with each other."

"Look, I have so much to do here before I finish my day. And when I'm done, I'm coming home and we can finish this conversation then", I tell him.

"Ok. Sounds like a plan. Drive safely and I'll see you when you get here", he tells me.

Kalin and I hang up the phone and the tears won't stop coming. I can't stop thinking how I've loved this man for so many years. We've gone through everything imaginable. We could have given up a long time ago, but we didn't. We stood the test of time, but he cheated on me and that's all I can think about right now.

Cynthia walks into the room while I'm deep in thought. "You're not going to believe who's in town", she announces.

"Who? Tell me!" I ask her.

"You ready for this?" Cynthia asks.

"Who is it?" I ask her.

"Stevie. Stevie's back in town."

CHAPTER 6

"Make Me Never Forget."

*F*inally making it home, my mind starts to drift towards my previous conversation with Kalin. As much as I want to continue our conversation, I'm more concerned about Sharelle right now. I haven't heard anything and it's almost 8pm. The officer said that he feels like she'll be home by dinnertime. *Something smells good coming from the house. Somebody is cooking something good! I wonder what Kalin has up his sleeves tonight. Is that what I think it is? Smells like Kalin is cooking my favorite dinner. Smells like cabbages!*

"Honey, you're home. I've missed you today", Kalin says, grabbing the things out of my hand at the front door. He takes my hands into his and we just stand there for seconds just looking into each other's eyes without saying a word. The moment is interrupted when Justice and Amber walk into the room.

"Mommy, where have you been? I need for you to sign this Field Trip form for me. Our class is going to Orlando to Universal Studios. And before you ask, it's only $40", she says.

"Ok, sweetheart. Let me get settled first and then I'll take a look at it. Just put it on my desk and I'll sign it. Did Sharelle call?" I ask, changing the subject.

"She's in her room. Where else would she be, Mommy?" Justice says, walking away.

Thank God Sharelle is here! I'm glad she's here, but I don't know whether to hug her and give her love or walk into her room and put a belt to her behind for putting herself in danger and making me and her father worry so much.

"I was just about to tell you that she made it home about twenty minutes ago. Somebody in a blue car dropped her off. She hasn't said a word to me or her sisters since she's been home. Baby, I love you", Kalin says, as he kisses me gently on the lips. "And later on, I want to show you just how much I love you. Your favorite dinner is on the stove and now that you're finally home, we can eat."

"This is all so nice, Kalin. But, why are you being so nice? What did you do that you are silently apologizing for?" I ask. Kalin frowns up and walks away confused.

I can't believe it, but after all these years, I still love this man. When he looks at me a certain way, I *still* get butterflies in my stomach and honestly, now that Sharelle is home safe and sound, I want to take him up on the offer of a night of lovemaking. Hopefully, this time, I won't think about Patrick. *Did I just admit that I think about Patrick when I make love to my husband?*

Sharelle's door is open so I walk right in. She looks up and sees me, so she takes the earplugs out of her ears.

"Sweetheart, what's going on with you? Talk to me before I pop a vessel in my head about why I had to get a call at work that you ran away from school. Why on earth would you do something like that?" I say to her, not stopped for even a breath of air. "We were worried sick about you!"

"Well, we don't ever have money like we used to and I wanted to go shopping so a friend took me shopping", she admits.

"Shopping? You skipped school and jumped in the car with God-knows-who to go shopping? Do you have any idea how crazy this sounds?" I ask her.

"Well, it's the truth", she says.

"And where does *this friend* get money to take you shopping?" I ask her.

"He has a job, Mother. He didn't steal it."

"I see! And how is it that you are friends with someone old enough to work? You're only 12 years old for crying out loud. I'm so angry and disappointed with you right now. You'll definitely live to regret these poor choices that you're making for your life. Trust me on that!" I yell.

"Momma, just let it go! I mean, just.....", she says, before I interrupt her.

Before I know it, my back hand pops Sharelle in the mouth. She grabs her face and looks surprised that I did it. "What is wrong with you?" she yells.

"There's nothing wrong with me. You need to get up and get ready for dinner. We'll talk about this later", I tell her, walking off.

I walk into my office where there's a mounting pile of papers from two nights ago. Most of this pile consists of junk mail, but there's one envelope that stands out from the others. It's a letter from Attorney Richards in Middleton. Seeing his name printed on an envelope is like seeing a ghost from the past. I carefully open the letter and the first thing I notice is that there's a check inside for $6500! According to the letter, Laura had it planned for checks to come at certain times of Princess' life and the timing couldn't be any more perfect. I was just wondering how I'd pull off a birthday party for her.

"Honey, dinner is served", Kalin yells from the other room. I don't want Kalin to know about this check, but I'll conveniently mention over dinner that we'll have a birthday party

"Coming! I'll be there in just a minute", I say, putting the check into my top drawer.

By the time I make it to the dining area, everyone is already seated and making comments about the delicious smelling dinner that Kalin has prepared. I can tell he's enjoying the attention. The man is already patting himself on the back.

"So how was everyone's day?" I ask, looking around at everyone.

"Mine was just wonderful, Mommy", says Amber, who's holding up her progress report with all A's on it.

"Great job, Amber. Keep up the good work, honey. And what about you, Justice?" I ask her.

"Mine was fine too. I'm doing ok in all of my classes, so I'm okay, too", she replies.

"And who's turning a year older this weekend?" I ask.

"Me!!" shouts Princess.

"That's right and who wants to help me plan her birthday party?" I ask. Kalin looks up and glances over at me.

"Me! I do! We have to help you so it will be awesome", they all comment. Kalin still looks a little surprised because I haven't discussed it with him just yet.

"Cool! I get to invite my friends over! Way to go, Princess!" Amber adds.

Small talk around the dinner table is my favorite part of the day. And Kalin didn't do too bad on the dinner either. He did everything just the way I like it. Now, it's time for a shower and some much needed time alone with my husband. I wonder if we'll spend our time talking or making passionate love. Kalin and I eventually dismiss the children to their rooms so that we can clean up the kitchen to give them a break for the evening. Between the two of us, there's plenty of flirting and smooching until we retire to our bedroom.

"I need to get a shower, honey", I say, stripping down and walking into the shower stall. Much to my surprise, Kalin is right behind me jumping out of his clothes. We haven't done this in a long time. I almost forgot how relaxing it is to take a shower with my husband. Feeling him rub my back and shoulders reminds me of the good 'ole days. His hands are magical. His manhood is getting bigger so I can only imagine what's in store for the rest of the evening. To be honest, I can't remember the last time we made love. It's funny how we take each day for granted, forgetting how important it is to keep each other satisfied in all ways. All we want to do right now is for the both of us to make each other feel good.

Kalin kisses me on the back of my neck, sending a tingling sensation to the rest of my body. He knows just what to do to me. Just thinking of what he's going to do to me is starting to erase my special moments with Patrick. This is the man I remember. Kalin turns off the shower, wraps the towel around me, dries me off, picks me up and carries me to our bed. His lips kiss every single part of my body. This passion between the two of us is intense. Kalin is the best lover I've ever had. Now that I think about it, maybe *this* is why I never left him.

"Baby, does this feel good to you when I do this?" he asks, as he takes his warm hands and places them between my legs. Kalin continues to touch me there. Hearing me moan gets him even more excited. He spreads my legs apart and begins to kiss me in my most sensitive spot. I've completely surrendered myself to my husband and I'm allowing him to give me the pleasure that I've wanted and needed for weeks now from him. This intense passion brings on the most intense orgasm I've experienced in months.

We continue to satisfy each other until we eventually fall asleep in each other's arms.

The alarm clock goes off and it feels like I just closed my eyes, but it's time to get up and start a new day. Kalin isn't in bed. He must have gone downstairs to see the kids off to school. From across the room, I can tell that my cell phone is lit up so that tells me that someone has left me a message. I pick up the phone and it's a message from Patrick. *I really shouldn't look at this message because Kalin and I just had a very special evening together and anything from Patrick can potentially cause me to forget it all.* I put the phone away in my purse and decide to jump in the shower instead. Just as I'm about to get out, I smell coffee brewing from downstairs, which means Kalin must've gotten up just to prepare breakfast for us. *Things could potentially get better for us if we continue having nights like last night. That really was amazing. Feels like old times.*

"Honey, breakfast is ready for you!" Kalin shouts from downstairs.

"Okay, honey. I'll be right there!"

I slip on my bathrobe and join Kalin in the kitchen. He has prepared breakfast for the family and the girls are already sitting at the table eating.

"Morning Mommy!" Justice says.

Stepping away from the stove, Kalin walks over and kisses me on the lips. "I love you and last night was magical!" he whispers.

"Get a room!" Amber says, as she pours syrup on her pancakes. Kalin and I both give her a crazy look and laugh. It seems like today is getting off to a great start, with one exception. Sharelle isn't sharing in this wonderful family breakfast. She refused to get up when the girls went to knock on her door. I guess she's going to keep up this rebellious stage until it's finally broken somehow.

Right now, I can't be happier with how things are going with me and Kalin. Granted, I'll have to get over all that has happened if our marriage is going to survive his acts of infidelity, but after last night, I realize that I really do love this man. Leaving the house with a different attitude about life, I'm taking a different route today to avoid the bumper to bumper traffic on Dolphin. I plan to have a stress-free today, but right now, there's someone following me. *Who is that? Why does the car make a turn every time I make a turn?* It looks like the car in my rearview mirror is Patrick's. *Is he following me?* Seconds later, I realize the person in the car *is* Patrick.

When I realize that it's Patrick, I pull over into the shoulder of the road. He walks to my side of the car. "Why aren't you returning my calls? I've called quite a few times. I've missed you, Melissa. I need you", he says, sounding desperate. "Don't you need me? Haven't you missed me?"

"Patrick, this is crazy. Why are you following me like this? Of course, I've missed you, but I'm married and you know that. I live with my husband and things are very complicated right now and I just...." I say before he interrupts me.

"What? You don't want me anymore? Are you telling me that you're going to reconcile with your husband, the man who hurts you and doesn't take care of you? Is that what you want? Tell me that you don't want me anymore and I'll walk away from you right now, Melissa, and you'll never hear from me again", Patrick says in a demanding tone. "Tell me right now that you don't love me and I'm gone!"

"Patrick, please! Don't do this! Not now!" I plead with him.

"No. I think that now is definitely the right time. All I know is that I tried to reach you all night and I was sick to my stomach thinking that you were making love to him. I know that you have to do that to keep up a façade until you decide that it's completely over, but were you? Were you loving *him* last night, Melissa?" Patrick's eyes fill with tears and he looks away. I guess because I didn't answer him right away, he believes that just maybe, I still have something for Kalin.

"Patrick, please don't cry. Don't do this. You know that what I feel for you is real. Everything is just so complicated right now in my marriage. I don't want anyone to get hurt, so please, be patient in this situation until I figure things out. Will you do that for me? Please, baby, please just be patient", I beg.

"Okay, Melissa. I can do that. I will do just that. I've missed you", he says.

"And I've missed you too, Patrick. So, please, have a good day today. I have to get to work and so do you. We'll talk later on. And then we...", I say until Patrick cuts me off by kissing me.

"Goodbye sweetheart", he says, walking back to his car. I watch him get into his car and drive away. *That was so hot, but where in the word did that come from? That man has a way with his mouth. Whew!*

I have finally made it to the office and Cynthia seems extremely anxious about giving me some news. She's waving for me to hurry up into the office.

"What's the big hurry?" I say opening the door to the front office.

"Guess who the headliner is for the big comedy event on Friday? We have to go!" she says excitedly.

"Ok, tell me. Who?" I ask her, curious to know.

"Stevie! He's coming to town to headline the biggest comedy event Miami has ever seen. Now, tell me that you want to go! It'll be so much fun!" she pleads with me.

"I don't want to go! Cynthia, I'm not interested in seeing Stevie. That relationship and those feelings for him are long gone. He and I were several years ago. I'm over it!"

"Come on, Melissa. Are you going to tell me that you're not the least bit interested in what he looks like or how he is doing or anything after all these years?" Cynthia says to me.

"What I'm saying is that I'm married now and I can't risk bringing myself or my concerns for his life into my thoughts and ...", I say, before Cynthia interrupts me.

"Ah hah...so there *is* something? You're afraid that if you see him or talk to him, those old feelings will re-surface. I understand that. But, look at it this way. I'll be there with you and that should make it a little easier. Come on! You haven't gone out to do anything fun in a long time and neither have I and I wanna go. Will you at least think about it?"

"Okay, Cynthia, you got me! I'll think about it. Can we get some work done now? Any messages? What's going on?"

"No messages. All is well for the property as usual. What's going on with Patrick? He called here this morning looking for you, and he sounded a bit concerned. What's going on with that *and him*? Are you still seeing him Melissa?" she asks me.

"I'm so confused about my feelings for Patrick. I know I'm a married woman, but I find myself becoming very fond of him. Kalin and I had the most amazing evening last night. When I got home last night, he had fixed a wonderful dinner and when we went to bad last night, we made love like we used to, Cynthia. And then when I got up this morning, he fixed breakfast. You should have seen the smile on my face. But then, when I was on my way to work, guess who was following me in their car, forcing me to pull over?" I say.

"I don't know. Who?" she asks.

"Patrick. He was concerned that I didn't return his calls and was wondering if I was home making love to my husband. This is just getting crazier and crazier by the day. What am I going to do?" I say, rubbing my forehead and looking puzzled.

"I don't know, but I told you or I at least hinted to you that this would happen. Patrick has fallen for you and he's not going to just walk away so easily. You need to really think about what it is that you want to do, MeMe, before someone gets hurt", Cynthia warns me.

"This would be so much easier if Kalin hadn't cheated on me with Wendy and it looks like with Diandra as well. I don't know if I can trust him anymore. He has too many secrets and I hate secrets. It just isn't right for a husband to have secrets from his wife", I say, standing up to walk towards the window. *Thoughts are entering my mind as to why Kalin was so nice last night. Does he know something that I don't know? Or was his attention towards me out of his guilty conscience?*

"Then you really have quite a bit to think about. You have children and history with Kalin and you have an infatuation with Patrick. Is Patrick serious about wanting to have a future with you or is he just trying to get in bed with you? These are the things that you have to consider", Cynthia advises.

"To change the subject, did I tell you that we're celebrating Princess' birthday? Her birthday is this coming weekend and I want Brittney to be there. Do you think you can give her a call and set it all up for me? The party will be this Friday night and I'd love to surprise Princess with her Aunt Brittney showing up; and besides, Brittney has always wanted to bring her kids here. Never mind, I'll call her myself, but I need help with finding a birthday planner. Can you do that?"

"Sure. I'm on it. I'll have someone by the end of the day", she assures me.

I walk into my office, put my things away, and dial Brittney's number. She picks up right away. "Hello, MeMe!"

"Well, hey there my friend. How are you today?" I ask her.

"I'm doing okay", she responds. "Is everything okay?"

"Yes, everything's okay. Just wondering what you and the kids doing this weekend."

"Nothing that I know of right now. Why?" Brittney asks.

"We're having a birthday party for Princess and I want to surprise her by having you and the kids there. It's my treat, of course. What do you say?"

"Oh my goodness!! I'd love to come to Florida to see my niece and celebrate her 18th birthday. The kids are going to be so happy when I tell them that we're finally going to Florida!" she shouts.

"Well, good. I'm glad you're happy about it. I'll either email you the details or I'll call you back. Either way, start packing girl!" I say.

"Thank you so much, MeMe. We got lots of catching up to do. I'm so happy my friend", she tells me, sounding quite pleased.

"You're quite welcome, B. We go a long way back. Laura was our girl and her daughter is turning into a woman now and it just makes sense that her girls are there to wish her baby well", I tell her.

"True. So true, MeMe. Okay then, I'll see you this weekend", she tells me.

"Ok. Call me if you have any questions about anything, okay", I tell her.

"Okay. I'll do just that", she tells me.

My phone has beeped several times since I've been on the phone. It looks like a Michelle Granger is trying to reach me. I wonder what this is about. Picking up my cell phone, I hit "missed calls" to return the call. She answers right away.

"This is Melissa Thomas and I just received a few calls from you. Is everything okay?" I say into the phone.

"Mrs. Thomas, it's about Sharelle", she begins to say.

"Oh God no! Is she okay? What's wrong *this* time?" I ask.

"I was just calling you to make you aware that a court hearing has been set for Sharelle. We received your request for a hearing to make her accountable for violating the Judge's orders and the hearing is today. I apologize for the short notice, but I just received it myself. It's this afternoon at 2pm. Can you make it?" she asks.

"Geez, well, first I'll have to drop by her school to get her. One thing's for sure is that she definitely needs to be held accountable. Tell me. Which courtroom is it?" I ask.

"Courtroom C", she responds.

"We'll be there", I tell her.

"Cynthia!" I shout, after hanging up the phone. Cynthia rushes in to my office.

"What's wrong? Oh my goodness!" she says, looking confused.

"Oh, I'm sorry to startle you, but I just received a call from the courthouse and they have finally set a court hearing for Sharelle's violation of the court's rulings. So, if I have any afternoon appointments, they will now have to be canceled", I tell her.

"What did she do?" she asks.

"Not going to school, breaking her curfew, talking back. You name it!" I say.

"And you went down to the courthouse and reported it, didn't you?" she asks me.

"And you know I did. Sharelle knows what the Judge's orders were from the last time she was running away and she just completely ignored them and decided to do that she wanted to do what *she* wanted to do. These kids are something else. Well, she won't do what she wants to do in my house. If they lock her up, they just lock her up", I say.

"Wow. For real? Yeah, you gotta do this because she has to learn", she agrees with me.

"Yes she does. So, please go ahead and make arrangements with the planner. I trust your judgment. You know what I like and what I expect from this planner; so, I'm leaving a blank check with you to get her hired. Have her come here and show you what she has and go ahead and pay her today. Tell her to update me with everything via email. And let her know that my friend, Brittney Snow, will be flying in from Alabama to arrive Friday and she'll need to make arrangements to pick her up from the airport. The details of her flight are still up on my computer, so make sure she gets that", I tell her.

"Yes ma'am. I'll handle it all for you. And Melissa, you know everything is going to be okay with Sharelle, right?" Cygnthia asks.

"I do know that one way or the other, it'll be okay. So, I need to get out of here now and get over to Sharelle's school to get her if we're ever going to make it to the courthouse on time", I say, preparing myself to leave.

"Absolutely. Drive carefully. I'll take care of everything", Cynthia assures me.

Traffic on I-95 is a bear right now and I really hope I'm able to get to the courthouse in time. Sharelle has no idea what's in store for her, but she brought this on herself. According to the sign, I'm minutes away from my exit to Sharelle's school. It looks like I just did miss the afternoon school pick up traffic, so I need to get in here and get out and then, jump back on I-95.

This is the most perfect day for everything to work the way it needs to. No issues whatsoever at the school. The Staff says goodbye to Sharelle, but they have absolutely no idea where we're going.

"So, Ma, why did you pick me up? Where are we going?" she asks, sounding a little concerned.

"Well, do you remember all of those days when you broke your curfew, skipped school, and totally disrespected me?" I ask, looking her way briefly.

"Ma, what's this about?" she asks.

"Today's your court appearance to meet with the Judge and tell her why you felt the need to violate her orders", I respond.

"You telling me I'm 'bout to go to court? You saying that the Judge gon' put me back in jail?" she asks.

"I'm saying that the Judge will most likely have some type of punishment in store for you because of your poor behavior at home and school", I say, noticing that she's starting to get upset. "Who are you upset with? Don't even try it! If you're going to get upset with anyone, look in the mirror", I tell her.

"Why are you doing this to me?" Sharelle shouts. "I've been trying. You're just being mean to me. I know you like the other kids better than me and I just know…", she begins, before I interrupt her.

"Are you serious? Don't you dare try to play like the victim! You've brought this on yourself. Nobody told you to do what you did. You wanted to be grown and this is what you get when you play those games. This has nothing to do with your sisters and brothers. You have the same opportunities they have, but you decided to do something else with yours. So, now, you'll have to deal with whatever consequences comes as a result of your poor choices", I remind her.

"Ok. It's like that, Ma. It's like that, huh?" she says, turning her head to look out the window.

"Sharelle, I love you. I know that you may not understand this right now, but I'm doing this to save your life. You are going to …..", I say, before she throws up her hand.

"Save it, Ma. I don't want to hear it. It doesn't even matter right now. What's done is done, but I am not going back to jail", she murmurs under her breath.

The parking lot is quite full by the time we arrive and thanks to my new GPS system, we arrive at the courthouse, with 15 minutes to spare.

The courthouse looks like a teen convention. Most of the parents look extremely frustrated and annoyed that they're here. All over the place are little groups bunched here and there of an attorney in a blue suit with a pad, a parent, and some youth standing there looking away as if he or she is annoyed with the conversation. I just heard a bailiff warn a few teenagers about the "no sagging in the courthouse" rule.

Courtroom C is where we are directed to have Judge Madison Calhoun hear our case. On the way into the courtroom, my cell phone vibrates. Cynthia is calling.

"Cynthia, is everything okay?" I ask, without even saying hello.

"There's an emergency at one of your properties. It's Symone from Carter's Landings. She sounds like she really needs you. I told her that I'd give you a call and have you call her back. She sounded like she was crying, Melissa", she said.

"I'll call her now. We were just about to walk into the courthouse. Thanks for the heads up", I say, hanging up the phone with Cynthia.

Symone answers the phone right away. "Symone, is everything okay?"

"Mrs. Thomas, I hate to bother you because I know you're at an appointment with your daughter, but my ex mother-in-law just called me and told me that my daughter was in the car with her father and they had a serious car accident and both of them are at the hospital. Nobody knows how serious it is right now, but I have to get over there right away!" she says, crying and barely getting the words out without a slur.

"Oh my God, Symone! I'm so sorry. Of course you need to get over there right away. Put a sign on your door saying that due to an emergency, the office is closed for the remainder of the day. Everything will be okay. You know that, right?"

"Yes ma'am. I'm just so scared", she says, crying.

"Please call me this afternoon and let me know if you think you'll be able to be at work on tomorrow so I can get your property covered", I say, now heading towards the courtroom.

"Okay and thanks so much, Mrs. Thomas. I appreciate it", she tells me.

"Think nothing of it, Symone. Take care of your family", I respond.

The courtroom is crowded today, but I get the feeling that everyone was told to be here at 2:30pm. Sharelle looks scared, but we take our seat towards the back of the room. The Judge has just entered the room and the court secretary calls the first case. Several cases have been called at this point and I'm starting to wonder when Sharelle's case will be called. The bailiff is coming this way. *Maybe I should walk outside with him to ask him.* Sharelle doesn't look too happy when she sees me follow the bailiff outside.

"Sir, how much longer will it be for them to call Sharelle Williams?" I ask.

"Let me see", he says, looking on his clipboard and scanning the list. "Looks like there are 2 people more to be called and then Sharelle."

"Ok. That sounds good. Listen, I'm sure you've seen a lot in this courtroom, but my daughter is here for breaking the Judge's orders. Is the Judge known to send youths back to jail if they violate? I ask the bailiff.

"Nine times out of ten, she will send her to jail for violating her orders", he says, walking away to help another parent.

When I make it back into the courtroom, Sharelle seems to be agitated so I sit down next to her. I wonder if she senses what I'm feeling right now. I wonder if she can tell that I am more relieved and more at ease knowing that we are about to be called.

"Ma, I gotta go to the restroom", Sharelle says, as she hurriedly leaves the courtroom, not giving me a chance to say anything. But for some reason, when she gets up, I get the feeling that she may not come back. So, I get up to make sure she's actually going to the restroom and when I get there, I call out for her and quickly discover that Sharelle didn't come to the restroom after all. So, if she didn't come to the restroom, where did she go? *Did she run away?*

Walking past the elevator, I get a sick feeling inside that Sharelle may have gotten on the elevator and when I step back just to see, she is and is waving goodbye to me as the elevator closes.

"Sharelle!! Get off the elevator! What are you doing?" I yell. Sharelle looks me dead in the eyes and continues to shake her head and wave goodbye. Instead of trying to chase her, I decide to go back inside the courtroom to tell the bailiffs to warn the security guards downstairs to be on the lookout for Sharelle. After giving them a description of Sharelle and what she's wearing, I sit back down and wait to hear that they have caught her.

"Mrs. Thomas, please come forward", the Judge announces.

Hopefully, they're about to let me know that Sharelle will have to go to jail for violating the Judge's previous orders. "Ma'am, the guards did not catch your daughter. I don't know how she did it, but she was able to get by them", the Judge begins.

"Are you telling me that my daughter outsmarted your guards? How can this be? Now what?" I ask.

"I'm putting a bench warrant out for her, so when she's found, she'll be arrested. Until she is caught, she will continue to have court hearings and even if she's still missing, you'll have to come in her place", the Judge instructs.

"So you're telling me that I have to be punished for what my child has done here today?" I ask.

"If that's the way you see it, then I guess the answer to your question is "yes", she says, somewhat dismissing me and my concerns. "Step aside and the court clerk will give you the next appointment."

I feel like I've been hit in the stomach. I came here to make sure Sharelle gets punished for violating the Judge's orders and I end up getting punished. On the way to my car, I'm reminded of what just happened when I pass by a security guard. Tears fill my eyes because not only am I being punished for what my daughter has done, but my daughter is missing *again*. The ride back to the office seems so much longer but I'm snapped out of my daydream when my cell phone vibrates. Looking down at the phone, I can see that it's Kalin calling. I wonder why he's calling at this time of the afternoon.

"Hello. Honey, how are you?" Kalin says, when I answer the phone.

"I'm fine; just leaving the courthouse", I respond.

"How did it go?" he asks.

"Horrible! Sharelle ran out of the courtroom and these crazy behind cops couldn't find her. My 12-year old daughter outsmarted them! And now, I have to keep showing up for her court hearings even if *she* is not there", I explain.

"That doesn't seem fair at all. Honey, are you okay? All we can do is just pray for her at this point. She has chosen this way of life. There is nothing you or me can do about it. Okay?" he says, trying to comfort me.

"I'll be okay. I have to get back to the office", I tell him.

"I was hoping that you and I could talk. We were supposed to have a conversation the other night but after you got home, we went to bed and you know what happened then", he says.

"What do you want to talk about, Kalin?" I ask.

"Our marriage, our future, the kids, you know, normal things that couples discuss. "You were very upset the other night and I want to address your concerns about Wendy and Diandra. You should know the truth."

"Oh, I see. Now, you want to tell me the truth. I already know the truth, Kalin. There isn't anything you can tell me more about Wendy than the fact that you got her pregnant and she aborted your child. And knowing this, you went and lived with her and her husband. I don't know if there is anything more you can say to me about that. You lied to me, you cheated on me; you pretty much broke my heart and I stood by you when most women would have told you to go to hell", I say, starting to sound angry and bitter.

"So, you have all the answers, right? That's part of our problem right there. You don't want to listen and talk things through", he responds.

"Go to hell, Kalin. That's what you can do, okay. I'm so tired of you always trying to explain things away when you have done something wrong. How would you feel if I had done something like this to you? You lied about Wendy and then you had a secret email going on with this Diandra chic", I say, pulling to the side of the road to talk to Kalin.

"I explained the Diandra thing to you, Melissa. I met her when you put me out of the house and I went to Alabama. She was nothing but a friend to me", he says.

"Give me a break, Kalin! Don't worry about it, though. We all have to be accountable for our actions. I was here every day trying to figure out how to feed and clothe your children. I can't believe that you'll attempt to say anything to me about Diandra. I have all of the emails saved in my computer. So, please stop trying to pass off to me that you and this woman were just friends. Do what you want! I have to go back to work. We can discuss how we want to handle everything later", I say, putting the keys into the ignition.

"What does *that* mean? Are you trying to tell me that you still want a divorce?" he asks.

"No. I think you're saying it. I have to go", I say before disconnecting the call.

CHAPTER 7

"Where's Your Father?"

"What time is the concert tomorrow night?" I ask, walking into the office in a much different mood than expected.

"So, you going, right? I'm so glad you've decided to go out and have fun. You've had a very stressful week and going to this comedy event just may be what you need, Melissa", Cynthia says.

"Yes. I think you may be right, Cynthia. So, what time should I expect you?" I ask.

"Let's say around 6. We can get some dinner first and then head over to the Arena."

"Sounds like a plan to me! We'll have fun. I'm curious about how good Stevie is on that stage", I comment.

"I heard that the guy is funny. Can you please tell me why your phone keeps lighting up?" Cynthia asks, pointing to my cell phone sitting on the top of my desk.

"Grown folks' business", I say, picking up my cell phone to see who is sending a text message.

The message is from Patrick. *I haven't stopped thinking about you and I can't wait to see you again. The smile on my face is because of you, Melissa. I hope that you are having a good day. Love, Patrick.*

Several text messages follow with similar messages as this, all from Patrick.

I have to be honest. Cynthia was right about one thing. I'm curious as to what Stevie looks like these days, but there's no way I can tell Cynthia that. In her eyes, I'm a married woman, so it's important that I maintain a certain image that I am 100% dedicated to my husband even though people may know that he cheated on me. It's just a matter of a few days and my questions will be answered.

All of my properties are doing well and none of them are in the red so that's always a good thing. It's been a long afternoon, and I'm finally ready to sit down at my computer and check my messages. Symone's message pops up first. It looks like her daughter is in stable condition and will have surgery on Monday, but she'll be at work on tomorrow. That's great news. Let me respond to her. *Symone, I am happy to hear that your daughter is stable and my prayers are with her for the surgery on Monday. I will either be at your property or I will have a temp cover the property. Take care of yourself and call me if you need anything at all.*

Knowing myself, I will most likely go to the property myself. The property is already in good shape, so this will be more of an opportunity to catch up on some paperwork. This might not be such a bad idea after all.

Not only am I concerned for Symone, but, to be honest, I'm not looking forward to going home tonight and having more conversation with Kalin. From the looks of it, I just may get my wish because his car's not here! I get a sick feeling in my stomach. *Is he coming home? Who is he with?*

Hours have passed by and Kalin is *still* not home. To make the time go by quicker, I'll just look for the email that the party planner should have sent me. I'm curious to see what she's come up with in this short time span. Whatever she pulls off, I'll be happy because I have only given her a few days to pull this together. We gotta get on it because in a couple of days, all of the kids will be here, along with Brittney, all ready to celebrate Princess' birthday. I even promised the girls that I would take them shopping on Saturday morning to pick out a new outfit to wear to the party. With all of this on my mind, I almost don't see Justice heading towards me.

"Mommy!" Justice says, running out to the driveway.

"Hey sweetheart. How was school?" I ask her.

"It was good. I have a field trip coming up and need for you to sign my permission slip and pay $20", she explains.

"Of course, I will. Put it on my desk and I'll look at it tonight. Is your father home?" I ask, already knowing the answer to the question.

"No, Daddy ain't here yet, Momma", she says, looking through my lunch bag as always.

"Ain't? Is that how we speak, Justie? Excuse me", I say to her.

"Sorry, Mommy. Daddy isn't here yet. And neither is Sharelle. She didn't make it home from school, so I don't know where she is", she says, running back into the house.

My heart is heavy right now worried about Sharelle and where she'll sleep tonight. I know the kids will wonder where their sister is, but I'm not trying to ruin Princess' birthday that's just two days away. All I can do is pray for Sharelle that God will send the angels to watch over her and keep her safe. I don't know why she keeps running away like this. And finally, when I make it into the house, I am pleased to find that Princess and Amber have prepared the dinner already. They made us chili hot dogs and French fries.

"This is so nice, girls. Mommy really appreciates the extra hand today. I need to talk to you all about Sharelle", I begin to say.

"Oh no! What did she do *now*?" Amber asks.

"We had court today and your sister was definitely not happy about it; and, just before they called her name to speak to the Judge, she jumped up and ran out of the courtroom", I begin to tell them.

"She did what?" Princess questions.

"Yes, she ran out of the courtroom and the worst part is that she got away. I don't know where she went and I haven't heard from her", I tell them.

"Oh no, Mommy! This is not good, is it?" Amber asks.

"Praying for her is all we can do for her at this point. So, how was everyone's day?" I ask, changing the subject.

"Mine was great!" Justice answers.

"Mine too", mumbles Princess and Amber.

"So, girls, are you excited about the birthday party? I haven't forgotten that I told you we would go shopping on Saturday. We'll definitely do that! We need to make sure that our birthday girl is at her very best. So, Princess, how does it feel that you'll be turning 18?" I say, with a smirk on my face.

"Feels good, Ma! It feels good!" she responds.

"Your Mother would be so proud of you. I'm so proud of you. You're a beautiful and smart young lady and I love that. And you remind me so much of your mother when she was your age", I say, getting up to fix my plate.

"Ma, may I ask you a question?" Princess asks.

"Sure, honey, anything."

"Who is my father? Do you know him? Is he still alive?" she asks.

This has caught me off guard. Princess and I have never really discussed Rock or his whereabouts. I guess I should have known that this question would surface at some point.

"Yes. Your father's name is Abernathy. We call him "Rock". I know him. And Yes, he's still alive", I respond.

"Does he know that I exist?" she asks.

"Yes."

"And does he want to know me? Does he care about me? What happened between him and my mother?" she asks.

"It's somewhat complicated, Princess. The truth is that Rock just wasn't ready for you when you were born, but he loved you. I'm not sure where he lives right now, but I'll try to locate him and see if I can't set up a meeting between the two of you and you can ask him all the questions you want. Is that okay?"

"That would be wonderful, Ma. Thanks!" she says, finally taking a bite of her food.

We all sit down to enjoy our dinner and decide not to talk about anything serious for the rest of our time together. When dinner is over, the girls take care of the dishes and I retire to my office to check my emails. The first email I see is the one from the party planner with a description of the party and what to expect. After scanning over the details, it looks like Cynthia has done a great job of making sure the planner meets my expectations. I'm impressed. Further down in my emails, I see that there is one from Patrick. He has sent me a beautiful card and flowers via email. *How is it that this man's emails always seem to come when I need it the most? He's so romantic and sweet and it has me feeling so good right now. I want to call him, but I know that I shouldn't. I really need to figure out what it is that he and I are doing. What really has my mind going is where Kalin is. Why isn't he home? Who is he with?*

It's getting later and still nothing from Kalin. He isn't here nor has he called. When I dial his cell phone number, it goes straight to voicemail. I try again and again and again and the same thing happens, which tells me that he's turned his phone off. *Where can he be that he has to turn off his phone? That tells me that he's most likely spending his time with another woman.*

I'm tired of waiting for him so I might as well retire to bed. After my steaming hot shower, I climb into bed alone, but with one quick thought of Patrick on my mind, Giving in to those thoughts of him, I give him a call. It turns out that he's having a "lonely moment" right now, so we end up being there for one another. Patrick's voice puts me in a very sensual mood and I can tell from our conversation that we have finally gone too far.

CHAPTER 8

"I Tried to Forget."

*I*s *this Brittney calling me? I wonder what she wants.*

"Hey B, how are you? Is everything okay?" I ask, without saying hello.

"Hey MeMe! I just wanted to thank you for making the arrangements for us to travel to Florida for Princess' birthday. I think this is so nice and so sweet of you to do", she says.

"Well, I thought that you and the kids could use a mini-vacation. You can all stay at my house so don't worry about trying to make hotel accommodations. We're a family!" I say.

"That means everything to me to hear you say that", I respond. "Tell me. What should I get Princess for her birthday? What does she like? What's her favorite color?" she asks.

"You being there is present enough for her, B", I respond.

"I was thinking about getting something to take with her to college where she'll always be reminded of her Aunt B", she responds.

"Of course. Of course. Whatever you get, I'm sure she'll love and appreciate it. But I know for a fact that she's going to be so surprised to see you. That's the best gift of all", I say. "I need your help on something."

"Sure. What is it?" she asks.

"Have you seen "Rock" around there lately?" I ask.

"As a matter of fact, I have. He's doing well for himself. He recently opened up his first barber shop and his girlfriend just had twin girls. Why the sudden interest in "Rock"?" Brittney asks.

"For the first time ever, Princess asked about her father. She wants to meet him. What do you think about that?" I ask.

"I think it's time. "Rock" is at a much better place right now. His head is on good and I believe that he'd be open to meeting Princess and having a relationship with her. I can have him call you if you'd like", she offers.

"Could you? Would you? Please. I appreciate it, B", I say.

"Absolutely. Anything for Princess", Brittney agrees.

"Ok. So, I will see you guys in two days. I can't wait to see my niece and nephew."

"And they're definitely looking forward to seeing you and Mickey", Brittney responds.

"Well, Mickey is over there in Orlando, but I can make sure they see Mickey when they get here", I say. "I gotta go now but I'll see you when you get here."

I hope that "Rock" will act civilized and responsible and will want to meet his daughter. *Maybe this, too, can be part of her surprise!* My thoughts are interrupted when my cell phone rings. It's Cynthia!

"Girl, what do you want? I'm on my way to the office", I say.

"It's Sharon from Corporate. She just called looking for you. She wanted to know what time you normally get into the office and when you would be in the office. It was strange. She wants you to call her when you get here", Cynthia says.

"Okay. Not a problem. Is everything else okay? Are you okay? You don't sound too happy", I comment.

"I'm okay but honestly, I just didn't like the way she sounded, Melissa. I think you need to hurry up and get here so you can call her back. I just didn't like how she sounded, that's all", Cynthia repeats.

"You worry too much. Everything's okay. I'll be there shortly. I'm just around the corner and I'll call her when I get into the office. So, did she sound upset?" I ask.

"I don't know, MeMe. She didn't sound the same as she normally does. I know that."

Moments later, I make it into the office to find Cynthia sitting behind the computer deeply involved in what she's doing, but she briefly looks up when I pass through to get to my office.

"Glad you could make it", she comments. "Hey, I know you're going through a lot with the kids and all but, let's try our best to have fun tonight. Are you excited?" she asks.

"I'm thinking that maybe I shouldn't go, Cynthia. I mean, with Sharelle gone and Kalin....", I begin.

"Oh no ma'am. You *are* going! We've planned to go and we're going. All you can do is pray for Sharelle. I'm sure she's safe. And don't you dare let Kalin stop you. Do something for yourself. I'll be there at your house around 6. End of story!" she says, walking towards the lobby.

"Just like that, huh? You're something else!" I say, laughing.

"No, you're something else; coming in here with that nonsense", she says. We both laugh. "Please call Sharon now and squash whatever that is."

I make into my office and the first order of business is to return Sharon's call and she answers right away.

"Sharon, it's Melissa. How are you? Cynthia told me you called. I'm in the office now. Is everything okay?" I say.

"I need to talk to you about Pinnacle Shores", she says. "Just need to clarify a few things."

"Okay. Let's talk. Do you want to do it now or will you be coming to the property or what?" I ask.

"No. Let's talk this afternoon. I'm in the area, but meeting with another client today. So, what does your schedule look like for 2:30 this afternoon?" she asks.

"2:30 sounds just fine. I'll see you then."

As soon as Sharon and I get off the phone, I call the property to speak with the manager, Mabel, to have her send me certain reports.

"Good afternoon, Mrs. Thomas", Mabel says after answering the phone. Mabel has been with the company for several years and I was thrilled when she agreed to manage this property for me. I think I like her because she reminds me of myself and how I managed my properties when I was a resident manager. She's one of the kindest people I know and I trust her with this property.

"Hey Mabel. How are you? How's everything with the property? I rode by there and it looks good", I tell her.

"I'm good. The property is good. Our numbers are solid. We are 94% occupied and we have quite a few prospects that we're following up with. Maintenance is caught up with work orders, we don't have any customer complaints right now, and we only have $8300 or so delinquent right now. And over $6000 of that is already committed", she explains.

"Wow! It looks like you're on top of it. You are always on top of things. I love that! I have a meeting this afternoon with Sharon from corporate regarding your property and I need you to send me some reports so that I am able to rattle off numbers with her when she asks and trust me, she'll ask", I tell her.

"Okay. Where do you want me to send them?"

"Send the reports to my email so that I can have a printed copy for her as well as an email version of it", I respond. "Everything certainly sounds good. I'm not quite sure what it is that she wants to discuss with me about the property, but I'll certainly let you know as soon as I know", I tell her.

"Ok, Mrs. Thomas. Have a great afternoon!" she says.

Within minutes, Mabel has sent the documents to me and I am reviewing the stats. She's right! The property is in excellent shape right now with the numbers, so I have no idea what it is that Sharon needs to discuss with me about this property unless, of course, she wants *someone else* to manage it.

"What did she say?" Cynthia says, barging into my office.

"She's coming by this afternoon to sit down and discuss Pinnacle Shores with me. I just spoke with Mabel and the property is at 94% for crying out loud! What in the world could she need to talk about? Guess I'm going to have to wait and see what it is that she wants to discuss. Now, about tonight?" I say, standing to my feet.

"Yes. What about tonight?" Cynthia asks. "Somebody has been thinking about Stevie, haven't they?"

"Ok, so I have to admit that I'm a *little* curious as to what he looks like now. Not gonna lie. But, I'm more curious as to how his comedy is. He better make me laugh. You know that reminds me. I haven't heard from Kalin today. He didn't bring his behind home last night", I say, looking away from Cynthia. *I don't want to make contact with her, just in case I start crying or something.*

"I had no idea. Did you call him? Why didn't he come home? What's going on with the two of you?"

"We had a conversation the other day and honestly, it wasn't a good one. To tell you the truth, I'm so over him. He cheated on me. He's the one who made our relationship bad with his cheating and his untruths. I think I'm ready to close this chapter. I think that...", I say, starting to elevate my voice.

"Melissa, ok, forget him for now. It's time to have some fun. Now, you know that I'm your closest friend and I happen to know how you felt about Stevie. You probably never really got over him. Remember how the two of you parted. He left to follow his career. And I know that you were supportive to him for leaving, but very broken hearted. It's okay. Your secret is safe with me. That's what friends are for", Cynthia says, offering her shoulder to me.

On the way back into my office, a strange call comes into my phone and it says "Restricted". I don't know if I should pick this up or not.

"Hello", I say.

"Hey", says the person on the other end of the call. "Just wanted you to know that I'm safe."

When she says this, I realize that it's Sharelle on the other end of the phone. It does my heart good to know that she's safe and sound.

"Sharelle, please come home, honey. Why are you staying out there? I'm worried sick about you. We're all worried about you. Come home and we can work out whatever it is that we need to work out. Are you really ok? Is anyone hurting you out there?" I ask, hurriedly.

"Ma, I'm okay and you'll be happy to know that I'm staying with friends. I gotta go, but just wanted to call so you won't worry about me", she explains.

"Sharelle, I'm your mother. Of course I'm worried about you! Honey, please come...", I say, and the phone suddenly disconnects. "Noooooooooooo!"

Cynthia rushes into the room. She asks, "Is everything okay? Why are you yelling?"

That was Sharelle. She called just to let me know that she's okay and when I tried to tell her to come home, she hung up on me. Oh my God, Cynthia! My baby is out there all alone", I say, as the tears begin to flow heavily.

"Don't do that, Melissa. You've done all you can do. These kids grow up and have their own minds and they don't want to listen. All you can do is pray that God watches over her and keeps her safe. That's all you can do", she says, rubbing my back and drying the tears away from my eyes.

"You're right. I'm such a crybaby. Must be that time of the month or something", I say, and we both laugh. "At least I know she's alive. Well, it's almost time for me to meet with Sharon. She should be here any minute now."

"Ok, Melissa. This thing will turn around one day. Just keep the faith", Cynthia encourages. Just as Cynthia walks into the clubhouse, she notices that Sharon is coming through the double doors. The 'honor roll' kids are already there, patiently awaiting to receive their sweet treats we promised them.

"Good afternoon, Sharon. How are you? Those are some nice shoes, but you always have on nice shoes. Melissa's in her office."

"Ok. I'll let myself in. It was good to see you, Cynthia."

"Same to you, Ms. Sharon", Cynthia says and then puts her attention back to the children waiting for her.

Sharon walks through the front office until she makes it to my office. "Hello, Melissa. How are you this afternoon? The property looks great!"

"Thanks, Sharon. We try", I say and we both laugh.

"Now, Melissa, I want to talk to you about Pinnacle Shores. The property looks good, your manager is doing great, so it's nothing bad. So, please relax", Sharon begins.

"Well, thanks for clarifying that because I've been worried sick all day wondering what it is that we need to discuss about Pinnacle Shores."

"The truth is that we need the occupancy level to be higher. I know it's sitting at….", she says before I interrupt her.

"94%, with several prospects", I continue.

"Yes, I know, but the truth is that we are in loan status and the higher the occupancy percentage, the more money we can get approved on the loan", she explains.

"And the Open House that the manager has planned for the weekend should bring in at least 10 new residents. We are getting tons of traffic and referrals from current residents. We'll be okay, Sharon", I say, trying to ease her mind of the occupancy percentage.

"I have an idea that I think will work. You ready to hear it?" she asks.

"I'm always open to new ideas to bring the property to the level where it needs to be", I respond.

"We need to move in fake residents and their move-in deposits to raise the occupancy percentage, print out all the reports that the bank is requiring that we need for the loan, and then move them out of the system. This will ensure that we have a higher occupancy percentage, thereby satisfying the requirements of the loan that will secure us just what we need from the banks. What do you think?" she asks.

Is she crazy? I am livid with this request but I know that this is my head manager so I will try to control myself. So, is this how they get ahead? What happened to hard work and dedication, which is what I teach my managers to do? How could I ever look my managers in the eyes and request of them to do something as unethical as this?

"Sharon, are you serious? You're joking, right? I've been in property management for several years and not only have I kept a clean record, but I've never had an executive manager make such a request to me. I'm speechless, Sharon, and I don't know what to say. I'm just..", I begin before she interrupts me.

"Just say you'll do it."

"Absolutely not, Sharon. I won't ruin my career for the 6% that I am short of being 100% at a new property way ahead of schedule. I can't do that, Sharon", I say. She looks shocked that I'm saying no to her.

"You won't do it?" she asks.

"No, I won't do it. And if that costs me my job, then so be it. I won't do it. I won't compromise myself for this job, Sharon. Would you do it? Would you put your name on something like this?" I ask her.

"If it meant keeping my job, I sure as hell would. But that's just me", she says, changing the subject and shrugging her shoulders. "So, how is everything going with this property? It looks nice."

"It's going just fine. 98% occupied with less than $5000 delinquent and it's the 10th of the month. Renewals are coming back signed to renew for another year. We don't have to advertise, so I would say that this property is doing just fine", I respond.

"Well, if that's it, I'm going to head back over to the corporate office. Please call me if you change your mind", Sharon says as she is getting up packing her briefcase with the reports I hand to her.

"Have a safe ride back over there. You should beat this Friday traffic before it gets too bad", I say.

Sharon leaves the office, but deep down in my soul, I feel that this little meeting just may cost me my job. Cynthia comes in shortly afterwards. "What did she want? She didn't look too happy when she left", Cynthia comments.

"You're not going to believe this. She wants me to make up some fake people and move them into the system for Pinnacle Shores to get a better occupancy percentage and I told her "no". How can she ask me something like this? I don't play that. I'm not going to compromise my name as a clean record manager for this company. No way!" I say, getting more upset even after she is gone.

"Are you serious? You know, Melissa, I've heard they do this type of thing a lot. Just to get more money for the properties. But I have also heard that if you don't do it, they'll fire you", Cynthia tells me.

"I don't care, Cynthia. I'll lose my job if I have to, but I'm not getting mixed up in fraudulent activity with this company. I won't do it. And besides, this won't be the first time I will have lost a job for not doing something unethical. What would my children think of me? They don't pay me enough money to do that. If it's God's Will that I be fired, then I'll be fired. It's just that simple. You don't know me! I despise this kind of thing", I say, slamming shut the folder sitting on my desk. Patrick must subconsciously know that I need to hear a good word right now because my phone is vibrating and it says, "message from Patrick". *"You already know what I want to tell you..one word..black!"*

"So, what you smiling for?" Cynthia asks. "Somebody sent you something on that cell phone that made you smile."

"Nobody! So, let's get out of here so that we can go home and get dressed for our girl's night out.

Cynthia and I close the office right at closing time just so we can avoid the Friday traffic on I-95. She goes south on I-95 and I travel north. "Ok, I'll see you at 6, right?"

"Yes ma'am, you will", Cynthia responds.

I pull into the driveway and didn't really expect to see Kalin's car. He didn't come home last night and I wasn't really worrying about it too much today. As soon as I get out of the car, he comes over to me to try to explain his situation and why he didn't come home.

"I don't want to hear it, Kalin. You're a grown man. You don't have to explain your whereabouts to me", I say, walking past him.

"I'm your husband and you deserve to know where I was last night. And why you weren't able to get through to me and....", he explains.

"Husband? You think that's what you have been to me? A husband? Give me a break, Kalin, but fortunately for you, I don't care anymore about what you do or who you do it with. I have plans this evening and I need to prepare myself before Cynthia gets here. So, if you'll excuse me", I say, pushing him aside.

"Plans? What plans? Where are you going?" Kalin asks, walking behind me.

"If you must know, I'm having a girls' night out with Cynthia and we're going to a comedy event. Don't wait up for me either!" I say, rushing into my shower.

Kalin heads towards the office and shuts the door. *What does he think? He stays out all night and has the nerve to think that I'm the least bit interested in what the hell he has to say. Hell no! I sat in that bed last night waiting for him. That is the last time I will ever sit up at night and wait for any man to come home to me.*

Cynthia will be here in the next 15 – 20 minutes and I have to be ready when she gets here. With a few minutes to spare, I call Papa Johns to order pizza for the girls and then I'm out of here to enjoy my evening. In the corner of my eye, I can tell that Kalin is just standing there watching me. "Why are you so happy? Who is he, Melissa?"

"Kalin, give me a break. Why? Because I'm happy and it has nothing to do with you. This is your fault that I want to go out with my girlfriend to enjoy myself. When I was sitting up and waiting for you last night, I realized that it's not something that I want to get used to, so if you want this marriage, you need to get your stuff together because there will come a day when I really won't care who you're with and you can trust that!!" I say, picking up my things and walking towards the front door. Cynthia just pulled up in her black shiny Volvo.

"What time will you be home?" he asks, trying to grab my arm.

"When I get home", I say, tearing away from his grasp and walking towards Cynthia's car.

I get in the car and Cynthia quickly lets me know that she saw that brief interaction with Kalin. "So, was he trying to get you to stay home or what?"

"No, worse than that; he wanted to know when I was coming home", I say. We both laugh. "Then he had the nerve to try to explain why he stayed out all night. I told him that I didn't want to hear it. But tonight is our night. Let's get something to eat. What do you feel like eating?" I ask.

"It really doesn't matter to me. You make the suggestion", Cynthia says.

"Ok. What about *Enchanted*?"

"Enchanted? Where is it?" Cynthia asks.

"Downtown. It's a very nice restaurant. I've eaten there a few times. What do you say?"

"Sounds good to me", Cynthia agrees.

What if I run into Patrick in here? Will I act as if I don't know him? Will Cynthia pick up on anything unusual between us?

When we pull up to the restaurant, I can tell that Cynthia is impressed. She has no idea that Patrick is the owner of this beautiful restaurant, nor is she aware that there are meals that he put together that are related to me. We walk inside and from that moment on, the service that we receive is impeccable. Cynthia and I are seated at a beautiful table in one of the back rooms. The jazz music is playing through the sound system and the mood is so relaxing. Our waiter brings us our drinks of choice right away, along with the menus.

"Melissa, since you've been here before, what's good?" Cynthia asks.

"The meal, *Ella Enchanted,* is to die for", I respond. "It's very delicious. You should try it."

"Ok. I will."

Our waiter returns and we order two *Ella Enchanteds.* "So, Cynthia, did I make a good choice?"

"Yes. Absolutely. This place is beautiful. Whoever runs this place has done a great job. They make you feel so welcome. I love it. This just may become a regular place for me", she comments.

Oh boy! I don't know if I want to run into Cynthia in here one day with Patrick. It will all make sense to her if she sees me with him, but she may not understand the whole story.

"Really? How sweet!" I respond.

The waiter finally returns with our meals and for the next 45 minutes or so, we sit and talk and laugh, enjoying every minute of our girl's night out. My phone vibrates and I check the message. *"You are sexy as hell to me and I can't wait. I am glad to see that you're enjoying your meal. Love, Patrick..xoxoxoxoxo".*

I must have a big smile on my face because Cynthia looks at me funny. "So, what has you sitting over there with that big smile on your face? I know it can't be your husband because you just left him and you left somewhat angry with him, so the only person I can think of is, perhaps, Patrick", she says, with a smirk grin on her face.

"Eat your food!" I say, jokingly.

For Patrick to send this message, he must be in the restaurant watching us. He probably saw us from the moment we walked through the doors. *How sexy it is to know that he's watching me right now. I wonder what's going through his mind. This is starting to turn me on and*

I'm finding it difficult to remember that I'm actually sitting here with my girlfriend in a public place.

Cynthia and I eventually finish our meals and opt out for dessert. We leave a very generous tip to our waiter, Jonathan. He did an excellent job serving us tonight. Cynthia and I leave the restaurant, jump in our vehicle, and head for the Arena. Traffic is somewhat slow tonight; no doubt it's because of this big event that's going down at the Arena. Cynthia must have some connections because we just parked in "VIP".

"Wow, somebody must know somebody for us to get to park in VIP", I say to Cynthia.

"Girl, you're crazy. But, isn't this better?" she asks.

"Of course it is. Now, let's get this party started. I'm excited about seeing Stevie do his thing on stage", I comment.

This is certainly one time that I'm glad that we don't have to go through the regular channels to get in because the line outside seems about as long as Dolphin Parkway. The only problem is that I have no idea to whom my gratitude should be for.

"Cynthia, who do you know that got us this hookup? It doesn't get any better than this" I say. We both laugh.

Where we're sitting, we can see the entire Arena. It definitely looks better up here. I can certainly appreciate these seats so much better than the seats I would normally sit at in this Arena. *I wonder who Cynthia knows that got us VIP treatment tonight. I am sure her husband must know somebody who knows somebody, but I don't care and it looks like the show is about to begin.*

"Ladies and gentlemen, you are about to see some of the funniest comedians the South has ever seen! If you're ready to get your funny on, sit back, relax, and help me introduce our lineup for the evening. Coming to you tonight is D-Ray Davis, Earthquake, a blast from the past Tommy Davison, a special appearance from Ced the Entertainer, and last but not least, our headliner for the evening, Steeeeeeeevieeeeeeeeeeee!!"

The crowd erupts with applauses. I look up on the screen and it's a giant size photo of Stevie in an off white suit and for a brief second, my mouth drops. Gorgeous is the first thing that comes to mind.

"Looking good, isn't he?" Cynthia asks, noticing how I'm staring at his picture on the screen.

"Yes he is! My boy! I'm so proud of him", I respond. "I'm so glad that you talked me into coming tonight. God knows I need this time to just relax and laugh, where I can try to forget my problems, even if it *is* just for one night."

"That's right! You deserve this, Melissa! So, let's enjoy the show and the rest of our evening", Cynthia says.

D'Ray is crazy! I loved his stand-up on the All Star Weekend. His performance tonight is even funnier than that. And now, Earthquake is on stage and I'm in stitches. I always love his performances. And just like always, he has a drink in his hand while he performs. Tommy Davison comes out on stage and immediately disrobes himself. For a skinny guy, he's somewhat sexy to me. Ced the Entertainer is one of my favorite comedians and he rocked the house tonight. He gets his funny on, but his main job is to introduce our headliner.

"This next guy coming to the stage is our headliner for the evening and is funny as hell. He grew up right here in Miami, but left to pursue a career in modeling out in L.A. You've seen him in the movie, "The Punisher"; he's been on the cover of Ebony, Essence, Jet, and a few white magazines. Your headliner, Steeeeeeeevieeeeeeeeeeeeee!" he announces.

The crowd erupts and immediately stands to their feet. Stevie walks out on stage in a red and black suit. He always did look good in red. He is walking across the stage and waving to the crowd, and blowing kisses. He has to settle the crowd down just to get in a word. "Hello Miamiiiiiiiiiiiiii!" he yells. "Ya'll look good out there!" They yell back to him showing him lots of love. At the end of Stevie's performance, I'm left speechless, but very impressed. He made me laugh several times, which is hard for *any* comedian to do.

"Is this some type of dungeon exit or something?" I ask, jokingly, as Cynthia and I are being led down a long hallway.

"No ma'am. You wanna meet the comedians, don't you?"

"Cynthia, who do you know that got us this hookup?" I ask, looking towards her. She is looking straight ahead with a smile on her face, pointed forward and says, "Him". I am curious to see the guy who she knows and when I turn around, I'm looking eyeball to eyeball with Stevie.

"Well, well, well, if it isn't Melissa Williams! Hello, Melissa!" he says, with the most gorgeous smile on his face.

My head swiftly turns towards Cynthia and I know she can read my mind. How did you…?" I begin to ask before Cynthia interrupts.

"Well, let me tell you how it happened. Stevie called the office one day looking for you and when I told him that you weren't there, he asked me for a favor. He started out by telling me that he was coming to town for this comedy event and he needed me to make sure you come. As soon as he said the name, Stevie, I knew who he was. So, for weeks now, I knew and this morning, he dropped by the office to bring me our tickets. *He's* the reason we had the VIP treatment tonight. Now, didn't I get you? You're surprised, right?" Cynthia asks.

"Ahh, very surprised!" I say, turning to Stevie. "You did a great job out there tonight! You actually made me laugh", I say, grabbing his arm.

"Wow! I'm glad to hear that. You look great, Melissa!" Stevie says, looking me up and down.

Cynthia excuses herself so that Stevie and I can have some privacy.

"Now, why did you feel like you had to get my assistant to get me here tonight? You could have just asked me yourself", I say, laughing slightly.

"I didn't want to take any chances on being here in Miami on the biggest night of my life and have one of my dearest friends *not* show up. So, I did what I thought was necessary", he adds. "And besides, you're my daughter's mother and have always believed in me. I'll never forget, Melissa."

"That's so sweet, Stevie. Thank you so much. You're too kind", I tell him.

"Speaking of my child, how is she? What's going on with her? Does she look like her beautiful mother or what?" he asks.

"It's a long story, Stevie. She isn't doing too well these days. We can talk about it at a later time. But she is 5'7" or so right now and in the 7th grade. She will, no doubt, be tall just like her father. She's beautiful and smart, but she's definitely going through those pre-teen stages", I respond.

"I would love to see her before I leave and...", he begins.

"And when will that be? When will you be leaving?" I ask.

"2 weeks. I'll be here for 2 more weeks", he answers.

"Okay. We'll see if we can't set something up for the two of you to have some time together", I respond. *Now, how in the world will I explain it when I have to tell him that she is actually not in my house at the time but that she has actually run away from home?*

"And what about you?" Stevie asks, standing with his arms folded.

"What do you mean? What about me?" I ask.

"Will you set some time aside for *me and you* to spend some time together?" he asks.

"Stevie, I'm a married woman", I respond. "And, aren't you married too?"

"Honestly, I'm going through a very rough divorce from my wife. We never had kids and …", he says, before changing the subject, "I really don't want to talk about this here. What are you and Cynthia doing after you leave here?"

"Nothing", Cynthia says, coming back over, right in time to answer the question.

"I have plans. Maybe we can get together at some point before you leave", I tell him instead. He looks puzzled, but accepts my answer.

"That's fair. It was really good to see you and thanks so much, Cynthia, for getting her here", Stevie says, reaching out for a hug.

I move in closer to give him a hug. And the honest truth is that I remember now just how safe he always made me feel with his hugs. My mind goes back 13 years or so and I remember our night at the Gaylord Palms in Orlando more than anything. He was so into me that night. But the reality right now is that I can't leave here with this man. We hug for what seems like an eternity before he gives me his card.

"And I need a hug from you too, Cynthia. Listen. Any friend of Melissa's is a friend of mine. Thank you both for coming and I'm delighted that you enjoyed the show. Would you ladies like to meet the other comedians?" he asks.

"Sure", we both say in unison.

Stevie walks right over to Ced the Entertainer and Tommy Davison, disrupting their conversation, just to introduce us to them. "Hey guys, stop talking for a sec. I have some beautiful ladies I want you to meet. Melissa and Cynthia, Ced and Tommy", he says.

"Nice to meet you both", I tell them.

"Oh my goodness! So nice to meet both of you. I enjoyed your performances tonight", Cynthia says, handing me her camera for me to get a pic of her with them, until Stevie tells me to get in and offers to take the picture himself.

"Smile everybody."

D-Ray and Earthquake are in a conversation about where they want to get a bite to eat and Stevie also interrupts them to introduce us. We take a picture with them as well. I'm just so shocked at how 'down to earth' these guys are. It was so nice to meet them all and I owe it to Stevie for making all of this happen.

"Well, I need to speak to a lot of people right now, but I just wanted to see you, Melissa, and I'm glad that I did. Enjoy the rest of your evening", Stevie says and walks away.

Cynthia and I head straight for the exit. On our way out, the guy who escorted us backstage gives us signed pictures from each of the comedians. "Plans?" Cynthia asks, looking puzzled. "Did you say that just to get rid of Stevie?"

"No, I actually do have plans tonight. You got me! My secret is out. I didn't tell you earlier because I knew that you would try to tell me that I should go home and talk things out with Kalin and all that and I am not trying to hear it right now. I'm going to my secret place and a friend is meeting me there, Cynthia. And please don't try to talk me out of it. I'm going! So just be my friend and understand", I say, looking forward. I notice that Cynthia is staring at me from the side.

"Is it Patrick?" she asks.

"Yes. Yes. I'm meeting him at *our* secret place", I respond.

"Our" secret place? I don't understand", she says.

"A while back, Patrick purchased this condo for me whenever I need to get away from Kalin, work, kids, etc. He has a key and he's meeting me there tonight. We've been planning this since the night that Kalin didn't think it was necessary for him to come home", I explain.

"Wow, Melissa. I can't believe this. I don't know what to say. That was nice of him to care for you like that. I will say that, but are you sure about this? Aren't you scared to be intimate with him? You know, that changes everything once you cross that line."

"I know that, and of course, I'm afraid, Cynthia. He and I have been friends for quite some time. This man has been there to encourage me and everything. We didn't make plans to sleep together. It's just spending some quiet time together. If it's supposed to happen, it will have to happen naturally", I respond.

"Melissa, I'm your friend for life. I won't judge you, but I want to know how you feel about your husband" she asks.

"I've loved Kalin for many years and have given this man the best years of my life. He hurt me when he slept with Wendy and got her pregnant. And then, when he had the secret email account with Diandra from Alabama, that just crushed me even more. And then most recently, just the other night, this man didn't come home and wouldn't answer my calls when I called. So, I just feel like it's time for me to be happy and if Patrick wants to make me happy, I'll let him put a smile on my face", I explain.

"I understand that, Melissa. I really do", she tells me.

Cynthia just pulled into the condo. "I see that Mr. Patrick is already here. Am I picking you up here tomorrow morning?" she asks.

"Yes. In the morning, I have to take the girls to the Mall to shop for their outfits for Princess' birthday party", I respond.

"And what will you tell your husband when he starts calling you and wondering where you are?" she asks.

"That you and I had a little too much to drink tonight and I had to stay with you", I answer.

"I see. Melissa, you're my friend and I love you and I just want the very best for you. That's all. I've seen you go through so much and I'm ready to see you live the happy life", she explains. "Why not just pray about this like you do everything else?"

"Me too, Cynthia. Me too! Good night", I say, opening the door to her car. I hate to act as if I didn't hear her question, but I'm ignoring it for now.

"Good night."

As soon as I turn the key to go into the condo, the door opens and Patrick is standing in front of me looking ever so handsome in his jeans and white tank top, exposing his chiseled arms. He reaches for a hug and I give it to him. He smells so good. We continue to hold each other for what seems like an eternity. *This feels like the perfect moment for a sweet kiss, but I dare not attempt it first. I can't force this moment.* Without warning, Patrick takes my face in his hands and gives me the sweetest kiss I have ever felt on my lips. Patrick is in total control of this kiss. He's taking me places with his tongue as it explores my mouth. I drop my purse and hold him tightly around his waist. The passion between the two of us is super intense. I didn't know that it would be like this. My phone vibrates and interrupts our fiery contact. The caller ID is saying that this call is coming from my house. It could be the kids, but it could also be Kalin. "So sorry", I whisper to Patrick. "I have to take this call."

"I know. Of course", he says, walking away to give me privacy.

"Hello", I say into the phone.

"What time are you getting home?" asks Kalin.

"I'm not coming home tonight. I'm with Cynthia at her house. We had a little too much to drink and I'm staying with her", I explain to him.

"I just called Cynthia and she said that she didn't know where you were", Kalin says.

"Kalin, please stop playing games with me. I know where I am. Is there anything else that you want?" I ask.

"I guess not. Who is he? Who are you with tonight?" he asks.

"Goodbye, Kalin", I say, hanging up the phone.

Turning my attention back to Patrick, he says, "Giving you a hard time, huh?"

He wanted to know when I was coming home", I respond.

"If it weren't for the children, you wouldn't need to go back home at all", he comments.

"And what is that supposed to mean, Patrick?" I ask, looking surprised that he went there.

"I mean. You could just stay here at the condo", he responds.

"Where were we?" I ask him, putting down my purse, ignoring his last comment.

Patrick takes my face in his hands just like before and kisses me passionately, using his tongue to explore my mouth, leaving a tingling sensation all over my body. His mouth is all over my neck planting soft kisses. "You wore black just like I asked you to", he says, in between kisses. I also asked you to wear sexy black panties. Are you? Can I see, baby?" he asks.

"Ahh, what is that smell coming from the kitchen?" I ask, tearing away from him with a smirk on my face.

"You're driving me crazy, sexy woman!" he says. "You know how much I love Italian food, so I prepared a little something just for you. I know you told me that you and Cynthia would have already eaten dinner, so I prepared just a *little* something. And to help you relax, I have your favorite wine chilling."

"Speaking of dinner, you were obviously in *Enchanted* tonight because of the text message you sent", I say. "That really caught me off guard, Patrick."

"Actually, I had stopped in to check on things on my way home. I was in my office and when I'm in my office upstairs, I can see all the customers come in. And in walks this beautiful ebony woman that caught my eye. I knew it was you because I can tell your walk anywhere. When I looked closer, it was you *and* your girlfriend. I watched you until you sat down at your table. I watched how you chewed your food and how you put your drink to your mouth. You were seducing me and you didn't even know it", he says, tracing his finger along my lips.

"You're turning me on, Patrick", I say, grabbing his hand and licking his middle finger. He seems to like when I do this. This time, I grab his face and I have full control of the passion in the kiss. My tongue is deep in his mouth and we're starting to venture into a point of no return.

"Baby, I want you. Can I have you, Melissa?" he asks, passionately.

"Not now baby. We have all night. Let's take our time and enjoy each other completely", I suggest. *I'm so nervous right now. I haven't been with anyone but Kalin for the last 15 years of my life. I don't know what it's like to have another man touch me in this way.*

"Yeah, you're right because I'm about to devour you and say to hell with the Italian food", he says, jokingly. We laugh hysterically.

"So, why don't I get a shower while you're finishing up the food?" I ask.

"I guess I can stand to be away from you for 15 minutes or so", he says.

I leave Patrick standing there to get my shower. My favorite lounging clothes from *Victoria's Secret* are already tucked away in my drawer. In the bathroom now and taking off my clothes, I get the feeling that I'm being watched. *I know I may not see Patrick, but I can feel his presence very strongly.* I look around, but there's no one there. It's a shame he won't get to see me in the black lace panties that he sent to my office the other day. As soon as I slip off my panties, I get this sudden urge to touch myself. It feels like Patrick has already started a fire between my legs.

"Don't stop, baby", Patrick says, startling me and walking into the bathroom.

"How long have you been standing there?" I ask him, blushing. Patrick's eyes say *I want you and I need you right now.*

"I thought I left you in the kitchen", I say, placing my arms around his neck. I can feel the fire coming from his body.

"You did, but I started thinking about the black panties that you were wearing for me and I had to take a peek. I hope you don't think I'm some kind of pervert", he says, laughing.

"Baby, I was hoping you were watching, so I won't think of you as a pervert if you don't think of me as a freak", I say, jumping up and wrapping my legs around him. Patrick places me on top of the countertop and continues to kiss me, but his hands begin to wander and end up on my breasts. My left breast is being devoured by him, taking his time to tease my nipples, one at a time. Before I know it, he has his warm hands between my legs and exploring every part of me. His fingers are inside of me and going deeper and deeper each time. He seems to get even more excited when I let out a loud moan. We are enjoying each other and the passion intensifies with each kiss. Patrick turns on the shower and continues taking off my clothes. Now, standing in the shower, Patrick and I are making love and it feels that we're the only two people left on the face of the earth. It feels as if we can't get close enough. With each thrust, his manhood hardens more and more. *I know now that the myth about white men isn't true. He's more than enough for me.* From the shower to the bed to the floor, we go all night like two sex starved teenagers.

Falling over to our side of the bed from sex exhaustion, Patrick rolls over, looks at me, and says, "So, baby, how do you feel now?" He takes my hand in is and waits for my answer.

"I feel like royalty! You served me with your best and it felt so good", I say jokingly. He laughs at me.

"There's more where that came from, Melissa. You mean so much to me and I'm glad that it actually took us this long to make love because it was well worth it. You taste so good to me, baby. I won't ever get tired of you. As a matter of fact, I *still* want you", he says. Patrick positions himself, opens my legs apart and starts to please me orally. Well into the night, we make love over and over. We can't seem to get enough of each other. Around 3 in the morning, we finally leave the room to eat the food that he prepared for us. At this point, Italian food sounds good because we've certainly worked up an appetite.

"This food is delicious, Patrick!" I say, taking the first bite.

"Glad that you like it, sweetheart. Melissa, I need to tell you something", he announces.

"What is it?" I ask, sounding worried.

"I don't know how to say this so I'll just blurt it out. I love you, Melissa, and I have felt something for you since our very first kiss sitting in my car at Starbucks. Do you even remember that?" he asks.

"Of course I remember that. That moment changed our lives, Patrick. I tried to forget about you after that. I tried everything that I possibly could to tell my heart that I was wrong for feeling what I was feeling for you. And when you showed up at the trial a few years back to show your support, I was blown away. Kalin never liked you. He always told me that you wanted me and I denied it on so many occasions when your name would come up in our conversations. But I can't deny what I feel right now. You might as well know the truth, Patrick. I love you too!" I confess.

"I'm the happiest man right now, Melissa! You're the reason this big smile exists", he comments.

"But Patrick, the reality here is that I'm still married and I don't know what to….", I say, and then he plants a kiss on my lips.

"That is what I think of that. I know it'll take some time for us to be together, but I'm hopeful that we'll be together one day. Is that how you see it?" he asks.

"I have never actually thought of it before tonight. I never thought that you would want me like that. What are you saying?" I ask, looking somewhat serious.

"I want you and me to be a family one day. I want to marry you someday", he proclaims.

"And how do you know that?" I ask.

"I don't ever want to sleep alone again. You make the bed feel so much better", he says. We both laugh hysterically.

"Sweetheart, Cynthia dropped me off here last night and she'll be here any moment now. Princess' birthday party is tonight and I promised the girls that I would take them shopping this morning for something to wear to the party", I say.

"May I get something for Princess for her birthday?" he asks.

"I don't think that would be a good idea, Patrick", I respond.

"Okay", he says. "Mom knows best. But, you haven't responded to the idea of us being married one day. I'm anxious to know how you feel about that", he repeats.

My phone is vibrating and Cynthia is texting me to let me know that she's outside waiting.

"My ride is here so I have to leave now", I tell him. "Later, okay?"

Patrick gets up and holds me in his arms and plants a very passionate kiss on my lips. "I hope this will hold you until we see each other again."

I'm a mess! This man has brought his "A" game and I'm feeling like some schoolgirl walking on a cloud. What did I just do? I broke my marital vow and made love with a man who I have had feelings for but never acted on it until my husband betrayed me. That is probably no excuse for doing it, but I did. What's done is done. Do I ever want to again? I think I do. How am I now going to go home and face Kalin knowing this secret of mine?

"Good morning", Cynthia says, as I approach her car. "How was your night?"

"Don't even ask. Please don't ask me that question because I don't want to lie to you. You're my best friend", I answer.

"So, don't lie to me. I asked a simple question. How was your night?" she asks again.

"I had the most amazing night ever! He made me feel something that I haven't felt in a long time. I needed what he gave me. I felt one with him, Cynthia. And I know I was wrong for breaking the marital vow, but I have no regrets whatsoever", I say, positioning my seatbelt.

"I hope it was worth it, Melissa. I'm glad that you and Patrick had a good time. Now what? Where does he want to go with the relationship?" she asks.

"He said that he wants us to be a family. I'm not ready to even think about that at all. Right now, I need to focus on my Princess' birthday party. He offered to buy her a gift, but I told him that I didn't think it was a good idea. I hate to go home and face Kalin, but I have to", I admit.

CHAPTER 9

"We Need to Talk."

"Well, well, well. Look who's working in the yard", Cynthia says, letting down her window to speak to Kalin after pulling into my driveway. *I guess this is Kalin's way of being able to check who's dropping me off.* "Good morning Kalin! I see you're getting the yard ready."

"Good morning, Cynthia. Thanks for bringing my wife home to me", he says, coming towards the door to open it for me to get out. "Good morning my beautiful wife! So nice of you to come home to your husband and kids", he says sarcastically.

"Bye, Cynthia! And thanks for last night", I say, totally ignoring Kalin's comment.

I get out of the car and walk past Kalin, who is standing there as if he's ready for a battle. "So, you're not going to acknowledge that I'm standing here?" he asks.

"Look, I'm not going to do this with you today. It's all about Princess and you're not going to ruin this day for her, so if you want to argue, pick another one of your ladies to do it with because I'm not trying to hear it!" I say, going into the house.

As soon as I get into the house, the girls make sure I know they're ready to go shopping. "Mommy, where have you been? We thought you forgot that we were supposed to go shopping", Justice shouts.

"No, sweetheart. I didn't forget. I spent the night with Auntie Cynthia. She's coming to the party tonight too!" I say. "Let me change clothes and check my messages and then we can go! Is that okay with you all?"

"Yay!! That's awesome! I'll let Amber and Princess know that we're leaving soon."

I walk into my bedroom and become somewhat upset when I see that my bed isn't made and there are clothes all over the floor. *What in the world went on in here and why didn't Kalin at least make the bed? I know what he's doing. He's really trying to piss me off and start a fight with me, but I'm not going to give him the satisfaction. I'm going to jump in the shower, get dressed and take my girls shopping. To hell with Kalin!*

While I'm in the shower, I can tell that Kalin just walked into the bathroom, no doubt ready for an argument. "So, how was your girl's night out with Cynthia?" Kalin asks.

"My night with Cynthia was fun, Kalin, if you must know. For the first time in a long time, I laughed and enjoyed being me. We had a great time!" I respond, talking over the running water.

"Where did ya'll go?" he asks.

"Why do you feel that it's necessary for you to know where we went? Where were you when you stayed out all night and wouldn't answer any of my calls? You practically turned your phone off. So, when you tell me where you were, I'll tell you where I was", I say to him.

"Is that right? I'll tell you where I was if you want to know, Mrs. Thomas. I went to a business meeting out of town and ended up staying at my cousin's house because it got too late and I didn't call you because I fell asleep and I ...", he begins to explain.

"Kalin, if you think I believe that, you're crazier than I thought. So, why didn't you at least call before you went to the meeting to tell me where you were? Look, I don't care. That's you! But right now, I need to get done so I can take my children shopping", I respond, getting out of the shower.

"You still didn't tell me where you went last night", he says, grabbing my shoulder.

"We went downtown for dinner and then to a comedy show. Are you happy now?"

"Yes. I'm happy now. Was that hard? That's all you had to say, Melissa", he says. "Why is everything so difficult with you these days?"

"Oh well! So, do you mind if I finish taking my shower and getting dressed?" I ask.

Kalin leaves the bathroom and I start feeling sick to my stomach. I'm sure it's the guilt I'm feeling from last night after having made love with Patrick. *I still can't believe that I did that. His charm got the best of me and I gave in to him. But the truth is that I wanted him and I needed him just as much as he wanted and needed me. We took care of each other and I can't stop thinking about it.*

Needing to check on a few things, I walk into my messy office, turn on my computer and not surprised at all when I see that I have 435 unopened emails. There's a pile of unopened mail on the top of my desk at least 2 weeks old. And I have to act just like I don't see it because right now, I'm only interested in certain messages. A message from Patrick just came in for me.

Good morning sweetheart. I hope that you're having a fabulous day and preparing for Princess' birthday. Tell her that I wish her a very happy birthday. And I just want you to know that I enjoyed our time together last night. You were amazing and you felt so good to me. As a matter of fact, I want more. I want to see you later. I can't get enough of you. I can still smell your scent, baby. I meant what I said when I told you that I wanted you, Melissa. If you can get away later, I want to see you. .... Love, Patrick.

The door to my office suddenly opens and it's Amber. "Mom, are we leaving soon?" she asks.

"Yes, honey. I just needed to check my emails first, but when I'm done, we're out of here! Give me 10 more minutes", I tell her.

Looking down the list of emails, I finally get to the one that most matters. It's the email from the party planner. She is confirming, step by step, what is going to take place regarding Princess' party. Her big gift is being delivered here and I just confirmed with my boy, Tony, that it will be here towards the end of the party. This will shock Princess! Mrs. Thompson has made sure that Brittney is on her way here and what time she will arrive. Princess has no idea that all of her sisters and brothers will be here later and so will one of her mother's best friends, Brittney Snow, and her children. I'm also relieved that "Rock" called her and wished her a happy birthday. She said that their phone call was just what she needed. This is going to be one very interesting birthday party for my beautiful daughter who is now 18 years old and ready to take her place out here in this world. I can only hope that Kalin and I have trained her to at least know how to treat others and how to lean and depend on God. Scanning the emails, I don't see any others that are that significant that can't wait. I grab my purse and yell out to the kids, "Let's go girls!"

The girls and I are finally on our way to the International Mall. "So, Mom, where were you last night?" Princess asks.

"I stayed over to your Aunt Cynthia's house. She and I had a little too much fun last night and neither of us wanted to drive so we parked it at her house", I respond.

"That's not what daddy said. He said that you were probably out with your boyfriend or something like that. Didn't he, Amber?" she says, looking to Amber to agree with her.

"Yes, he did, Ma", Amber agrees, looking out the window.

"Don't listen to him, girls. He's just saying that because he was out all night the other night and was just trying to be funny. I was with Aunt Cynthia", I say. "So, Princess, do you have any idea what store you want to get your outfit from?"

"*Forever 21* has cute clothes, so I figure we can start there. Are you and daddy getting a divorce?" Princess asks. I can tell that she obviously wants to talk about mine and her father's marriage and *our* issues.

"Why would you ask that, Princess?"

"I overheard him talking to someone on the phone last night and heard him say the word, *divorce*, and I just assumed that…", she begins.

"My beautiful daughter, today is your day and I don't want you to think about anything but enjoying yourself tonight with your family and friends. Let me worry about your daddy. He's just a big baby sometimes. I'm not going to pretend with you girls, but daddy and I do have things that we need to discuss, but none of it has anything to do with either of you. We both love you all very much and whatever we decide to do in our marriage has nothing to do with you. Do you all understand that?" I ask, trying to look at them through the rearview mirror.

"Yes ma'am", Justice whispers. The others slowly chime in and say *yes ma'am* as well.

"Look! We're here and it's jam packed today. We head for the entrance and the first thing I need to do is find the directory to see which direction we need to go to find *Forever 21*. I'm not surprised that this place is packed with teenagers on a Saturday afternoon. Amber, Justice, and Princess get lost and start going through the racks like they're on a mission. Kalin is ringing my cell phone. I wonder what *he* wants.

"Hello Kalin. I'm here with the girls. What do you want?" I ask.

"I just called to tell you that I love you and I want you to save me a dance tonight", he says.

"Boy, you're crazy. Is that *really* why you called me?" I ask, laughing into the phone.

"Yes. That's why I called *and* to tell you that I think you are still the most beautiful girl in the world", he responds.

"I know what you trying to do, Kalin. You think you're getting some later. Your smooth talk doesn't work anymore. I thought you knew that", I say to him.

"The good thing is that you're still my wife and I'm still entitled to sex with you. Don't make me go there with you, Melissa. And until you are no longer my wife, I suggest that you control yourself and not sleep around with other men before I do something that you're not going to like", he threatens.

"Entitled?" I ask. You think that you can do whatever the hell you want to do, sleep with whomever you want, make babies with whomever you want, have secret email accounts with whomever you want and I'm supposed to just act like none of it happened. Did you remember that I was your wife when you were doing all of *that*?" I ask, starting to get angry.

"You're crazy, Melissa. You come up with all kinds of stuff in your head and you're actually starting to believe it!" he shouts through the phone.

"Listen to me asshole! I'm not crazy and for years, you've made me believe that. But, that is where you're wrong! I've just caught on to you and I'm mad as hell because you took my life away from me, Kalin. But you better believe that I'm taking it back and I'm taking control. Your lies and schemes don't work on me anymore. I'm much stronger today than I have ever been in my life. So, honestly, you can go straight to hell!" I say, hanging up the phone.

Oh my goodness! What did I just do? Whatever it is, it felt so good. Did I just stand up to Kalin? Did I just release my fear? I did! I did! I feel as free as a bird.

"Ma, I like this one. What do you think? Do you like it?" Princess asks, showing me this emerald green dress with sequins at the top and a bubble at the bottom.

"I think it's gorgeous and it looks beautiful on you! You're going to look so pretty tonight. Let's go to another store for the accessories. It doesn't look like they have any good stuff in here. Did your sisters find something to wear?" I ask.

"They're both trying on outfits. I think Justice should get something from Tilly's. These clothes are more for us older girls", she says.

"I agree. We can go there next and get everybody's accessories at Tilly's. They have better accessories. But before we go to Tilly's, let's get some lunch", I suggest.

"That sounds like a plan. I want Chic-Fil-A!"

"That's my girl. Chic-Fil-A it is!" I shout.

Justice and Amber head our way with cute outfits as well. "Mommy, what do you think?" they both ask.

"I think that you're both going to look beautiful as well. I was just telling Princess that we should go to Tilly's for the accessories. They have better jewelry there, but let's get some lunch first", I say again.

These girls are wearing me out. We have been in this store for 3 hours. I am definitely ready for a drink or something.

"That sounds good", Amber says, and Justice also agrees.

We finally make it to the Food Court, sit down, eat our food and are on our way to Tilly's when Princess runs into some of her friends. "Hey girl! We're coming to your party tonight! We heard that it is going to be off 'da chain!" one of the girls says, after giving Princess a hug.

"I am so glad ya'll coming. Tell everybody for me, okay", Princess says. The girls say their goodbyes and we continue on our way to Tilly's.

Tilly's is crowded as well, but I have to keep telling myself that this is almost over. We walk over to the accessories and start mixing and matching everyone's outfits with the appropriate accessories. And the good news for me is that if you spend at least $100 today, you can get a discount of 20% off your purchase. I take advantage of this deal and decide to get some accessories for myself. On our way out of the mall, I stop by the makeup counter and get a concealer and some lipsticks. Our mall experience is over and we're finally on our way home, with the birthday party just 3 hours away.

As soon as we turn the corner and onto our street, the girls notice that their sister's car is parked in the driveway. "Mommy, Christy is here!" Justice shouts.

"Happy Birthday, Princess! That is your first gift", I say, giving her a hug.

"Are my brothers coming too?" she asks.

"Well, you'll just have to wait and see", I say.

The girls rush inside without taking any of the bags. When I go to grab them, I look up and Kalin is standing behind me. "Now, you know you were wrong for hanging up on me", he says.

"Kalin, can we please not do this tonight? Let's not ruin Princess' day. Can you at least do that for your daughter?" I ask.

"We don't have to do any arguing, Mrs. Thomas, if you just act like you have a husband who has needs and take care of him at least once a week and …", he begins.

"Is that what this is about? You want some sex, Kalin? I wanted sex the other night when I had to go to bed alone. I had to end up masturbating myself to take care of *my* sexual desires because my husband didn't see fit to call me and tell me where the hell he was. And when I tried to reach him, his phone went straight to voicemail. And my husband shows up the next day, without an explanation at all. Now, I want to enjoy this evening for my daughter and you're not going to ruin it for her!" I shout, grabbing the bags and heading inside. I leave him standing there with tears in his eyes. Before I make it in the house, I can hear him say, "I don't want to lose you, Melissa."

When I make it inside, I can see that the girls have surrounded Christy. They love their big sister so much and she loves them too. She hands Princess a bag from *Gucci* and says happy birthday to her. Princess takes the bag and puts it on the make believe gift table. It looks like Cynthia has dropped off her gift as well. The girls all head upstairs to start doing what girls do to prepare for a party, so I take a sit next to Christy to find out how things are going in her world.

"So, how's everything in Atlanta?" I ask.

"Things are going quite well, Ma. I was just recently put up for a promotion, but I'm patiently awaiting their decision as to who will get it. There are lots of good people up for the job. It's a management position", she says.

"Oh, honey, that's just wonderful. I'm so proud of you whether you get it or you don't. You seem to really like Atlanta. Anyone special, yet? I ask.

"Ma!" she yells. "I'm not thinking about that and I'm way too busy to even think about a relationship. I am, however, considering going back to school to pick up my Master's", she says.

"That would be just great! You truly are awesome! Now, changing the subject; what time do you have to pick up Darren and Kameron from the airport?"

"Their plane arrives at 7. I should be leaving in about 30 minutes. I just need to catch more of this LA game. The Lakers are losing and they're really pissing me off!" she says, now turning up the volume on the television.

"Christy, what have I always told you?" I ask.

"I know, Ma. It's just a game!"

The party is now just an hour or so away, and I now need to get dressed. The house looks beautiful. The party planner came over while we were out and took care of all the decorations. The caterer is due to arrive shortly and right about now, Mrs. Thompson should be at the airport waiting on Brittney's flight to arrive. *I can't wait to see her and the kids.*

When I make into the bedroom, Kalin is in the shower and he asks me to join him. After I decline, he jumps out of the shower and pulls me in with him anyway and my clothes get wet. He starts kissing me and I try my best to resist him. *I can't block out my intimate evening with Patrick. I feel that these are his lips and I feel like I am cheating on Patrick now. How crazy is this!!*

"Don't you miss the way we make each other feel, Melissa? You know you always liked when I did this", he says. Kalin rips my blouse open and my breast fall into his hands and he starts kissing them one by one. I can't resist him and immediately start giving in to him. I return his kisses harder and harder. He falls on his knees and start pleasuring me orally. He really is so good at this. But when he wants me to reciprocate, I can't do it. I just can't do it because I know that he has had sex with another woman and I can't picture tasting him when someone else has been all over him too. "What's wrong? Why can't you give me what I want?" he asks.

"Do you really want the truth, Kalin?"

"Yes, I want the truth! I'm sitting here and I'm hard as a rock and I want my wife to make love to me and instead of doing that, she's standing here arguing with me about sucking me!" he yells.

"I will never do that again because you had sex with another woman while you were married to me. I will never suck you and that...", I say, when without knowing what will happen, Kalin grabs me and thrusts himself inside of me. I can feel his hardness. So much so that I let out a loud moan. He grabs my legs and puts them around his waist and he makes love to me until he orgasms. He moans so loudly that I'm afraid he may startle the girls. "Dang girl, you got some good stuff! That's all I wanted and now, you won't have to worry about me for the rest of the evening. That will always be mine, baby", he says, and gets out of the shower.

I just had sex with my husband, but I feel so dirty. I feel like I should run off to Patrick to tell him what happened. I feel like it should not have happened. He pushed himself on me. I didn't really want it to happen, but the truth of the matter is that I had sex with him and I don't ever want to do it again. The sex we just had made me feel like a piece of meat. He doesn't desire me the way a man should desire his wife. He just treated me like a piece of meat and now I feel dirty. I never thought a husband could make his wife feel like this. I didn't even have an orgasm with him. But Patrick, on the other hand, made me feel special and desired.

When Kalin gets out, I turn on the shower to bathe myself. Kalin took his shower and is probably downstairs fixing himself a drink. As soon as I step out the shower, my phone rings and the caller id says, *restricted*, which tells me that this must be Sharelle. I pick up the phone and say hello.

"Mom, hey!" Sharelle says.

"Hey sweetheart. I miss you so much. I love you, too", I say.

"I know, Ma. I miss ya'll and love ya'll too", she responds.

"Sharelle, please come home. I'm so worried about you being out there and not having anywhere to sleep or any food to eat or...", I say, before she interrupts me.

"Ma, I have people taking care of me. Don't worry. I just called to speak to the birthday girl", she says.

"Okay, let me get her for you. Princess! Princess!" I say, and within 15 seconds, she is standing in front of me.

"Ma, what's wrong? Is everything okay?" she asks.

"The phone is for you. Someone wants to talk to you", I say, handing her the phone.

"For me?" she asks, but grabs the phone. "Hello".

Princess and Sharelle stay on the phone for at least 5 minutes before I hear Princess say, "Bye, sis, and take good care of yourself and just know that you can always come back home. We all love you." Their call is disconnected and Princess seems to be so happy to have heard from Sharelle. I'm just glad that my girls have a tight relationship amongst themselves.

"Ok, Ma, gotta finish getting dressed!" Princess says, running out of my room; but, just when I'm putting the finishing touches on my makeup, I can hear the doorbell ringing. That must be the caterers. I call downstairs for Christy to let them in.

Within minutes, Christy is upstairs in my bedroom to let me know that the caterers have a few questions for me. I'm so glad that I am finally done getting dressed so that I can handle these small details. Before I make it downstairs, I can already smell the aroma coming from the food just delivered. It smells delicious!

"Sorry to bother you ma'am, but we just need to confirm where you would like the food placed", the gentleman says. With his authoritative disposition, I am sure he is the head caterer or possibly even the owner of the business. He is a very attractive man, standing at least 6 feet tall, with manicured hands, perfect teeth, and dark brown hair. For a second, I am staring at him, but quickly snap out of it because I realize that he just asked me a question.

"Oh, please, put it right here, sir. It smells delicious", I comment.

"Almost as delicious as you", he says, throwing his hand up and apologizing. "I didn't mean to be disrespectful ma'am. It just came out like that. Sorry", he says.

"It's okay, sir. What's your name?" I ask, extending my hand out to him.

"Oh, I'm sorry. My name is Brandon. And you must be Mrs. Thomas?" he asks.

"Call me Melissa", I say. For about 5 seconds, we just stand there looking at each other with no words. Brandon reminds me of someone. I am not quite sure at this moment, but he does. "Well, thanks for bringing in the food, Brandon. You can put it all right here on this table. The party planner will be in soon and she already knows how and where she wants everything", I tell him.

"A party planner, huh? You have a beautiful home, Melissa. Did you decorate it yourself?" he asks.

"As a matter of fact, I did, Brandon. My husband did quite a bit of it as well because he is an interior designer, but the color scheme was all my idea, but we both picked out the furnishings ourselves", I respond.

"Well, it is beautiful! Is your husband around?"

"I am not sure where he is. I think he is out back somewhere", I say. Just when I say that, I can hear Kalin walk up behind me.

"I am Kalin, *her husband*. And you are?" Kalin asks, extending out his hand to Brandon.

"I am Brandon, sir. I was just telling your wife how lovely I think your home is and I understand that you both had a hand in decorating it", he comments.

"Yes, me and *my wife* decorated it", Kalin says, placing emphasis on *my wife*.

I think Brandon gets the hint. He moves over to the table and starts moving the food where I previously instructed him to move it. Kalin gives him such a hard time that he eventually gives me an apologetic look for being a little flirty. *I don't really care about that because I enjoyed being teased by an attractive man and too bad if Kalin doesn't like it. The worst thing he could have done was mess over a good woman who always had his back. And now, I'm going to enjoy being me.*

From what I can see here, there will certainly be a house full of happy teenagers by the end of the night. And finally coming down the driveway is the van that belongs to my party planner, which means one thing! It means that Brittney and her children are here! This is going to be another big surprise for the birthday girl and it looks like Christy's coming down the driveway right behind her. So that also means that her brothers are here too! It seems as if everything is going to be right on point for my birthday girl!

As soon as the van stops, Brittney runs right over to me. We hug each other for what seems like 10 minutes. "I miss you girl! Thank you so much for loving me enough to let me be here tonight for Princess' party. You're the best friend a woman could ever ask for and I love you, MeMe!" She almost sounds as if she's crying.

"Ahh B, you know you my girl and I'll always love you. We'll be friends forever. So, I just want you to enjoy this weekend and let's speak nothing of the past. All is forgiven. Now let me look at my beautiful niece and nephew", I say, letting go of Brittney and taking the hands of her children and kissing them both on the cheeks. "Wow! You two have gotten to be so big!" Just as they are giving me a hug, I hear a male voice say, "Well hello Mother!" I turn around and there's Darren and Kameron standing there looking ever so handsome.

"Hey boys! How are ya'll? Look at my boys looking so handsome!" I say, when B interrupts me.

"Please don't tell me that this is Kameron and Darren coming up here looking like two very handsome grown men", she says, giving them a hug at the same time.

"Hey, Aunt B", Darren says, and Kameron follows. It's so good to see you here in Florida. So glad you could make it!"

"Me too! Somehow I feel that this weekend is going to be a blast!" Brittney exclaims.

"Okay guys. Let's make our way inside to surprise our birthday girl", I say. "Mrs. Thompson, the caterers dropped off the food, so you can set up the tables however you like. Please let me know if you need anything", I tell her.

Just as soon as we walk inside, the girls are coming down the stairs and immediately start yelling when they see their brothers. "You made it!" Princess shouts, running over to Kameron and Darren. Neither of them notice Brittney or the girls so I had to interrupt their little hug fest and say, "And Princess, look who also made it to your party. It's Aunt Brittney from Middleton and your two cousins and they all came...", I say, before she interrupts me with a loud scream. "Oh my God, Auntie! It is so nice to see you here! Thank you so much for coming!" she says, giving Brittney and her children big hugs.

I'm so happy right now because it looks like things are really coming together for Princess' birthday party, but what's on my mind is what happened earlier tonight with Kalin. I don't want him to think that our relationship is once again solid because I let him sneak one in on me. The fact still remains that our marriage is in trouble right now and I'm still contemplating divorcing him, but I dare not bring this topic up tonight and ruin Princess' birthday.

"Mommy, how do I look?" Princess asks, twirling around for me to see her entire dress.

"Sweetheart, you look so beautiful. You look just like your mother. She would be so proud of you right now. Come here and take a picture with me and your Aunt Brittney", I say, handing the camera to Kameron to take the picture.

The doorbell rings and my guess is that this must be Cynthia because she should be here by now. "Somebody get the door!" I yell. In walks Cynthia looking as beautiful as ever. "And where is the birthday girl?" she asks, walking right over to Princess. "Sweetheart, you look beautiful! I know you've heard that a million times tonight already", Cynthia says.

The birthday party is officially underway. Guests continue to pile into our home, showing up with gifts for Princess. The music is blasting and Princess and her friends look like they're having the time of their lives. Like most teenage parties, the adults gather in the back den area, while the teenagers dance the night away in the family area set up for them. Princess looks so happy opening all of her gifts and then, to everyone's surprise, the DJ announces that there's a final gift presentation for the birthday girl.

"Thanks to all of you for coming out tonight to celebrate with Princess on her 18th birthday! I won't embarrass you, I promise, but I really want you to know that your family loves you so much and we believe in you. And sweetheart, I want to personally congratulate you for working so hard and earning your way into college. For those of you who don't know already, Princess has been accepted into Howard University. Congratulations, sweetheart!" The crowd erupts with applauses and cheers for Princess. "But, this final birthday gift is something that you will need when you run off to college and I want everyone to follow me outside for *this* gift."

As many that can get through the door, they follow me outside, where a car is parked in the driveway. Princess looks so surprised. She covers her mouth and runs over to me. "Mommy, thank you so much! This is the best birthday ever! I had no idea that you were giving me a car. Mommy! Mommy! I'm so shocked!" she shouts, over and over again.

Motioning for the crowd to settle down, I say, "There's one more very special thing about this car that I think you should know. This was your mother's car in high school. When she passed away, this is one of the things that she left behind for you that she wanted you to have on your 18th birthday. And just *one more* special surprise, sweetheart. She paid for this party, the DJ, the food, everything! She asked me and Kalin in her Will if we would let her do this one. And one *Final* thing!! She wrote you a letter before she died that she wanted you to have tonight. But that is for you personally when you retire to your bedroom."

I don't think that there's a dry eye in the building. This speech has brought to tears, not only Princess, but her friends as well. Some of them start coming up to her to give her hugs and wishing her happy birthday. My work here is done and I'm exhausted. There's at least one hour remaining for the party, so I go back into the room where the adults are and we continue having our drinks and enjoying ourselves too. Kalin looks so peaceful and happy talking with Cynthia's husband. My phone lights up and it's a text message from Patrick. *So, how is the party going?*

How is our birthday girl? I hope that she's getting all that she wants. Baby, I miss you so much. I have done nothing but think of you all day. When can I see you again? Love, Patrick..xoxoxoxoxo

I respond to his text and say, *We need to talk.*

CHAPTER 10

"Is This Your Daughter?"

I know I promised Symone that I would sit in at her property today, but I think I should call the Agency to bring in a temp. I have way too much work to do in the office. I'd rather go tomorrow after getting my work done.

Traffic is crazy on I-95 this morning, but I finally make it to the office and immediately notice that Cynthia's car isn't in the parking lot. *Am I losing my mind?* I just remembered that she sent me a text earlier letting me know what happened with her husband's truck and how she has to now take him to work. She should be in around 10 or so.

It seems like hours, but Cynthia is finally walking through the door and I realize that I've been here since 8 and I'm ready for a much needed break. "Cynthia, I'm so glad you're finally here because I need some fresh air. I'll be back in an hour or so", I say, as she walks in the door.

"Okay. Is everything okay? You don't look so happy right now", Cynthia says, observing me as I grab my briefcase.

"I'm fine but I have so many things on my mind and no, I don't want to talk about it", I say, before she gets a chance to ask me.

"Well, dang! I didn't even get a chance to get it out. You seem to be pretty pre-occupied so, I won't bother you. Take your time. I'm here now", she says.

While I'm packing my things to go, my cell phone vibrates and Patrick wants to meet somewhere and talk. *I don't think I'm ready to talk to him. I don't know if I should tell him that it's over between us or not. And then Kalin; do I want to make an attempt to fix my marriage or should I just let him go and be by myself right now?* "Melissa, are you okay?" Cynthia asks, noticing that I'm looking off into space.

"Yes. I'm okay. I just need some air", I respond.

"You know that I'm right here if you need me. Take it easy, hun. Think you'll be coming back to the office?" she asks me.

"I doubt it. I'm gonna take some of my work with me, but please call me if anyone from Corporate calls", I suggest.

"Of course I will. I have quite a bit of work to do myself", Cynthia tells me, closing the door behind me.

Cynthia, finally getting settled into her work, is interrupted when she gets a call, but to her surprise, it's Miami General Hospital. Not knowing who or what this could possibly be about, she picks up the phone.

"May I speak with Mrs. Thomas?" the woman on the other side of the phone asks.

"She's not in. How may I help you?" Cynthia asks.

"This is Janet Jones, head nurse at Miami General, and we believe we have her daughter here", she begins to explain before Cynthia shouts, "Oh God no, not Sharelle. Oh God no!"

"We're not sure if her name is really Sharelle. She gave the officers a different name, but she matches the description of Sharelle Williams from the missing person's database and lists this as a number to reach her mother. We tried her cell phone number, but there was no response. Do you have any other way of reaching her?" the Nurse asks.

"I'll find her. How is Sharelle doing?" Cynthia asks.

"I'm not able to give that information to anyone but her parents. Please have her either call me back at (305) 555-1276 or just come by the emergency room at Miami General. I appreciate your help", she says.

Cynthia has to find Melissa so she calls Kalin to see if he has heard from her, but he claims that he hasn't. He went on to say that he hasn't seen her nor has he talked to her since she left the house this morning. Thinking for sure that Melissa would have contacted her sister, Cynthia calls Diana. No luck there, either! *Where in the world can Melissa be? Cynthia wonders.* Diana's been trying to find Melissa, but instead of sitting around and waiting, she heads over to the hospital so someone will be there when Sharelle wakes up. Cynthia has tried everyone else, so she makes a final attempt to find Melissa and dials Stevie's phone. He answers right away and Cynthia is relieved that he believes he knows where Melissa may be. He also admits that he hasn't heard from her but now sees that she sent him a text about 45 minutes ago. Promising me that he'd find her and call me back, he sounds nervous and afraid.

"Cynthia, by the way, is everything okay? Is there an emergency?" he asks.

"There is, Stevie. There's something wrong with Sharelle. I don't know the details, but I do know that she's at Miami General Hospital, so when you find her, tell her to please call me", Cynthia says, starting to cry.

"My Sharelle! Oh God, no!! I have to find her. I just have to find her, but please don't cry, Cynthia. I'll find her", he says, and hangs up the phone.

The temperature is starting to change outside. It looks like it's going to rain, almost as if a storm is headed our way. Sharelle's in the hospital and her mother has no idea of it. Cynthia is starting to worry because it's not like Melissa to not answer her calls.

If it ain't one thing, it's another, Cynthia mumbles.

Melissa Has Some Secrets
Torn 2: Passion, Pain & Promise.

CHAPTER 11

"Do You Think I Believe That?"

*A*fter receiving the call from Cynthia, Stevie knows that he needs to find Melissa. The good thing is that he knows just where she would go to clear her head, which is probably why she sent him a text message. Whenever Melissa had heavy thoughts on her mind, she would always go to their Park and sit under the tree by the lake and throw rocks into the water. Stevie makes it to the Park and sees Melissa's car in the parking lot. He can't believe she's still here because it's starting to get dark.

The closer Stevie gets, he can see that this *is* Melissa and she's exactly where he thought she would be. She can hear him coming and looks around.

"Oh my God!! You scared me", Melissa says, when she sees Stevie.

"I knew that I would find you here. How are you beautiful?" Stevie asks.

"I'm okay. Glad you're here. Thanks for coming", Melissa says, standing to her feet. She notices right away that something isn't right with Stevie. He has a look of worry on his face.

"Well, I can't take all of the credit for being here. What's going on with your phone? People are trying to reach you. I'm actually here because I received a call from Cynthia wanting to know if I had heard from you. I have to tell you something, but I really don't need you to freak out", Stevie explains.

"You're scaring me, Stevie. What is it?" Melissa asks, going into her bag until she locates her cell phone. "Oh no!! I forgot to take it off "silent"."

"Melissa, the hospital called about Sharelle. Cynthia received a call from the hospital saying that they believe the young lady that they have in their emergency room is Sharelle. We have to get….", Stevie says, before Melissa interrupts him.

"I have to go!! What hospital? Did Cynthia say?" I ask, jumping up and heading to her car.

"Miami General. Let me drive!" Stevie suggests.

Stevie and I jump in his car and within a few minutes, we're already on I-95, weaving in and out of traffic. Now, I can see that I missed several calls from Cynthia, my sister, the house *and* Miami General. The first call I make is to Diana and she answers right away. "Melissa, where are you?!! We've been trying to reach you for a couple of hours now. Where are you honey?" Diana asks.

"I'm on my way to the hospital. Stevie found me and told me what was going on. My phone was still on "silent" because I forgot to change it when I left the office", I explain to her. "Will you please meet me at the hospital? I need you, sis", I say.

"I'm already here. I came as soon as the hospital called me. Sharelle is asleep. She hasn't opened her eyes yet. I didn't want her to wake up and nobody was here. Get here as soon as you can."

With Stevie whipping in and out of traffic, we finally make it to Miami General and the emergency room is busy as usual and the front desk clerks are just as unprofessional as they usually are. "Yeah, may I help you?" the clerk says, chewing her gum.

"Yes, I received a call that my daughter, Sherelle Williams, was brought in earlier. Can someone please tell me how my daughter is doing?" I ask, with tears in my eyes.

"It's going to be okay, Melissa", Stevie says, rubbing my back.

"Ma'am, please go through the double doors and to the right and into room #12", she directs us.

Stevie and I go through the doors and immediately, I feel sick to my stomach, not knowing what to expect. 14, 13, and now 12… We pull the curtains back and Sharelle is sedated, with an IV already taped to her arm, but she still looks so peaceful.

"Oh my goodness, Melissa. She's so beautiful! So very beautiful!!" Stevie says, starting to cry.

"Don't cry! You're going to make me cry. We just have to be happy that she's alive. Let me find a nurse who can talk to me about what happened", I say, leaving the room.

I walk out to the nurses' station and get a sense that *Cheryl* must be the nurse assigned to Sharelle because she immediately fills us in on the details of what got her here.

"First of all, we need to properly identify that this is your daughter, Sharelle, because we…", she begins to explain, before I interrupt her.

"Yes, that's definitely my daughter in there, so please, tell me what happened to her", I demand.

"Step over here, Mrs. Thomas", Cheryl says, directing me to the side. "Your daughter was in the car with a man and 2 other women. Apparently, his car was being watched by police and when they closed in on him, he tried to make a run for it. They chased him, but, it didn't end well at all. The car spun out of control and your daughter was thrown around in the car. Unfortunately, the seatbelt that she should have been in didn't work. The driver was banged up quite a bit and is in surgery right now. The other girls in the car received minor bruising, but they'll be just fine. They've already been released from the hospital", she explains.

"I'm speechless! Oh my God! Is she going to be okay? What's wrong with her?" I ask, wiping away my tears.

"I might as well tell you now. She'll need a blood transfusion. Your daughter has lost a lot of blood. She's in severe pain in her back and that's why we have her sedated. When we were giving her the meds to put her out, she gave me a message to give you when you got here. She wanted me to tell you that she loves you and that she's sorry for putting you through all of this", Cheryl explains. "The doctor is going to be here a little later to explain to you the options regarding the blood transfusion, but if you need anything else, please do not hesitate to let me know. I'm here for you, okay", she says.

"Yes, please have the doctor come speak with me when he gets back", I say, turning to go back to the room.

Stevie is sitting by Sharelle's bed and is holding her hand with tears in his eyes when I walk into the room. "Melissa, I'm so sorry that I haven't been here for her more. I'm so sorry that I went out to do my career and left the two of you here to fend for yourselves. Will you please forgive me?" Stevie asks, crying.

"Please don't do that. Sharelle is going to be fine and when she wakes up, you can tell her yourself. She'll be so happy to finally get to meet you. Okay?"

"Okay. I'll do that."

"Stevie, the nurse just told me that Sharelle has lost a lot of blood and will need a blood transfusion. So, it is a good thing that you *are* here. But, the doctor is going ….", I say, but get interrupted when Diana and Kalin walk into the room.

"How is she, Melissa?" Diana asks, looking on.

"She's doing okay for right now, but she's going to need a blood transfusion. I was just telling Stevie that it's a good thing that he's here because I'm sure that they'll want the parents tested first", I say. Without looking in his direction, I can already see the look on Kalin's face.

"Stevie? So, you're Stevie?" Kalin asks. "Since when did you make it into town and how is it that you knew he was here, Melissa?"

"Not here and not now, Kalin. This is not the place to have this conversation", I respond, starting to get a little upset.

"Why not? Why is it that I didn't know that my wife's ex-lover was in town and that my wife was spending time with him?" Kalin asks, moving closer to me.

"Listen, man, it's not like that. Respect your wife right now. Don't you see that she's going through something? The two of you can talk about all of this when you get home, but for right now, my daughter needs her mother, so if you don't mind….", Stevie says, before Kalin cuts him off.

"I don't need you to tell me what to say to my wife. I will do whatever...", Kalin begins to say but the doctor walks into the room.

"Good evening everyone. I'm Dr. Shatinoff and I'm the attending physician for this young lady and I need to speak with her parents", he announces. I step forward.

"Please explain to me, Doc. What's going on with my daughter?" I ask.

"She's going to be fine, but keep in mind that she took a nasty hit when the car crashed simply because she didn't have on her seatbelt. She lost a lot of blood, but we stopped it, but now she needs a blood transfusion. Once she's responding well to it, she should be able to go home at that point", the Doc explains. "So, where are my donors?"

Stevie and I step up and the Doc tells us to follow him. We leave Diana and Kalin in the room with Sharelle. The Doc takes blood from each of us and tells us to sit tight and that he would be back soon with the results.

"So, what was that all about back there in the room, Melissa?" Stevie asks.

"Well, that is what I was going to talk to you about. Kalin and I are having the worst issues in our marriage right now. I'm even on the verge of divorcing him. He cheated on me some years back with this woman and got her pregnant. She aborted the baby when she realized that he wasn't going to leave me to be with her. But then later on, I put him out of the house and he went to Alabama to be with his family and he met a girl there and when he came back, I realized that they had their very own email account and was communicating back and forth with each other", I begin to explain. Stevie's mouth is wide open the entire time I'm talking.

"What?!!!!! Are you serious? You went through all of this and you're still with this man? I'm speechless, Melissa! Just speechless!" he says.

"Well, tell me something. Am I crazy for wanting to divorce this man? What do you think about all of this?" I ask.

"First of all. I think your husband is an absolute jerk. He couldn't control himself even for the sake of Sharelle. Doesn't take a rocket scientist to see that ya'll got some issues so you need to think carefully about whether you want to stay with him or not, but I do know this. If you decide to stay, I think ya'll need some counseling to learn how to trust each other again", he recommends.

"But, there's one thing I left out, Stevie", I say.

"What is it?" he asks, paying close attention to my every word.

"In the midst of all of this, I met a guy named Patrick who has really been there for me emotionally and just recently, those feelings led to a physical exchange", I say.

"You slept with him, Melissa?" Stevie asks, stepping away from me.

"Yes! I slept with him, Stevie. And I enjoyed every minute of it. He made me feel like a woman in every way possible. And what's worse is that I want him again and again and again! I can't stop thinking about our special night and he wants our relationship to go further", I say.

"Wow! Girl, this is some stuff for Oprah! Melissa, I have known you for several years and honestly, I can't blame any man for wanting you because not only are you beautiful, but you are the sweetest woman I have ever met and either of these men would be lucky to have you. I hate that I left you and hurt you the way I did. But, I guess this is a good time to tell you that I thought of you every single day and I wanted to call so many times, but if I had done that and heard that sexy voice over the phone, I would have been back to Miami in a heartbeat!" he confesses.

"Stevie, you have no idea how long I've waited to hear you say that", I admit. Stevie and I get caught up in the moment and he reaches over and kisses me on my lips, but in a friendly manner. "What was that for?"

"Just my way of saying that after all of these years, I still think you're hot and let's just say…", he says, before I interrupt him with a passionate kiss on his lips in return.

"Don't say anything else because I may have to walk out of this hospital with you, take you to a hotel and I think you know what comes next with us", I say, teasingly.

"No. Why don't you tell me what you would do to me? I want to hear. I like to hear it, Melissa", he teases back.

"Seriously, Stevie, we can't do this. But, back to my problem. What in the world do I do with all of this? I never meant to fall for Patrick. I didn't know that my feelings for him would progress the way that they did. He's been calling me all day and so has Kalin and that's why I went to the Park. I needed to clear my head. I really don't know what I should do", I say, with tears in my eyes.

"Oh, honey, don't cry. I can't give you that answer. Go to God on this, Melissa. I know that you love your husband or you would NOT have stayed with him all of these years, but he changed on you and that's where your problem lies. He's not the same man that you fell in love with and I can see it in your eyes that you don't necessarily trust him either. You're in a pickle and I really feel for you. I can't tell you to go with your heart because you are in love with two men and this decision will have to be between you and God", Stevie says.

The doctor has just returned to the room and motions for me to come outside.

"What's wrong?" Stevie asks, looking puzzled as I follow the doctor outside.

"Hold on. I'll see. I'll be right back", I say to Stevie.

When we get outside, the doctor starts shaking his head.

"What's wrong? Why did you take me out of the room?" I ask the doctor, looking scared.

"I don't know how to tell you this, Mrs. Thomas, but that man is not a match for your daughter. And I didn't want to tell you in there with him. I think that this is probably something that you should tell him yourself", he explains.

"Are you saying that Stevie is not Sharelle's father? Is that what you're telling me, Doc?" I ask, now in total shock.

"I'm sorry, ma'am, but no, he is not her father. Your blood matches and unless there is someone else, we can always get a match from our Blood Bank. That won't be a problem. So, will you go back in there and tell him or should I?"

Oh my God! Oh my God! I can't believe this!! If Stevie is not the father to Sharelle, then it must be Juan, the one night stand! It just can't be! Stevie and I were always intimate and it was the one night with Juan that got me pregnant! How in the world am I going to look at this man and tell him the truth?

"Mrs. Thomas, are you okay? Are you sure you can do this?" the doctor asks.

"I'm sorry, sir. I'll tell him. Thanks, sir."

When I walk back into the room, Stevie is turned around and facing the wall, but turns around as soon as the door opens. When he sees the look on my face, he knows that something is wrong.

"What is it, Melissa? Just give it to me straight. What's wrong with me that I can't help my daughter?" he asks.

"Stevie...", I stutter.

"What is it, Melissa? Just tell me!" he demands.

"There's a problem with the blood test, which means that there's something that I have to tell you", I begin. "I'm so sorry, Stevie. I'm so sorry and I hope that you'll find it in your heart to forgive me for what I've done."

"What is it, Melissa?" he asks, grabbing my face.

"She's not your daughter, Stevie. I'm so sorry. I'm so sorry. I didn't think that a one-night stand would mean anything, but it did. She's not your daughter. I'm so sorry. I didn't mean...", I say, when Stevie jumps up and hits the wall with his fist.

"What the f---, Melissa? How could you do this to me? How could you? I can't believe this!! I hate you! I hate you for hurting me like this!! How could you?" he shouts and runs out of the room.

I can't move. I'm numb. I'm in total shock right now!! How could this have happened? I can't believe that I just hurt Stevie like this! Oh God, please forgive me! Please let Stevie find it in his heart to forgive me for this. Please help me to forgive myself for this!

I go back into the room where Sharelle is and Stevie is already leaving out and avoids me like the plague. He doesn't look in my direction, but storms out of the hospital.

"What's wrong, Melissa?" Diana asks when I walk back into the room. "What's wrong with Stevie and why is he crying? What did the doctor say?"

And now, I'm crying uncontrollably. Kalin reaches for me and holds me. "Baby, please tell us what's wrong. You're starting to scare us. Your sister is sitting here crying. So tell us what's wrong", Kalin demands.

"Sharelle is not his daughter and the blood test just proved it", I blurt out.

"Oh my God, Melissa!" Diana says, covering her mouth in total surprise.

"Oh no! I feel for the guy. I really do. I can only imagine what he's feeling. Oh no, Melissa! I'm her father *anyway*. That is my daughter over there in that bed and we'll make it through this. As far as I'm concerned, she has always been my little girl. Don't beat yourself up, Melissa. This, too, shall pass", Kalin says, comforting me with his arms around me.

Diana doesn't say another word, but sits in the corner completely quiet. I'm sure that she'll tell me later how she feels about all of this. Right now, the most important thing is making sure that Sharelle gets the transfusion successfully. The doctor finally comes in and announces that he's getting the staff prepped for the surgery and will be back for Sharelle in the next 10 minutes or so. Kalin has a look on his face that I've never seen before. For the first time ever in our life together, he looks like he's afraid. So, I reach out to him.

"Kalin, everything is going to be okay with Sharelle. She's going to make it through this. I'm sure of it and I'm not worried about it either. You believe me?" I ask him.

"Yes. I do. I believe, Melissa", he responds.

"I believe too, sis", Diana mumbles.

The doctor comes in and they take Sharelle away. Diana lets us know that she's going to the cafeteria and asks if either I or Kalin need anything. We both decline.

"Well, I'm going to leave so that you two can talk. I'll be back in a little while because I need to get some fresh air myself."

As soon as the door shuts behind Diana, Kalin reaches out to me for a hug. I accept it and we stand there for minutes just holding each other. *I can't remember the last time Kalin and I have held onto each other this long without some type of confrontation. He feels good right now and God knows I can use this hug even if it is from Kalin.*

"I love you, Melissa. I know that we've been through so much over the years, but you are and will always be my number one girl. Nobody will ever take that spot from you. I know you're upset with me because of things that you have no idea about, but I love you and I'm still in love with you after all of these years, but I don't think that you look at me the same as you used to", he says.

"Kalin, I have always loved you and I think you know that by the things that I've shown you throughout our life together. I proved it to you over and over no matter how much I may have hurt by the things that *you* did, but it has come a point in my life where I need more for me. I need someone who believes in the same things I believe in and is willing to give up everything he wants in life just to be with me. I need to be the most important thing to him, second to God. You used to make me feel that. I used to believe that you loved me like there was no love, but you allowed someone else into our marriage and into our bed and although I have forgiven you, I don't know if I will ever be able to trust you, Kalin. You have no idea how much that hurt me, especially knowing that I was there for you in all ways possible", I tell him, finally glad to be able to tell him the truth about how I feel. *I was never able to do this before because of my fear of him.*

"You weren't always there for me, Melissa. When I went to jail for spanking Sharelle, you hardly came to see me in there. I was scared, honey, and I needed you and you came when you wanted to come and ...", he begins to say, but I interrupt him.

"Are you serious? I came when I could. I had to still work and provide for our children with my income only. You weren't able to provide for them, so I did what I had to do and took another job and I feel sorry for you if you can't understand that", I say, walking away to the other side of the room.

"I understand it now, Melissa. Now, I know that you loved me with everything that you had to give. Now I understand why you did what you did and....", he begins to explain.

"But now, it's too late, Kalin. It's too late", I say, pulling away from him.

"It's not too late! It's not too late! Don't say that, Melissa. We still love each other, so please don't say that. Let's try to work things out! Please, Melissa. Please!" he begs.

"I don't think I want to try anymore because honestly, I'm starting to feel something in my heart for someone else now, Kalin", I confess.

"You what? You seeing *someone else*? Don't do this, Melissa!! Please don't tell me that this has something to do with Ms. Rita's doctor? Why in the world would that white man want your black behind?" he asks, trying to hurt me.

"This conversation is over. Why in the world did I think that we could have an adult conversation? You are impossible to talk to and ...", I say, before he interrupts me.

"Why? Because I don't want to know that my wife is starting to feel something for another man? Why don't I want to talk at this point, Melissa? No. I don't want to hear this garbage that you're telling me. I don't want you to want someone else. What man would want to hear something like this? You tell me! Who? I'm not a happy...", he says, until I jump in and interrupt.

"Wait a minute! Let's just put it out here. This is your fault, Mr. Thomas. You're the one who sent me out here to meet someone else and let them make me feel like a woman. While you were out there taking care of Wendy and Diandra, you should have been taking care of your wife. You should have been holding my hand and making love to me. Men like you are so stupid because you have it all right here at home and you go out there and find a woman who could care less about you", I say, starting to sound angry.

"I'm sorry, baby! I'm so sorry that I hurt you, Melissa! But baby, please, he doesn't love you. He will never love you like I do. We have a family together. What about our children? Have you thought about what this will do to them?" he asks.

"I have not thought about everything, but I'll do whatever I have to do to keep them safe and loved and to grow into responsible young ladies who will always make wise decisions", I respond.

"You think you're going to run off with someone and take my kids with you? Well, you have another thought coming. I won't let that happen. You hear me? Never!" he yells.

"Kalin, I would never do anything like that and keep you away from your children. I'm not *that* heartless and I know that they love you. I just want to be happy. And then the other night when you stayed out all night, that was the icing on the cake for me and you were so arrogant with it. You didn't call or anything. And what's worse; you didn't give a care in the world about me or my feelings."

"Melissa, I explained about that night and..", he begins.

"Yes, you did, and it was complete bs!"

Diana walks back into the room with her drink in hand. "I have to admit that the cafeteria food doesn't taste as bad as other hospitals", Diana states, noticing the tension between myself and Kalin. "Melissa, would you like to take a walk and talk to your big sister?" she asks.

I try to make eye contact with Kalin, but he looks away and doesn't look my way at all, so Diana and I leave the room. "I think it's time for you to talk to your big sister. What in the hell is going on around here today? And why did you show up here with Stevie? Please stop me and answer me at some point", she demands.

"Oh God, Diana. I should have called you some time ago to talk to you about my life and what's been happening. I think I was just too embarrassed and didn't want to hear you say that you were right all along about Kalin. I do need to talk. Let's walk down to the courtyard."

"Melissa, you're my sister and I love you and I've always known that Kalin was not the man for you. Think about it. He was still *married* to his wife when you met him and what did he do when he decided that he wanted to marry you? He just got up from that house and moved into yours and for crying out loud, the man quit his job, leaving you to have to feed him and your kids. It's like you gained another child to take care of. As your sister, I was mad as hell about that because anyone could see that he was using you", she says.

"I never looked at it that way", I admit.

"I know you didn't. He charmed you with his good looks and sweet talk and because you're such a nice person, you took him in and accepted whatever he gave you and you forgot all about your dreams and everything. He made you think that your family was the enemy and that he was the only person who cared about you. Am I right?" Diana asks.

"Something like that, D. But now, I'm divorcing him because I can't take this anymore. I don't want to be with him anymore and I need your support. Tell me I'm doing the right thing here", I plead with her.

"I'm definitely here for you, but I won't tell you what's right for you. You have to know that deep down in your heart. If you're ready to divorce this man after 15 years, I'll support you, but the only advice I will give you is to make sure that this is what you want. Make sure that you aren't just doing this because you're mad at Kalin. Divorces can be nasty and people get hurt", she tells me.

"No, no, no. I'm doing this because I'm no longer in love with Kalin the way a woman should be in love with her husband", I admit, with tears in my eyes.

"And not because you met someone else?" Diana asks.

"Although I met someone else, I promise you that he's *not* the reason I'm leaving Kalin. Kalin messed up over and over again; first, by getting another woman pregnant, then running off to Alabama and having a fling with a woman there. Can you believe this man had the nerve to set up a secret email account for him and her to communicate?"

Diana is completely shocked. She's standing across from me with her mouth wide open, which is a dead giveaway that she had no idea about any of this.

"Close your mouth before a fly goes in", I say, jokingly. "I know you had no idea, but this is what I have been dealing with over the last years. It hasn't been easy since he got out of jail. The man I fell in love with is still incarcerated", I admit.

"Oh my goodness, MeMe. Why didn't you talk to me about what you've been dealing with? Nobody had any idea!! I thought that you were just busy with work and didn't have any time for anything else", Diana says.

"Now you know. And I just...", I begin.

"Who is he, Melissa? Who is this man who you have feelings for and does he have them for you?" she asks.

"Do you remember the Doctor who was there for Rita before she passed away and who was able to get the confession from her?" I ask.

"Yeah! That was the guy who basically helped you get your kids back", she comments.

"He's the man, Diana. We became closer and closer throughout the years and I have to admit this, but we turned it physical just recently", I say.

"What!!! Girl, you going crazy 'round here! You slept with the man?" Diana asks.

"Yes. I did. He made me feel so good, Diana, and I can't stop thinking about him. He's been texting me all day and I have not returned any of his text messages. I told him the other day that we needed to talk and I haven't reached out to him at all since I sent that message. There is no telling what he must be thinking", I admit.

"What are you going to do? What does your heart say do, Melissa? Really?" she asks.

"I love Patrick and I want to be with him. I don't think I'll ever be able to trust Kalin again, Diana. He killed it! And then, I didn't tell you this. He had the nerve to stay out all night. He didn't think it was necessary to offer me any type of explanation until I asked him days later. He had some lame excuse that he was at his cousin's house and fell asleep", I admit to her.

"And I know you didn't believe that!" she tells me.

"Of course, I didn't and I told him I didn't believe that bs! The night after that, I found myself in Patrick's arms. I guess I was craving the attention so much that I gave in to him, but honestly, I enjoyed every minute of it", I confess.

"Ok..so now that you've done it, do you have any regrets?" Diana asks.

"Heck no. None whatsoever", I say.

"And what's this about Stevie not being Sharelle's father? What the hell was *that* about?" she asks, looking totally shocked.

"I don't know, sis. Honestly, I thought that there was no way anyone else could be Sharelle's father. He and I were sleeping together non-stop, but one night when Stevie wasn't returning my calls, I went out with one of my girlfriends who was going to a Pajama Party that night and invited me along. I went with her and there was this guy there, named Juan, who was flirting with me all night. And you know how I am. I flirted back with him and one thing led to another and before you know it, he and I were having sex. It was a one night stand and I never saw him nor talked to him again. He is the only other possibility of a sperm donor for Sharelle. It just can't be true!!"

Neither of us has been keeping track of time, but we have been down here talking for at least an hour, but we really need to head upstairs to check on Sharelle. As soon as we make it upstairs, the first thing we see are the two police officers standing outside Sharelle's room. The male officer approaches me. "Ma'am, are you Sharelle's mother?" he asks.

"Yes sir. I am. What's the problem, Officer?"

"We need to speak with you in private regarding your daughter", he says.

"This is my sister. You can speak with me openly", I say.

"Ok. I'll get right to it. Your daughter's going to jail when she's released from the hospital", he blurts out.

"Oh God! What's next? Why is she going to jail, sir?"

"Your daughter was in the car with a trafficker, who is also a registered sex offender. Your daughter was working with him pushing drugs and prostituting and she...", he explains.

"What!!!!!!!!!!! Please don't tell me this!! My daughter was selling drugs and prostituting? She is only a baby!!! Oh God! How do you know she was selling drugs?" I ask.

"She had drugs in her possession. They were in her purse and the girls in the car also confirmed it. The other girls in the car were also pushing and prostituting, but they were over 18. Your daughter was the only minor in the car", he explains.

"And what about the guy who was driving? You said that he was a registered sex offender. So that means, he should not have been with a minor in the first place", I ask.

"That's correct, ma'am."

"Well, is *he* going to jail?" I ask.

"He was already taken to jail this morning. And I understand that your daughter will be released tomorrow morning and when she's released, she'll be taken over to the Juvenile Detention Center", he says. "Do you have any questions?"

"No sir. I don't have any questions. Thanks for letting me know."

The Officers leave and Diana and I just stand there in surprise. *I don't know whether I should be angry first and then sad. My daughter has been prostituting on the streets for a man who is not even supposed to be around children and not only that, but she was selling drugs for him. What in the world should I feel right now? How could Sharelle do this to her body? How can a man sleep with my young daughter and think that she is an adult? I want to scream and hit something or hit someone!!*

"Melissa, I know what you must be thinking", Diana finally says.

"Diana, you have no idea what I'm feeling right now! I'm angry and I just want to scream!! Oh my God! How much more can I take today?" I shout.

"I know it hurts, but you have to remain calm when she comes out of surgery. She doesn't need to hear anything negative or hear anything that reminds her of what she dealt with out on the streets. God has brought your daughter back to you. Thank him for that! And depend on Him to help you deal with the issues", she demands.

"You're right, sis. You're definitely right. I'm just thankful she's finally off the streets even if it had to happen this way. And honestly, I would rather her be in jail because she can't run again", I tell her.

My earlier conversation with Kalin must have been too much for him because he left. The nurse said he left about twenty minutes ago. He loves Sharelle so much, but he couldn't wait around and see how she'd be doing after the surgery.

So much time has passed and they're finally bringing Sharelle back into the room. The doctor approaches me and says, "Mrs. Thomas, surgery was a success! Your daughter did wonderful in there. Her body accepted the blood without any issues and after a good night's rest, she can go home tomorrow", he tells us.

"That's great news! Thanks so much for your help on everything!"

"Anytime! I'm just glad she's going to be okay. And you ladies have a great evening", the Doc says and walks away.

"Diana, did you notice how he looked at me?" I ask.

"Girl, you crazy. Isn't one doctor enough for you?" Diana asks, jokingly.

"I guess you're right!! But he sure is sexy to me. It must be the white coats or something", I admit.

After a good laugh, Diana and I turn down the lights so that Sharelle can sleep peacefully.

CHAPTER 12

"Talk to Me Like a Man."

"Why hasn't Melissa called me?" Patrick asks Cynthia.

"I don't know, Patrick. She's still at the hospital with her daughter", Cynthia answers.

"Her daughter? What happened to her daughter?" he asks, sounding concerned.

"I can't say. I don't know if she would want you to know. I mean, it is…", Cynthia tries to explain.

"Cynthia! I love this woman and I need to know what's wrong. Please tell me!" he pleads with her.

"Her daughter was taken to the emergency room yesterday from a bad car accident. I got a call from her this morning that Sharelle is going to be okay. She had to receive a blood transfusion, but she should be getting out today if all went well last night", Cynthia explains.

"It's good that she's getting out today. What should I do? Please tell me", Patrick pleads.

"Do nothing. Wait on Melissa to tell you what you can do. Let her come to you to talk about this. She'll come to work after Sharelle is released. I'm sure of it!" Cynthia advises Patrick.

Patrick, reluctantly, listens to Cynthia and decides to wait for Melissa to make contact with him, but he's not patient at all. So, to make it easier, he decides to go into the office to catch up on some paperwork. When he pulls into his parking lot, he recognizes the car that's parked next to his space. It's Kalin's car. Patrick pulls into his parking space and Kalin gets out and approaches his vehicle.

"Hey, man, please step out the car and talk to me like a man", Kalin demands.

Patrick puts his car in park and gets out. "What is it that you want with me, Kalin? And why have you come to my place of business to act like a fool?" Patrick says.

"I haven't said anything yet. I'm not trying to cause a scene or anything. It's just me and you standing here talking", Kalin says.

"Ok. Fine. Let's go into my office if you want to talk", Patrick says, leading the way.

The two men walk past the front desk and into Patrick's office. Kalin shuts the door behind himself.

"I'm going to get right down to it, Dr. Patrick, and I want to know one thing. What in the hell do you want from *my wife* and what gave you the right to take *my wife* to bed?" Kalin demands.

"Please have a seat, Mr. Thomas", Patrick calmly says. "This may come as a surprise to you, but *your wife* is a grown woman and she's smart enough to make her own decisions. When I met Melissa several years ago, I immediately felt something for her because of her beauty *and* her intelligence, but she was married to you and she made that very clear to me and I backed off. And then when she re-appeared in my life at the Trial, I wanted to run out of that courthouse with her, but again, I respected the fact that she was married. But, when our paths crossed again and I saw how unhappy she was, I couldn't stay away. She needed me", Patrick admits.

"What do you mean "she needed you"? She has a husband. What would she need *you* for?" Kalin asks.

"Her needs weren't being met. Men like you can be so weak and stupid. You had a beautiful, intelligent, working woman, and instead of getting your stuff together to make sure she was well taken care of, you allowed another man to meet some of her needs and that, my friend, is a recipe for disaster because the man she ran to is more than capable of meeting all of her needs. She couldn't depend on you for anything, Kalin. Is that *my* fault? No, that is *your* fault!" Patrick says, turning on his computer. "Is there anything else, Mr. Thomas? I have quite a bit of work to do."

Kalin is very upset at this point. He feels so helpless and for the first time since falling in love with Melissa, he finally realizes that it may be time to let Melissa go. There isn't anything else that can be said. He realizes that he's the reason he lost his wife and it hurts. "Why can't you just get out of her way so that she can work things out with her husband?" Kalin asks.

"Mr. Thomas, again, Melissa is a grown woman and if that's what she wants, she knows how to tell me. I've never forced her into anything. But, I'm not going to stand here and deny my feelings for her just because you've shown up here at my office and you're upset. I care a great deal about her. So, if there isn't anything else to discuss, I have a great deal of work to do", Patrick says, standing to shake Kalin's hand.

Kalin refuses the handshake and leaves the office angrily. Patrick sits back down at his computer and starts his day, hoping that Melissa will eventually make contact with him.

The ride back home for Kalin leaves him puzzled about his relationship with Melissa. He struggles with the thought of whether to contact an attorney or not. The idea of losing his wife to a man like Patrick is somewhat troubling for Kalin because Patrick certainly has much more to offer Melissa than he ever could. Finally making his way back to the house, Kalin decides to temporarily move out, thinking that, perhaps, this just may be time for that separation from Melissa.

CHAPTER 13

"Something Just Hit Me."

"The detectives are here, Melissa", Diana announces. "They just got here a few minutes ago. I saw them in the lobby when I was coming from the cafeteria."

"Ok. So, I guess my daughter will have to face her punishment for what she has done. And as much as I know she has to do this, Diana, I'm so upset by all of this and I …", I say, but Diana stops me right here.

"Melissa, this isn't something you caused. Your daughter made these decisions to do whatever she did and she's the one who has to pay the price", Diana begins. "You have other children who need you right now and this is not the time to put yourself down. This is NOT your fault! Do you understand me?"

"I do. I do. I was just saying that…", I say.

"I know what you're saying. I'm a mother, too. Now, here, drink your coffee before it gets cold", she says, handing me my cup of coffee she got from the cafeteria.

"Did Kalin call?" I ask her.

"Not that I know of", she answers. "Kalin is the least of your worries right now."

"I know. I'm just a little concerned about him because he was really upset when he left here last night. And Stevie? Oh my God! I hope that he can forgive me for what has happened", I say.

"I'm sure that he will, Melissa. He's a nice guy and he seems to care about you a lot, so I think that all of this will work itself out one way or the other", she responds.

"I have to be honest. There's someone else on my mind this morning, too. There's no telling what he must be thinking. I haven't communicated with him in a few days. I think it's time for me to come to grips with everything and have a conversation with the both of them. What do you think?" I ask.

"I think that you definitely need to come to grips with everything and make some decisions. I believe that once you finally stand your ground on these issues, you'll begin to heal and everything will look differently to you", Diana comforts.

The Doctor walks in and gives his blessing for Sharelle to be discharged. He is; however, interested in seeing her again just to make sure that everything is okay with her. We make the appointment for next Thursday, at his office. When the doctor turns to leave, Sharelle finally wakes up.

"Mommy?", she says, barely opening her eyes.

I walk over to her. "Yes, sweetheart. I'm here. Glad you woke up, sleepy head."

"What am I doing here? Why are you and Aunt Diana here?" she asks.

"Sweetheart, you were involved in a car accident and you got hurt and they brought you here, but the good news is that you're being released today. You're doing so much better now", I tell her.

"You mean I'm going home? Am I finally going home?" she asks. Diana looks away to hide her emotions.

"You're being released, sweetheart, but to the Juvenile Detention Center. On the night of the accident, the police found drugs in your purse, so they're charging you with possession of marijuana and you'll have to....", I begin to say, until she interrupts me.

"But those weren't mine, Mommy!! Those were his drugs. He put them in my purse because He said that if I got caught with them, they wouldn't do anything to me because I'm a minor. Those aren't my drugs! Mommy, you have to believe that!" she exclaims.

"It's not for me to believe, Sharelle. You have to convince the Judge on tomorrow. Right now, I want you to get some rest. The detectives are already here for you, so don't panic when you see them. I need for you to be a big girl about this and accept whatever punishment comes as a result of these decisions that you've been making", I say.

"I'm so sorry, Mommy. I'm so sorry to put you through all of this. Will you please forgive me and not hate me?" she says, with tears in her eyes.

"Sweetheart, you're my daughter and I love you and there's nothing you can do to change that. Do you understand that I have real love for you? We'll be waiting for you to come home", I say.

"Is Kalin still there?" she asks.

"What kind of question is that? Why wouldn't he be there, Sharelle?" I ask.

"Just wondering", she comments. "I love you Mommy. Please take care of yourself."

"Okay, sweetheart, I will."

The detectives walk in and start signaling that it's time to take Sharelle away. Diana and I move out of the way so that they can handle their business with her and within minutes, she's gone. My baby is out of my sight once again and I'm in tears. No matter what my daughter has done or will do in the future, she's my child and I love her and it hurts when she makes these decisions that keeps sending her to jail.

"Diana, I need you to take me to my car. I left it at the Park yesterday", I say.

"Sure, sis. No problem."

Diana and I leave the hospital and head down Dolphin Parkway until we make it to the Park. My car is still intact, but the closer I get to my car, I can tell that there's a note on my car. *Who left a note here?*

I pick up the note and it's from Stevie. *I will never forget you. For the time that you and Sharelle were in my life, you made it special. I'm glad that I got the chance to see you, but I'm leaving tonight to go back to California and I just wanted to say goodbye. I really hope you work out your marital issues. You are a beautiful woman, inside and out, and I know that you didn't mean to hurt me. So, with that said, I am not upset with you. I was hurt last night and I wanted to hate you, but I can't. We have been friends for a long time and we have been through many things together. Take care of yourself, MeMe, and know that I am always here for you.*

"Girl, what did he say?" Diana asks.

"Here, read it for yourself", I say, handing her the note. "What forgiveness he has in his heart! That is the most beautiful thing I've read in a long time. He forgave me, Cynthia! He forgave me! That just warms my heart."

"This is so nice, Melissa. See! Not everyone is mean and hateful. This man was so hurt last night, but he forgave you", Diana says.

"I know! I don't know what to say. Thanks, sis", I say, driving off.

What a night! I know that Patrick needs to hear from me right now, but I need to get home and get a shower and get into the office. Oh no, Cynthia! I haven't called her to get any updates or anything! My life is a mess right now. My husband and I are on the verge of a divorce. I had Stevie thinking for years that Sharelle was his daughter and she isn't so I hurt him. Patrick is falling in love with me and I have been avoiding him like the plague.

Dear God. I haven't spoken to you in a while and maybe that is part of the problem. I have really made a mess of things in my life. This is not where I thought things would end up with my marriage. I loved this man so much and he betrayed me, Lord. I wanted to forgive him and move on with our relationship, but he messed up again by not coming home the other night. So then I went and slept with another man to ease the pain. I know that I was not right for sleeping with a man who is not my husband, but he made me feel good, Lord. He made me forget the pain I was in and I hate to admit it, but I'm starting to feel something for him. I'm not in love with Kalin anymore and I don't feel right being with him and not being able to give myself completely to him.

Lord, please hear my prayer. Please forgive me when I'm weak and when I fall short of the things you would have me to do. Please show me the right way and the answer for my life. These and other blessings I ask in your son, Jesus' name...Amen.

When I pull into my driveway, I can see that Kalin has his car backed in and it looks like he's taking things out of the house. "What are you doing?" I ask him, as I approach his car.

"What does it look like I'm doing? I'm moving out. This is what you really want so I'm giving you the space that you need", he says, still putting things into the trunk.

"Do you not want to talk about things *first?*" I ask.

"Well, I already talked to your lover, Patrick, and I know all....", he begins, until I interrupt.

"You did what?" I yell. Why are you communicating with Patrick?" I ask, yelling.

"I wanted to know why he felt that it was okay for him to sleep with my wife", he says, locking his eyes with mine.

"You have a lot of nerve, Kalin Thomas! And you're such a hypocrite!! Did I ever approach Wendy about her affair with my husband? No, right? You're such a jerk and I can't believe you did that!! And besides, what makes you think I slept with him?"

"Yeah, well believe it! But, I won't bother either of you anymore. I'm moving out and doing my own thing so that I can take care of my children", he says. "And I know you did, Melissa. I know you did!"

"Well, that's a good thing. I hope you know you still have the responsibility of taking care of them", I say. "I didn't have these kids by myself, you know, and I shouldn't have to do everything for them. You sit around and think the world owes you something and it doesn't. You have to get out here and get it like everyone else. What makes you think that....", I begin to say, but Kalin snaps and punches me in the face with his fist, pushing me hard into the side of the car. I feel immediate pain, agitating my neck and back. I can't believe he would hit me like this, knowing I have a bulging disc in my neck from the car accident. The wrong blow to my head or neck could kill me.

"I don't need you to tell me what I need to do for my children, you b----! You worry about your kids and let me worry about mine! I'm so tired of hearing you tell me that", he says, without looking at me to see if I'm okay.

"Why did you do that? What did I say that was wrong? Feel like a man, Kalin? If that's what makes you feel like a man, go ahead and hit me again. Kill me if you want!! If that's what it's going to make you feel better, do it, Kalin! Do it!" I shout at him.

"Melissa, please stop! Just go away okay. Leave me the hell alone and let me get out of this house!" he says, pushing me away.

"I can't believe you did this to me! I can't believe you hurt me like this! You slept with another woman and you got the nerve to judge me! This is all your fault, Kalin! If you hadn't done that, you'd still have your wife. It's not Patrick's fault or anyone else's fault for that matter. But I forgave you for that, but then you went and stayed out all night the other night and lied to me *again* like I believed that story you gave me. You're the reason you're packing your things. Own up to it and take responsibility for once in your life. I'm done! Go ahead and get the heck out of here! I don't care anymore!!" I shout, walking into the house and slamming the door.

All I want to do at this point is just run away. I want to run away into my secret hiding place where it's just me and God. I feel so alone in this world. It's like I live in a world, surrounded by complete strangers. By the time I make it into my bedroom, I can clearly see that his man has lost his mind. He has thrown clothes all over the bedroom as if he went into a temper tantrum or something. I don't have time to focus on this right now, so I force myself to look past all of it and head for the shower. *Oh no! I just remembered that I have to go to Symone's property today. Maybe I should get a temp there again today. But I needed to call the Agency yesterday. I have to keep my word and get over there. I can actually get some of my work done sitting in her office.*

Kalin walks back into the bedroom once I step in the shower and he mumbles something to me, but I completely ignore him because I just want him to go so that I can get dressed for work and move past this moment. He mumbles something again, but this time I turn off the shower and yell, "What!"

"I need to see you for a second, Melissa. Please hurry."

I get out of the shower and Kalin is in bed expecting for me to give him sex one last time. *Is this man crazy? He just punched me in the face and he thinks I will spread my legs for him. He must be out of his rabbit mind.*

"You must be out of your mind if you think I'm going to give you sex after you've just treated me like a piece of trash and punched me in the face. I suggest you get it wherever you've been getting it because you won't get it here anymore. If you can't have more respect for me than that, why should you get the benefits of even having a wife? Thanks for the invitation, but I'll pass", I say, walking back into the bathroom.

"So, what? You gon' run to your white boy and get some loving? Is that what you want, Melissa? Is that who you want to make love to you?" Kalin yells.

"I think you need to get out of here because you're starting to act crazy and I'm not good with that. I have a long day ahead of me and need to get out of here, so…", I begin to tell him.

"Come here and give me my p----", Kalin demands, grabbing the towel and pushing it to the floor.

"What's wrong with you? I don't wanna have sex with you, you jerk! What do you think this is? You think you can just treat me any kind of way and I'm supposed to just accept it? That was the *old* Melissa and I don't have to be treated this way, so you can go straight to hell, Kalin!" I yell.

"So, it's like that? It's like that?" Kalin asks.

"Yes. It's like that!" I say, walking away.

Kalin grabs me and throws me to the bed and forces himself on me. He forces my legs open and enters me with great force as if he's trying to hurt me.

"Stop, Kalin! Stop! Why are you doing this?" I ask him, starting to cry.

"You're my wife and I'll be damned if I'm going to let another man please my wife!" he yells. Kalin continues to force himself inside thrusting harder and harder. "This is mine! Do you understand that?"

At this point, I'm crying and asking him to get off me, but he ignores my requests until he's "done" with me. He crawls off of me, puts his pants back on, and leaves the house. I get back in the shower just to wash his scent off of me. *Am I supposed to call the cops and tell them that my husband raped me? I can't believe he did this. I can tell he's angry. I should just let this go and get to work and move forward with my day and my life and let God deal with Kalin.*

My drive to work is somewhat peaceful. Time for a Yolanda Adams CD. I still like the Oldies. Her music still does it for me. Driving and listening to gospel gives me a little time to reflect on what has happened in the last 24 hours and just find some peace with it all. I have to stop by the office first and *then* head over to Symone's property. I'm sure that Cynthia has some updates for me.

"Well, well, well, look what the cat drove in here", Cynthia says, when I open the double doors to the Leasing Office.

"I miss you, too, Cynthia! I'm so glad to get back to work. This is one thing that doesn't stress me. Forgive me for not calling you last night, but, Sharelle is fine. She was released this morning, but was released to the custody of the Juvenile Detention Center. Apparently, she had drugs in her purse, so she's being charged with Possession", I explain.

"What! That's crazy! But you had to know that something like this was going on out on those streets", Cynthia says.

"I guess so! I guess so! But the most embarrassing thing happened last night, Cynthia. I wish you could have been there for me, girl", I begin.

"What happened?"

"Sharelle ended up needing a blood transfusion and because Stevie was with me, it just made sense for him to give his blood as well as me", I stutter.

"Of course. And what was wrong with that?" she asks.

"Well, his blood didn't match", I say, dropping my things on the desk.

"You mean to tell me that he is...", she says, hesitantly.

"That's correct! He is NOT her father! And that means only one thing. That the guy I had a one-night stand with is Sharelle's father!"

Cynthia just stands there with her hands over her mouth. "Oh my God! Oh no, Melissa!!

"And you know the worst part of it all?"

"There's more?" Cynthia asks.

"Yeah, he's married and has no idea that I was pregnant with his child. I hope this doesn't get too ugly. I think it's time he knows that he has a daughter. And the sad part is that Sharelle has no idea either", I tell her.

"You didn't say anything to her at all?" she asks, getting up from her desk.

"No, I didn't tell her. She slept through the whole thing. I can't even think about that right now. But the good thing is that Stevie forgave me for it. He left a note on my car and said that he forgives me. Isn't that sweet of him?"

"That's beautiful and that's what you call a real Christian. I don't know too many people who could have forgiven you for that", she tells me.

"Did I get any calls?" I ask.

"Yes. I left all of your messages on your desk, but there's one that I'm sure you'll want to know about", Cynthia says.

"Who? Tell me."

"Patrick called here earlier this morning and was very concerned for you. I hope you don't get mad about what I'm about to say, but I told him that you were at the hospital with your daughter, but I also told him to please wait for you to come to *him* with it. You're not mad, are you?" she asks.

"No, I'm not mad. It's okay, Cynthia. I guess I should call him. Can you believe that Kalin went to Patrick and questioned him about having sex with me? Unbelievable!!"

"No, he didn't. Whats 'going on with Kalin?"

"You don't want to know. But, good news, he moved out of the house this morning. I'm definitely going to change the locks when I get home tonight", I say.

"So, you two are really going to do this divorce thing, huh?"

"I think it's best, Cynthia. And I'm finally at peace with it. But, I'm only here briefly because I have to get over to Symone's property today. I'll be working from there", I tell her.

"Yeah, she called this morning wanting to make sure that you would be there."

"Do me a favor and pull the best route for me. My GPS is on the blink", I say, walking into my office. "And pull the end of month reports for all of my properties.

Cynthia walks away, but mumbles something to me as she's walking away.

"What did you say, Cynthia?" I ask her, trying to get her attention.

"You got another personal call on yesterday and it was from a guy named Stuart Peters", she says.

"Oh wow! Stuart? I haven't heard from him in a long time. What did he say?"

"Oh, nothing, but just to call him back", she tells me.

Cynthia takes just 15 minutes to get everything to me and I'm finally on my way to Symone's property. It's a beautiful day here in Florida and I'm starting to see why I've lived in Florida since 1991. There isn't a cloud in the sky. I've never gone this route before and although it's unfamiliar to me, it seems to be better. At any moment now, I'm expecting a call back from the Agency. *That must be her. She usually works her magic for me at such a short notice so let's see what she has for me.* Perfect timing! I'm stopped at a traffic light so I pick up the phone, but right when I say *hello,* something hits me out of nowhere and a white flash is the next thing I see. I can hear muffled sounds and it feels like everything is going in slow motion and there's an indescribable pain in my head. I've never felt anything like this ever in my life. The phone flies out of my hand and all I can see is the back of the 18-wheeler that's stopped in front of me. *What was that? Oh my God! Am I dead? My head hurts. I can't turn around. My neck hurts.*

Struggling to find my phone, I pick it up and the caller is still there. "Mrs. Thomas, are you still there? What happened?" she asks. This is Sandra from the Agency."

"Oh God, no!!! Something just hit me. I'm in so much pain. Please help me. Please help me. Can you please call Cynthia to tell her what happened? Call my family. Oh Jesus! My head hurts!! Please, somebody help me", I begin to say over and over again. People are knocking on my window right now", I say, slurring my words.

People are shouting at me from the outside wondering if I'm doing okay. I let down the window and even though they're talking to me, I can't comprehend what they're saying at all. "Ma'am, can you hear me?" one guy says. "The ambulance is on the way. Just sit tight. You'll be okay", another says.

It wasn't long and these young men were rushing and putting a brace on my head and slipping a board carefully underneath me. "Ma'am, my name is Brian and we're going to get you out of this car and put you in the ambulance and take you over to the hospital", he says, slowly. "Do you understand what I'm saying to you?"

"My head really hurts, sir. Please give me something for this pain in my head. It feels like my head is going to explode! Please help me!" I beg.

"Ma'am, we can't give you anything yet. The doctor will look at you when you get to the hospital and it will be his decision what you get for the pain", he explains.

"Okay. Okay. I need to call my family and let someone know what has happened."

"Ma'am, we really need to get you into the ambulance as quickly as possible. You can have one of the nurses do that for you when you get to the hospital. We need you to be seen as quickly as possible to make sure you're doing okay", he explains.

I eventually let the young men get to work and do what they came here to do. *I can't believe this! Instead of sitting at the property and catching up on my work, I'm riding in the back of an ambulance, looking up at the lights wondering what just happened. My pain is getting worse and worse. I'm thinking about all that is important in my life right now. This could have been worse. I could have been dead right now, but God spared me. Things like this makes you want to grab the people you love and hold onto them for dear life. I can see a vision of my kids right now and how they would feel if God had allowed me to die here today. Would they have missed me? What about Kalin? Would he feel bad for all of the things that he did to me? Calm down, Melissa. Everything is going to be okay.*

I finally make it to the hospital and due to my circumstances, I'm given a room right away. The nurse walks in to announce that I'm going to XRAY in the next 15 minutes. She removes my earrings, bracelets, and anything that will interfere with the examination. "Ma'am, I need to contact my family and let them know what has happened."

"Okay, let me get you the phone", she says, walking over to give me the wall phone.

"Thank you so much."

I dial Diana's number, but get her voice mail. I try to leave the message in a way that she won't worry too much. Then, I dial the office number to see if Cynthia answers and she does. "Cynthia, did the lady from the Agency call you and...?" I begin to ask.

"Oh my God, Melissa! Yes! She called. I was so worried. You have us over here worried sick about you. Kalin *and* Patrick have both been calling to see if I'd heard anything. What hospital are you at?" Cynthia asks.

"I'm at Miami Southern Hospital."

"Okay. I'm coming. I can't let you go through this by yourself. I 've already called Manhattan next door and their leasing agent is going to come over here to sit at the property for the rest of the day. So, don't think about it. I'm coming!"

"Drive carefully, Cynthia. Drive carefully."

CHAPTER 14

"Will He Know Where I Am?"

"Sharelle Williams", the bailiff shouts. Sharelle holds up her head and walks to the front to be addressed by the Judge. Sharelle's public defender announces why I'm not in the courtroom due to an accident that happened on yesterday. Sharelle is just finding out about the accident and she's totally surprised. "Is my mother okay?" she asks. "Please tell me. What's wrong with my mother?"

"Sir, please have your client calm down", the Judge orders.

"Sorry, Judge, but she's just finding out that her mother was involved in a car accident." The public defender turns to Sharelle and tells her that he would speak with her in a few minutes about it, which calms her down.

"Ok. Sorry Judge. Please carry on", he tells the Judge.

"Thank you, Sir. Sharelle, you're being charged with possession of marijuana. What's your plea in response to these charges?"

"Not guilty", Sharelle mumbles.

"Speak louder, young lady", the Judge says.

"Not guilty", Sharelle says a little louder.

"Ok. Make note that Sharelle is taking a plea of not guilty. A court date has to be set at this point. Madam Reporter, what do you have?" the Judge asks.

"Thursday, 2 weeks from today", she responds.

"Ok. The date is set and you'll receive a letter in the mail confirming this appointment. Ms. Williams, you're free to go home. Please make sure that your family arrives no later than 5pm to pick you up", she says.

"Your Honor, due to the fact that Sharelle's mother is in the hospital, we'll need temporary permission for someone else to pick her up", the public defender requests.

"Ok, Sir. Please submit the name of the person who will pick her up to the Department for them to get approval to pick her up."

"I'll do my best to make contact with the Mother to see who'll pick her up. Thanks Judge."

You would think that Sharelle would be happy to be going home, but it's hard to tell because she has a sad look on her face, which could easily be because of the news she just heard. It's starting to dawn on her that it's actually been a long time since she's been home and it may take some time for her to get used to being there again and getting back into the swing of things.

"Sharelle, please go home and get back in school and do the right things. You're a beautiful young lady with a bright future ahead of you. Don't waste it away by trying to be an adult too soon", the public defender encourages.

"Yes sir. I promise I'll try my best. So, what's gonna happen to the guy that was in the car?" Sharelle asks.

"What do you mean?" he asks.

"Is he going to get out and will he know where I am? I'm pleading not guilty because he was the one who put those drugs in my purse because he said I wouldn't get in as much trouble as he would if I was caught", Sharelle explains.

"Here's the deal, Sharelle. You *will* have to testify to that when it comes up. And he'll probably be in the courtroom when you do. Do you know that this guy is a registered sex offender?" he asks.

"No. I didn't know that", Sharelle responds.

"Well, he is and he's hurting young girls like yourself. He's taking young girls across state lines and prostituting them. He's *not* a good guy", the public defender says.

"Yeah, but you don't know what he's capable of doing. I'm afraid to testify against him while he's watching me. I don't know if I can do that", Sharelle tells him.

"I don't see how we'll be able to put him in jail forever *without* the testimony of any of you girls that he's hurt. Not testifying will put him back out there to do it again. He bonded out of jail this morning and will probably be right back at what he was doing", the public defender explains.

"You don't understand. I don't want him to hurt me or my family. I'm afraid of him so I'll have to think about this and I'll have to really think about whether I want to testify or not", Sharelle says, walking away with a sad look on her face.

Sharelle returns to her seat and waits for the bailiff to take her away to wait to go back to the Center. At least for now, she's going home to her family and to her warm bed.

CHAPTER 15

"Who's Taking Me Home?"

"*M*rs. Thomas, you have a visitor", the nurse announces before Cynthia walks in her room.

"Oh, hey Cynthia! It's so good to see your face", I say.

"Don't try to get up. It's okay", Cynthia says, placing her fruit basket on the table. "I thought you might want something to snack on."

"Thank you dear. That's so nice. So, what exactly did Sandra tell you when she called?" I ask.

"She said that she was on the phone with you when you were hit and said it was so loud", Cynthia says.

"Yeah. It caught me by total surprise. I've never felt this kind of pain in my life. I'm still in pain. They won't give me anything until all the tests are finished. This thing around my head hurts. My back is in so much pain. I would much rather be at work right now. Did you make arrangements for Symone's property for me?" I ask.

"Would you stop thinking about work for once?" Cynthia says jokingly. "But, yes, I did. Sandra sent that same Temp that was there yesterday. I told Sandra to just have her go in for the rest of the week. When I talked to Symone, she was actually relieved to take the rest of the week off so that she can be there for her daughter's recovery."

"Thank you so much for doing all that you do. Is the Corporate Office aware of what has happened?" I ask.

"Yes. I spoke with Sharon personally and she was asking what hospital they took you to. She wanted to know if there was anything you needed and to have you give her a call if you needed anything at all. She seemed genuinely concerned for you", Cynthia adds.

"That's good. I'm in so much pain right now and I'll be so glad when these tests are over so that I can finally get something for this pain!! Oh God, Cynthia! I can't take too much more of this", I tell her.

"Hang in there. It'll be okay", she says, rubbing my head. "Do you want some water?"

"Yes, please", I tell her.

The doctor walks in and announces that the Lab residents will be in shortly to take me for further tests of my back and neck. *I don't think I'm scared. I just have to trust God no matter what happens here today. He is with me and I know it. If He weren't, I would have been in worse shape right now, but I am alive and that is what matters. So many things are going through my mind right now. What if there is some permanent damage? Will I recover? Will Patrick still want me if I am hurt? Will I have to end up damaged?*

"Do you have any questions, Mrs. Thomas?" the doctor asks.

"No. I don't. I just want something for pain as soon as possible", I respond.

"I hear you. I know it hurts, but it gives us an inaccurate read on the tests if you're medicated, but I have ordered some strong pain meds for you as soon as the tests are done. We'll give you a shot in the rear to make it better for you", he says and smiles.

"I don't have a problem taking it in the rear, Doc", I say, when Cynthia taps me on my hand. *I just realized how that must sound.* The doctor carries on without much thought of what I just said.

"Great! Once they bring me the results of the lab tests, I'll be in to discuss them with you", he says.

He leaves the room and the nurse comes in to check my vitals again. "Mrs. Thomas, there's a man outside who's very anxious to get in here to see you, but I want to make sure that it's okay with you", the nurse tells me.

"Who is it?" I ask.

"He says that his name is Dr. Patrick Norwood", the nurse tells me.

Cynthia looks at me and smiles. "Let the man in, Melissa."

"Sure. He can come in. It's okay."

The nurse leaves the room and in walks the most beautiful sets of green eyes I've ever seen. He pays no attention to the fact that Cynthia's in the room, but walks right over to me and kisses me on my lips. "Baby,

I was so worried when I got the call that you were in a car accident. I love you, baby. I love you so much", he says.

"I love you too, Patrick."

Cynthia clears her throat. "Hello Patrick. Good to see you too", she says and then laughs.

"I'm sorry, Cynthia. I didn't see you sitting over there. I love this woman right here so much", he says, pointing at me.

"That's so sweet. I'm happy for the two of you. If this is what you both want, I am happy for you", Cynthia says, setting off a whole new conversation.

"Is this what we both want?" Patrick asks.

"Not here, Patrick. Not now, please."

"Okay, beautiful. You're right. We'll discuss that later. Let's just get you better and get you out of here. What has the doctor said so far?" he asks.

"They'll be coming shortly to take me to get XRAYS and then the doctor will discuss the results with me and we'll just go from there", I say, looking up to see Kalin coming through the door.

"What the hell are you doing here man? This is not *your* wife. It is not *your* job to be here", Kalin says, walking through the door.

"Kalin, please don't come in here with all of that. I'm okay with him being here so you need to just chill with all of that", I tell him.

"Kalin, please", Cynthia begs.

The lab techs are here and are ready to take me upstairs for my tests. *I am so afraid to leave the two of them here, but thank God Cynthia is here. She is good at keeping things peaceful, so I know things won't get out of hand with her around. What is Kalin doing here? I really would much rather go through this without him.*

"She'll be back in about 30 minutes or so", the lab tech announces.

After adjusting my bed, I'm taken away. All of a sudden, I become concerned with these tests and don't want to find out that there is something seriously wrong. *Oh God! I just remembered that Sharelle had her hearing this morning and I missed it. I need to find out what happened at the hearing. I can't forget to do this when I get back to the room.*

"So, why *are* you here man?" Kalin asks Patrick.

"Man, listen. I'm not going to go through this with you. I was informed that Melissa was in a car accident and because I'm her friend, I thought that being here for her is what she needed during this time. She didn't object to my being here so I don't really care what you have to say", he says, calmly.

"Really, huh? Did she tell you that we made love just this morning? She'll always be mine. Do you understand that?" Kalin says in a very mean tone.

"Wow. Good for you. It doesn't look like you'll have that job too much longer. You might as well enjoy it while you can. I don't have anything to do with what you and Melissa do, man. So, please stop trying to make that known. Do you know how crazy you sound?" Patrick says, getting up and walking towards the door. "Cynthia, I'm going to get something from the cafeteria. Would you like something?"

"No, Patrick. Thanks for asking", Cynthia says.

Patrick leaves the room and Cynthia uses this opportunity to talk to Kalin. "What is wrong with you, Kalin?"

"I hate that m-----------", Kalin responds.

"Why? What did he do to you? Patrick is a very nice guy and he hasn't done anything wrong here. If you have any issues, it is with yourself for losing your wife in the first place. Don't be stupid! He's here because she wants him here. He knows that and he's not going to leave so you might as well chill out with all of that drama. He loves her, Kalin", Cynthia explains.

"I can't believe you're standing here telling me this. You're probably the one who told that white man that she was even in the hospital and now, you want me to just walk away and give this man my wife? I can't do that, Cynthia. I just can't do it!" Kalin shouts.

"What you don't understand is that it isn't up to you anymore", Cynthia explains. "If you ever want to try to save your marriage, don't pressure her right now and for God's sake, stop putting Patrick down because you're just pushing her into his arms when you do that", Cynthia advises.

"I hear what you're saying. I do. It's just that seeing him here being there for her makes me sick. There was a time when she would look to me to do that for her. I blew it Cynthia. I hurt my best friend and I just don't know how to make it right with her. I believe she must really like him being that he's here and everything", Kalin says.

Patrick walks through the door with his items from the cafeteria and takes a seat by the bed. He doesn't interfere with mine and Kalin's conversation. But when he sees that we stopped talking, he says, "Cynthia, do you know the doctor's name that's caring for Melissa?"

"I think his name is Dr. Mitchell", Cynthia responds.

"Dr. Mitchell, hmmmm, I think I know him. I'll see when he comes back. I know quite a few doctors from this hospital. I did my residency with many of them. He didn't come back yet, did he?" Patrick asks.

"No. He didn't. He'll come back after ...", Cynthia begins, but is interrupted by Kalin.

"Hey man, why do you care? You're sitting here and asking questions like this woman has already divorced me and she's single or something. That's a married woman that we're talking about here and you just show up here like you're already her man and I just...", Kalin begins.

"Listen, Kalin. I'm not here to cause any problems. I'm here for Melissa in her time of need like a good friend does. And please, don't let this white skin fool you", Patrick says, sitting back down in his chair.

"Guys, please. Let's keep it peaceful for Melissa. I don't want her to come back here and all hell has broken loose. I'm so sure that she's worrying herself sick about what she *thinks* may be going on in here. When she comes back in here, she does not need to come in here listening to two grown men bickering back and forth", Cynthia scolds.

"You're right, Cynthia. I care about her way too much to stress her out", Patrick says.

Cynthia, Patrick, and Kalin sit in silence until I make it back into the room. As soon as I come through the door, Cynthia runs to me and says, "How did it go? It wasn't too bad, was it?"

"How did it go in here? Tell me the truth. Did anyone get crazy while I was gone?" I ask.

"I'll tell you about it later", Cynthia whispers to me.

"How do you feel, Melissa? Kalin asks. "I heard that you got hit from behind while you were just sitting there", he says, walking over to my bed.

"I am in a lot of pain right now, but the doctor will be giving me something for pain soon. As soon as I was hit, I immediately felt pain to my head and neck. I couldn't move my head at all. It sure did scare the hell out of me!"

"I bet it did. I'm glad that you're doing okay. It could have been worse."

I notice that Patrick is extremely quiet and looks like something is on his mind. Something must have happened here and I need to find out because I don't want him having information that I haven't explained.

"Patrick, are you okay? You seem quiet", I turn to him and say.

"No. I'm just thinking about different errands that I'll need to run when I leave here. How are you feeling? Still in pain?" he asks.

"Yes. The nurse will be in at any moment to give me the shot in my rear to help me with the pain. Thanks for being here. I know you probably got so much that you need to do and I'm sorry that I took you away from it', I say.

"Oh please! I'm the boss, remember? It's okay."

In walks the nurse with my relief! "Finally!" I shout.

Everyone steps out of the way while the nurse flips me over to administer the shot in my rear. Within minutes, I'm already feeling some relief. "Cynthia, I just remembered that Sharelle had court today and I missed it. Will you please contact the Public Defender and find out what happened? His number is stored in my phone under "Public Defender". I know you let him know about the accident, but I need to know what the Judge decided for Sharelle. If she ends up getting released, I will definitely need for you to pick her up for me", I say.

"And you know that I'll do that for you. Don't worry about anything but getting better", Cynthia demands.

Dr. Mitchell walks in and announces that he's ready to discuss the lab results so it's time to clear out the room. Everyone steps outside.

"Did that shot in the rear do it for you?" he asks. "You should be feeling good right about now".

"Yes. I feel great. Thanks so much. So, give it to me straight", I say.

"The lab results are actually not that bad. There is some curvature in your spine. But I'm going to recommend that you make an appointment with a chiropractor immediately for therapy. You'll experience severe headaches and muscle spasms as a result of this accident, but don't worry. I'm prescribing meds for the spasms and for the pain and this will temporarily relieve you, but the therapy will definitely help. Now, I can't let you drive tonight, but from the looks of it, you have more than enough people willing to give you a ride home, so I won't worry about that. Do you have any questions for me?"

"Curved spine? Will that ever be fixed?" I ask.

"Therapy will help get things back in place as it should be. I'll be honest. Even though you will get therapy, you'll probably still feel pain in your back and neck from time to time", he admits.

"That's no good! But, I can't complain. I'm alive. I could have died in the car accident", I admit.

"I love your attitude, Mrs. Thomas. I wish more people...", he says before I cut him off.

"Please call me Melissa. You're being too formal."

"Ok, *Melissa*. Like I was saying, I wish more people looked at things in this manner", he says.

"As far as I am concerned, it is the *only* way to look at things, Dr. Mitchell."

The doctor and I continue our conversation until I get a clear understanding of my condition. He leaves, but sends in the rest of my family. Looks like I'll be busy over the next six months with a chiropractor.

"I need a ride home. So, who's taking me home?"

CHAPTER 16

"Don't Tell Your Mother."

"Good afternoon, Mr. Watson. How are you?"

"I'm fine, thank you", he responds. "Who's this?"

"This is Cynthia and I'm a friend of Mrs. Melissa Thomas and she asked me to give you a call regarding her daughter, Sharelle Williams", Cynthia explains to the public defender.

"Oh yes! Yes! I was expecting a call from someone. Thank you for calling", he says.

"No problem. Being that Mrs. Thomas is in the hospital, I was hoping you could inform me of her daughter's status", Cynthia requests.

"Sure. No problem. I understand. How is she doing?" Mr. Watson asks.

"She's doing much better. She'll have to go to therapy, but she's alive, but just very concerned about her daughter", Cynthia says.

"Well, there's good news! Sharelle gets to go home to be with her family. She does; however, have court next week, but for now, she *can* go home. She just needs someone to pick her up no later than 5pm at the Juvenile Detention Center", he explains.

"That's not a problem. I'll pick her up if that's okay", Cynthia suggests.

"Sure, Cynthia. I'll alert JDC that you'll pick Sharelle up because her mother is in the hospital and unable to do so", he confirms.

"Thank you so much. I'll be there."

Cynthia knows that for her to be able to get everything done, she'll have to pick Sharelle up on her lunch break. But now, Cynthia is wondering how Sharelle will be able to get into the house if Cynthia is at the hospital and she doubts if Sharelle will have a key. The only other person with a key would have to be Kalin, but Melissa won't like the idea of Kalin showing back up at the house.

Melissa will just have to understand that she has to do this to get Sharelle into the house. She, reluctantly, calls Kalin.

"Hello", Kalin answers.

"Kalin, it's Cynthia. How are you?"

"I'm ok. What's up?" he says.

"I have to pick up Sharelle from JDC, but I don't want to just drop her off without knowing that she can get in the house. Will you please meet me at the house just to let her in? Princess is not in town so I can't get her to let her in and I don't want to bother Melissa with it because she probably doesn't even have her keys" Cynthia tells him.

"Sure. I don't have a problem with that. So, Sharelle is going home, huh? That's really good. Does she know about the whole father situation?" Kalin asks.

"I don't know and I don't think *you* should be the one to tell her. That's Melissa's job, Kalin", Cynthia adds.

"I wasn't thinking of doing anything. I was just wondering. So, what time do you want me to be at the house?" Kalin asks.

"I'm leaving here in 30 minutes to pick her up, so I'll get to the house no later than 2 o'clock", Cynthia tells him.

"Fine. I'll see you then. How's your friend today?" he asks sarcastically.

"She's just fine, Kalin. She's extremely sore, but other than that, she's doing just fine."

Cynthia finishes up the postings she was doing in Rent Roll and heads north on Dolphin to get over to JDC through the rush hour lunch traffic. She shows her ID and is cleared to pick up Sharelle. The process is underway and to pass time, Cynthia pulls out her November issue of Ebony magazine and begins to read. Surprisingly so, Cynthia's phone doesn't ring at all while she waits. When Sharelle walks through the double doors, she seems genuinely happy to see Cynthia. She walks over to her and gives her a big hug and whispers in her ear, "thank you Auntie".

"How's my momma? I cried all night after finding out that she was in a car accident. Is she okay?"

"Sweetheart, now you know that your mother is a tough cookie. She was hit pretty hard from behind, but she was in her car seat. There are no scrapes and bruises, but she is in severe pain. Her back and neck really hurts her. She *will* have to go to therapy to help her with that, but she'll be just fine", Cynthia responds.

"Oh my God! If anything were to happen to my mother, I would lose my mind. I know that I have disappointed her, but I love her, Auntie", she says, now walking towards the car.

"And she loves you too, Sharelle. She talked of nothing but you the entire time you were gone from the house. That woman would sit in her office all the time praying for you to come home. She wanted to just get in her car and ride until she found you and brought you back to the house", Cynthia says.

"There's NOT a day that went by that I didn't think about my mother and my sisters and brothers", Sharelle says.

"And what about Kalin?" Cynthia says, smiling.

"I hate that man!" Sharelle says, catching Cynthia by surprise.

"Why?" Cynthia shouts. "That's not nice, Sharelle!"

"He's a liar and a cheater and I hate him. I hate him for hurting my mother and making her cry. I can't respect any man who does that. My mother deserves so much better. That's all I'm saying", Sharelle says.

"Why do you say he's a liar and a cheater?" Cynthia asks.

"I don't want to say right now, Auntie. Can we please change the subject? How are my sisters doing?"

"You can talk to me, Sharelle. I won't tell your mother if you don't want me to tell her", she says.

'I know, but I just want to concentrate on being positive today and if I talk about him, it will *NOT* be positive. How are my sisters?" she asks.

"They're doing just fine. Everyone is just worried about Mom", Cynthia admits. "Well, I might as well tell you that I had to ask Kalin to come and let you in the house because Princess is out of town and I just had no other choice but to get him to do it."

"I'm cool with him. I just don't trust him at all for my mother. Not anymore! Not like I did when we were little", she confesses.

"Can you get along with him for me?" she asks.

"Not a problem."

"Good, because we're here and it looks like he just pulled in behind us", Cynthia says.

Cynthia pulls into the driveway and Kalin parks right beside her. He jumps out of the car and goes to Sharelle's side of the car.

"Hey sweetheart. It's so good to see you alive and well. How are you feeling?" Kalin asks Sharelle.

"I'm doing better today. I was feeling bad yesterday, but not today. I was so scared when I was out there on the streets, but I'm really glad to be home", Sharelle admits.

"And we're glad that you're home", Kalin says, giving her a hug. "Are you hungry?"

"I'm starving! The food in JDC is disgusting. I'm not kidding you when I tell you that I'm so glad to be home to eat my mother's cooking", Sharelle says with a giggle.

Cynthia helps Sharelle into the house. "Sharelle, you good? I'm going back to work now, but I'll call your mother and let her know that you've made it home safely so she won't have to worry."

"Yes, I'm fine, Auntie. I'll be just fine. I promise. Don't worry."

Cynthia leaves and Kalin fires up the stove to make Sharelle a homemade burger and fries. "So, I guess I should tell you that I've moved out of the house and your mother and I are contemplating a divorce", Kalin says. Sharelle's facial expressions change just a little and Kalin notices.

"How does that make you feel?" Kalin asks.

"I don't have a comment on this because I don't know what has been going on around here. That's between you and my mother to work out. You're both adults and you should know what's good for the both of you. I'm sorry that you guys can't figure out how to make things work, but if you're not happy, then you're not happy", Sharelle comments.

"Wow. That is such a grown up response. Who have you been talking to?" Kalin asks.

"I've learned quite a few things being out on the streets and no, I don't want to talk about any of that", Sharelle says, getting a soda out of the refrigerator.

"I understand that. Well, make sure you help out your mother when she gets back here. She's definitely going to need your support", Kalin tells her.

"You bet I will. I love her and I don't want to see her hurt anymore", Sharelle says, looking away.

"What's that supposed to mean, *hurt anymore*?" Kalin asks.

"Just what I said. She's been hurt enough in her life and I'm tired of *my mother* being hurt. She deserves so much better than that", Sharelle says, almost with an attitude.

"You almost make it sound like *I ha*ve hurt her", Kalin comments.

"I'm just saying; but, if the shoe fits, Kalin", Sharelle says.

"Sounds like you have something on your mind, Sharelle. Do you feel like talking about it?" Kalin asks. Kalin can tell that Sharelle really means what she's saying because her attitude has changed completely from the time she walked into the house. He's not sure if he wants to keep prying or if he *really* wants to know what she's talking about because it sounds like this conversation could get a little heated.

"Sure you wanna know?" Sharelle asks, taking a bite out of her sandwich.

"If there's something you feel that you need to say to me, by all means, please do so", Kalin tells her.

"Ok. I'll tell you. I know your little secret. I know what you've been doing and how you've been telling my mother something else. I know all about your little "fling" with Mr. Carl's wife. I saw you one night when you thought you were hiding. And the only reason I haven't told my mother is because it would break her heart into pieces knowing that her true love is busy with another woman", Sharelle says.

Kalin is in shock. He doesn't understand how Sharelle knows so much. He's sure that his expressions are telling Sharelle all that he's thinking.

"Yeah! My mother deserves better than you", Sharelle exclaims.

"Sharelle, wait a minute! You may have things totally out of context. It's not like that!" he tries to explain.

"Listen. That stuff doesn't work quite as well on me as it does my mother. She's so blinded by what she thinks is love, but I can see straight through it. It's just a matter of time that she sees you for who you are and move on. I don't have anything against you personally, but I know that my mother has men at her all the time and for some reason, she has chosen to stick by your side after all these years", Sharelle says.

"I didn't know that you felt this way about mine and your mother's marriage, Sharelle", Kalin comments.

"Now you know. I didn't always feel this way. You did this, Kalin. And since I saw you that night all cuddled up with that woman and knowing that my mother was probably sitting here in this house wondering where you were or crying her eyeballs out, I lost a lot of respect for you. She doesn't deserve that. And with *that woman* of all people", Sharelle says, with a disgusted look on her face.

"Sharelle, I think that you got this all wrong", Kalin tries to explain, but Sharelle is very convinced of what she saw.

"I don't want you to share anything with your mother. She and I are already having major problems right now. She wouldn't understand if she heard something like this", Kalin says.

"Stop telling her lies. Let her go to be with someone else. You wanna be with that woman so be with her. My mother is beautiful and she'll be just fine. She'll always have her children", Sharelle says.

"I can see that we won't see eye to eye on this, so let's just stop talking about it", Kalin suggests.

"Fine with me because you can't feed me those lies you feed my mother", Sharelle tells him.

Kalin finally leaves the house. In so many ways, Sherelle would much rather get familiar with her room again with Kalin gone. His car is completely out of the driveway, so Sharelle heads down the hallway to her bedroom, looking exactly like she left it. With nothing but time on her hands, Sharelle decides to clean the house so that it'll be comfortable for her mother when she's released from the hospital. It'll just be one less thing that she'll have to worry about after getting home. Sharelle decides to spend the rest of the afternoon washing dishes, cleaning bathrooms, sweeping the garage out, and cleaning the refrigerator.

With Kalin gone, Sharelle realizes that she will now have to grow up to help her Mom with the girls and suddenly cope with being alone.

CHAPTER 17

"It Wasn't Like That at All."

*T*he time away from work puts Cynthia behind just a little. When she makes it back into the office, the voice messages are full and a few residents dropped by with rent checks and renewal signatures. Cynthia quickly recognizes that there's an urgent message flashing and it's from Sharon.

After listening to the message, Cynthia is surprised at Sharon, knowing I was just in a car accident; but, because of Sharon's tone in her voice, Cynthia is trying to decide if she should tell me about this message or just handle it herself. She decides to tell me because not only are we co-workers, but we are also friends and she doesn't want me to be railroaded.

I'm finally being released from the hospital today, but decide to take some time off to recuperate until I get a call from Cynthia.

"What's going on Melissa? What did the doctor say?"

"Good news! He's releasing me now. I'm just waiting on Patrick to pick me up. Why? Is everything okay? You sound like something is wrong" I tell her.

"Okay. That's nice of Patrick. Tell him that I said hello when he gets there. You really like him, don't you Melissa?"

"I do, Cynthia. He makes me feel so beautiful even when I *know* that I'm not beautiful. We laugh together and never discuss life's problems. He's certainly a lot less complicated than Kalin. Is everything okay? What are you *not* telling me? What did Mr. Watson say about Sharelle?" I ask, trying to get it out of her.

"She was released and I went ahead and picked her up from JDC, but I might as well tell you now that I had to get Kalin to meet me at the house to let her in and so I….", I begin to explain.

"And did he?" I ask, in total shock.

"Yes. He met us there and let her in. When I left, he was still there. I'm sure that he's gone by now", I add.

"I hope so. It would be a total disaster if he's still there when I get home, especially since Patrick is taking me home. I don't need the drama. Not today and Lord knows, not ever!" I tell her.

"He seemed to be in a fairly okay mood and he even seemed happy to see Sharelle, but honestly, she's not so happy with him these days. I asked her to talk to me about it, but she refused; so, I just want to give you heads up on that", Cynthia warns.

"That child always has a problem with somebody. There's just no telling about her and him. They used to have the best relationship Ive ever seen with a father and his daughter, but for the last year or so, her attitude has really changed towards him", I say. "But, I have to go now because *Green Eyes* just walked into the room."

"Okay. Have a safe trip home and Melissa, enjoy letting someone else take care of you. Patrick is more than capable of taking care of you. Let him pamper you", Cynthia advises before hanging up.

"Good afternoon beautiful! How are you feeling today?" Patrick asks.

"I'm doing just fine, now that you're here", I say, giving him a hug.

Right in the middle of our hug, the nurse walks into the room. "Young lady, you're all set to go. Here are your discharge papers. The doctor wants you to follow up with a chiropractor first thing Monday morning. Get as much rest as you possibly can. You will be very sore, especially when you wake up tomorrow morning. But, in this packet are two prescriptions. One for the muscle spasms and one for the pain", she describes.

"I'm going to definitely need the one for the pain", I say, smiling.

"I'll make sure that these prescriptions are filled and that she gets her rest", Patrick says to the nurse.

"Well, that's just wonderful", she responds, looking up and down at Patrick and trying to decide if he's with me or not. He notices it as well.

Patrick and I leave the hospital and head to Rick's Tow Yard to look at my car and to get my belongings. When we get to the Yard, I have to prove that I'm the owner of the vehicle and now trying to explain to the guy that my things were left in the car, but for some reason, he's just not getting it. Patrick, in his ever so professional tone, explains and now there's understanding. I have no idea of what to expect when we see my vehicle. Patrick notices it first. "Oh no, Melissa! Look at your car, honey. It looks like a total loss to me", he comments.

"It sure does. Wow! I must have been hit pretty hard for my SUV to look like this. I just have to say *Thank You Jesus!* If my car looks like this, I can only imagine what the other car looks like", I say.

"I can get the pictures for you honey", Patrick states.

He pulls out the camera and takes several photos of the Escape from different angles. I just purchased this SUV not even a month ago and now it's totaled; but, it's just a car. I am thankful to God because I'm here to tell about it. It could be worse.

"Okay. I think I got all the shots that you'll need. When I get home, I'll download these and send them to your email and all you'll have to do is forward the email to the adjuster", he says.

"You're so good to me, Patrick. I appreciate you so much", I tell him, giving him a hug. *I can tell that Patrick is a little distant from me today. Why, I wonder. I'm trying to think if I said something or did anything that could have offended him, but I can't think of anything. I don't know if I should ask him because I don't want to ruin our mood, but I am very curious.* "Is everything okay, Patrick?"

"Why would you say that?" he asks.

"You seem a little different today. Don't get me wrong. You're being very helpful, but the other day, you said that you loved me and you wanted to step things up between us and today, it seems as if you barely want to touch me", I tell him.

"Honey, you were just injured in a car accident. I don't want to do anything to hurt you", he explains.

"C'mon Patrick. You and I both know that's crap. Aren't we supposed to be friends? So, please tell me the truth. Did I say anything to offend you?"

"Melissa, I would much rather not talk about this right now. The most important thing is getting your prescriptions and getting you home to get rest. You heard what the Nurse said. Another day and we can discuss things", he says, grabbing my hand.

"No. What is it?" I ask again.

"Why can't you understand that I don't want to discuss it right now? Will you please respect what I need for once?" he says, with a little more force this time, so much so that I move away from him.

"Oh I see. So, now, I don't respect you? Is that what you're trying to say, Patrick?" I say, getting a little angry.

"Melissa, sweetheart, that's not what I mean and you know that. I've had a long day and I just want to keep things simple. I care about you and all I want to do is take care of you today. So, please let me, baby", he pleads.

We leave the tow yard, but with very little conversation in the car. Because he had already called in the prescriptions, they were ready when we stopped at the pharmacy. As we're driving on my street, I notice that there's a car parked next to the tree next to my house. *It looks like Kalin's car. Please don't tell me that this man is waiting to see who will bring me home just to start something. I'll call the police on him if I need to do that. Why won't this man just move on knowing all the stuff he has put me through and how he has cheated on me with Wendy and God knows who else?*

"Okay, honey. We're here. I'll get your things and bring them inside. You just go in the house and greet your daughter and get ready for bed", Patrick directs.

"Patrick, I don't want to alarm you, but that's Kalin parked by the tree, but don't mind him if he says anything to you", I tell him.

"Sweetheart, Kalin is the *last* thing I'm worried about. His bark is much louder than his bite", he says.

Once I open my door, I notice that Kalin is getting out of his car and walking towards me and Patrick. Before he gets to us, he starts yelling, "What the hell is this? You think you just gonna move in and take my place? I know you hear me!"

"Melissa, just go inside. I got this. He's not going to make a scene out here and disrespect you and me like this. Just go!" he tells me, grabbing my things from the trunk.

I do as Patrick suggests and go inside, but Kalin keeps talking. Once I get inside, I look out the window to see what happens. They're exchanging words back and forth, but Patrick walks off from him and heads towards the front door, with my bags in his hand.

"Man, don't walk off from me! I'm talking to you!" Kalin yells.

Patrick turns around and responds to him. "Listen, I'm *not* your problem. You were never married to *me* and hurt *me*. Deal with your demons. Move on with your life and never approach me again with this. Now, if you don't mind, I need to get these bags inside and take care of my friend before I get back to work", Patrick calmly says.

Kalin doesn't like how Patrick quieted him down, but he has to respect the man for standing his ground instead of throwing punches like any other man would have done. I'm watching and also impressed with Patrick's soft spoken demeanor; but even more surprised when I see Kalin go back to his car and leave.

"Ok, Melissa. I've grabbed everything out of the car", Patrick says, walking into the kitchen. Melissa and Sharelle both walk into the kitchen.

"Hello young lady. You must be Sharelle. I've heard so much about you. Nice to meet you", Patrick says, extending his hand to Sharelle.

"Hello, Mr. Patrick. Thanks so much for taking care of my mother. I'm so glad that she has a friend like you."

"It's my pleasure to be your mother's friend. She's such a beautiful woman, inside *and* outside", Patrick compliments.

"Oh stop, Patrick!" I giggle.

I'm starting to get tired. Patrick follows me into my bedroom and puts my things in the corner. He taps the bed, which is my cue that he thinks that I should get in it. It only takes me a second to walk into the closet and slip into my pajamas and into my comfy bed I go. Patrick tucks me in and kisses me on the forehead. I'm shocked that he doesn't go for a passionate kiss. *Maybe he just doesn't want to disrespect my home or something, but somehow I feel it's much more than that.*

"Well, my work is done here for the day. You're home and safe and sound in your bed. Get some rest and call me if you need anything at all", he says.

"I can't thank you enough for all that you have done, Patrick. Thank you so much and if ….", I begin, but he interrupts me.

"No thanks required, Melissa. We're friends and that's what friends are for", Patrick says, getting up from the side of my bed and walking towards the door.

"Patrick, kiss me", I say, causing him to turn around immediately.

Patrick is now standing right next to me. I get out of the bed and place my arms around him and kiss him on his lips and say, "Thank you baby."

I notice that Patrick doesn't return the kiss to me as I expected he would, but he did say earlier that he didn't want to talk about it. *I need to find out what is bothering him. Did somebody say something to him? I hate this distance between us. He is usually way more attentive, especially if our lips touch. I miss his sweet kiss on my lips the way we did that night at our Spot.*

"You're welcome, baby", he says. Patrick wraps his arms around me and squeezes tightly. I can tell that he wants to say something to me, but he doesn't. For a few moments, he just stands there and holds me without saying a word.

"Baby, is everything okay? Why won't you tell me what's wrong? What happened? Please talk to me, Patrick. I won't be able to rest if things aren't good between the two of us", I say to him.

"Melissa, you wanna talk, right? Ok, here it is. Did you have sex with Kalin?" he blurts out.

Oh my God! Kalin told him about yesterday. But he doesn't understand that it was rape. How will I be able to explain this?

"He asked me if you told me that you slept with him. That would mean that you came back here and made love to him *after* our special evening together. I know you don't really owe me an explanation, but to me, that was somewhat foul because I did nothing but think of you after our night together", Patrick says, looking somewhat sad.

"Patrick, please let me explain because it wasn't like *that* at all."

CHAPTER 18

"Not That Night."

"*M*elissa, please get Charlotte Anderson from Section 8 on the phone for me", I tell Cynthia.

"Ok. I'll get her, but we have several move-ins and we don't have time for the inspections. What are you going to do?" Cynthia asks.

"I got this. Don't worry. I have a good name down at Section 8. Watch God's favor and see how I get approved *without* the inspection. She'll do it…", I begin to say. Cynthia interrupts me.

"How in the world are you going to do that? There's no way they'll approve the apartments without an inspection. They've never done anything like that."

"That's why it's called *favor*", I respond.

Cynthia calls Ms. Anderson, but she's not in, so I end up leaving a message for her to call. The 3 section 8 residents who are anxious about moving into their new apartment just walked in the front door. What are we going to do?" Cynthia asks.

"Move them in. I'll take care of Section 8. I know she'll approve the units. Don't worry. I'm very familiar with their processes and because my name is very credible at Section 8, we'll be just fine; and besides, we need to get these units occupied", I remind her.

"Okay. This one's on you. I've never seen you do anything outside of protocol before, but *you are* the boss", Cynthia says.

The residents have walked the new unit with Cynthia and are very pleased with how it is being presented on Move In Day. *Of course they love it! I am very specific and thorough when it comes to a turned unit being made ready for move in. My special touch is fresh flowers and chocolates.*

This treatment seems to get more and more residents coming our way without having to advertise.

"Melissa, you have a call on Line 1", Cynthia announces.

"Ok. I got it! Hello", I say.

"Hey Melissa! How are you?" the person on the other end says. *I don't quite catch the voice. It almost sounds like Brittney, but I'm not sure. This person almost sounds like they have a cold.*

"Hey! Is this Brittney?" I ask.

"Wow. I haven't been gone for 3 weeks and you've already forgotten who I am", she says laughing.

"I'm sorry. It's just been a long day already. How is it going for you and the kids?"

"It's going just fine. They went on and on for days about how they loved it there and can't wait to go back. You really outdid yourself spoiling them", she comments.

"That's an auntie's job for sure", I say.

"It's just that it's coming up to the anniversary of Laura's passing and I think it would be cool if we planned some type of small ceremony here in Middleton for her. I think that your kids could get a kick out of it. When was the last time you came home?"

"You have a point. It *has* been awhile since I was home. Let me talk to the girls and see what they say and I'll get back with you on that", I tell her.

"That's wonderful and when you come, you all have to stay at my house", she demands.

"Okay. We will."

"Brittney and I disconnect our call, but now that she's off the phone, I think that a trip to Alabama might be a pretty good idea after all. It would be just me and the girls. *A girl road trip! Sounds just like what the doctor has ordered. I could use some time away from Florida.*

Cynthia walks in looking exhausted. "Girl, I could use a drink!" she shouts.

"Me too! Let's go to the Blue Martini's and get one drink. What do you say?" I ask her.

"What about the kids? Aren't they home alone?" she asks.

"Yes, but they'll be okay. It's just one drink, Cynthia. Will your husband survive if you don't come home right away?" I ask, jokingly.

"Let me call him", she says.

While Cynthia is making her call, I decide to check my personal emails and I'm surprised when I see an email from Kalin. I don't know what got into me, but I was curious to see what he had sent me. I open it up and it's a pornographic photo that he and I had taken during sexual intercourse at one time during our marriage. I think it was 2 years ago. *What is he trying to prove with this? I know what he looks like underneath his clothes? Does he think that he's seducing me? Does he not know that I only liked this when we were happy and in love?* I close the email without responding but wait, I see that he also sent the email to Diandra. *He must think I'm buying all of this! I am second to her now and I have finally come to grips with it. My heart can't love Kalin even if I tried. He hurt me so badly. A few weeks ago, I would be crying and breaking down right now, but I'm actually starting to heal and be done with him. I told him that this day would come. I always told him that the day I STOP asking him about what he's doing and who he's doing it with is the day that he will know that I'm over him.*

"Girl, you act like you've seen a ghost!! Why are you looking at the computer screen like that?" Cynthia asks, walking back into the room.

"No. I'm fine. I was just thinking."

"Another email from Patrick, huh?" Cynthia asks, smiling.

"No. Not this time."

"Have you had your talk with him?" she asks.

"No. Not yet. Why didn't you tell me what Kalin said to Patrick at the hospital?" I ask Cynthia.

"I really just didn't want to be involved with this, Melissa. I heard him tell Patrick and the look on Patrick's face told the story of how he felt. You could clearly see the hurt in his face and Kalin was eating it up. But, this is between you, Kalin, and Patrick, and I would like to remain neutral in this situation.

"I understand. I really do. I don't blame you! Patrick and I haven't sat down and talked about it. I don't really know how to explain this to him because it's like…", I begin to say.

"Tell him the truth, Melissa. You slept with Kalin. He caught you by surprise and slipped one in over your head and you gave in to it. That's the truth, right? How will you have anything with Patrick if you can't tell him the truth about this? He deserves to know the truth", Cynthia suggests.

"You're so right, girl. *If only she knew the truth. This one wasn't my fault at all.* You're right. I really care about Patrick and I just have to be honest. I know that I'm not in love with Kalin. I know that I don't…", I say, walking towards the office door.

"Are you sure? Are you sure that you're done with Kalin in your heart? I know you, Melissa and I know that you would not have given in to having sex with him if you didn't desire him. Be very sure, my friend. We are not talking about a boyfriend where you and he break up every other week. This is your husband we're talking about. We're talking about 18 years and 2 kids. I'm just saying….", Cynthia says.

"Yes. I know you're right about what you're saying, but this is the same man who cheated on me first and got a woman pregnant and never told me the truth about it. If it had not been for the state attorneys, I would not have found out the truth about who Kalin really is. So, I'm not going to forget these things. No, I *am* making the right decision to end our marriage. I'm not in love with him and I don't think I can ever get that back. There has just been too much damage, just too much."

I pick up the picture of the girls sitting on my desk and start reminiscing about the day the picture was taken. We had taken the girls to Disney over in Orlando and Kalin and I made out in the pool after everyone had gone to sleep. That was a fun time!

"Be honest with yourself, Melissa. Did you forget that you *also* slept with him the night of Princess' birthday party?" Cynthia asks.

"Well, not that night. I mean, no, no…he didn't", I say.

"What does that mean, *"not that night"*?" Cynthia asks.

"Nothing. Nothing. Move on, please", I say.

"No! What does that mean, Melissa?"

"Cynthia!! Oh God, please help me! Kalin…he…he forced himself on me the morning of the accident. I didn't want sex with him and he walked into the bedroom, pushed me to the bed and forced sex with me and starting yelling obscenities about Patrick. It was crazy! I got over it! Not like it hasn't happened before. All men hurt me. That's just how it always ends, okay. End of conversation, okay. I don't ever want to be with Kalin ever again. I'm done with him, Cynthia. That man has caused me so much hurt. So, please let's move on!"

"Oh God, Melissa! Honey, you really do need to talk to somebody. Why don't you let me…", Cynthia begins to say, but I interrupt her.

"No! I want to move on and forget it ever happened. Please respect me on this one, Cynthia!" Melissa pleads.

"If you say so, Melissa. Well, there's really nothing else to say about Kalin then. So, you're right. Let's move on. What a jerk!" Cynthia comments, walking out of the office.

I get the feeling that Cynthia will have a totally different attitude about Kalin now. She didn't like the comment I just made about him forcing himself on me. She'll eventually get to see him for what he really is just like everybody else.

Moving in the section 8 residents without having the inspection done is unheard of and I have no choice so I really hope that the call that just came in is Ms. Anderson because I'm going to hear about this if I don't get these units approved. "Melissa, Ms. Anderson is on Line 2", Cynthia yells from the other room.

"Good afternoon Ms. Anderson", I say, picking up the phone.

"Yes, Mrs. Thomas. I just received your urgent message. Is everything okay?" she asks.

"It depends if you can help me with a very urgent matter that I have here", I respond.

"What is it?"

"I have 3 units that are section 8 and because Corporate is putting so much pressure to get these units occupied, I had to go ahead and get these units occupied, so I moved the residents in without the inspection that I *know* I have to get done prior to their moving in. So, I really need your help in approving these units and signing off on the Contract", I explain.

"Now, Mrs. Thomas, you know that we are supposed to inspect the unit first and I can't….", she begins to explain.

"I know that. I really do know that and I've never done anything like this before and that's why I'm asking for this one favor to approve these units for me. You know that our units are in great shape."

"That doesn't matter, Mrs. Thomas, because we have certain guidelines regarding the inspections", she says.

"Ms. Anderson, I can assure you that I personally walked these units and can confirm that these units were without any issues. I apologize and won't do this again, but I need your approval on these 3 units", I tell her.

"Okay, Mrs. Thomas. I will do this for you this time, but in the future, please make sure to allow enough time to schedule your inspections so that we don't go through this again", she says.

"Thank you so much, Ms. Anderson. I won't do this again. Thank you and thank you", I say to her.

"Send over the form so that I can sign off on it and get it processed so that we can get you in the system to receive your checks on the first of next month", she advises. "Are you coming to our brunch tomorrow?"

"Of course I'll be there. And thanks again, Ms. Anderson", I say, relieved that she's agreed to sign the contracts.

That was a close call! I felt like she would do it for me, but she made me work for that one. But at least we got the approval.

"Cynthia, come in here!" I shout. She comes in with a surprised look on her face.

"What! What's wrong?"

"Ms. Anderson is signing off on those contracts as we speak. Tell me God ain't good?"

"Are you serious? She's signing off on the contracts *without* having done the inspection? That's unheard of! She's very strict. I can't believe she's doing this. I guess you got your *favor*", Cynthia says, jokingly.

"And I give God all the glory for it! Remind me that I have a brunch on tomorrow at the Section 8 building. I promised Ms. Anderson that I would be there", I comment. "Now, let's get out of here and get our drinks!"

CHAPTER 19

"Mommy, Don't Look!"

"Hey girls! What do you want to do today? It's a beautiful Saturday outside. Any suggestions?" I ask, while preparing their breakfast.

"I don't know about anyone else, but I'd love to go to the Mall and see what sales they're having now that the holidays are over", Justice says.

"Well, I'm off work today, so I'm in", adds Princess.

"And what about you, Sharelle?"

"Okay, Ma. Sounds like fun! Looks like we'll have a girl's day out", Amber chimes in.

"Alrighty then! So, let's finish with breakfast, get the kitchen cleaned, and we can be our way", I say, but just as I say that, my phone vibrates. It's Patrick. *I just realized that I haven't spoken to him since the night he dropped me off. I don't want him to think that I don't want to talk to him so I answer the phone.*

"Hello stranger", I say, trying to break the ice.

"You know that I've been waiting to speak with you some time now, Melissa. You don't love me anymore?" he asks.

"Patrick, you already know the answer to that question. I've just been super busy at work and with the kids, but I have thought of you every single day", I tell him, leaving the kitchen to have privacy.

"Really? What have you been thinking?" he asks, sounding serious.

"About you. About us. About everything", I tell him.

"So have I, but you know what I keep playing in my head over and over?" he asks.

"No, why don't you tell me, Patrick?" I ask him.

"I've been thinking about how the woman I adore had a moment with her husband, who she claims she doesn't love anymore. I can't get the picture out of my head of you and him making love. It's driving me nuts, Melissa!" he says.

"I'm not in love with him anymore, Patrick, and you're going to have to believe me", I say.

"So, will this become a regular with you and him? I'm not interested in sharing you with him, so tell me now. I know he's still your husband, but I don't want to be in the situation like the other night. I mean, if you feel that you need to work things out with him, then tell me that. Tell me the truth, Melissa", he demands.

"Patrick, sweetheart. Listen. I'm about to leave home now to spend the day with the girls. Let's get together at the condo for some dinner tonight. What about that?"

"Yes. That sounds like a plan. We need to talk. I'll see you tonight."

"Okay, baby. Tonight it is", I tell him, hanging up the phone.

He sounds like a man in love. Does he really love me? Is that possible? Can a man really love me, adore me, and cherish me like I've always wanted. They all start out good. I'm looking forward to spending time with Patrick tonight. This is my one shot at trying to explain what happened with Kalin. I think I need to tell him about the rape.

"Mommy, we went ahead and washed the dishes since you were on the phone!" Justice yells, walking into my office just as I hang up the phone.

"Yes. Let me slip into some jeans and a blazer and then, we can go", I announce.

"Ok. Hurry! And don't put on makeup because then, it will be 2 hours", Amber adds.

The girls and I are on our way to the Fashion Mall on the other side of town. Sharelle is sitting up front with me and Amber, Princess, and Justice are sitting in the back seat. We stop at a red light at Waters and Cummings Avenue and out of nowhere and without warning, Sharelle hits the floor.

"Honey! What's wrong? What happened? Why are you doing that?" I shout.

"Mommy, don't look!! Don't look!! It's the guy that I was in the car with the night we had the accident. Please don't look over there! He'll kill me if he sees me. Please don't look!" she yells, sounding panicked.

"Sharelle, get up from there. Nobody is going to do anything to you, sweetheart. You're safe now. It's okay. You don't have to be afraid. You're safe now. You're safe now. It's okay, honey", I say, trying to console her. I pull the car over into the closest parking lot to grab my daughter and comfort her.

"It's just that he always told us that he would kill the ones of us who get away from him because he doesn't want us to live to tell about all the things that happened", she explains, "and since I'm one of the ones who got away, he'll surely come after me."

"Why is he out of jail? Isn't he a registered sex offender, who was just with a minor and should not have been? This system really sucks here in Florida!"

"They don't care about that. He has money and he can buy anybody he wants. Let's just go now. I'm okay. Let's just go", Sharelle says, getting off the floor of the car.

"Are you sure? Do you want to go home?" I ask.

"No. I'm not going to ruin everybody's day. I'll be fine. Let's go to the Mall", she says.

After making sure that Sharelle is better, the girls and I continue on until we finally make it to the Mall. It's so crowded today with after-the-holiday-shoppers looking for those bargains just like we are. We end up in Forever 21 where we spend the rest of our day, shopping, going from rack to rack looking for the bargains. The girls are eager to spend some of their money that they got from Christmas from their grandfather.

"I'm exhausted! Let's get some lunch", I suggest. I'm sure they're all tired. Surprisingly, they let me pick out the place, so we're off to Chic-Fil-A. Little did I know that I would soon regret this choice. *Are my eyes deceiving me? This is not the person I want to see right about now. God knows that I don't want to make a scene right now, but is that Kalin sitting in the corner? And is that Wendy with him? I really hope the girls don't see him over there. I hope they're too busy eating to notice. Good, they're leaving! And thank God that he didn't see me.*

"Order what you want, girls. I need time to think about what it is that I want", I tell them.

Because the restaurant is extremely crowded today, we have to wait just a little longer for our food, but they make it worth our wait when we're offered a free salad for our meal. We finally sit down to enjoy our lunch and decide that we've had enough shopping. At this point, I just want to get home as quickly as possible. The only way I know to do that is to jump on the Expressway and pay $5 for tolls. We load the trunk with all of our bags and finally leave the Mall. On the ride home, nobody's saying anything. The girls are exhausted! My 94.5 FM station is on point with the old school music. The kids must be sleep because they would have commented on my music at this point if they were awake.

Justice startles me when she speaks up. "Mommy, we had so much fun!"

"I'm so glad, sweetheart. That's what it's all about", I reply.

"Mommy, may I ask you something?" Amber asks.

"Sure, honey. What is it?" I say, not aware she was also awake.

"Who was that lady that daddy was with?" Amber asks. I'm totally shocked because I didn't think that they saw him.

"It was probably a client of his, Amber", I respond.

"Ok. So, why didn't he at least speak to us? He acted like he didn't see us", she says.

"Maybe he didn't see you, honey. Just call him when you get home, okay", I suggest.

"No. When I get home, I'm taking a shower and getting a nap. I'm exhausted!" she says.

"I'm gonna beat you to the shower!" Justice shouts.

"I already called it! Mommy, tell her I already called it", Amber repeats.

"Ladies, I can't believe you're fighting for the shower. One of you can take a shower in my bathroom if you're *that* anxious", I say, laughing.

I'm so glad that they are fighting over the shower and have given up on wanting to know who the woman was with Kalin. There is no way I could tell that he was with his mistress.

"Girls, when we get home, there's something that I need to tell you. There are some things that we need to discuss", I announce to them.

"Lemme guess. It's about you and Daddy", Amber says, slouching back into her seat.

CHAPTER 20

"Only the Best For You."

*P*atrick's mood has changed so much since his conversation with Melissa. He's looking forward to their dinner tonight. He's hoping that they'll be able to put the whole Kalin thing behind them once and for all. In preparation for their dinner, Patrick heads over to the Market to pick up some special ingredients that he likes to use when preparing his famous pasta dish. It's nothing for him to have an expensive bottle of wine to seal the deal on the most romantic evening.

At the hospital, his patients are all doing well so Patrick has no problem with leaving the office a little earlier than he normally would. He wants his dinner with Melissa to go perfectly. He's hoping that the florist delivers the flowers on time and that they get the right tulips, which are Melissa's favorite. He wants to make sure that his sweetheart feels special from the moment she enters the condo.

"She must be special because you haven't been in here in a long time for these ingredients", the clerk says, as Patrick checks out at the Family Marine Market by South Beach.

"She is. She really is", he responds.

"They're bringing the wine from out back. We didn't have any left in the rack. It's the most popular wine we have. Aaah, looks like it's here now", the clerk tells him, handing it over to him.

Now that he has all that he's come for, he leaves the store and heads over to the condo, but he stops by Victoria's Secret first to pick up a nice gift for Melissa. Within 3 hours, Melissa will be knocking on the door and he wants to make sure she enjoys their first evening together since the night they made love.

Patrick hopes Melissa can appreciate the scented candles lit throughout the condo. It smells so good and the mood is just right. It's the mood for lovers. Patrick wants to forget about the conversation they had the other day that involved Kalin and just enjoy their time together.

If it's possible for a man to have "butterflies", Patrick certainly has them right now, anticipating the look on Melissa's face. He's somewhat startled when he hears keys in the door. *That's right! Melissa has her own keys to the Condo.*

"You look exquisite", Patrick says, when he sees Melissa coming through the door. "Good enough to eat and I do mean eat." They both laugh.

"You look very handsome, too, Green Eyes. I love that shirt on you. So, I see you found it. Someone has really nice taste", I say, sarcastically.

"It was, indeed, a very nice surprise, Melissa. Thank you. Come on in, sweetheart. Would you like a glass of wine? It's already chilled", Patrick says.

"Of course I would. Is that the kind that I like that you always get from the Market?" I ask.

"Yes, it is my sweet lover. Only the best for you", he responds, pouring two glasses of wine.

"Ohhh, I see what you're trying to do. You want to get me all drunk so that you can take advantage of me, huh?"

"Baby, you walked in the door wanting to give me that sweet love. You and I both know that you're so hot for me and you've been thinking all day of how you want to give it to me", Patrick says confidently, looking into my eyes.

"Wow! You think you know me", Melissa says, laughing, taking a sip of her wine.

Patrick takes my glass from me and puts it on the coffee table. "I bet you if I were to put my hand underneath your skirt right now, you're already wet", he says, sliding his hand up my thigh. *What got into this man? He's laying it all out tonight with the good food, wine, candles, clean condo…all the things I love.*

"Oh yeah", I say, moaning, making a weak attempt at trying to stop his hand from going up my thigh, but his hand feels so good on my flesh. My body is starting to tingle all over and he knows exactly what his touch does to me.

"I knew it. Baby, you're so wet. You want me, don't you? Come here", Patrick says. "Kiss me."

I must be under his spell because right now, I might do whatever this man tells me to do. He smells so good. Patrick and I share the most intense and passionate kiss ever. It is almost as if I can't get *enough* of my tongue in his mouth. He kisses me behind my ear, on my neck, and pays special attention to my supple lips. Patrick stops right before things get too heated and hands me a bag from Victoria's Secret. "Oh, I can only imagine what this is", I tell him.

"I hope you like it baby", he comments.

"You're always so thoughtful", I tell him, giggling, but, something tells me that you were thinking about yourself when you went out and bought this sexy nightie."

"Go put it on for me, baby. I want to see you in it", he says.

I go into the bedroom to change, leaving Patrick on the sofa sipping on his wine. While in the bedroom, I slip on my favorite Love CD that I always listen to when I'm here. Patrick looks up and sees me dancing my way back into the room, with his mouth wide open. "Ohhhhh baby, you look so beautiful!! I am one lucky man. I like the way you move. You're turning me on right now, Melissa", he says, focusing on my breast.

"You like? Well, I want to make you feel good tonight. Are you okay with that?"

"I'm definitely okay with that. You are one sexy woman, you know that?" he comments, while I continue to grind on top of him with my lap dance. I slowly unbuckle his pants and slip off his pants, throwing them out of the way. Patrick doesn't seem to mind at all when I take charge of our lovemaking, causing him to orgasm over and over. I'm starting to lose count. "Did you enjoy that, baby?"

"Yes, baby, I totally enjoyed that. You really do know how to make your man feel like a King, don't you?" We laugh.

Patrick takes my face into his hands and gives me a kiss, whispering the words, "I love you" at each breath. I respond to his passion by saying, "How do you know you love me?" He stops, looks me dead in the eyes, and says, "I can't think of anything else but being yours, I can't stop wondering what our life together would be like, I dream of you, I talk to you when you're not here, I come to this Condo just to remember our times that we have spent here, and when I close my eyes, I see your face, baby. That's how I know I love you", he responds. Our kisses intensify. Patrick kisses my neck, my breast, one nipple at a time, my belly button, and then he looks into my eyes as he spreads open my legs. His face is hidden between my legs and his magic tongue goes to work waking up every nerve in my body.

"Oh, baby, that feels so good. Please don't stop, baby!" I say, moaning louder and louder.

We make love well into the night, totally forgetting about our dinner. Patrick and I fall asleep in each other's arms, waking up around 3am. All of this lovemaking has certainly worked up an appetite for the meal that's already prepared in the kitchen. Patrick decides that we should eat our meal together in bed. "How would you like this to be our life every day, Melissa?" he asks.

"What do you mean?"

"I mean. Would you ever consider being mine after you divorce Kalin?" he asks, taking his place back in the bed.

"I haven't really thought about it, Patrick. I'm just getting out of one marriage and I just want to heal from everything first and then, let's see where it takes us. Is that okay?"

"I think it's fair, baby, but I want you to know that I love you and you're the only woman that I talk to, Melissa. I'm so busy at the hospital that I hardly have time for anything else and that's one of the reasons I never had a girlfriend because nobody is able to put up with my schedule. They become frustrated and I can't blame them. They accuse me of not giving them the time that they are so deserving of and it pushes them away. I hope it doesn't push you away, Melissa", he explains.

"It won't, Patrick. It won't. I'm very busy as well, so it works out just fine for me. Hey, how is Evan? I bet he's getting so big", I say, changing the subject on purpose.

"He is! He's with his mother tonight. I'm taking him to Orlando this weekend to Universal Studios. He's so excited because he loves all of the parks up there. Maybe one day, we can all go together", Patrick says.

"That would be nice. I hope you boys have fun", I tell him.

"We will. We'll definitely do that. You're so beautiful, Melissa", Patrick says, looking into my eyes.

"Come on! I know I must look pretty rough after that wild sex that *we* just had", I laugh.

"That's what makes you beautiful. Did you know that you make the cutest look on your face when you're having an orgasm?" he asks me.

"Are you serious? Too funny!!" I comment.

Patrick and I sit for the next few hours just talking and getting to know each other better. Neither one of us brought up Kalin's name. We are having so much fun that we're just enjoying this time learning about what each of us like. I have to admit it, but he's quite the comedian at times, sending me into hysterical laughs with some of his comments. We both realize that our special evening has to come to an end because I have to get home to the children before they send out an APB looking for me.

"When will I see you again, Melissa?" Patrick asks.

"Let's just play it by ear. Let's just let this happen naturally and see where it takes us, but let's enjoy it", I say.

"That sounds like a plan. I can do that, baby. I enjoyed you so much and I'll certainly miss you until I see you again."

"Same here. I enjoyed you too. I enjoyed getting to know you better than anything", I say, holding his hands.

"Anything? Better than me putting my tongue on you and having you cum in like 30 seconds from it?" he says, laughing.

"You're funny! I gotta go!" Patrick and I laugh as he walks me to the door. We share the most intimate goodbye kiss.

On my ride home, I play back the entire evening in my head and I can't remember the last time I felt like this. I didn't want to leave. I wanted to stay there with him all day, cuddling and kissing in between like two teenage lovers. He brings that out in me, but my reality is that my children are home and will start wondering where I am. I'm surprised that they haven't tried to call me.

Please tell me that Kalin's car is not in my driveway. That is Kalin's car in my driveway! What the hell is he doing here? I don't feel like getting into it with this man right now.

As I get closer to the back door of the kitchen, I can see people moving around. They must be up and preparing breakfast already. I'm definitely not looking forward to any confrontations so I plan to walk in here and be cheerful, hoping that there won't be any type of misunderstandings.

"Good morning, family", I say, opening the door.

"Well, well, well, look who decided to be a woman and come home", Kalin remarks.

"Good morning to you, too, Kalin", I say, unmoved by his comment.

"Where have you been all night?" he asks, walking towards me.

"Kalin, I don't believe I have to answer to you anymore when it comes to where I am or who I'm with. Do you *not* get that?"

"When it comes to *my* children, you do! I called last night and they said you weren't here, so I called again around 3am and they said you *still* weren't here, and that is when…", he says, until Justice interrupts him.

"But we told him that we were okay, Mommy!"

"Sweetheart, don't worry about it. Why don't you guys go upstairs and let Mommy and Daddy have a discussion", I say, giving her a hug and pointing her upstairs.

"So you two can argue, right?" Amber says, leaving the kitchen.

Now that the girls are completely out of sight, Kalin and I can continue our conversation.

"You are such a jerk, Kalin. When will you stop? You don't run this anymore! This is over and you don't control me anymore. I'm free and I'm the happiest I have ever been! The girls were okay and they weren't afraid. There was no reason for you to come barging over here to rescue them. Just so you'll know, I *will* be changing the locks so please, don't get comfortable with thinking that you will be able to come in and out of my house" I say.

"You have become the ultimate b----, haven't you? I don't know who you are anymore", he says.

"That's a good thing because the woman that you turned me into is dead; she is dead!! I just want to live my life now and be happy, Kalin. You have obviously moved on so why do you keep bothering me? Huh, why?" I ask, walking over to make me a cup of coffee.

"What do you mean that I have moved on?" he asks.

"You might as well hear it from me. I was out with the girls yesterday and we stopped into Chic-Fil-A to have lunch and they saw you there with Wendy. I told them that she was a client, but I don't think they bought it. So, don't be surprised if they ask you about it. They were shocked that you didn't come up to them to speak", I explain.

"I saw ya'll, but I didn't want a scene in front of my children and me …", he responds.

"A scene? I don't want you anymore. Trust me when I tell you that. I don't want you. She won. She can have you. Let her take you in and take care of you and deal with the stresses that I have had to deal with over the last few years and then you tell me who won", I comment.

"So, is that it? I was a burden to you? Is that what you're saying, Melissa?" he asks.

"What I'm saying is that you fell asleep in this marriage. You forgot that you had to take care of me just as much as I had to take care of you. Other people became more important to you and those decisions cost us our marriage and that's all I'm saying", I answer, turning away from him.

"I still want to try with you. I'm still in love with you. I will always love you, Melissa. You're the woman I love. You're the mother of my children and no woman can ever say that and I....", he begins, until I interrupt him.

"No, you do have *another* child with *another* woman, but that child just didn't live", I correct him. "You took that away from me of being able to say that I am the mother of your children."

"Let's work on things and see...", he begins.

"No. I don't want to work on things. I am starting to heal and I don't want you back into my life to disrupt that", I say.

"Why? Is this about that white boy? Are you serious, Melissa? You think that man want you? That man just wants to sex you and then he's going to drop you! You can't be serious", Kalin says.

"Let's not go there. I don't need you to tell me anything about Patrick, because the truth of the matter is that this has *nothing* to do with him. You messed up. You had me, but you took me for granted, forgetting how to make me happy and you let other people become more important than me; so, you're the one who lost me. You had me, you had me, and you just pushed *me* to the side and now, I don't want to hear it."

Kalin and I agree that the conversation is over, but before he leaves he mumbles something about me going out all night leaving the kids home alone just to be with my white lover. *I don't know why he is so against the fact that Patrick is white. I never knew that he was this prejudice against another race.*

The girls come back downstairs when they hear the door shut, which alarms them that Kalin has left the house.

"Did he leave?" Justice asks, looking around.

"Yes he did", I tell her.

"So, he left us without saying goodbye?" she asks.

"He said to tell you that he will call you later", I lie.

"Mommy, do you still love Daddy? He said that you love someone else. Is that true?" Justice inquires.

"Honey, your father doesn't know what he's talking about. I love my girls. That is who I love. But, I do want to have a talk with you girls. Go get your sisters for me", I tell her.

Justice rushes out of the room yelling for her other sisters, while I take a few more sips of my coffee, noticing that the girls have already eaten breakfast, but nobody bothered to clean the dishes. Now that they're all here, I can speak freely with them.

"OK. We're here, Mommy. Justice said you needed to speak with us. What is so urgent?" Amber asks.

"I want to talk to you girls about Mom and Dad and what's going on with us", I begin, but Amber interrupts me.

"Ohhhh..here we go! The "D" word. So, come on, out with it; you're getting a divorce, right?" she asks

"Girls, please hear me out completely. Your father and I have been together for s-o-o-o-o-o-o- many years and from our relationship came the both of you and for that I am extremely proud. But the truth is that sometimes adults grow apart from each other and become distant and eventually just stop talking to each other", I explain.

"Wow. Being an adult is not so fun, is it?" Justice comments.

"Ugh, no sweetheart, it isn't always fun. That's for sure", I respond. "Daddy and I have decided to live in two separate places while we go through the divorce. We need you both to understand that this has absolutely nothing to do with you. This thing is on me and him only. We just don't see eye to eye anymore, so we feel that it's best we just not live in the same house", I explain to them.

"This really sucks Ma! One of my friends in my classroom is going through this and she said that it's so hard because *her parents* fight all the time now that they are going through a divorce", Amber admits.

"We'll try *not* to argue because it's not the best way to handle problems anyway", I say. "You don't deserve that."

"Does this have anything to do with that woman he was with on Saturday?" Sharelle asks.

"Why do you say that?" I ask, surprised that she, too, noticed.

"Because when he walked her to the car after sneaking out of Chic-Fil-A, he kissed her in the parking lot when he didn't think anyone was watching", Sharelle blurts out.

"Daddy kissed *another* woman!! How could he?" Justice shouts. "That's just not right, Mommy! Why did he do that?"

"I don't know the answer to that, sweetheart. Who knows? But, that is *not* what this little meeting is about. I need for all of you to trust me to make the best decisions for our household. And there's one more thing", I say.

"What is it?" Justice asks.

"Mommy does have other friends that she may talk to from time to time. I just don't want you to be alarmed if a friend calls me or asks me out to dinner or anything and it will only be....", I begin.

"We have a father already and we don't want another one!!" Justice yells, running back upstairs.

This didn't quite go as well as I had planned, but after talking to my girls, I realize that they know more than I have given them credit for knowing. I'm certainly glad I did differently than most who decide to stay with their husband for the kids' sake. I truly believe I would be doing them more harm than good. Tomorrow, I will have to contact Mr. Abney and move forward with my divorce.

CHAPTER 21

"Just Ask My Mother!"

Sharelle has court today and I have no idea what will happen. Getting there earlier will give me the opportunity to speak with Public Defender Watson for him to review the case with me.

"Mom, I want you to know that I'm not afraid for what may happen today", Sharelle says, as we scour the parking lot looking for an empty space.

"Really? I'm proud of you for saying that because the truth is that it *is* time for you to face the consequences for your actions. Whatever happens in here, I got yo' back, okay", I tell her.

"Thanks Mom. I appreciate that. I really do", Sharelle says.

Sharelle and I walk inside. The courtroom is busy as usual. It's filled with angry mothers, upset that they have taken off *another* day from work, or youth who look as though they could care less what their families have to go through to have them in the courtroom. We look for Mr. Watson and find him in the corner having, what looks like to be a discussion, with one of his clients. He finally looks up, sees us walk in, and continues consulting with the parent and her child. *I am sure that he will be over as soon as he is done with them.*

"Mommy, look at all the kids in here. Is this not horrible or what?" Sherelle asks, while we wait.

"Yes it is, actually. This is not what you should be doing right now. You're about to be 13 years old and should be having fun at sleepovers with your friends, hanging out at the mall, and just doing "kid things", but instead, you're here going through this and for what, Sharelle? Was it worth it to be in the car with that guy that night?" I ask.

"No, it wasn't! Unlike *some* of the girls out there in the streets, I didn't have to be. I had a loving home that I could have been at, but I wanted to be grown *too* fast and look at where it landed me", Sharelle confesses.

"But, we *are* here and we have to ask God to give us the strength and the patience to deal with whatever happens in here today."

The Public Defender is heading our way, but he has someone else with him. It must be his assistant or something.

"Good morning, Mrs. Thomas and Sharelle. How are you both doing this morning?"

"We're doing just fine. What about yourself?" I ask, looking at both him and the gentleman with him.

"Well, thank you. Let's get down to it. This is Mr. Griffith and *he* will handle Sharelle's case moving forward. I was appointed to the young man in the car that night and I can't represent you both due to a conflict of interest, but Mr. Griffith can take care of her, okay", he explains.

"Ok. Fine. It was nice working with you, Mr. Watson", I say, extending my hand to him.

"And you as well. Good luck to you, Sharelle", he says, walking away.

"Ok. So, let's get down to it. Honestly, Sharelle is looking at being sent to a Program. She has been in front of the Judge too many times and I can tell you that the Judge is getting a little irritated with it. And now, you're in here for a possession of drugs and battery on a police officer while resisting arrest", the new Public Defender explains.

"You make it sound horrible", I comment.

"I know and I'm sorry for that, but this is real life", he responds.

"Tell me about these *programs*. Where exactly do they send you and what happens in there?"

"Judges will typically try to keep you in Florida, but they have them all over the country. These *programs* are designed to keep the youth from going into their adult life as offenders. Completing this Program could mean that Sharelle's record will be clean and it won't look like she ever did a day in the Juvenile Detention Center. If she *does not* complete the Program, she will have to come out and do her time for these crimes committed. But, it is all up to her", he continues to explain.

"Do you hear what he's saying, Sharelle?" I say to her.

"Yes ma'am."

"These Programs range from low to high risk and that's based on what type of security the child needs. My guess is that they'll give you Moderate security. But today, the Judge is going to review the evidence in this case and if it's credible, then we already know what's next. Do you understand, Sharelle?" he asks.

"Yes sir. I do understand. I just want this over with. Is that guy going to be in the courtroom today?" Sharelle asks.

"What guy?"

"The guy that was in the car that night. Is he going to be here today?" she asks, looking around.

"He'll be in the courtroom because we're basically hearing the evidence and the Judge may have some questions for him", Mr. Griffith explains.

"NO!!! Please NO!" Sharelle exclaims.

"No. Calm down, Sharelle. He'll be in the courtroom, but through a monitor. He is at the Miami-Dade County Jail and he…", he responds.

"But I thought he got out of jail", Sharelle says.

"He did, but he was re-arrested on a totally different charge. This guy is trouble. How in the world did you meet him, Sharelle?"

"On the streets. He took care of me and made sure I ate and all I had to do was sleep with some men and get paid. It was hard at first because I didn't make the money he thought I should make, so he would beat me up and send me *back out there.* I eventually learned how to make the $1000 per day that he demanded out of me", Sharelle says, looking away.

"It's okay, honey. Let's not talk about this right now. We can do that later. Let's just concentrate on what we're here for today", I suggest. She looks like she's about to cry.

"Any questions from either of you?" he asks.

"No. We're good for now", I say, nodding.

Now that the bailiff has opened the door, we follow the other parents into the courtroom. To make sure that we don't miss hearing her name called, Sharelle and I take our seats near the front. Looking around, I can easily tell that the Florida Juvenile system is seriously failing our children. As a parent, I wanted my child to start getting punished when she starting getting into trouble several months ago. Unfortunately, Florida has what is called a "points system" and the juveniles can mess up as much as they want, but until they have reached enough points as required by Florida Statute, the JDC is a revolving door, wasting the taxpayer's dollar.

The way I see it is this. Sharelle is here for resisting arrest on an officer and I know that Florida is known for punishing people who disrespect the police. Unfortunately, it didn't matter too much to the State when Sharelle pulled my hair, threatened to jump out of my moving vehicle, put her sister's lives in danger, and sold my digital camera. The lack of respect that she had for me, her mother, *should* have been enough to land her in county time, but she would show up in court, time and time again, get a warning from the Judge and be sent home with me after only 24 hours in JDC.

"Sharelle Williams. Sharelle Williams", the clerk announces.

Sharelle and I walk past the bailiff and take our place at the microphone, looking at the Judge who doesn't look too happy right now. "Ms. Williams, I see you're back in my courtroom. I see you got time to hang out with your friends forgetting all about school and out there getting in trouble with people that you have no business being with. What do you have to say for yourself?" the Judge asks.

"I messed up. I messed up again, but I want to do better. I've been home with my mother and haven't gotten into any trouble", Sharelle explains. "Just ask her!"

"And that's good young lady, but we have a serious matter before us. You were hanging out with these older people with drugs in your purse. And not only that, you were resisting arrest from a police officer and you kicked him when he tried to arrest you. That is completely unacceptable, young lady", she says.

"Yes ma'am", Sharelle says, just above a whisper.

"And Mom, what do you have to say about all of this?" the Judge asks me.

"I have to admit that this is all very horrible and Sharelle *should* be held responsible for her actions, but I have seen a child who seems to be ready to make a change so that she can get her life back on track and I want to do everything that I can do to help her get where she needs to be", I respond.

"I'm so glad that she has your support, Mrs. Thomas, because so many children come through this courtroom whose parents never show their support and this place is just a revolving door until they finally end up in prison", she explains. "But, I think that the best thing for Sharelle is to be placed into a residential program, designed for kids like her. This Program will teach her how to make better choices for her life so that this cycle will end and not lead into more crimes. Mr. Griffith, have you discussed this option with your client and her mother?" she asks.

"I have, Your Honor", he answers.

"Very well then. Mrs. Thomas, there will be a meeting this week between Sharelle's attorney and representatives from Dept. of Juvenile Justice to discuss a plan of action for your daughter. Do you understand?"

"Yes ma'am."

"Sharelle, do you understand why I have to do this?" she asks, looking at Sharelle.

"Yes ma'am, I do."

"Okay. Mr. Griffith, your office will be contacted by DJJ and you both will set something up this week, and Mrs. Thomas, you and Sharelle will both be in that meeting to offer your input", she tells us.

The Judge has spoken and it's settled. Sharelle will be going to a residential program. My daughter will be going away this time, but at least this time, she is going away to get some help, which is what I have always said she needed. I look over at Sharelle and she looks to be at peace.

We came into the courtroom one way, but we're finally leaving with an appropriate course of action this time that will give my daughter the help she needs. "Sharelle, are you okay?" I ask.

"I am now, Ma. I'm so sorry for everything I have put you through. I'm so happy because you've always been here for me and I appreciate you so much", she says, giving me a hug. My daughter and I just stand there embraced in a hug and the way she is holding me, I can tell that she truly is sorry and *wants* to make a change.

"Mrs. Thomas, I will have my secretary give you a call in a couple of days to let you know when and where the meeting will be", Mr. Griffith says, extending his hand to me.

"Great. Thank you, sir."

The ride back home is a quiet one. Sharelle is most likely reflecting on everything that just happened in the courtroom. I have that and many other things on my mind. The truth is that there are so many things on my plate right now that sometimes I don't know if I'm coming or going.

"Mommy, are you okay?" Sharelle asks.

"Yes, sweetheart. I'm doing okay. "What about you? How are you holding up?"

"I'm doing just fine. I'm glad that I'll finally get some help", she says.

"Me too. I want you to go into the Program with your head on right, do as you're told and before you know it, you'll be coming home", I tell her.

"I will, Mommy, she responds. "Just look at it like this. I'm just going away to Camp for a couple of years or so", she says, trying to comfort me.

"That's a good way of looking at it", I say, laughing slightly.

By the time we make it to the house, I realize that I promised Mr. Abney that I would stop by his office today. "Honey, I have another appointment, so go ahead inside and fix you some lunch. Your sisters should be home soon."

"Where are you going?" she asks, getting out of the car.

"To meet with the divorce attorney", I answer.

"Good for you, Mommy. You deserve better. It'll be okay in the end. I hate to say it, but I'm glad that you're divorcing Kalin. He doesn't deserve someone as nice as you", Sharelle says, shutting the door behind her.

As she's walking away, I drive off and it hits me like a ton of bricks what she just said. *She is right! I do deserve better and I don't think I ever realized it until just now.*

"Mr. Abney, we need to talk", I say, after he opens his office door.

CHAPTER 22

"Tomorrow Is Not Promised."

"Things must not have gotten better since we last talked", Mr. Abney says, showing me to the chair beside his desk. His office looks even more put together today than before. I would love to have the name of his decorator because they have done a fabulous job with this room.

"No. They didn't. They have actually become even more complicated", I say.

"Please explain, Mrs. Thomas."

"You sure you have time?" I say, sarcastically. He laughs and gets up and fixes me a cup of coffee. "Here it is. I'm just not in love with my husband anymore. After the cheating, lies, and emotional abuse, I am done, Mr. Abney", I begin to explain but he interrupts me.

"Please call me Kelvin", he says.

"Ooohh...okay", I apologize. "Like I was saying, I'm just not in love with him anymore. I really tried to be there for him no matter what. But it's just not enough anymore and I'm ready to be happy", I explain.

"And you're sure about this?" he asks.

"I'm very sure about this", I respond.

"What if it gets ugly?" he asks.

"Then, I'll have to take the good with the bad, but I want my freedom from this man", I say, sitting in the chair in front of his desk. "I have to find my way back to happy because I look in the mirror and don't recognize who I am anymore."

"Then, have a seat and let's get started", he advises. Mr. Abney and I spend the rest of the afternoon strategizing over what could potentially be a nasty divorce. After collecting all of the information, he agrees that it will take a week for him to put it all together to have Kalin served with divorce papers. *I know I want this, but divorce? Really? Am I really going through with it this time? Is it because of Patrick or am I really done with him? All I know is that I'm tired of this man hurting me the way he does. I'm tired of him putting his hands on me, yelling at me, and treating other women better than he treats me. I'm tired and just like R Kelly says, "When a woman's fed up, there is nothing you can do about it".*

"Is there anything else you want to tell me? I don't like surprises in the courtroom", he asks.

"There *is* one thing", I admit.

"Ok. What is it?" he asks.

"Patrick. Dr. Patrick Norwood", I tell him.

"What about him?" Mr. Abney asks.

"I started seeing him and Kalin could possibly try to bring this up and…", I begin to explain.

"Really? That's not good, Mrs. Thomas. I really wish you…", he begins before I interrupt him.

"But, he has been having an affair with his friend's wife for years, so please let him bring that up and things will get real ugly real fast", I say. Kelvin stands up and walks over to his file cabinet and brings a document and places it in front of me. "Is this Patrick?" he asks.

I look down at the document and it's a photo of me and Patrick together standing at the doorway of the condo.

"Oh my God! Where did you get this?" I ask, sounding surprised.

"It was mailed into this office. I believe Kalin may have had you followed, Mrs. Thomas", Kelvin explains.

"This is getting a little scary. He must have been following me or had someone else do it. Can this potentially hurt me if I don't have proof of *his* affair?" I ask.

"Honestly, it would be your word against his. He can use this to try to get the kids or anything. Now, if you have some kind of proof that he had an affair, it might get him to lay off this and stick to other things", he explains.

I know just how to shut Kalin up. "Don't worry about it, Mr. Abney. I know just the thing to take care of this.

"Very well, then. I'll go ahead and prepare everything and unless I get an address on him, we'll have to serve him the papers at his job. And when he contacts you, and I know he will, please direct him to me. Give him my phone numbers and simply tell him to speak to your attorney if he has any questions", Mr. Abney says.

Walking past the receptionist, down the elevator, and out through the double glass doors, I realize now what just happened. I just signed off on papers to have my husband served with a divorce. All of the years that I gave to Kalin is summed up in one day and will soon be completely over.

I hate when I have to rush, but I have to get back to the property. Cyndi just sent me a message that Sharon is onsite and is very anxious to speak with me. *I wonder what this is about this time. Is she trying to force my hand to move in fake residents again? It doesn't matter to me what she says because I am not doing anything illegal for this company? It is not worth it and if it costs me this job, so be it!*

Driving onto the property and not knowing what to expect, I grab my briefcase just in case I have to explain the numbers for one of the properties. When I walk into the office, I don't see Cynthia at first, but I catch a glimpse of her in the supply room talking to Sharon. The conversation looks pretty intense. I can only imagine what that is about, but I can't pay it too much attention because I need to get into my office to prepare myself for this meeting.

"So, you made it?" Sharon says, walking into my office. She's not alone this time. She brought Roger and Caitlyn along.

"Yes, I made it and what do I owe the pleasure of having all of you guys here at the property?" I ask.

"We need to talk", Sharon says, shutting the door behind her. Neither Roger nor Caitlyn makes eye contact with me, which tells me that this is probably going to be a reprimand of some sort. *There is a huge lump in my throat. And suddenly, I am unable to breathe and it feels extremely cramped in this office.*

"Melissa, for some time now, we have been reviewing all of your properties and they have been doing pretty good so far this year, but we were really hoping for a quicker response at Pinnacle and ..", she begins, before I interrupt.

"Sharon, is this about moving the fake people in? I can't do that. There is just no...", I say, before she chimes in and says, "What are you talking about? Please let me finish and then you can speak. Okay?"

"Sure. Please. Go ahead", I say.

"Okay. Like I was saying, we were hoping to see things move a little faster at Pinnacle as this property completely depends on the occupancy ratings for its loan amount. And on top of that, I was also informed that you moved in some residents without getting them approved through Section 8, which is a direct violation through the Tax Credit program. This mistake could have cost us lots of money. I was shocked that you did this, Melissa, because you have never done anything like this before and I have to say that I ...", she says, but then I interrupt her.

"...but I got the units approved anyway. How many people do you know could pull that off? I know that it was risky, but I was still able to get it done and ...", I say, but Sharon interrupts me.

"Melissa, that is not the point. It should not have been done. Your performance is being questioned by the owners lately. We call and you're never at the property, but seem to be in some court hearing, or some other of your many obligations. Because of that, your properties are suffering and the company feels that it is time for us to separate. We are going to have to let you go", she says, looking down at the papers in front of her.

Did I just hear her say "let me go"? With everything I have given to this company, they are firing me!! Is this really happening to me? After 5 years of busting my behind, day in and day out, collecting their money, taking care the residents, they feel that it is time to let me go. I can't believe this is happening. Is this how it feels when you feel like God has abandoned you? I can't put it into words! I feel so alone right now. I want to die. I literally would rather die than to feel this pain right now.

"I guess this is final and there's nothing I can do", I say, looking down at the papers in front of me. I try my best not to let them see me cry. I'm completely shocked right now. Neither of them can look me in the face, all avoiding eye contact with me. I can't believe that Roger is sitting here with nothing to say when just the other day, he sat in *my* office crying about his marital problems with his wife and how he hasn't been able to concentrate on the job. *I wonder what Sharon would say if I told her how unprofessional Roger really is. I bet she would probably re-think this if she knew what his behavior is really like. Maybe that is why he is avoiding eye contact with me because he knows the truth. But, there is something deep down inside of me that won't let me bring that up right now. Dear God, please give me peace right now. I want to cry. I want to scream.*

I want to be angry. I can't believe they are doing this to me right now. Oh God, no!!

"Melissa, you can take all the time you need to gather your things. I already spoke with the owner and he agrees that we should give you pay for the next 3 months just to make this transition a little easier for you. Do you have any questions?" she asks. *I know that she is talking to me, but her voice sounds muffled. I am fighting back tears because there is no way I will give them the privilege of seeing me cry. And if I talk, I know the tears will come and I do not what them to see me cry.*

"No. That's fine. Everything I need, I already have. Thanks for the opportunity to have worked with the company for as many years as I have. It's been my pleasure to serve. Although I disagree with your decision, your decision is your decision. As long as *I* know that I gave this company everything I have to give, that is all that matters to me", I say, standing to my feet. Taking them all by surprise, I stand to my feet and extend a handshake to each of them and walk out of the office. *Come on feet, move. Don't let me down now. Hold up your head, Melissa. Walk out of here with your head up. Lord, please no tears! Not in this office. I am better than that.*

Cynthia catches a glimpse of me walking into my office and when she sees me come out of the office with my purse, my briefcase, and my laptop computer, she doesn't look surprised. She looks sad. She begins to cry and rushes over to me and gives me a hug. *Oh no! Are the tears coming? No! Not here!* "Cynthia, it's okay, honey. I'm going to be okay. Please don't cry. This is just one more thing for God. I'll be okay. We'll talk later. You just keep doing a good job here, okay?" I say, to her, placing my hand on top of hers and walking out of the office before the tears fall.

I walk to my car and there is so much grief on my heart. I can feel that they are watching me leave, but one thing that they will have to all agree on and it is that I walked out of the office with my head up and not down.

Oh God, no! Why have you abandoned me? Why have you put me out here to sink and die in this world? Why didn't you just let me die when I wanted to die? Is this what you saved me for? I would have been better off dead than to have to deal with all of this heartache that the world offers. Are you serious with me right now? Did this just happen? I gave my all to this company and they let me go! Why?!! What am I going to do now? This is all I have done for the last several years. What will my children think of me? What about the divorce? I can't do this! I just can't! I need to get out of here and get a drink or something. God, I can't believe that you let me down and have left me out here to die!

The first call I make is to Patrick, but his phone goes straight to voicemail. *Where is he? And why has he shut off his phone?* By now, the tears are flowing heavily and I have had to pull over because I'm so upset and crying. My head is starting to hurt from crying so much and I just remembered that I was waiting to get to work to eat, so I'm starving right now. My phone beeps. A call is coming in. It's Patrick.

"Hello, honey. You okay?" Patrick asks. "I saw that you just called."

"Honey, no, I'm not okay!" I shout into the phone.

"Sweetheart, calm down. What's wrong?" he asks. "Baby, tell me what's wrong."

Sobbing heavily and without clear speech, I mumble, "I lost my job. What am I supposed to do now? Huh? What? I can't believe they did this to me after all of these years? Why can't I ...?" I say, before he interrupts me.

"Honey, where are you? Talk to me."

All of a sudden, I start feeling that I don't want to talk to Patrick anymore. I don't really want to talk to anyone right now. "Patrick, I need to go."

"No! Melissa, I don't want you to be by yourself right now. Please meet me at the condo. I can be there in about an hour. I just need to get a few more things done and I'll get someone else to finish up for me today. You need me and I want to be there for you. So, I'll see you in about an hour", he says.

"Ok, sweetheart. Are you sure? I don't want to put you in a bad spot", I tell him.

"No. It's not a problem at all."

I wipe the tears away and start the engine. After having driven for a good ten minutes, I can already feel myself starting to move towards the acceptance phase of my separation from the company. At some point, I *have* to come to grips with what happened today. When I wake up tomorrow morning, for the first time in over 10 years, I don't have a job nor do I have a clue as to what to do with myself. I have depended on this job to do that for me for several years.

Before heading over to the condo, I decide to take a little detour to Crispers for my salad. Every time I go into this facility, I always see someone I know and today, I want to just get in and get out. My phone is ringing and the caller ID says "Kalin". I answer.

"Hello, Kalin."

"Melissa, are you okay? I called your job and they told me that you didn't work for the company anymore. And the lady who answered the phone had a nasty attitude about it. What happened?" he asks.

"It's fine, Kalin. I'm very upset right now, but I'm sure that after it settles in with me, I'll be okay. I appreciate your concern. Thanks", I tell him.

"Let's have lunch. I'm on your side of town and I can meet you somewhere", he offers.

"I appreciate that, but I'm having lunch with someone else."

"Don't tell me you're talking about white boy. Are you still messing with him? You haven't figured out that he doesn't want you?" he asks.

"Goodbye, Kalin. I'll talk to you at a later time. I really have to get going."

"Ok. So you mad now, huh? You don't like when I talk about that white mutha…..", he says, raising his voice a little.

"You're so predictable, Kalin. I'm in a horrible mood today and instead of you calling up to be a friend, you have to be "you". How typical! Look, I gotta go!" I say.

Why can't this man care about someone besides himself? Why couldn't he just call me up to talk without bringing up racial slurs about Patrick? Does he not get it that I don't see a white man, but I see a good man? Patrick is good to me and that is why I fell for him. Kalin is not and that is why I fell out of love with him. I need to just get my salad and get out of here.

Right as I'm leaving, the cashier looks at me and says, "It's going to be alright, Melissa."

What! What does she know? Did I say anything to her about my business? Where did that come from?

"Thank you, Cheryl", I say, looking at her name tag. "But, where did that come from?"

"I'm not sure. I just felt like I needed to say it to you", she says.

Oh my God! Where did that come from? Does she know what happened to me today? How could she know that I lost my job? I receive it in the name of Jesus.

Driving to the condo to meet with Patrick is just what I need right now. I just want him to hold me and take care of me and tell me that everything is going to be okay. I need to get right before I go home to explain to the children what has happened. Looking at the bright side of things, they're giving me 3 months of pay before they cut me off. That gives me at least 3 months to find a job and with my skills, that should be no problem.

When I pull into the driveway, I can see that Patrick has not made it here yet. That gives me enough time to eat my salad, take a shower, and calm down. What a surprise when I walk through the door! He had ordered several dozens of roses and placed them throughout the condo. How thoughtful is that! Wow!

My phone is ringing *again*. It hasn't stopped ringing since I left the property. News certainly travels fast in the company. I'm sure that there are lots of questions as to how a woman who earned "Best in Collections", "Property Manager of the Year", and "Best Maintenance Team" year after year could have done something to get fired. Little do they know that I didn't really get fired for my lack of performance, but instead, it's because I didn't want to play ball with Sharon. I didn't want to be fraudulent with the occupancy rate at the Pinnacle property and honestly, I would do it all over again. I'll call Cynthia later just to let her know that I'm okay.

This condo is so comfortable. Hearing the keys rattling at the door tells me that my sweetheart is here. I jump up to greet him.

"Hey Melissa. How are you sweetheart? Come here and give me a kiss", he says, holding his arms out to me.

"I am now! I appreciate you for taking the time off work to be here for me and I just…", I begin to say before I start crying.

"Baby, don't cry. It's going to be okay. I'm going to take care of you. You don't have to worry about anything. It's going to be okay. It's their loss", he says, hugging me and kissing me in between.

"Thank you sweetheart. It means so much to hear you say these things to me", I respond.

Patrick and I hold each other for the rest of the afternoon. He fixes us both a glass of wine. With the wine, the soft music, and this gorgeous man, my afternoon is going much better than it started. "Melissa, I have to tell you something", Patrick says.

"Oh no. I can't handle hearing more bad news today. What is it?" I ask. He gets up and walks over to the window and stares outside.

"It's about my health, Melissa", he says.

I get up and run to him. "Tell me. What is it?" I ask, grabbing his face towards mine. A tear falls from his eye. "Baby, what is it? You're scaring me now!"

"Melissa, I went to the doctor for my regular check-up and my prostate check came back irregular", he blurts out.

"No!!!" I shout. "This can't be happening to us, Patrick. They can fix this, right?"

"Melissa, I don't know yet. I don't know", he says, beginning to cry. "I was just told about it this morning. That's where I was when you called me. I just got this news", he says.

"Oh my God, Patrick! Oh my God! What is going on?!!!" I shout.

"We have to hold it together, Melissa. We have to be here for each other. I promise to be here for you and …", he begins.

"…and I promise to be here for you", I say, completing the sentence. "I will go to the doctor with you. Just tell me when we go back and I'll be right there with you."

"Do you mean that Melissa?" he asks, looking deep into my eyes. I wipe the tears from his eyes.

"Of course I mean it. I love you and I care about you. You have always been here for me and I want to do the same for you. Let's just sit here and enjoy the rest of our afternoon before we have to leave and go home", I say, leading him back to the sofa.

Patrick takes me into his arms and kisses me. We kiss for what seems like an eternity. Before we knew it, we had fallen asleep only to wake up and find that it's dark outside. Patrick looks so comfortable when he sleeps. I love playing with his curly hair and rubbing the back of my hand across his face. When he wakes up, he looks up at me and asks, "How long have you been up?"

"For a little while just watching you sleep. You look so peaceful, Patrick", I tell him.

"I never want this moment to end, Melissa. I want to feel like this for the rest of my life. And I know you want it too. I can see it in your eyes. I say we just make it…", he begins before I interrupt him.

"I thought we would just take it one day at a time", I remind him.

"Tomorrow is not promised to any of us and I don't want to waste anytime from my life. You and Evan would totally complete my life", he comments.

"One day at a time, Patrick. Please", I say.

A few more hours have passed and it is finally time for me to go home and break this horrible news to my children. I have no idea how they'll react. I know they'll like seeing me home when they walk in the door from school, but problem I have with that is that I've always worked. I don't know what to do with myself being home all day.

Patrick and I say our goodbyes and I go one way on Merritt Island Parkway and he goes the opposite direction.

Dear God. Please give me strength right now. I'm trying my best to trust you when I don't understand things, but I'll be honest with you, it's getting harder and harder to trust. It seems like the more I trust you, the worse things get. I don't understand why you would allow me to lose my job when you know that this is how we eat and everything else. I didn't do anything wrong. I didn't deserve this, especially when there are so many people within the company who could care less about it or the residents. Why me, God? Why me? I don't understand this and I'm so hurt right now that I don't even know how to pray for this situation.

The tears are flowing heavily down my face at this point. My heart hurts and it certainly doesn't feel like God is with me. I don't know how much more I can take of this. All of these heartaches are coming one after the next. It is almost as if I don't have time to breathe before there is another crisis.

CHAPTER 23

"I Thought We Were on the Same Page."

This drive home at this time of the day feels so weird. The school buses are slowing up traffic. Children are everywhere. At this time of the day, I'm usually sitting in an office at one of my properties preparing my weekly updates for Corporate. I have to admit that the time I spent with Patrick has made this a little easier. I have to now go home and explain what has happened to me.

"Mommy, you're home!" Justice says, opening my door for me. "Mommy, why are you crying?"

"I need to talk to you girls. Is everybody in there?" I ask, wiping the tears away.

"Yes." Justice runs into the house yelling for her sisters to come down because she sees me crying.

By the time I make it into the family room, they're all there waiting for me. "Ma, what's wrong?" Amber asks.

"Your daddy probably did something to her", Sharelle comments, sending Amber into a frenzy.

"Ma!!!!!!!!!! Did you hear what she said?" Amber asks. The girls go back and forth for a second until I yell, "Enough! This has nothing to do with Kalin. Please, hear me out."

"Ok, sorry Ma", Sharelle says. "And sorry to you too, Amber."

"This is the bad news of the day. I lost my job. I don't understand it either, but I went in to work today and my boss was there and she just said that they had to let me go", I explain.

"But Mommy, you have been there for so long with them. Did you make them mad or something?" Justice asks.

"I must have made somebody mad, Justice. I don't understand it myself", I respond.

"What are we going to do?" Princess asks.

"Survive. We will survive like we have always done."

Each of the girls walk over and give me a hug, which makes me cry even harder. They depend on me for everything and I feel like I'm letting them down. I feel like a total failure right now.

"Mommy, let's just watch a movie. We already ate some hot dogs, so you don't have to worry about cooking for us. I'll pick out the movie", Amber says.

"That sounds like a great idea. A movie would take my mind off of this for a while. Let's order a couple of movies. Somebody, make some popcorn while I take a quick shower and put on my pajamas. These girls do a great job of trying to convince me that they don't worry about anything, but I know that deep down inside, this sudden loss of income scares them just as much as it does me.

We watch television well into the night until we all fall asleep in the family room on the sofa. It's 2am when I wake up and send everyone to their bedrooms. Closing my bedroom door behind me, I notice that my cell phone is beeping. It looks like I've missed a few calls, all of which are from Patrick. He didn't leave a message, but I wonder what is so important that he would call 4 times. I hit "call back" on my cell phone, but there's no answer. I dial again and still, there's no answer. I rush to the computer to see if maybe he sent an email, but nothing. *Now, I'm getting worried about him. What's going on? Oh God, please watch over Patrick right now, Lord. You know what is going on and I just ask that you watch over him and keep him safe. In Jesus' name. Amen.*

No sooner than I finish my prayer, my cell phone rings and I run across the room to grab it, only to find out that it is not Patrick. It's Kalin calling. I probably sound like I have an attitude. I pick up the phone without saying hello and just say, "What?"

"Dang! What's wrong with you? Mad because you home alone while your white boy out there enjoying his life", Kalin says.

"What are you talking about Kalin?" I ask.

"Yeah, I just saw him out at the restaurant tonight having dinner with someone else", Kalin says.

"So! The man has to eat. I'm not upset about that. Give me a break, Kalin. What do you want?" I ask, sounding a little annoyed with him.

"Is this what you call me for at this time of the morning? You could have saved it because I already knew he was going out to this restaurant with this woman." *I don't know what possessed me to lie like that. The truth is that I am wondering who this woman is and why he didn't mention this to me. Perhaps, that is why he was calling me.*

"Ok. My bad. Sorry to bother you. I just thought you would want to know", he says.

"I already did. So, please, goodnight and find something else to do", I say, hanging up the phone.

I try Patrick's number again and this time, it goes straight to his voicemail. Now, I think I'm starting to get upset. I didn't think I liked him this much to get me upset. I guess I keep thinking about all the times Kalin hurt me and I'm starting to think that Patrick is capable of doing the same thing. My mind is definitely starting to wander. I need to call someone, but it's already so late and I'm sure Cynthia is fast asleep, but I bet Brittney is wide awake. Knowing her, she's probably just getting home. I need to tell somebody!

"Hello", Brittney says after two rings.

"Hey girl. How are you? I knew you would be up", I say.

"Is this MeMe?" she asks. "Is everything okay? Why are you calling so late?"

"I need someone to talk to, girl. Are you busy? I ask her.

"I'm never too busy for you, but let me do this. I just got in from the club, so let me take a shower and I'll call you right back. Are you okay?" she asks.

"I just need to talk. That's all", I say. The sadness in my voice must have made Brittney re-think her decision to get off the phone.

"Never mind. I'll shower when we're done. Talk to me, friend. What is it? What's going on?"

"It's everything! You know that me and Kalin are going through a divorce and I...", I begin but she interrupts me.

"No! I didn't know that. Why didn't you call me and tell me? I had no idea. Ya'll seem so happy. What in the world is going on?" she asks.

"He hurt me so badly with other women and then he became abusive. And then on top of that, he wasn't working and basically told me that I wasn't worthy of him getting a job. He would sit on his behind every day while I went to work. Sitting here watching porn all day is what he was doing. I tried to hang in there, you know, because I believe in marriage, but I just couldn't do it. I can't be with this type of man. So, I went downtown and filed the divorce papers", I explain.

"So, did he try to stop you? What did he do? How did he respond?" she asks.

"At first, he tried to win me back, until he realized that I was seeing someone else and falling for him fast", I respond.

"What!!! You already have someone else?" she asks.

"He and I are just friends, taking one day at a time, but yes, I'm fond of him, Brittney", I confess.

"Now, you know what I'm about to ask you now, don't you?" she asks.

"Let me guess. You're going to ask me if I slept with him yet and I'm going to answer you that I have."

"Melissa! You're bad, girl! How could you?"

"I know it isn't right to do it because I am still legally married, but it happened mutually between us and we were just both feeling good that day. It happened and I have no regrets for it at all."

"Oh my goodness. You're right! There's just so much going on", she admits. "So, is Kalin still in the house or what?"

"No. He moved out, but the reason I'm so sad tonight is because not only did I lose my job after 6 years today, but I got a call from Kalin telling me that he saw Patrick out at a restaurant with another woman. I pretended to know about it, but I really don't know what that was about. Being honest about everything, I have to say that Patrick did try to call me, but I missed his calls. What puzzles me is that he didn't leave a message", I explain.

"Wow! And how long has all of this been going on?"

"For several months. To be honest, I've been contemplating divorce for the last year or so. I just recently filed", I tell her.

"So...when we came for Princess' birthday, you and Kalin were having problems then?" she asks.

"That's correct. Before the party that night, my husband forced sex with me", I confess. "It got to the point that I just didn't want him touching me anymore. I no longer had a desire to sleep with him. I was staying up all night to avoid going to bed. It had even gotten so bad to the point that I was having sex with Kalin, but I was thinking about Patrick and wishing it was him that I was having sex with.

"Whewwwwwww, Melissa! Now that's bad", Brittney says.

"I agree with you. I agree. I'm just being real with you about what happened. I'm not proud of myself, because I should have just let him do what he was doing, go to God in prayer, and wait for him to change. I confess today that I did it for as long as I could. But, I was so lonely for a man's touch that I eventually gave in to Patrick one night and we had sex and it was beautiful. The truth is that I was already in love with him when I had sex with him", I admitted.

"But now, he's out with some woman and you have no idea who she is?" Brittney asks.

"That's right. But you better believe I'll get to the bottom of this. I went through hell and back with Kalin and I'm not going to ever let another man dog me. You can believe that!"

"Did I hear correctly that you lost your job too?" B asks.

"Yes. You heard correctly", I say.

"What are you going to do? How will you survive? Kalin is out of the house. You won't have any money coming in. Will Patrick help you?" she asks.

Knowing that Patrick and I never really talked about this, I can't truly answer this question. Come to think of it, he never said anything to me today about helping me with my bills or anything of the sort. Can I just assume that he will help? Should I assume that he loves me this much? Sure, he helped me on a few things a while back, but is he willing to do it more consistently now that I'm unemployed. For crying out loud, he's out with another woman tonight. The only thing I can do here is lie.

"Of course. Patrick told me that I didn't have anything to worry about because he would help me and the girls. He even bought this condo for us so that we would have somewhere to spend time together. He's such a sweet man, Brittney", I say.

"Okay. I hear ya. But, are you trying to convince yourself of that because he's actually out with someone else tonight?"

"I'm so sure that it's nothing and I'm also sure that he was calling me to tell me that he was going out with someone else", I say.

"So, what will you do, Melissa? Seriously, you still need a roof over your head for you and the girls. What happens if you can't find a job quickly enough?" she asks.

"I don't know, B. I really don't know."

Brittney and I talk for at least another hour about what's been going on in Middleton, *her* love life and the kids, but it's now 5 in the morning and I need to go to sleep. The kids will be up soon moving around and trying to wake me up for our Saturday outings. Kids move on quickly when bad things happen, but we're the ones who sit around and mope all day, which is exactly what I want to do.

Moments later, I'm comfortably underneath my bed sheets looking up at the ceiling wondering how I ended up here. *Dear God. I'm almost without words right now. I am hurting so badly right now. I don't even know what to pray about. It feels like I took a huge step backwards by losing my job. I am trying to believe you, Lord. I really am, but it feels like the more I trust you, things seem to get worse and worse. I am really not trying to complain and question you, but I can't understand this. I can't understand how a person like me who gives so much can be terminated in this manner. And it hurts too. What am I supposed to do? What will I do with myself not having a job? How am I going to pay for the things that my family needs? And what is going on with Patrick? I know that being with Patrick is out of your order of doing things, but I truly care about him, Lord. Is he playing with my emotions? Will he eventually hurt me like Kalin did? Is it your Will for me to be with anyone? Lord, I do have so many questions. Please help me to rest now. Please let me have a peace of mind, Lord. I don't want to lose my sanity over this. Forgive me for not trusting you. Forgive me for questioning you. In Jesus' name. Amen.*

God must have answered my prayers because the sun is peeping through the windows and the clock reads 12:30. The children must have agreed to let me sleep. I can hear the Saturday morning cartoons and muffled noises. I'm so glad that the kids recognize that I need to sleep.

"Good morning sleepy head", Justice says, as I walk into the kitchen where they are.

"You guys didn't wake me up?" I ask.

"No, Mommy. You looked so peaceful so we agreed that you needed to sleep and we decided not to worry about what we normally do on Saturdays", she responds.

"That's so sweet, Justice. Thanks to all of you. I appreciate it so much", I say, watching them prepare their breakfast. "So, I'm getting up now to take a shower and get my day started."

I go back into my bedroom to take a shower, and that's when I notice something flashing in the corner and right away, I remember that it's my cell phone. Picking up the cell phone, I'm shocked when it's finally Patrick calling.

"Hello", I say into the phone.

"Good morning beautiful. How are you this morning?" he asks.

"I'm fine, Patrick", I say, sounding a little cold.

"Are you sure everything is okay? You didn't ask me how I'm doing this morning", he says, sounding disappointed.

"I'm just a little confused with what your intentions are, okay. I thought that we were on the same page and then I hear that you're out at dinner with some woman. I'm not about to let you humiliate me like this. And then, to make matters worse, I had to hear it from Kalin that you were out with this woman, so I was here last night….", I say, before he interrupts me.

"Wait a minute! Is that what's bothering you this morning? You thought I was out on a date with a woman last night in *that* kind of way. Baby, please listen to me. Melissa, listen", he begins.

"Don't worry about it, Patrick. You don't owe me an explanation. I'm not your wife. Please spare me. I don't want to know about it. I have way too many things on my mind these days anyway", I respond.

"No! I won't have you thinking that I would play you like that. No! You're going to listen to my explanation. Let's do lunch. Do you have plans for lunch?" he asks.

"No, I don't have plans". I admit.

"Great. Meet me at Logan's on Citrus Blvd. by 1", he says.

I agree. We hang up the phone and for some reason, I feel better already and I feel even better that Patrick wants me to know exactly what's going on with him. I feel like he cares about me enough to do so.

Rushing past the girls, I let them know that I'm having lunch with a friend and before I make it to the front door, Amber says back to me, "Mommy, Princess is taking us to the Mall when she finally gets done cleaning her room."

"Everybody got money?" I ask.

"Yes, Mother, we do!" Justice answers.

"Well, ya'll have fun!" I say, grabbing my keys, my purse, and shutting the door behind me.

It's such a beautiful day outside, just perfect for a picnic. Traffic is not heavy at all heading down Citrus Blvd. The air on my face feels differently today. It's more of a gentle breeze than yesterday. It's almost as if I'm actually in the presence of God. The peace that comes across my heart is a peace that I've never experienced. It almost feels as if yesterday didn't happen. But the truth is that right now, I just want to enjoy being in the company of a good friend. I know I have to call Cynthia. I don't want her to worry about me because she has called at least a dozen times. I just don't want to talk to anyone right now and I hope she understands.

The parking lot is full today at Logan's, but I'm pretty excited that Patrick suggested this place. When I make it inside, Patrick is sitting in the front waiting for me. He stands up to greet me when I walk through the door.

"You look so beautiful, baby", he says, kissing me on the lips.

"Thank you, sweetheart", I say.

Patrick and I are taken to our table located in the back. This is the perfect spot. Our young waiter approaches our table, "What can I get you both to drink?" he asks.

"Strawberry lemonade for me", I answer.

"And give me what my lady is having", Patrick says, winking his eye at me.

"Certainly. I'll be back with your drinks", he says, walking away.

"Sweetheart, let me tell you something. I love you, okay", Patrick begins.

"I want to believe that, Patrick. I do. But, you *were* out with someone else last night. And I don't know who she was or why you were with her", I say.

"Baby, she's a friend in the business. She's on my Board of Directors and I was getting her advice about my condition. I tried to call you a few times just to let you know that I was having dinner with a woman, but you didn't answer and I didn't want to leave a message like that on your phone because it would have made you angrier and I ...", he begins, but I interrupt him.

"But, if Kalin had not told me, would *you* have told me?" I ask, looking away.

"Melissa. Sweetheart. I just told you that I called you to tell you about it. I need you to trust me. I've never been questioned like this because I'm a very honest man and I won't do anything to hurt you, sweetheart. I need you to trust me right now", he pleads.

"You're right, Patrick. I'm so sorry. I should have known that it was nothing because you've been very consistent in making sure that I know how you feel about me. Please forgive me. Yesterday was just a horrible day, other than the time I spent with you and the girls.

"How are they, by the way?" he asks.

"They're all shopping at the Mall today. I'm surprised at how well they took the news of my unemployment", I tell him.

"They're strong just like their mother. You're strong, baby, and I know you'll come out of this. I promise you. I just know it", he consoles me.

"I appreciate your support. It means a lot, sweetheart."

Patrick and I kiss, totally forgetting where we are. "Now, do you believe me, Melissa?" he asks, holding my face in his hands.

"I believe you. I believe you. Sorry I doubted you, baby", I say, kissing him one more time.

The waiter returns with our drinks, but clears his throat to get our attention. "Here are your drinks", he says, placing them in front of us. "Are you ready to order?"

"Yes. I'm gonna have the salmon salad, but please add pecans and strawberries", I respond. Patrick orders the same. While waiting for our food, we cover quite a few topics, all having to do with our future together. *I'm not sure where all of this is headed, but I'll keep going with the flow.*

"So, how is the divorce coming?" Patrick asks.

"Let's see. I've already made the initial visit to the attorney. As a matter of fact, he's currently drawing up all the paperwork, but he promised me he'd let me know the moment that Kalin is served", I respond.

"Kalin contacted me, Melissa", he says.

"What?!! When?!!", I yell. "I can't believe that. Why would he do that?"

"Sweetheart, I knew that he was the one who told you that I was out because he called me last night. How did he even get my phone number?" Patrick asks.

"I had no idea that he called you. He most likely got the number from my phone while he was still at the house. It eventually got so bad at home with him that I stopped trying to hide what I was feeling for you, but Kalin practically handed me to you. I just didn't care anymore. That was when I realized that the marriage was over", I say, looking away often. "But, I didn't know that…", I say, but Patrick cuts me off.

"Sweetheart. I told him the truth about my feelings for you. He's so disrespectful. The man kept calling me "white boy". He actually told me not to hurt you because you're a very special woman", Patrick says.

"Are you serious? I had no idea he felt that way. I'm so glad that he's finally come to grips with all of this."

"Hold up; I didn't say all of that. He made it very clear that if you ever forgave him, he would fight to have you back because he still loves you. The man acknowledged that you are definitely the best woman he's ever had and he regrets every single day that he messed up and …", Patrick explains.

"But *you* need to understand that I'm with you now, Patrick. My heart belongs to you and I want to get to know *you* better and it doesn't matter to me what he *now* thinks and..", I say.

"I want you to make sure that I'm what you want. You know that I'm not well, Melissa. Maybe you *should* try to make things work out with your husband", Patrick suggests.

"Are you serious? Do you hear yourself? Do you not want me anymore? Is that what you are *really* trying to say?" I ask, moving away from him.

"Don't you do that, Melissa", Patrick says, placing his hands on top of mine. "How can you think that *I* don't want you? I want you to be happy and that's all I've ever wanted, Melissa. You're being unfair right now. I want nothing more than to make you happy and to make you mine. We're just talking and…", he tries to explain to me.

"Listen. If I wanted to be with Kalin, I would be with Kalin. I understand that I made a vow to love him forever, and yes, I'm all about marriage and making marriage work, but the marriage between me and Kalin is no more. He doesn't really know how to love me and I'm tired of waiting on him to figure it out. Do you get that?" I ask, looking directly into Patrick's green eyes. "I want you", I say, grabbing his face and kissing him as if we're the only two people in the room.

"Alrighty then!" Patrick says, grinning from ear to ear. "You have made me a happy man, Melissa."

"Yes. I can see that", I laugh, looking between his legs, paying attention to his hard-on.

"Wow! Look what you're doing to me, girl. I know what I want for dessert", Patrick comments.

"I bet I know what you want for dessert, too", I say, laughing out loud.

The waiter returns with our food and places our food onto the table. "Is there anything else that I can get either of you", Joshua asks, with a slight grin on his face.

"No, that will be all for now, Joshua. Thanks!"

Joshua disappears and Patrick and I eat our food, kissing in between. "My salad is tasty, but not as tasty as this beautiful and sexy woman sitting across from me right now", Patrick says, looking directly into my eyes.

"What are you trying to do? Are you trying to get me to take you right here Dr. Norwood?" I say, grinning.

"Whatever floats your boat, Melissa", he says. "What are your plans for today when lunch is over?" he asks.

"I'll most likely go home and take a warm shower and get some work done in my office", I answer, jokingly.

"I have something better in mind", he comments.

"Really? What do you have in mind?" I ask.

"I was thinking that we could go back to the condo, sit on the balcony and snuggle and catch a sunset. We could even share a glass of wine and see where our evening takes us. I want you to spend the night with me tonight. I don't want you to go home", he says.

"Really? Are you sure?" I ask.

"I'm very sure. So, call your sister and see if she can go to the house with the girls so you don't worry yourself all night. I want you to relax and enjoy our evening. Do you think you can make that happen?" he asks.

"Let me call Diane and see where she is." I dial her number and she answers right away.

"Girl, where are you? I've been worried sick about you. Cynthia called me and told me what happened at the job. Are you okay, Melissa? You have put so much time and sweat into that job so I know you must be hurting, but it's okay, Melissa. God's gonna work it out. You know that, right?" she asks.

"Of course I do. I'm okay. It is what it is. I know that I didn't do anything wrong, so I don't care what they say. *I really wish she wouldn't bring this up. I am trying to forget about all of that for at least a day. The more she talks about it, the more I start to lose my happy. Please stop saying anything about it. Maybe if I stop talking about it, she will stop talking about it too.*

"Melissa, are you listening to me?" she asks. "I'm just worried about you."

"I'll be just fine, Diana. What I called you for was to see if you could sleep at my house tonight", I say.

"Sure. Where are you going?" she asks.

"I'm spending the evening with Patrick. As a matter of fact, I'm here with him for lunch", I tell her.

"Thank God for Patrick. I'm so glad that you are out enjoying yourself and not sitting around feeling sorry for yourself about that damn job! Hell yes, I will go to your house and stay with the kids. Enjoy your time with Patrick. At least there is a man who knows how to put a smile on your face!" Diana says, raising her voice to express her approval.

Patrick seems happy because he can tell that she's saying "yes". He's shaking his head, as if he agrees with Diana. "So, what did she say?" Patrick asks when I hang up the phone.

"She said, *"heck yeah, I'll watch the kids because there is finally a man who knows how to put a smile on your face"*, I tell him. "So, it looks like you have a house mate for the evening."

"I am soooooooooo happy about that, too. Are you finished eating? Let's get out of here!" he says, leaving a tip for the waiter who has done an excellent job serving us.

Patrick and I leave the restaurant and decide to go straight to the condo to drop off my car. Because we are eating in tonight, we have to also go over to the Farmer's Market to pick up items to prepare our dinner. "Ok, honey, I'll see you at the condo", I say, jumping into my car.

"Ok, honey. Go straight there. I'll see you in a few minutes."

CHAPTER 24

"Where Did That Come From?"

"*A*unt Diana, where did you say that Momma was?" Justice asks.

"Your mother had to run out of town to check on one of her friends over in Orlando, so she won't be home and she asked me to come here and stay with you girls", she says, while walking over to the refrigerator to get some cranberry juice.

"Really? She didn't tell us about it", Amber comments.

"I know. She just found out about this like an hour ago", Diana responds.

"But she didn't take any clothes with her", Sharelle comments, with a smile on her face, as if she's being sarcastic.

"I'm sure that your mother will figure it out. I'm sure of it", Diana says, tapping Sharelle on the hand as if she notices that Sharelle is being sarcastic. "So, what would you ladies like to do tonight?"

"I would love to go to see Twilight", Justice yells.

"Of course you would", Sharelle comments.

"Is everybody else okay with that?" Diana asks, looking around at the three girls. Princess is at work and won't get off work until after we are gone.

"Yeah, yeah, yeah! That's okay with me too", agrees Amber and Sharelle.

"Ok. So let me get on the computer and pre-order our tickets so we don't have to wait in line", Diana announces. She heads towards Melissa's office to complete the transaction, while Amber, Princess, and Sharelle rush upstairs to get dressed.

Everybody is all seat-belted in and heading towards Regal Cinemas off Dolphin Parkway. This is the most popular theatre for all of the teenagers. It's where all of the teenagers go on Saturday nights and Diana believes that tonight won't be an exception.

They pull into the parking lot and it looks like every single teenager in Miami has come out to see the movie, Twilight. The girls are in for a surprise because Diana paid a little extra money to get tickets to sit in the balcony for them to get a better view. The girls always love spending time with their Auntie Diana because she always goes all out for them.

Their night is simply amazing, but on the way home, the girls become even more concerned about their mother and father's divorce.

"Auntie D, what do you think about divorce?" Amber asks, as soon as they get back into the car.

"Where did that come from sweetie?" Diana asks.

"I was just wondering. You know that Mommy and Daddy are getting a divorce, so I was just wondering what you think about it?" she repeats.

"I think that sometimes it's necessary. I think that people sometimes get married that *should not* be married. And if they are mature about it, they can go through the divorce without anybody getting hurt", Diana responds.

"Do you think our mom and dad should have been married?" Justice asks, looking directly into the mirror at Diana.

"I think that we need to stop this conversation and talk about the movie. How did you all enjoy Twilight? Are you glad we came?" Diana asks, changing the subject. It must have worked because the girls talk no more of their parents' divorce.

"I am definitely Team Edward", Justice confesses.

"Yeah, me too", agrees Amber and Sharelle.

"Can we call Mommy and tell her about the movie?" Amber asks.

"Let your Mother rest! I'm sure that with her driving all night, she's tired. She'll be home tomorrow and you can tell her all about it", Diana suggests to them.

"Okay. That sounds fair. Auntie, can we stop for some ice cream?"

"Okay. You three are expensive!! Sure, Ben and Jerry's is straight ahead and we can stop for ice cream and then we're going home!" Diana exclaims.

CHAPTER 25

"You Know What I Want to Eat."

"So, what would you like to have for dinner, honey?" I ask Patrick, getting out of the car at the Farmer's Market.

"Do you *really* want to know the answer to that question?" he says, shutting my door for me. Patrick gently posts me against the car and kisses me.

"You, baby. Eating you is good enough for me. I'm sure you'd enjoy it because I'm very hungry for me some Melissa today and you know what happens when I'm hungry", he laughs.

"Yes, I do. You are so crazy!"

"Just telling you what's real, baby. You know I love how you taste", he adds.

"Okay, lover boy. But, I mean, what are we going to purchase in the store to cook for our dinner tonight?" I ask, pushing him forward gently.

"I was thinking that we could prepare steak and twice baked potatoes", he suggests.

"Cool! I'll call my friend, Amy, because she is absolutely the best at preparing this meal. That sounds like a plan. It's been awhile since we had steak. Is this okay for you to eat, honey?"

"Baby, I can eat whatever I want!" he answers.

"Speaking of your health, when was the last time you went to see a doctor and what is he saying?" I ask, changing the subject and tone of the conversation to a more serious one.

"Melissa, no, not tonight. We're not going to talk about anything serious tonight. I just want us to enjoy each other. Deal?"

"But....", I begin.

"But nothing! Not tonight!" he demands.

"Okay, but tomorrow, I want to discuss this. I'm not trying to be a bother, Patrick. It's that I love you, okay?"

"Okay, honey."

Patrick and I continue shopping for everything we need to prepare our meal. Once we have everything that we need, we jump back into Patrick's car and head back to the condo. He makes a surprise stop to this stand next to the Farmer's Market and Patrick disappears around the corner. I might as well use this time that he's away to check my messages. Luckily, I only have a message from Diana letting me know that she's taking the kids to see Twilight and for me to have a good time being happy with Patrick. I can see that he's coming back now. *What in the world was he doing?*

"For you, my love", he says, as he takes his hand from behind his back with a dozen red roses.

"Oh my goodness, Patrick! That is so sweet of you to buy me roses. Honey, thank you so much! They are so beautiful", I say, hugging his neck and giving him a sweet kiss. "And what is this for?"

"Just because! I don't need a reason to tell my sweetheart that I love her", he responds. "I love you and I appreciate you for coming into my life and opening up your heart to love."

For years to come, this will be mine and Patrick's special moment that I'll remember forever. *I feel like I can say the words "I love you" to him, but if I do, there is no going back. I won't be in control anymore. He'll be in control and he'll have my heart. This timing is perfect. That is for sure. What will he think if I say it? He has already said it to me and I know he must be wondering if I love him too. I mean, it has been years.*

"I love you, Patrick", I say, not letting him go, but looking directly into his eyes. Patrick looks extremely surprised, but yet, so happy to hear these words roll off my tongue. I say the words without a care in the world. I say them without thinking that I just got my heart broken by a man I was in love with for 15 years. I say them, hoping that he still feels the same way about me.

"Melissa, I love you too. I really mean that and you see how you feel today?" he asks.

"Yes."

"This is how I want you to feel for the rest of our lives together. I've been in love with you for a long time, sweetheart. I remember our first kiss in my car outside of Starbucks. As plain as day, I remember saying to myself *that night* that you would be my wife. Don't get me wrong. I respected the fact that you were married to Kalin, but I knew that I wasn't going to just let you walk away", Patrick explains.

The tears are flowing down my face. I have not felt like this in years. *Oh no! I said it! I put it out there. I wonder what Patrick is thinking now. Where do we go from here? What is next for us? I don't know about that, but for right now, I just want us to get home so that we can just enjoy being in love. When we make love tonight, it will be real.*

"Oh Patrick! You make me so happy. Thanks for putting this smile on my face. I'll always cherish this moment."

Patrick and I form a bond that I don't think will ever be broken. What has just become apparent to me is that I have always carried him in my heart, but I gave my husband the priority, but the truth is that Patrick was always there and we were just waiting for our time to come. We make love tonight with tears in our eyes because neither of us has ever experienced love like this.

After such a romantic evening, I wake up and Patrick is gone. This room feels so empty without him in it. Looking around, I don't see anything out of hand. I walk in the bathroom and he's not here, but I can tell that he *was* here. When I call out to him, I don't get an answer, but as soon as I walk over to the bed, I find a note beside the bed that reads, *"Good morning beautiful. I enjoyed last night. You really do know how to take care of me, but I was even happier to take care of you too, baby. I have a doctor's appointment today, but I didn't want to wake you up, so I left. Breakfast is on me. Here's money for you to get some Starbucks. Today is the anniversary of our first kiss. I love you and will call you later. Love, Patrick…..xoxoxoxoxo*

It Feels Like I've Been Here Before
Torn 2: Passion, Pain & Promise.

CHAPTER 26

"She Must Be Special."

"*P*atrick, the best thing for us to do is begin some form of treatment immediately and hope it decreases the size of your tumor, caused by your rare blood disorder", the doctor explains.

"What's gonna be the least painful way of doing it?" Patrick asks.

"There is no easy way to care for this disease that you have. It's just not enough information on it, so I have to go with what's available right now", the doctor explains. Patrick is listening and complies by shaking his head.

Before he leaves Dr. Nelson's office, Patrick makes arrangements to begin treatment, but he knows that he can't do it until *after* the trip he's planning. He knows that this treatment may have him cranky, but he just wants to enjoy a romantic weekend with Melissa before treatment begins.

"Ok, Patrick, I've spoken with the hospital in Connecticut and they have you set up to begin treatment in 3 weeks. We don't want to wait any longer than that. It'll give you enough time to take your trip and rest before beginning the treatment", Dr. Nelson explains.

"That's perfect. And do you believe these treatments will cure me of this disease?" Patrick asks.

"Nothing is guaranteed, Patrick. Nothing. But, I can tell you this. It will certainly decrease the size of this tumor. This technique has been tested and has worked so far and I don't see why it won't work for you. We just have to remain positive and believe. Can you do that for me?" Dr. Nelson asks, writing the prescription. "In the meantime, take these pills to ease the pain that you're having, but let me know if you start to experience any side effects not listed here", he explains, pointing to the brochure he is handing to Patrick.

"Okay. Thank you, sir. Because of the new love in my life, I have to remain positive about all of this. You know we *just* talked about starting our life together and now this!"

"Have you talked to your new love about your condition?" the Doctor asks.

"No. I haven't and I don't think I will. This is going to be just fine and I won't really need to alarm her. She doesn't need to see this", Patrick continues.

"I disagree with you because I personally think she should know. She should know what you both are up against with this disease", Dr. Nelson states.

"Ok. I'm going to get out of here and head over to the travel agent. Thanks so much, Dr. Nelson. I have a trip to plan, but I'll let you know when I make it to Connecticut", Patrick says, standing up to leave the office. He shakes his doctor's hands and walk out of the office.

Patrick has Miami Travel on his speed dial, but just as he's dialing their number, Melissa calls. He switches over to take the call. "Good morning beautiful", he says, as he answers the phone.

"Baby, I was worried about you. How did it go at the doctor's?" I ask.

"It was great, honey. Everything is going to be just fine. I'm getting better. The doctor put me on some pills that should make me feel better" he says, feeling horrible that he can't tell her the truth.

"I knew it. God is so good. I prayed for you, baby, when I woke up and saw your note", Melissa says.

"That's great. Did you go get your breakfast?" he asks.

"I did. I'm here at Starbucks now, remembering our night and wanted to call you. It was our first kiss. I tried my best to resist you, but I can't do it any more today than I could that day", I confess. We both laugh.

"Is that right?" he asks. "You're so special to me, baby. What are your plans for the day?"

"Nothing much. I just need to catch up on some work, so I'll most likely be at home for the majority of the day", I respond.

"Okay. Me too. I have some phone calls to return. Clients, you know? All boring stuff. Let's talk later okay. I have a surprise for you", he says.

"You're full of surprises, aren't you?" I say, laughing.

"Yes. Only the best for my baby", he says, making me blush. "I love you, Melissa."

"I love you too, Patrick."

"Well, get home safely. I'll call you later", he says, with tears in his eyes. He's glad that Melissa can't see him right now.

"Ok, baby. Later."

Patrick hangs up with Melissa and starts to cry. He knows that the life ahead of them will be hard if this treatment doesn't work out in Connecticut, but Patrick has an issue with bringing this serious problem up to Melissa because she has enough on her plate. He doesn't want her to start thinking the worst. It's time for them to move forward with a life together so he hopes that this Connecticut trip will put *this* issue to rest once and for all.

Patrick finally gets Miami Travel on the phone. "Hi, Dr. Norwood. It's been a long time since you've scheduled a trip. Where are you going?" the agent asks.

"To a place that will put the biggest smile on my sweetheart's face, London. Put together a package to travel to London and email it to me so that I can look it over and sign off on it. I want this trip to happen as soon as possible because when we return, I'll have to then travel to Connecticut", Patrick tells the agent.

"So, are we talking about a flight out for when?" the agent, Lisa, asks.

"Next Friday and I want the accommodations to be for one week at the nicest hotel in London. I want a tour guide to take us to all the romantic places there. Make sure to use Destination Europe because they're very quick on getting a response to you on the package. Email the package details to my personal email", Patrick instructs.

"You got it, Doc. Whoever she is, she's a very lucky woman", Lisa comments.

"She is a very beautiful woman and deserves to have the very best vacation", he comments.

"Yes. I sure will. And your email is patrickdocfl@hmail.com, right?" Lisa asks.

"That's correct. I've never traveled to London, so it'll be an adventure for the both of us", he says. "I'm most definitely looking forward to spending this special time with her."

"Are you celebrating anything special?" Lisa asks, not looking up while looking at Destination Europe's website.

"You never know. You just never know what kind of magic will be made in London. I just know that when we return, I may not be able to spend as much time with her, so I want her to really know how I feel", Patrick explains. "She's going to be so shocked because she's always wanted to travel out of the country. So, if you'll jump on that, I will greatly appreciate it", Patrick tells her.

On the way home, Patrick starts thinking ahead to make sure that he hasn't forgotten anything. He's already starting to pack for the trip and later on tonight, his secret will be out of the bag and Melissa will know what he's been up to for the last couple of days. The reservation is made at Café Prima Pasta on South Beach. They have the best pasta dishes in Miami. Melissa mentioned one day that she wanted to go there so tonight, she will.

CHAPTER 27

"Where Are You Taking Me?"

"*M*omma, I'm okay and I've accepted that my last day here is next Thursday. I've actually made peace with myself over it", Sharelle says,

"Really, Sharelle? I'm so happy to hear you say this. You might as well accept it. Think about it this way. The sooner you get started on the time they gave you, the easier it will be and before you know it, you'll be back home", I respond.

Sharelle and I walk into the family room and put the TV on Lifetime. Our favorite times together are spent watching Lifetime. Both of us really get into the movies that come on this channel. By the end of the movie, we're both crying.

"Are you and my sisters gonna be alright Ma?" she asks, grabbing the remote.

"We're going to be just fine. You just make sure to stay focused, Sharelle. Don't go in there to make these people's jobs any harder. You're there to be rehabilitated so that you don't come back out here doing the same crazy stuff", I tell her.

"I know, Ma."

Our movie starts. *Now, why can't I write a story one day that could be good enough for Lifetime? God knows we have had enough drama for a series of stories. I wouldn't even know where to begin; who am I kidding?*

Sharelle and I are cuddled on the couch spending this quality time together because I know that in a few days, I'll have to turn her over to the State of Florida to do her time at the residential facility in Stuartville. The other girls recognize this and go upstairs and play games in their room.

"Sharelle, you wanna come help me pick out something to wear tonight?" I ask.

"And where are you going, Miss Lady?" she asks.

"Well, if you must know, Patrick is taking me out to a nice restaurant tonight. He said that he has a big surprise for me", I answer.

"Really! That's nice, Mommy! I'm so happy. I really like this Patrick dude. He puts that big smile on your face and that makes me so happy knowing that he'll be out here with you while I'm away and ...", she begins to say.

"And it doesn't upset you at all?"

"No! Why should it upset me?" she asks, looking puzzled.

"Because of Kalin and...well, you know", I say.

"Mommy, Kalin is a joke! He has had you crying for many nights. You don't think I saw it? I am the observant one, remember? I saw everything, and I do mean everything! I heard all the arguments that y'all had. These walls are thin, Ma. It's a good thing that he's gone. He was not the right man for you because he broke your heart so many times. But, I'm a kid. What do I know?" she says, grabbing my hand and pulling me up off the couch. "Let's find you something to wear! Come on!"

Sharelle and I rush to my closet to pick out the sexiest black dress in my closet. We decide on a fitted black dress with tie up sexy shoes and all the accessories to match. Tonight, I'll pamper myself with warm milk in my bath and my favorite Victoria's Secret body wash. Using the body oil to match, I moisturize my entire body, down to my pinky toe. Sitting down at my lighted mirror, I'm now ready to put on my face. Sharelle is standing by to flat iron my hair. She and I are both happy with the finished product. Just as we are wrapping up, Justice and Amber walk into my room. "Mommy! Where are you going? You look pretty!" Justice says.

"Mommy is going out to dinner tonight and aren't we happy for her?" Sharelle says, barging in.

"I guess so. Who with?" Amber asks.

"A friend of hers", Sharelle says, not giving me a chance to answer any of the questions.

"Mommy, you're ready to go, so go out and enjoy yourself. You look beautiful", Sharelle says, grabbing my purse and keys and leading me out of the room, with her sisters following.

"You girls gonna be alright?" I say, looking back at them.

"I got them. We're just fine. You ordered the pizza, right?" Sharelle asks.

"Yes. It's paid for and everything. It'll be delivered in about 30 minutes. The tip is on the countertop in the kitchen. Give it all to him", I say, with a smirk on my face. The girls stiffed the last driver and didn't give him his entire tip that I left behind.

The girls shut the door behind me and I can hear that it locked. I'm finally on my way to the condo to meet Patrick and I can't wait to see him. I've thought about our plans all day. Driving down Dolphin Parkway feels differently tonight. I have absolutely no idea what Patrick's surprise is. Could it be that he's going to ask me to marry him? He wouldn't do that because he knows that I'm not divorced yet. I need to call Cynthia to see what she thinks.

She answers on the first ring. "Hey Ms. Thing", she says.

"Hi Cynthia. I know you must think I'm the worst friend ever by not calling, right?" I ask her.

"Girl, now you know that I know you. It doesn't matter to me if we go without talking for months, I know you love me and you know I love you and want nothing but the best for you", she says.

"So true! So true! Well guess where I'm headed."

"Where?" she asks.

"On my way to meet Patrick at the condo. He's taking me out to a nice restaurant tonight. Said he's got a surprise for me", I say.

"Surprise? Oh no! You don't think it's that he wants to....", she begins before I interrupt her.

"Propose? Absolutely not! How can he do that if I'm still legally married? I don't know what it could be", I say.

"Then just enjoy the moment, my friend. Enjoy the moment and let this man pamper you. He really does love you, you know? I believe that in my heart and you should too. I think that you are in love with him, Melissa. You should see how your face lights up every time you talk about him", she says.

"No, I didn't notice that", I say. We both laugh. "Well, I just pulled up to the condo and it looks like I've made it here before Patrick, so I'll just go inside and wait on him", I tell Cynthia.

"Okay. You know I want details. I don't expect to talk to you tonight, so we'll talk tomorrow, okay", she says.

"Okay. Good night."

"Good night."

Cynthia and I hang up and just as I put the key in the door, I realize that it's already unlocked. I can hear soft jazz music coming from inside. *Oh no! Has someone broken in here? I didn't see Patrick's car in the parking lot. Should I run out of here or what?*

"Come on in", the voice inside says. *That sounds like Patrick's voice. It is Patrick!*

"Honey, you scared me half to death", I tell him, barely pushing him forward.

"You look absolutely amazing! Baby, you are so beautiful! I am such a lucky man to have a woman like you in my life", he says, kissing me.

"Sweetheart, that's so nice of you to say", I respond.

"It's the truth, Melissa. It's the truth", he says, paying close attention to my cleavage.

"Eyes up here, honey", I say. We both laugh.

"I just can't keep my eyes off you. Damn, you're hot!"

"Ok. Ok. Enough. I see what you're trying to do. You're trying to get something started. You're so slick. Anyway, where is your car? I didn't see it downstairs.

"That's because it isn't downstairs and I…", he begins.

"So, how did you get here?" I ask.

"We're riding limo style tonight. I want us to relax and just enjoy being with each other. You know I always wanted to make love in a limo", he teases.

"I bet you have, you funny man! Are we ready?"

"Yes. I made reservations for 7 so we should be going."

We walk outside and head straight for the Hummer stretched limo. "Patrick, what a nice surprise, honey!" I say, kissing him on his lips.

"Only the best for you, Melissa. You deserve this and more, baby. Now, let's have a good time tonight. Let me pamper you the way you deserve to be pampered", he says, following behind me getting inside.

The driver closes the door behind us and our night of fun is just beginning.

I don't know if I have ever noticed this nice scenery at night in Miami. Dear Lord, how in the world did I get this? Thank you Jesus for loving me and giving me something more. I wonder where we're going for dinner.

"So, what do you think, sweetheart? Seems like you have something on your mind", he says, taking my chin in his hands to face him.

"I'm just so happy, Patrick. I've never felt like this in my life. No man has ever treated me like this. I was married to Kalin all those years and he never even took me out on a date for crying out loud. I didn't know that this is how a woman is supposed to feel. I'm just so happy. You just have no idea, Patrick", I explain.

"Baby, look at me. You're a precious woman and I can't imagine how anyone would ever mistreat you, but I'm happy that he gave you to me to love. I'm not happy that he hurt you, but you ended up with me and I won't hurt you, Melissa. I won't ever leave you. I will always support you and take care of you and the girls. Do you believe me?" he asks.

"I believe you, Patrick. I believe you, baby."

Patrick and I share the most intimate kiss and it feels like there is nobody else in this world right now, but me and him. All of a sudden, it feels like the limo is stopping. We must be here already. I'm anxious to know where we are and within the next few minutes, the driver comes around and opens the door. We get out of the limo and the first thing I notice is that I'm stepping down onto red carpet. *Did this man go through all this trouble to make me feel special? I don't believe this. I am in love! I never thought I was worth all of this trouble.*

"Patrick, did you do this too?" I ask, looking back at him.

"Baby, you're so worth it all", he says, escorting me out of the limo.

We finally make it inside and are seated at a table previously picked out by Patrick. The atmosphere in this restaurant is so romantic. Each table is lit with a soft candle. The jazz music playing in the background really sets the mood. I have to admit that the treatment that I'm getting tonight would make any woman feel like the most beautiful woman in the room and that's exactly what he has made me feel so far.

"Honey, this restaurant has the best pasta dishes you ever want to taste. I would like to do the ordering as I am sure you will be impressed with it. Do you trust me with the food that is about to go in your belly?" he asks, smiling and grabbing my hands.

"Yes sir! I trust you", I say, smiling back at him.

Patrick orders our food. "So, are you probably wondering what this evening is all about?" he asks.

"Uh yeah! I've thought about nothing but this dinner all day. Are you kidding? I'm so excited", I say, looking directly into his eyes.

"Well, well, well, I could torture you and make you wait all night, but I won't do that to you", he says. "Close your eyes."

Oh my God! No! Am I going to wake up and find a box in my hand? I can't believe it! It's about to happen! I'm going to pass out of this chair.

"And stick out your hand", he instructs. "No peeping, Melissa!"

I hold out my hand and Patrick places what feels like a booklet in my hand. "Now, open your eyes!"

I open my eyes and the words TICKET are the first words I see. "Open it."

On the envelope is a note that says "We are going to London for 1 week!" in bold letters on bright yellow paper.

"Is it true? Are we really going to London? Patrick, are you serious? Please tell me you're kidding!"

"I wish I could, baby, but I can't. We leave Friday and will be gone for one week. No interruptions of any kind; just you and me. The flight reservations have been made and we'll be staying at the Jumeirah Carlton Tower. This is one of the nicest hotels in London. A friend of mine recommended it. My buddy told me that it is paradise on earth and ...", he begins to say until I interrupt him.

"Nobody has ever done anything like this for me, Patrick. I don't know what to say. I am ..", I begin.

"Just say that you'll go to paradise with me", he says.

"There's no way I would miss it, Patrick. I'm so happy right now that I could just scream but these people in this restaurant would think that I have lost my mind. Baby, this is the best surprise! I mean it! Thank you so much. This is really nice!" I respond, grabbing his hand and kissing him as if there is nobody in the restaurant but me and him.

"I have another surprise for you later."

"Another surprise? Wow! You're really doing your thing tonight, aren't you?" I say, laughing.

"You're special to me, Melissa. I often think of the first time I ever laid eyes on you. You were doing what I love to see in a woman. You were caring for another human being, which is the most selfless act I have ever known. That is what made you so beautiful to me that day. Yes, of course, you were dressed nicely, your hair was in place, your face was flawless, but I saw past all of that and went straight to your heart and when I looked at your heart, I saw God. I will never forget that day because I fell in love with you right then", he says, looking directly into my eyes.

"I love you, Patrick. I love you so much. Thank you so much", I say, when right at that moment, the waiter returns with our food.

"Sorry to interrupt", the waiter says. "Your food is here."

He puts our plates down in front of us, places the wine on the table and tells us to enjoy our meal.

"Now, back to what I was saying, I love you, Patrick. I tried to resist you. I was married at the time that we met, but I was very loyal to my husband. I believe in the institution of marriage and to be honest with you, if Kalin had not started being abusive to me, I would probably still be with him. But, unfortunately, it had gotten to the point that people who had known me for years didn't recognize me anymore. *I* didn't recognize me anymore. So, I'm thankful that you were there to show me what real love feels like. You make me feel like the most beautiful woman in the room", I say, starting to tear up.

"You *are* the most beautiful woman in the room. I love you too, Melissa. Now, let's eat!"

Patrick and I continue to reminisce throughout dinner about all the things we've experienced together, while enjoying good food and wine. It feels like there's something *else* going on here.

Now that we've enjoyed this fantastic meal, it's time to head back to the limo. The limo driver lets us in and our journey begins. After a few minutes, I notice that we are not heading back to the condo. "Honey, where are we going? I don't remember seeing any of this when we came. I know that I can't be *that drunk!*"

"Just enjoy the ride. Come here."

I move in closer and Patrick gives me a passionate kiss. His hand ends up on my leg, then my thigh and before I know it, he's sliding off my panties and kissing me harder and more passionately. The music in the background is really setting the mood in this limousine. Patrick's special made Love CD is playing and Al Green's, Love and Happiness, is setting the mood right now. I was always amazed that he liked so much R & B music.

Patrick unbuckles his pants and exposes his penis. He takes me and sits me on top of his lap and kisses me more, running his fingers through my hair, sending electricity through my body. He looks deeply into my eyes and says, "I want you right now, baby. Can I have you, Melissa?"

"Please don't stop, Patrick. You make me feel so good."

Instinctively, my body moves with his flow and we're making love, with the driver not having a clue as to what is taking place in the back of this limo.

It feels like we're going up a hill, so I decide to look out the window and all I can see are trees. "Honey, where in the world are you taking me?" I ask him.

"You'll know very shortly", he responds, while fixing my clothes. I take my panties and place them in my purse because I can tell that we'll be to our destination shortly. The limo comes to a halt. The driver opens the door. Patrick gets out and helps me out. "Sir, is there anything else that you need this evening?" the driver asks.

"No sir. That will be all. Have a great night and thanks for a job well done." Patrick hands him what looks like two hundred dollar bills. He shuts his limo door and drives away. We're standing in front of this beautiful two-story home. His car is in the driveway. *Are my eyes deceiving me? Did this man bring me to his house? All of these years, I've never even considered his home or where he lives at all.*

"Is this your house, Patrick? Did you bring me to your house?" I ask in total surprise.

"Yes. Surprise number 2. I feel like you should know where I live. Our relationship has moved to that level now", he says, taking me by the hand and leading me inside. As soon as we walk into his home, I see a picture of him and Evan and Evan's mom. *Ooooohhhh, I don't know how to feel seeing that. I have to act like it doesn't bother me or he'll notice. Everything has gone good so far so I can't ruin the evening with a little jealousy. It's not easy because it almost makes me feel like he's still in love with her or something. I have to do some acting right now because seeing that just hurt a little.* "Come on in. I want you to make yourself comfortable. Would you like some wine?" he asks.

"Of course. That sounds good. White wine, please."

"White wine for me lady", he says in his interpretation of a British accent.

Patrick fixes our wine and leads me to what appears to be the family room. "Make yourself comfortable, baby. Are you surprised?" Patrick leaves and disappears upstairs, but returns within ten minutes or so.

"I'm totally surprised! You have surprised me like I have never experienced before and I'm looking forward to traveling to London with you. How long are we going to be there? I forgot to ask you that", I say.

"We're going to be there for an entire week. The plan is to fly out Friday morning and we'll arrive in London eight hours later. You're not afraid of flying, are you?" he asks, laughing.

"No!" I respond, playfully hitting him. Taking a sip of my wine, I look around and see several pictures of Evan throughout the years. "Evan is really a handsome young man. He looks just like his daddy", I say, kissing Patrick on the lips.

"You think so? Many people say he looks like his mother. I think he looks more like her."

"So, where is he tonight?"

"He got out of here when I told him that I was bringing my lady here. That's when he decided to sleep over at a friend's house", he responds. "Come here, baby, and dance with me." Patrick picks up the remote and hits play and this time, Teddy Pendergrass is singing for us instructing us to "Turn Off the Lights". "I love this song. Teddy really knows how to set the sexiest mood, doesn't he baby?"

"Yes he does. But I don't really need him to because I was ready the moment I stepped foot out of the limousine", I say, putting down my wine glass and taking his wine glass from him. I have had enough wine to give me the boldness I need to seduce him. I pull away from him and begin to dance for him seductively like a stripper.

He seems to really be enjoying it. "Aaah baby, you're making me so excited for you right now", he mumbles.

"Yes, I see just how much you want me", I say, looking down at his erection.

"So, why don't you come over here and give me my strawberry."

"I will give you whatever you want, but let's take our time. We have all night. I want to enjoy you like I've never enjoyed you before, baby."

Patrick can't resist me any longer. He picks me up, throws me onto the sofa, spreads my legs apart and begins to kiss me in my sweet spot. Electricity is flowing through my body. I see fireworks. Patrick has the magic tongue. He knows exactly where to put it and how to use it to bring extreme ecstasy. My orgasm is flowing uncontrollably. Our lovemaking is going to new heights tonight. Patrick's face is covered in my juices and he doesn't seem to be bothered by it at all. I take him by the hand and lead him to lie down so that I can crawl on top of him. He follows my lead.

"I love you, Melissa. You taste so good. I can't get enough of you", he says, grabbing me and leading me to sit on top of his manhood. Our bodies move together in love until we both climax sending us both into sexual convulsions. "Wow, baby, you were amazing. And we haven't even made it to my bedroom yet", Patrick says. We laugh.

We hold each other until we decide that we're ready to go upstairs. Patrick grabs the wine and our glasses and leads me towards the stairs. Going up the stairs, I notice more pictures of Evan. "Oh, are those your parents?"

"Yes. That's my mom and dad. That picture was taken last year when they went skiing in the Alps."

"Nice."

"Ok, we're here. You ready to enter?" he asks, laughing.

"What's so funny? What do you have up in here?"

"Nothing, baby. Come on in." He opens the door and we both walk inside. Patrick's room is so spacious and comfortable. *Is that a fireplace? This man is so romantic. I can only imagine the good times that he has had in this room with his wife.* "So, what do you think?"

"I love your room. This is really nice. And what a nice touch! You have rose petals from the door all the way to the bathroom." The bathroom has his and hers sink, a TV over the jacuzzi tub and his and hers closets. *I wonder if all of my stuff would fit in this closet. I really could get used to living like this. He has really built a nice home for him and his son. This is so nice and comfortable.*

"I'm glad you like it. Let me run a nice warm bath for you. So make yourself comfortable and let me pamper you", he says, putting down the bottle of wine and glasses.

Slipping out of my clothes, I step into the bathtub. Much to my surprise, Patrick decides to join me in the tub. The music is playing softly, candles are lit all around the tub, and Patrick is pouring each of us a glass of wine.

"I would love to give you this all the time, Melissa. You deserve it, baby. Do you think you could get used to this lifestyle?" he asks.

"I'm so sure I could get used to this. Just know that what is *most* important to me is waking up next to you each day, Patrick. That's all I want. All I want is you", I tell him. I appreciate nice things, but I don't treasure them. I treasure the love between the two of us more than anything. I just don't want you to ever forget to love me. It doesn't matter to me whether I have all of this", I say, holding out my arms to indicate the luxury surrounding us, "but what I do care about is that I'm always the woman in your heart." *Is he crying? Is Patrick crying? Are my eyes deceiving me? I never thought I would ever see this man crying.*

"Melissa, I've never felt like this before in my life. I've never had a woman make me feel that it was all about me. I'm overwhelmed right now with what you just said to me", he says, giving me a bear hug. Even though we're in the water, I can still feel Patrick's manhood getting hard in my back. He pulls me around to face him and grabs my face with his hands and kisses me. I place my arms around his neck and return his passion with a tight hug. Our wet bodies are very close. Patrick grabs me by my waist, lifts me up, and places me on top of him so that I can straddle him and wrap my legs around him. He places himself inside me and starts making love to me. Patrick's mouth is so warm when he kisses me on my neck. The music, the candles, the lovemaking in the bathtub is sending this night off in the right way.

"Tell me you love me", I say to Patrick.

"I love you, baby. I love you with all of my heart", he says. I can tell that he is about to have an orgasm. He always makes this cute face right before he does. "Oh God, Melissa. You feel so good to me. I need you. Don't ever forget that!" There's something about this lovemaking tonight that feels different than any other night. It feels like Patrick and I have really bonded in a way that we have never bonded before. With him bringing me to his home, it makes me feel as though he's serious about this relationship. Little by little, he's letting me in and now, we're going on a trip to London together and life just can't get any better.

CHAPTER 28

"She's In God's Hands Now."

"Do you have everything that you can take?" I say to her. "I think so, Mommy", she responds.

"We're gonna miss you, Sharelle!", Justice yells, running into the room. She runs right to Sharelle.

"I'm gonna miss ya'll too", Sharelle says, fighting back the tears. "I'll be home in no time."

"It won't be the same here without you", Amber comments. "Who's going to do my hair so cute like you do?"

"That's sweet of you to say, Amber", Sharelle responds. "Both of you, please take care of Mommy. I worry about Mommy", she says.

"You bet we will!", Princess says, from the doorway. "I couldn't miss your departure lil' sis, so I asked for a new time to go in today. We'll definitely make sure that Momma is okay. We'll take care of her, sis."

Sharelle runs to Princess and gives her a big hug. They stand there for a few seconds embracing each other in a sisterly hug. "Thank you, sis. I really appreciate that", Sharelle mumbles.

"Ok, everybody. Break it up! Let's get some breakfast and enjoy our morning before Sharelle has to leave. Before Princess has to leave, we sit down and have breakfast. Princess says her goodbyes and leaves the house.

The ride to the Detention Center is a quiet one. Nobody wants to talk because we know what's about to happen. Justice breaks the quietness. "So, Sharelle, you gonna write me whenever you can?"

"Of course I am, Justice. Of course I am. I'll write you and send some drawings for you to hang up in your room. I'll keep drawing to keep myself busy."

"That's very important, Sharelle. Staying busy will keep your mind occupied and will keep you out of trouble. Please do that for me, for yourself. Stay out of trouble. Now, you heard what that attorney said. If you go down there and get into trouble and don't finish the program, you'll have to come back here and answer to those charges against you", I tell her.

"I got it Ma. I got it. I'm not interested in getting into any more trouble. I'm going down there to do what I'm supposed to do so that I can come back home", she responds.

We finally make it to the Detention Center. This place looks so cold and uninviting. I guess the idea is to make it where kids hate it so much that they don't want to come back. But, for whatever reason, there are so many young people who return to this cold place over and over again, my daughter being one of them. "Ok, we're here, honey. Let me get your bag out of the car. Sharelle and Amber both get out of the car. "Give me a hug." As much as I want to cry, I can't cry. I don't want to make her think I'm being weak or anything of the sort.

Before Sharelle has to go, I decide that we should pray. *Dear God. Thank you for waking us up this morning. Thank you for watching over our family throughout the night. Thank you for bringing us safely to this place this morning. Lord, Sharelle has to leave and we come to you asking you to watch over her while she is away in this program. Comfort her when she is scared, lonely, or angry. Be her guide and give her wisdom. Protect her from any dangers. Lord, get her and the other inmates safely to their destination this morning. Be a best friend to her, Lord, when she feels friendless. Give us, her family, patience to endure the time that Sharelle is away. Keep her safe, Lord. These and other blessings we ask in thy son Jesus' name. Amen.*

We say our final goodbyes to Sharelle and watch her walk down the long sidewalk to the Detention Center, where they told her to report. They will transport her to Stuartville, where she will spend the next several months. Most likely, she won't be home for Christmas and will spend it in the residential program. I'll have to continue to trust God to give me the peace to deal with this. I know that it was her choices that put her in this position, but she's my daughter and I just want to hold onto her. My children are growing up and I don't want to lose them to this system. This just reminds me that I need to call all of my kids just to let them know that I love them.

Back home now, I need to take some time for myself. Seeing Sharelle leave like this has me in an emotional tailspin. That, coupled with the fact that I'm unemployed right now, has me feeling as if God has left me.

"Hey girls, can you do me a favor? Can ya'll just hang out for a while so that I can get some rest? I just really need to spend some time with God right now."

"Mommy, you okay?" Amber asks.

"I will be, honey. I will be. I just need to spend some time alone to think about things and relax. I'll be fine", I say to them.

"Ok, Mommy. Can we order a movie?"

"May I. It's 'May I order a movie'?" I correct her.

"Ok, Mommy. May we order a movie?" Justice asks.

"Sure. You may order 2 movies only. By that time, I'll be ready to get up and fix us some dinner."

Walking to my bedroom, I start thinking about everything. It's been a couple of days and I haven't heard from Patrick. We're supposed to be leaving out tomorrow for London. *What am I thinking? He's probably getting himself prepared for our departure and purchasing some items for the trip. I don't know, but what if he is out shopping for my ring right now. I mean, why else would he want to go to London? Now, I'm really losing my mind. What's this empty feeling that I'm having deep down in my spirit? Is it that I'm already starting to miss my daughter or is it that the Spirit of God is trying to warn me about something. I don't know what this uneasy feeling is. I should just get some rest.*

The picture of Patrick next to my bed gives me a refreshing feeling. He has the cutest smile in this photo. It reminds me of how we felt the night we went to my favorite restaurant and the photographer snapped our photo as we were getting out of the limousine. He treated me like a Queen that night. *I wonder what he's doing right now.* Curious as I don't know what, I pick up the phone and dial his number. It goes directly to voice mail, so I leave a message. As soon as he gets the message, I have no doubt that he'll call me back. *Don't tell me this man's going to stand me up.*

My bags are all packed and Diana is scheduled to come over tomorrow to stay with the girls while I'm away on my trip. She's so happy for me because she of all people knows that I desperately need to spend some time with a *real* man. I just remembered that Cynthia called and left a message for me while we were out. I hope she hasn't fallen asleep yet.

"Hey girl! You doing okay? Cynthia asks. "Ready for your trip tomorrow?"

"I think so. I've packed everything. I hope that I haven't forgotten anything."

"You got all your sexy lingerie in that suitcase, right?" she asks. We both laugh. "What time are you all flying out?"

"Now, you know I do", I tell her. "Our flight leaves at 11am. We just came from dropping Sharelle off to the Detention Center. I think I'm feeling sad about that. I miss her already and I worry about her being there, but I do trust God to watch over her. I don't really have a choice, but you remember that boy that got killed in one of those places a few years back, right?" I ask.

"Yes, I remember. Who doesn't? That was tragic. But, Melissa, trust God on this. Trust Him to have her back and watch over her. She's in His hands now. Leave Sharelle and that whole situation with God and don't you worry about it", Cynthia encourages.

"You're right! I prayed about it and now I have to leave it in God's hands. I have to. It's the only way."

"Okay, so cheer up! You sound sad. You're leaving tomorrow to go to a place that you never thought you would ever go to and you're going with a man who really loves you. Now, that's something to be happy about. But, go ahead and get you some rest. You'll need it. I'm sure that Patrick has all kinds of fun and excitement planned for the two of you. Do you need me to do anything for you while you're away?" Cynthia asks.

"You think you could find a job for me and have it ready for me when I return?" I say, sarcastically.

"Girl, you're crazy. Bye, Melissa!"

We hang up the phone with each other, but for some reason, I have a weird feeling in my gut and I don't know why. I don't know where it's coming from. *It just dawned on me that I have been talking to Cynthia for quite a while now and Patrick hasn't returned my call. Where is he? Where is he? I haven't heard from him. Melissa, stop worrying! The man is just busy. If there was something wrong, he would have called you by now.*

I crawl into my bed and pull the covers up to my neck. It's chilly in here. The girls must have turned the air conditioner down, but I tend to get colder than everyone else. My eyes are starting to get tired, so sleep is probably not that far away.

I know I need to get some rest. The chamomile tea is most likely going to do the trick and help me to relax and calm down my spirit.

CHAPTER 29

He Hasn't Been Here."

"*M*ommy, wake up! Wake up!" Justice says, jumping on my bed.

"Oh my God! What! What happened?" I ask, in total shock, having been awakened in this manner.

"You have to get dressed for your trip. It's morning!" she yells.

Did I sleep throughout the night? Why didn't the girls wake me up last night?

"Did I sleep all night?" I ask. "Why didn't ya'll wake me up last night?"

"You were sleeping so peacefully and we know you've been tired lately, so we figured you needed to sleep", she answers.

"Did Patrick call?" I ask.

"No. Not that I know of."

I grab my phone to see if he left a message or anything and nothing. Not a missed call, nor a text message, or anything. *Was he that busy that he couldn't return my call? What's going on here?*

Dear Lord. Thank you for waking me up this morning. Thank you for watching over me throughout the night. Thank you for watching over my children and keeping us safe. Lord, I don't know what this feeling of uneasiness that I have, but I ask that you will watch over us today as we leave this country to travel to London. Be with us, Lord. Go with us on that plane and fly with us all the way to London and protect us even after we make it to London. I ask you in Jesus' name. Amen.

"Mommy, get up! You're going to be late. Patrick's gonna come and you're not going to be dressed", Amber says, tugging at me to get in the shower.

I can hear keys turning in the front door. It's Diana! She has keys to my home in the event she has to pick the girls up for me or run errands of any sort. "Somebody is going to London today!" Diana yells, making her way into my bedroom. I'm already in the shower.

"Hey Diana! Thanks for coming!" I yell, from the shower.

"It's my pleasure to hang out with my beautiful nieces for the entire week. And besides, you're bringing me something back from London, aren't you?"

"Of course I'm going to bring all of you something back", I yell, from the shower. "Hand me my towel, please!"

I jump out of the shower and put on my comfortable, traveling clothes. Diana is standing by watching me apply my makeup and doing a verbal checklist with me to make sure that I don't forget anything. Everyone knows that I can be forgetful at times.

"Passport? Where is it?" Diana asks.

"In my purse, Diana. I'm not *that* crazy. That's the most important thing", I say, as we both laugh.

"Ok, so what time is Patrick supposed to be here?" Diana asks, looking down at her watch.

"Well, let's see. The plane leaves at 11 and we need to be there at least an hour ahead of time. He should be here soon", I answer.

"Did you talk to him this morning?" she asks.

"No. I didn't. I called him last night, but he didn't return my call. It's almost 9:30 and I still haven't heard from him, Diana. Oh God! What's wrong?"

"Stop worrying! I'm sure he's already on his way. Call him!" she suggests.

I pick up the phone and dial his number and it goes straight to voice mail. "Diana! It went straight to voice mail. Now, what do I do?" I say, almost sounding like I'm in a panic.

"Honey, I'm sure that there's a good explanation for this. Do you know the home phone number?"

"No. I don't. I know the work number. Let me try that number and see if anyone saw him there", I say.

I pick up the phone and dial his work number and I get his receptionist, Amy. "Amy, Hello. This is Melissa Thomas, one of Dr. Norwood's friends. I'm expecting him shortly and was wondering if he's been in the office today."

"I'm not supposed to discuss this, but I've seen you here a few times and he did tell us that he was going away with you, but I have to tell you this. He has not been in the office for the whole week. He wouldn't tell us where he was going, but just said that we should contact him on his cell phone if he was needed", she explains.

"Ok. Thank you, Amy."

"Did he not show up or something? Aren't you supposed to leave today?" she asks.

"Yes we were. I am really concerned about him now. Thanks again."

"So, what did she say?" Diana asks, standing by anxiously waiting.

"She said that he hasn't been in the office all week", I say, running to the bathroom. I haven't eaten anything, but I feel like throwing up. All of a sudden, the blood is rushing straight to my head. I slam the door behind me.

"Girls, go in the family room. Shut the door behind you. Let me talk to your Mother. She'll be okay. Okay, trust Auntie. I got it", Diana says, shutting the door behind them.

"Melissa, are you okay in there?" I ask through the door.

"Diana, please leave. I'll be okay. It doesn't look like I'll need you now. I just want to be alone. Please leave", I beg, trying to hide the fact that I'm crying.

"MeMe, I'm not going anywhere, so you might as well stop saying that. I'm going to be right here with you to walk you through this. Please unlock the door. Don't shut me out. Talk to me. I'm your sister and I love you. We will get through this okay", Diana says.

"I'm okay, Diana. I'm okay. Don't worry about me!" I yell.

"You're my baby sister. Of course I worry about you, so please, don't shut me out of your life this time. Let me be here for you through this."

I might as well unlock the door because it doesn't look like Diana is going anywhere. "It's unlocked!" I yell.

Diana opens the door and she finds me on the floor in fetal position. She runs over to me and makes me sit up. "Melissa, come on now. You didn't let Kalin take you down and you're not going to let this take you down. We are stronger than that. You pick yourself up and move on. I'm sure that there's an explanation for all of this. I don't believe that Patrick would do this to you like this. Come on. Let's go in the room and talk", Diana suggests.

I get off the floor and go back into the bedroom, throwing Patrick's picture to the floor. I can't stand to look at him right now. *Now, I know why I was having uneasiness in my gut. The Spirit was warning me that this was coming. I felt like something was wrong. I guess I knew something was coming, but I had no idea that it would be this.*

"Now, why did you do that Melissa?" Diana asks.

"Because right now, I hate him! I hate all men! They are all alike. They get a kick out of hurting us. They get us to fall in love with them and then boom, it's all over! This man made me feel like a Queen last week. He made me feel like he wanted me in his life and now he's gone! Just like that! No call, no letter, no text, no email message or anything. How could he do this, Diana? How? You tell me how this man who made me feel so beautiful, take my hurt away, and then turn around and rip my heart to pieces? I trusted him with my heart", I say, starting to cry uncontrollably.

"Let it all out, Melissa. Let it all out! Come here, sis!" Diana says, giving me a hug and rocking me like I'm a baby in her mother's arms. "God's got you, sis. God has never left and He never will. It doesn't matter who comes and who goes, He's always with you. Lean to him, Melissa. Don't beat yourself up over this."

"Here I was thinking that I had met a real man who loved me and really wanted to be a part of my life. He didn't do any better than Kalin. Maybe it's just not meant for me to have a man in my life who'll really love me for me. I'm so tired, Diana. I can only take so much. And then on top of all this, I'm going through this divorce from Kalin. It is just all too much hurt. How much am I supposed to take? Huh? Tell me, sis. When will I finally meet a man who can make me happy and give me what I used to believe I deserved?" I say, crying.

"Melissa, stop it! Just stop it! I'm not going to let you sit here and feel sorry for yourself. I'm not going to do it. I can't do it. Ok, so your marriage didn't work out. You should have left his raggedy behind a long time ago, if you ask me! Patrick messed up, but sweetie, please let the man explain himself. I'm sure that there's an explanation for this. Pick yourself up. Let me ask you a question. What is it that finally made you decide to leave Kalin? I was always curious to know that", Diana asks. "But hold that thought. I noticed that you have some Smirnoff in your refrigerator. Let me grab some and have us a good ol' sisterly time today. I know you gotta have some chips in here, too, somewhere."

Diana returns with a six pack of Smirnoff and a big bag of barbecue potato chips. How perfect! It's almost lunchtime anyway. The girls are content in the family room and enjoying each other's company. Princess left for work already. "The girls are okay. I told them that they can order a movie. I hope that's okay", Diana says, handing me my Smirnoff.

"It's fine. It's fine."

"Ok, so I am listening. Tell me. What was it?" Diana asks.

"What was what?" I ask, opening my Smirnoff.

"That made you finally leave Kalin. I can't wait to hear this because you were so in love with this man and wouldn't listen to anything anyone tried to tell you about him."

"It got to a point that I was no longer attracted to him because of the person he was turning into. He had started being mean to me and to the girls. I will never forget the day that he hit Justice in the head, punishing her for not doing something he asked her to do. That is exactly how he used to hit me in the head. I knew then that I had to get away from him and protect my children before all of us ended up dead", I say. Diana's mouth is wide open.

"Are you serious, Melissa? He had started being abusive to the girls?"

"Worse than that, he was even starting to call them "b------". Kalin said that if they act like that, then that is what they are", I tell her. "Can you believe a father would call his own girls by that name?"

"Wow, this jerk was actually worse than I thought he was. I swear I don't know what you ever saw in him. I hate him all over again", I say.

"Things were bad in the end, Diana. I was constantly going on his email account and seeing where he was still communicating with that lady, Diandra that he met in Alabama. He had been telling me all along that she and he were just friends, but their emails together were, to me, inappropriate for him to be a married man. He made it seem like I was the crazy one. He continued being friends with her even though he knew that she was interested in a relationship with him. He flat out told me that he would not discontinue a friendship with her. I stopped being the most important person to him and little by little, he would prove that to me", I say, taking a long gulp from my Smirnoff.

"Wow! I can't believe you endured so much with this man; but, yet, you always seemed so happy with him, Melissa", she says.

"Yes. I did, didn't I? I had to. He made me act that way to keep people out of our business. He was very manipulative and mean. People thought he was this really nice guy who always seemed to be the loudest one in the church saying "Amen", but he was horrible at home with his wife and kids. He managed to get people on the outside to love him, but in his own home, we didn't respect him at all", I explain.

"Did you still have sex with him even though you knew that he was cheating on you?" Diana asks.

"Yes. Yes I did. We had the best sex. That was one area where he mastered and that is probably the last thing we had to hold onto. He acted like he was in love with me when we had sex. That was the *only* time he acted like he loved me."

"You used to be able to hide it, Melissa, but I'm your sister and I know you. Remember? I'm the one you used to live with when you were in high school. We used to fool me back then when you and your little friends swore up and down that you were out studying and we know how that turned out, don't we?" she comments. We both laugh.

"Well, we were!" I say, laughing. "But seriously, Diana, I was so in love with him that it would just make me cry thinking about him sometimes. But, he changed. He changed and started treating me like I was the woman he was cheating with and his allegiance belonged to other women. I felt like he was more concerned about their needs than he was concerned about mine and …", I say, but she interrupts.

"But you stayed with him all those years and that's the thing that's so hard to believe. Why? How could you?" she asks.

"Because of my faith in God. I thought that I had to go through some things in the marriage to make it work. I thought that I was being an honorable woman by taking everything from him and my belief was that God would change him around at some point."

"There are so many women that believe just like you did and they're living miserable lives, thinking that what they are putting up with is God's plan for their life. Although I believe God creates marriages, I believe that they're meant to build you up and not tear you down. And you, my dear sister, were down! You had actually gotten to the point where you just stopped looking happy. Is that when you were finally ready to end the marriage?" Diana asks, taking a sip of her Smirnoff.

"I think so. I mean, I allowed myself to flirt with Patrick and that's something that I never thought I would have ever done. I used to look forward to receiving his calls, his texts, and his cards. He was so thoughtful and at first, I tried to resist him, but things *really* started to get horrible at home. I opened up to the possibility of being with him more and more. I don't think I even cared if Kalin caught me or not", I admit.

"And did he?" Diana asks.

"Did he what?"

"Did Kalin ever catch you?" she asks again.

"Yes, he did. Yes. He found a message that Patrick sent me once and he questioned him. Kalin even went to the man's job to question him about the two of us", I tell her.

"No he didn't! You mean to tell me that Kalin got balls? I can't believe that! And, how did Patrick respond to that?" Diana asks.

"He basically defended his love for me. He didn't back down and I think that his reaction to everything somewhat intimidated Kalin. But whatever happened that day, Kalin came home and packed his things and moved out of the house. I didn't apologize about Patrick. He was there when I needed it and Kalin, little by little, pushed me away", I say, grabbing a few potato chips.

"It sounds to me like you and Patrick have something special", Diana says.

"Yeah, I thought we had something special. Where is he, Diana? Where is he? He stood me up. He had me thinking that we were going on a trip to London together. I mean he laid it on. He didn't even have the decency to call me and let me know that he wouldn't be here. I haven't heard from him all week. And he hasn't even been to the job all week either. So, what did he do? Did he just skip out of town by himself? Oh my God! That's what he did! He went on the trip without me and took someone else!" I say, yelling, standing to my feet, and walking over to my phone to dial the airline to see if he loaded the plane.

"Melissa, who are you calling?" Diana asks, now standing next to me looking at the phone.

"I want to see if this a------ boarded that plane. How dare he do this to me, Diana? How could he? How could he hurt me like this?" I say, waiting on someone to pick up the phone.

A customer service rep finally picks up the phone and after giving her the reference number, she was able to confirm that Patrick did not board the plane to London. "See, Melissa! He didn't leave either! Now, will you stop with the foolish behavior! I'm thinking that something must have drastically happened to him. Has he ever done anything like this before?

Think about it, Melissa. I know your heart is broken, but something could be wrong", Diana insists.

Dear Lord. Thank you for everything Lord, the good..the bad..and even the things that I don't understand. I ask you Lord to please watch over Patrick right now. You know where he is and what he is going through right now. Send your Spirit to comfort him. Give him peace, Lord. Please, please, Lord. In Jesus' name, Amen.

By the time I'm done praying, my face is full of tears and my heart is bleeding. *I don't know how I will get past this. I don't know if I want to get past it. I feel like I want to give up right now. I loved Kalin and he hurt me to my soul. I loved Patrick and he hurt me to my soul. Why? Why? I didn't do anything to hurt him. I couldn't imagine hurting my worst enemy this way. The pain in my heart is making me have a loss of breath. I don't know if I have ever felt this kind of pain in my heart. I don't want to go on, Lord. This is it for me. Why did he hurt me like this? What did I do wrong? I loved him with everything I have to give and it wasn't enough.*

"Melissa, don't cry. Please don't cry. You're gonna make me cry. I don't understand it either, but just trust God, sis. You've always trusted Him for everything. You're the strongest woman I know", she says, starting to cry. "Give me a hug."

"I don't want to be strong!" I yell. "I want to be loved!"

"Sweetie, I know! I'm so sorry!" she says, consoling me.

Diana and I embrace in a sisterly hug. I don't think I can ever remember a time that she and I bonded this way. "Thank you, Diana, for being here. I really mean it. Thank you", I say, letting her go, wiping her tears away. "Let's watch a movie on Lifetime. This is the best time since our emotions are already all over the place."

We leave my room and go into the family room. It's Pick-a-Flick Friday and random movies are being selected. There's a good one on about a man who ends up cheating on his wife, but with a man. "Time for the popcorn! Looks like it's going to be an all-nighter", I say.

CHAPTER 30

"I Want My Life Back."

"What do you need me to do?" he asks.

"Sir, please put your urine in this cup?" the nurse instructs.

"Right here?" he asks. "I sure hope I can go."

"Yes. And when you're done with that, meet me in the Lab so that we can pull some blood", the nurse directs.

"Oh no! I hate needles", he laughs. "Look at me acting like a baby."

The tests are all done and the doctor walks into his office, where his patient is awaiting the results. "Good evening, Sir. How was your flight to Connecticut?"

"The flight was fine. I'm more anxious to know what's wrong with me?" he says.

"We'll get to that soon enough. How have you been feeling lately?" Dr. Phillips asks.

"Tired. Helpless. Drained. I take my vitamins every single day, but it doesn't do any good. I want my energy back. I want my good health back. I want my life back, Doc", he comments.

"I know. I know you do. Let's get to the results."

"Okay. That sounds good to me. That's what I need to hear right about now."

"Sir, are you okay for me to give it to you straight?" the Doctor asks.

"I can handle it. I'm a doctor myself. Just tell me, please", he pleads.

"Sir, there's a tumor that seems to be growing and from the tests that we have done so far, I'm not really sure why. There's still research being done about this rare disease that you have. So, because this disease is so rare, I'm going to bring in a specialist and friend of mine from London to look at it and give me his opinion", the Doctor explains.

"Oh, so the tumor is getting even bigger?" he asks. "And you don't know why?"

"Yes, it is. All of your vitals are looking good right now, which is the good news. I'm happy that, at least, there's no fever or anything else that looks out of whack. We just need to get this tumor out of you", the Doctor responds. "But, we need to keep it from growing. I don't like the fact that it's growing inside of you."

"So, tell me about this doctor who's coming from London?"

"His name is Shem. That's what I call him, but he's Dr. Smith. He's a good friend of mine and he's very knowledgeable when it comes to some of these unknown diseases. He should be here Friday, so I'll need you to stick around", the Doctor explains.

"Of course. I'm here for as long as I need to be. I have had to rearrange all of my affairs just to see about my health", he tells the Doctor.

"I'm sure that it wasn't easy to have to say goodbye to your family and friends under these circumstances."

"..and it's even worse when you don't say goodbye and just leave", he says.

"Oh no. That's not the way to do it. I'm sure they're all worried about you", the Doctor tells him.

"I know they are; especially, the love of my life. She's probably wondering why I left her just when we were discussing our life together", he says.

"And, you didn't think you could tell her the truth?" he asks.

"I didn't want to put her through this", he tells him.

"Oh, I see. Well, I'm going to have my nurse take your information. I'll see you on Friday. Try to get out of the hotel and get some sights in, but whatever you do, please try to relax."

"I'll try my best."

CHAPTER 31

"She's Done It Again!"

"Sharelle Williams!" the Officer yells.

"Yes ma'am. I'm here!"

"Stop goofing off and stay in line or you're going to find yourself back where you don't want to be. I'm not playing with you. We ain't here to play with you. Now, stop playing!"

"Oooh Sharelle, she told you", the girl standing next to Sharelle mumbles.

"Shut up!" Sharelle shouts.

"That's it, Sharelle! Come here!" the Officer yells, walking towards Sharelle.

"Ma'am, I wasn't talking to you, I was talking to her", Sharelle tries to explain, pointing to the girl standing next to her. The Officer is not trying to hear Sharelle's explanation, but instead, takes her away to confinement. She writes up the report and heads down to the main office to complain to the Director about Sharelle's behavior.

"She's done it again", the Officer tells Director Stephens.

"Who?" the Director asks.

"Sharelle. I don't know what the deal is with that child. She's very polite, which tells me she was raised the right way, but why is she always running her mouth? I don't get that. I think that you should give her mother a call and explain to her that if her behavior continues, we'll eventually move her out of this program and send her to a high risk facility", the Officer says.

"Alrighty. I sure will. Let me get her file and review it. This child is hard to figure out", the Director agrees.

Within minutes, she's flipping through the pages of Sharelle's file and getting mre familiar with her family structure and what it was that landed her in the facility. She doesn't know what to think when she reads how Sharelle was consistently, throughout the years, an honor roll student, served in organizations in her schools and church. But, she clearly sees where it all started. It was Sharelle's 7th grade year when she started missing school and running away, prostituting on the streets to support herself. It's no wonder that Sharelle finally got picked up one night while in the car with a well known pedophile, who called himself, "Darkness". His criminal background looks all too familiar. In this case, he's charged with sex trafficking and Sharelle just may have to eventually testify against him.

"Oh my goodness!" Director Stephens blurts out.

"Why? What's there?" the Officer asks.

"Now, you know I can't discuss that with you, but I appreciate you for pointing this young lady out to me. She definitely needs our help. Ok, you may be excused now", John tells her.

John reads over the file again, just to make sure he hasn't missed anything and makes a phone call. "Sheree, please get me the Counseling Group", she says.

"Ok", the receptionist agrees.

Within a few minutes, John is on the phone with Maria, the head of the Counseling Group, and they're going back and forth about Sharelle. "I see that this child has had some serious events to take place in her life and I want to make sure that she's getting counseling. Is she set up to receive counseling from your group?" John asks.

"What's her name again?" Maria asks.

"It's Sharelle Williams", John responds.

"No. I don't see that she's one of our patients just yet", says Maria.

"Well, I can't think of anyone who needs it more. Please come over and pick up a copy of her file and get her set up for counseling immediately", John instructs.

Maria makes it to John's office and gladly receives the file, flipping through the pages as if it's a good book. John can't help but notice how moved Maria seems to get after reading the family history.

"We need to help this young lady. It seems as if she's just been passed around from person to person in her life. Please get her in the program as soon as you can", the Director tells her.

"Ok. It's a done deal. I know we can help her. Thanks for bringing this to our attention", Maria says, turning around to leave John's office.

CHAPTER 32

"There Has to be a Reason."

"**H**ey Ma!" Darren yells from the other side of the phone.

"Hey boy! Why are you so happy today?" I ask him.

"Because I'm talking to the most beautiful mom in the world!" he shouts.

"Boy, stop acting crazy! What's wrong with you this morning and why are you calling me so early in the morning?"

"Oh, I didn't even think about what time it is there", he responds. "Mom, I have great news!"

"What is it? I would love to hear some good news."

"I'm coming home for two weeks! Aren't you excited?" he asks.

"That *is* certainly great news! I'm very happy about this. I miss having all of you here in the house. Is Kameron coming with you?"

"Now you know he is. He's using his vacation time to come home", he says.

"And you're coming just because?" I ask.

"Yes, Mother. We love you and I know that Sharelle is gone and Auntie D told us about what happened with Patrick and we just love you, Ma. We just love you."

"That's so sweet, Darren. When you all get here, maybe we can get a visit in to see Sharelle. Would you like that?" I ask.

"Of course. Of course I'd love to go see her. We're leaving out tomorrow night. So, please have my bed ready because I'm probably going to jump into it as soon as I get there", Darren tells me.

Hanging up the phone, I run to give the girls the good news. I'm not surprised with their reaction to this news. Justice is jumping around and chanting, "My brother is coming, coming, coming...my brother is coming home!"

Amber walks in and asks, "What's all this noise for? I'm trying to study!"

"Darren and Kameron are coming home in a couple of days! Isn't that exciting, Amber?"

"Mom, are they really?" Amber asks, looking towards Mom.

"You heard her!! They're coming home!"

Dear God. Thank you for my children and Lord, please look over Darren and Kameron who will be leaving Philadelphia to get on the road to travel to Florida. Keep them safe. Keep their eyes opened. In Jesus' name, Amen.

I know what I have to do now. I need to get their old room straightened up and take some of the things out of there so they can get in it. I had used their room to store some of my files. Guess it's time to put them back in the office. I might as well do something else because applying for these jobs is starting to get super boring and I still haven't had one callback for a job interview. *I had no idea that it would take me this long to find a job with all the skills that I have. I guess I have to stop looking at the sales jobs that I would always look right past, but whatever the case may be, I want my boys to enjoy their time here and I don't want to stress them with my issues. I have almost used all of the money from the severance check.*

"Mommy, you have mail!" Justice yells. "I almost forgot!"

She hands me the stack of mail that she pulled out of the mailbox and the first thing on the top of the pile is a letter from Mr. Abney, my divorce attorney. Ripping the letter open, I get a sick feeling in my stomach. I don't know why that is. It can't be that I'm having second thoughts about divorcing Kalin, can it? *Or is it? Am I making a mistake and walking away from this 18-year marriage? Do we have issues that can be worked out or am I just feeling lonely because Patrick is no longer in the picture?*

The first line of the letter let me know that there's still more to pull together before we can even think about going into a courtroom. It seems that there's more paperwork that I need to fill out, which is the paperwork that makes the court aware of what it is that I'm asking for in the divorce. I need some time because I never really thought about this at all.

It's been several weeks since Patrick has disappeared and I'm finally able to get a little more rest at night. Nobody has heard from him.

I've tried contacting his office and they're close-mouthed about his whereabouts. I even tried to make contact with his son, but no luck there. It's hard to prepare my heart to let him go. There are so many unresolved issues about this that I can't imagine walking away until they're resolved. I can't stop the tears from flowing. I try to hide it from everyone and make them think that it no longer bothers me, but I cry myself to sleep at night. I fell in love with him, but he left me just like that, without so much as a goodbye.

"Momma, when will Darren and Kameron get here?" Justice asks, taking me out of my trance.

"Oh! They'll be here by tomorrow afternoon. So, we have some work to do to get everything all straightened out for them", I tell her. "You wanna help me?"

"Sure, Mommy. I don't have a problem helping you. I'm glad they're coming. It'll be good to have them here again. How long are they staying?"

"I'm not sure, but however long it is will be fun, don't you think?"

Justice and I start moving all of the boxes out of Darren and Kameron's old room and start placing them in the office. The room is starting to feel better already. I have to admit that all of this household activity is making me feel better and causing me to think and worry less about Patrick. It doesn't last long because out of the blue, I start getting sad and have to excuse myself for a moment and go to my room to be alone.

"Mommy, where are you going?" Justice asks, looking puzzled.

"I'm going to my room for just a moment. I'll be right back", I tell her.

"Okay!" Justice has no choice but to accept this answer, so she walks into the family room and flips on the television.

On my bed and looking up at the ceiling, I decide that it's time to have a real conversation with God. *Oh God! Please help me deal with this sadness. Why did this man hurt me so much? Why did he do this to me? Why? Once I get over Patrick, I don't ever want to feel love in my heart like this for another man! Kalin hurt me to the point where I wanted to die! And now Patrick has left me. He made me feel like he really cared for me and loved me and wanted to take me to places I had never been. What did I do that was so horrible for this man or any other man to hurt me to the point of not wanting to breathe again? Dear God, please help me get through this! I can't do it without you. I can't!*

"Mommy, what's wrong in there? Are you crying?" Justice yells from outside my door.

I stop crying so that she won't hear it in my voice. "No, honey, I'm okay. That's the television!" I yell to her. I feel bad for telling this untruth to my daughter.

"Oh, okay! Well hurry back so that we can finish with getting the house ready!" she yells.

I know that I really don't have time to grieve through this process because my children constantly need me and whenever I get a moment to myself, it's always interrupted. *Maybe I shouldn't be grieving after all. Just maybe this is God's way of saying that I should be with my husband. I know I'm feeling very lonely right now. Maybe I'll call Kalin later on just to see how he's doing.*

"Ok, you ready to get back to work?" I say, opening my bedroom door and walking into the family room.

"Let's tackle the kitchen next", Justice says. Amber just walked downstairs and agrees to help.

We spend the rest of the afternoon getting our household chores done. Since they've done such a good job helping, I decide to take them both out for a late lunch. We jump in the car and head to Chic-Fil-A. They have the best chicken sandwiches in the world and anyone with half a brain knows that you can't deny that their ice cream is the best tasting homemade ice cream ever.

"Mommy, there's daddy!" Justice yells, as we pull into the parking lot.

Oh God! I hope he is alone and not with someone else because that is going to crush her spirit. Please God, let him be alone.

"He sees us and is coming our way. Can I get out, Mommy?" Justice asks, looking over at me.

"Sure, honey. Go talk to your father."

She and Amber both jump out of the car and run into his arms. *I have to admit that he looks quite scrumptious today. What am I thinking? No, Melissa, no! You are divorcing this man, remember?*

"Hello Melissa. You know you looking good standing over there. You can give me a hug, too, you know", he says, looking at me like he did many years ago. *Oh God! You know I want to. I miss being held, but I can't come off as weak before I end up doing something that I will later regret.*

"Nah, I'm good right where I am. Thanks, though."

We all walk inside and order our food. Since he's alone, he decides to sit down with us and eat lunch. It was good for the girls because they don't get to see him that much since we've separated. It appears that Kalin is extremely happy to see them. I know I've heard him say "I love you both so much" at least 5 times.

"Melissa, if it is okay with you, I'd like to pick the girls up on Saturday to take them shopping", Kalin says. *That is a nice gesture for him to make. I'm shocked and pleasantly surprised to see him make such an effort to spend time with his children. It would be nice if he would throw some money this way to help me take care of them.*

"That's fine with me, Kalin. Girls?" I ask, looking towards them.

"Yesssssss!" Justice shouts. Amber joins in. They both give him a hug.

"And one more thing, Melissa", he says, walking towards me.

"What is it?" I ask him.

"Next month, I'm traveling to Alabama for the Christmas holidays and I would love for Justice and Amber to go with me. My mother has not seen them in at least 2 years and it would mean a lot to me if you would allow them to go with me", he asks, looking quite sincere. I look at them and they look as if they agree with him.

"If they want to go, I'm fine with it. This year has been trying for all of us and I just think they deserve to have a good Christmas. So, if they want to go, I'm okay with it. How long will you be up there?" I ask.

"For 2 weeks", he answers. The look on my face must have spoken disappointment because Justice releases herself from Kalin and runs to me and says, "Mommy, I don't want you to be sad."

"No, sweetheart. Mommy will be just fine. I want you to go and enjoy yourselves. You deserve to. You know you don't want to miss out on grandma's good cooking", I tell her.

"Are you sure, Mommy?" Amber asks.

"I'm sure."

It looks like I'll be spending the holidays alone, unless Christy, Darren, and Kameron come home. Kalin will take them shopping this weekend and a month from now, they'll be on their way to Alabama. *I wonder if he will spend time with his so-called friend, Diandra, while he's there. He doesn't have to hide it anymore since the secret is out that we're getting a divorce. As long as he doesn't try to pull this happy family thing with him, her, and my children, we are cool.*

We head back home and the entire way back home, they're reminiscing about the last time we traveled to Alabama as a family. *The first thing that comes to my mind is how me and Kalin sneaked off to the laundry room while everyone else was asleep and had the hottest sex ever. We were really craving each other. Snap out of it, Melissa! What's with me today thinking about Kalin and the past? I must be even lonelier than I thought!*

By the time, we make it home, Darren and Kameron are already parked in the driveway. They have already let themselves in and are probably eating something. I open the door and they both come hugging on me like they did when they were little boys. "Ma! It's so good to see you. You look wonderful!" Darren says, kissing me on the cheek and lifting me in the air.

"Boy, put me down!" I yell. "Hey Kameron! Give me a hug, boy. Look how big you have both gotten. Neither of you are my *little boys* anymore", I say.

"No, Ma, we aren't", Darren says, heading back into the kitchen to finish making his sandwich.

"Hey big brothers!" Justice yells, giving Kameron a big brotherly hug. She jumps on his back and off to the family room they go. Darren finishes making his sandwich and he joins her. Flipping through the channels, Justice finds *"High School Musical"* and at first, the boys complain about watching this, but she convinces them to watch it with her. Because she's the youngest, she usually gets her way with her big brothers.

"Momma, I talked to Christy yesterday and she said that she'll be here for Thanksgiving", Darren blurts out.

"Did she?!!" I ask. "I had no idea that she was coming! This is just wonderful. All of my kids will be here except Sharelle."

"Oh yeah. How is she doing in that Program?" Jonathan asks.

"So far, so good", I say.

"Momma, did you hear from that guy, Patrick, yet?"

"No, son. I haven't heard from Patrick and I am ....", I begin to say before Kameron interrupts.

"He hasn't called you either?" Darren asks, shaking his head.

"No, son. I haven't heard anything. It's almost as if he dropped off the face of the earth and all I can do now is just pray for him that he's okay and …", I say, before Darren interrupts.

"Ma, just let it go! Forget him. You don't need him anyway. I'm tired of all of these selfish and no good men coming in and out of your life. And I hope Kalin punk ass don't come around here no more!" Darren says, grabbing the pillow and placing it underneath his head.

"Darren! How dare you use that kind of language in this house? How dare you disrespect me like that? What has gotten into you, boy?" I yell at him.

"I'm sorry, Ma! Sorry! I didn't mean to disrespect you. Please forgive me for cussing, but I meant what I said about your husband", he says angrily.

"Calm down, man", Kameron says. "Momma has been through enough."

The four of us finish watching the movie. For me, I'd like to pretend that this conversation never took place.

"Ma, what's for dinner?" Darren asks.

"Your favorite", I tell him.

"Cabbages! Yeah!" he says, kissing me on the cheek

When the movie is over, I head to the kitchen and prepare the food and put it on the table. Princess makes it home just in time for dinner. She seems to be happy to see her brothers.

"Ma, Sharelle's on the phone", Amber says, handing me the phone.

"Hello."

"Hey Ma! How you doing?" Sharelle asks.

"I'm doing fine, sweetheart. It's so good to hear your voice. Guess who's here!" I say.

"Who?" she asks.

"Kameron and Darren. They came down for the week. It was a surprise. I had no idea that they were going to be here until they called and told me."

"That's really awesome, Ma. You need them to be there with you so that you won't be too sad about Patrick. Has he called yet?" she asks.

"No, he hasn't. He hasn't called."

"Mommy, you sound sad", she comments.

"Well, I'm still sad, honey. I am. This really hurt me. But, at this point, I'm just worried about him", I respond.

"I can't talk long. I just wanted you to know that I'm okay", she explains.

"I'm glad to hear that. And Sharelle, please stay out of trouble."

"I will, Ma. Don't worry. This is a piece of cake", she says. "I should be out of here in no time."

"That's great news, Sharelle. I'm so happy to hear that. So, you're staying out of trouble and everything, right?"

"Absolutely! Get back to the family. I gotta go anyway, Ma. Tell everyone I said hey and bye and I love them."

"I sure will."

After dinner, everyone retires to their bedrooms for some much needed rest. It's been a long day for all of us. Now that I'm in rest mode, I just remembered my friends telling me about FACEBOOK and that I should go online and meet new people. They tell me that it's a good way to take my mind off Patrick. Honestly, I don't think that there is anything that could take my mind off Patrick. I'll try anything, though. But I just remembered that I don't have a sign in. I go through the proper channels to log in and start inviting people that I personally know to become my friends. This is pretty easy and one by one, I start seeing all of my old friends from my alma mater, Middleton High.

The phone rings. *Who could it be at this hour?* The only reason I decide to get up and see who is calling is because it's late and it could be an emergency. By the time I get to my cell phone and see that it's only Kalin, I want to scream, but I answer the phone anyway. "What do you want, Kalin?"

"Wow, you were waiting for me, weren't you?" he asks.

"In your dreams. Now, what do you want?"

"Just want to know if I can come over, Melissa. I miss you. You're still my wife, you know", he says.

"Kalin, give me a break. I'm really not interested in sleeping with you. We are over, remember?" I tell him.

"Come on. You know you need it. I heard about white boy, so I know you ain't getting none", he says.

"That's absolutely none of your business, Kalin. I have to go now."

"Come on. Don't go. We both need it. Let's take care of each other, Melissa. We can do it like we used to. You always did like making love to me. Let's have some fun. *I can't believe it but I'm starting to almost give in.*

I am in need of a touch from a man but, am I willing to let Kalin satisfy that need? Am I that lonely?

"Goodnight, Kalin. Thanks for the offer, but I'm going to have to decline. Going to bed now."

The nerve of that man! I have to admit, though, that I was about to give in to him. What is wrong with me? I know that it's not that I still love him, but I guess I am a little lonelier than I thought. I need to move on and meet other people and keep going forward without looking back, but Lord, please help me to do that.

The night is slipping away and all I can think about is sleeping right now. My eyes are tired and heavy from crying. I must have looked at Patrick's pictures and cards at least a hundred times. For some crazy reason, I decide to dial his number and just like the last hundred times, it goes straight to his voicemail. The smile on his pictures is what I remember most from our last night together at his house. When I last looked into his eyes, I saw a very happy man who wanted to spend the rest of his life with me, not a man who wanted to run away. There has to be a reason he left. Something must have happened after I left that he didn't want to talk about with me. But what? What could it be?

CHAPTER 33

"You Can't Say Anything!"

"Cynthia, is that you?" the man on the phone asks.

"Who is this?" Cynthia asks.

"Cynthia, it's me, Patrick. I'm sorry to bother you if you are busy, but I…", he begins to say, but Cynthia interrupts him.

"Oh my God, Patrick!! Are you okay? I know that Melissa must be so happy to know that you are okay. That woman has been worried sick about you and her….", Cynthia says, but Patrick interrupts her.

"She can't know that we talked", Patrick says. "I'm only calling you to see how she's doing. I really love her, Cynthia, and I care about her more than she will ever know", he says.

"This is crazy. What do you mean that *she can't know*? Why can't she know, Patrick?"

"I went away to protect her, Cynthia. I know she's angry with me and I know that she feels as though I abandoned her, but I left because I love her. Is she okay?" he asks.

"Is she okay? What kind of question is that? She's devastated! She's crushed! She cried for a whole week after you left. She is *not* okay, Patrick. Will you please just call her?" Cynthia begs.

"I can't. I'm very ill, Cynthia. I knew that I had to come to Connecticut for some therapy, so I planned the trip to London the week before I was supposed to make this trip, but before we made the trip, I got sick and had to come to Connecticut early and …", he begins to explain.

"Therapy? Did Melissa know about this? Therapy for what, Patrick? Are you okay?"

"I don't really want to talk about that. How is she doing? How is she *really* doing? I have done nothing but think of her day and night, Cynthia", he says.

"Patrick, that woman loves you so much. You have no idea what she has gone through day after day worrying about you, but you should at least tell her that you're okay and ...", Cynthia pleads with him.

"No! Cynthia, it's important that I keep her out of this until I'm better. I love her too much to let her feel any more pain. Just find a way to help her relax, Cynthia. I'll check in from time to time with you to see how she's doing", Patrick says.

"How can I reach you? I want to be able to call you if I need to tell you something", Cynthia tells him.

"No. I'll call you. Come on now. I know that if I give you the number, you'll just give it to her. I would do that for my friend in pain, too", he says.

"Okay. I'm glad to know that you're okay, Patrick. Thank God for that."

Cynthia hangs up the phone and everything in her heart tells her to contact Melissa and tell her that she talked to Patrick, but he asked her not to do that. He didn't really explain much about it other than he doesn't want to hurt her, but he doesn't realize that he's hurting her by not letting her know that he's okay. She decides to call her friend.

"Hello", I say, surprised to hear from Cynthia at this hour.

"Hey girl. How are you today? How is your time with the boys?"

"Having a blast. I miss these boys so much. They're the best. They cleaned out the garage for me today and told me that they didn't want me doing anything strenuous today because it was my day to relax. Isn't that sweet?" I tell her, sounding happier today than most days.

"But, with everything else, how are you?" Cynthia asks, hoping she will mention something about Patrick.

"I'm doing okay *with everything else.* I still cry myself to sleep at night wondering if Patrick is safe. I think I hate him for hurting me like he did, but I know that God would not be pleased with that. And, you won't believe who's trying to jump in bed with me?"

"Let me guess! Kalin! That snake!" Cynthia says.

"Yeah, that snake. And you know what else? I almost gave in to him, Cynthia. Now, what does that say about me? I'm divorcing him for a reason, but for a split second, I wanted him. Not gonna lie. I did!" I confess.

"But you can't give in to that, Melissa. You have come so far with your independence and feeling free in your heart. Why would you give all of that up just to be hurt again?" she asks.

"Listen. I gambled with my heart on Patrick. I let Kalin go and allowed myself to fall for another man and look at what *he* did. He hurt me just as bad as Kalin did. I could have stayed with Kalin if I wanted to cry and be hurt. I was *already* getting that", I tell her.

Cynthia wants to tell Melissa the truth, but she promised Patrick that she wouldn't do that. She's hoping that he will get himself together in Connecticut and eventually call her, hopefully before Kalin twists her mind and fools her into thinking that he loves her.

"Melissa, I know that Patrick loves you. I have to tell you something", Cynthia says. She can tell that she has my full attention because I completely stopped talking.

"What is it? Tell me. Do you know something that I don't know?" I ask in desperation.

Cynthia has to think what she will say next. For a split second, she wants to tell the truth, but feels that it will hurt Melissa even worse coming from her and not Patrick. So she goes a different route.

"I notice the way he looks at you, Melissa. Before the trip was supposed to happen, Patrick called me and told me how much he loves you and adores you. He went on and on about how you complete his life. That man is in love with you, Melissa. Don't give up on him. Do you trust me?" Cynthia asks.

"You're my closest friend. Of course, I trust you."

"Then trust me when I tell you not to give up on this man. He loves you, Melissa. Sometimes, men have a different way of showing it than we do, but it doesn't mean they love you any less. It just means that they do things differently. I *know* that he loves you. Pray for him and trust that God is working this thing out the way it should be worked out. Focus on other things right now and for God's sake, do not bring Kalin back into your bed", she advises.

"Wow, Cynthia. I never thought you cared *this much* about Patrick. I appreciate you for telling me this. I really do care for him, Cynthia. I really do", I say.

"Then, stick with that. Now, tell my handsome nephews that I said hello and I'll see them tomorrow. I'm coming over so we can hang out and throw some food on the grill", she says.

"Girl, things are a little tight on the budget right now. I don't have it like I used to when we would grill and put...", I begin before she interrupts me.

"I got you, Melissa. I just got my quarterly bonus, so the food's on me and ...", she begins to say.

"No!! I can't let you do that! I don't want you or anyone to start feeling sorry for me and giving me hand-outs and stuff like that. I just don't...", I tell her before she yells at me.

"Melissa, who are you talking to like that? Don't you dare go there like that with me? We've been friends through everything, girl. I ain't feeling sorry for you. I love my friend and I just wanna hang out. And that's that. And don't you ever get like that with me, *not me*. We're friends and that's just what friends do for one another. So, go ahead and let the boys spoil you today and I'll see you tomorrow", she says.

"Ok, Cyndi. I know you love me and you're just trying to help. I'm sorry. Please forgive me, okay?"

"Of course, I forgive you."

Cyndi and I hang up the phone and for a moment, I feel close to Patrick. It's almost as if he's thinking about me so strongly that our minds are meeting each other right now, but in a supernatural kind of way. Maybe when I close my eyes tonight, I'll see Patrick in my dreams and in it will be some kind of sign.

Dear God. I'm hurting right now and I don't know what your plans are for me. I wish you could clue me in on what you know. Am I supposed to be with Kalin or with Patrick? What is your best for me? I want to do Your Will, Lord. I don't want to be out of Your Will. Please comfort my heart. Give me the strength to go on from day to day. Help me find a job so that I can take care of my family. This family has never had to go without a job and I need you Lord. I need you to show me my way. What is it that you would have me to do? What is it? Why does it feel like you have just completely gone to sleep on me? Sometimes, it feels like you have left me to figure this all out on my own. Well, I can't! I am nothing without you. Nothing! Nothing! My heart aches and it doesn't stop. I want to stop crying. I want to stop hurting like this. It is destroying me, Lord. I ask that you send special angels to watch over Sharelle. Keep her safe, Lord. And please watch over Patrick. Be with him through whatever it is that he is going through. Bring a solution to his problems, Lord. Only you know what they are. And Lord, continue to watch over this family. Guide me. Lead me to follow Your ways. And Lord, when that day comes and you bless us to get our finances in order, I will be very careful to give You all the honor and the praise. In Jesus' name. Amen.

CHAPTER 34

"I Can't Do It Without Him."

"Sir, it looks like you're going to need chemotherapy because the therapy that we were attempting was not a success", Dr. Smith tells Patrick.

"Oh God, no! Are you serious? But I thought that…", Patrick begins.

"I know. I really thought that the therapy would somehow keep the disease from progressing, but it's taking a life of its own. What are your feelings towards chemotherapy?" Dr. Smith asks him.

"I've heard many things about it, mostly bad to be honest. I don't want to lose my hair and be sick all the time. The hardest thing I did was distance myself away from a woman that I love very much without even telling her where I am. I can't believe this!" Patrick yells, placing his face in his hands. He begins to cry.

"I know that this isn't easy for you and your family, Patrick, but do you trust God?" the doctor asks.

"I do. I do trust God", Patrick admits.

"Then, trust Him to work things out for your good. Trust that He knows better than even you and me", Dr. Smith tells him.

"You know something? You're absolutely correct about that. So, you're a believer, Doc?" Patrick asks him.

"Of course I am. I'm only a good doctor because of God above. He gives me wisdom daily. I couldn't do *what I do* without Him", Dr. Smith tells him.

"It's not everyday that I meet a praying Doctor, but it's always a good thing to know that the man who is working with me believes in God. I wish more doctors were like you", Patrick says.

"Ok. So, it's settled. Chemo will begin on Monday. Try to get some rest over the weekend", the Doctor suggests.

"OK. Will you be here when I return on Monday?" Patrick asks.

"Yes. I'll be right here. I won't be going back to London until I can at least see some progress", Dr. Smith responds.

"Thank you. I can honestly say I've never met a doctor like you before", Patrick tells him.

Patrick leaves the office and knows that he has to mentally prepare himself for chemotherapy. He has heard about Kent Falls Park as being one of the most peaceful parks in Connecticut. Patrick picks up some lunch and starts driving that way. Before he knows it, tears are falling down his face. He can't seem to get Melissa off his mind. For a brief moment, Patrick puts himself in Melissa's shoes and just maybe in some spiritual way, God is allowing him to feel what Melissa feels. Patrick has made it up in his mind that as much as he wants to hear Melissa's voice, he can't call her, but she does at least deserve to know that he loves her.

Patrick can't remember who told him about this Park, but whoever told him was on point. It's just what he needs right now to get his mind off everything. This reminds him that he and Melissa are supposed to be living it up in London right now. The plan was to visit some of London's most romantic spots while there.

The more the time pass, he starts to second guess himself about calling Melissa. He goes against everything he believes and dials the number. He's surprised when he hears the voice on the other end of the phone. The male voice throws him off guard and he hangs up the phone. *Has she already moved on, Patrick wonders. Who is the man who answered the phone? Melissa must have gotten tired of waiting.*

Patrick desperately wants to call Cynthia to find out if Melissa is already seeing someone else, but decides against it. He doesn't really want to hear Cynthia tell him that he's waited too long. Instead, he goes into his pocket and pulls out her picture, stares at it and begins to cry again. Although he knows that she deserves better than to have a man just leave her high and dry, he was confident that she would wait for him because of their true love. He wishes she could have understood what *he* was going through. But the truth of the matter is that Patrick hid it from Melissa. He didn't tell her what was going on, but made a decision to leave her to deal with the pain and feelings of abandonment.

To get through the task of chemotherapy, he realizes that he needs to make peace with God and himself. He looks to the skies above and feels at peace with what lies ahead for him. Dr. Smith is nothing short of a man sent by God to help in his time of sadness. Patrick is impressed at how he seems to really care about his patients. Patrick's reality is that on Monday morning, his life will change. He may lose his hair, but more than anything, he is hoping not to lose his faith.

CHAPTER 35

"Is There Anything Left?"

"*H*ey guys, I'm not feeling well, so I'm going to get some sleep. I know ya'll having fun watching your favorite shows, but please try to keep it down. When I get up, I'll fix us some dinner. Sound like a plan?" I ask.

"Sounds like a plan, Mommy!" Justice yells.

"Mommy! I'll get it!" Darren shouts, running to grab the phone. "Hello."

There's silence on the phone. Darren says it again. "Hello."

The caller waits a few seconds and then hangs up. Darren tries to see where the call came from, but the caller id reads "restricted". "People calling here and hanging up! What's up with that?"

"Who was it on the phone?" Kameron asks.

"I don't know. They didn't say anything. Just hung up!"

Justice makes a few bags of popcorn for everyone and they spend several hours just watching television and eating snacks. All of their favorite holiday shows are on and it's like the good ol' days. Brianna and Princess join them eventually.

I can't sleep anymore. I have to get up. Lying here in this bed just makes me feel worse. I don't want the kids to see me sad. They're here visiting and they want their mother to spend some quality time with them at some point. I have to find some kind of way to get over Patrick. I have asked God to bring him back, so if he does, he does, but if he doesn't, I know that I have to move on, but what he has done hurts me to the bottom of my heart.

"So, who's ready for dinner?" I yell, walking into the family room where all of the kids are gathered watching television.

"I'm starving, Ma", Kameron says, getting up to give me a kiss on the cheek. "How did you sleep?"

"I slept just fine. So, didn't the phone ring earlier? Who was it?" I ask.

"When I said hello, they just hung up. I said "hello" twice and they didn't say anything", Darren explains.

"Who was the call from? Did it say on the caller id?" I ask.

"The call came from a restricted number."

I wonder if that could be Patrick. I just wonder. But, why would Patrick call me from a restricted number? It must have been a wrong number or something. It's been 2 months. It is time to get over Patrick and move on with my life. If he cared about me at all, he would have contacted me by now. For all I know, he could be off in God knows where with God knows who. I have to face the fact that he's just another man who lied to me. Just another man who said he would never hurt me.

"Ok. So, what would my beautiful children like for dinner tonight?" I ask.

"It's Friday night, Ma. Let's have burgers and fries", Amber suggests. Everyone agrees.

I have to admit that sitting around at the dinner table with my children is a very good feeling. It makes everything else not feel so difficult. Darren and Kameron are both doing well in Philadelphia. I have to admit that I'm so glad that they're living there together. Amber and Justice seem to be adjusting well to the fact that Kalin is no longer here, or it could be that they know that they're going shopping tomorrow with their father. Princess will be leaving next year for college. Sharelle is away, but she should be home in no time if she continues to do well. My children have always been a saving grace for me. They have always made me see what was most important in life. I just need to find a job so that my family won't have to struggle.

"Ma, can I ask you a question", Darren asks.

"Boy, it's 'May I ask a question'?" I correct him.

"Momma, you have been doing that since I was a little boy", he comments.

"Yes. I know. I'm tired of doing it", I say, jokingly. We laugh. "What's the question, son?"

"Do you need some money? I mean, you're not working. How are you paying everything?" he asks.

"Darren, I'm fine. I'm not going to take money from my own child. We'll be okay. They gave me some money to last us for a minute or two", I tell him.

"But, Ma, I'm sure it's running out by now. You've been out of a job for 3 months already", Darren says.

"No, son, no. Thank you, but no thanks, okay. It's the responsibility of me and Kalin to take care of this household and ...", I try to explain, but he interrupts.

"Ma, that sorry behind man....", he starts to say, but stops, noticing that Amber and Justice are listening.

"We'll be okay. No more talk of it, D", I say, grabbing his face and kissing him on the cheek.

Darren gives me that look that he really wants to say more, but he realizes that this just may not be the right place to discuss this.

We finish off with Breyer's Ice cream and Oreo cookies for dessert. Like old times, the kids clean up the kitchen and put everything away just like I like it. Since everything's done, I decide to retire to my office to check my messages and to see if any interesting people have contacted me on my new internet toy, Facebook.

I wonder if this is the norm because I have almost sixty friend requests waiting for me to accept. Even though I recognize most of them from high school, there are also people requesting my friendship that I don't quite remember, but I accept all of the friend requests anyway. Deep down, I was hoping to get on here and find a message or a sign of Patrick. *This IS NOT what I am supposed to be doing in here. Stay on track, Melissa.* Unfortunately, there are still no emails from Patrick. *I have to find a way to get past this before it takes me out.* Every card, letter, or email that Patrick has ever sent me, I kept it. *Maybe what I need to do is just do what I have to do to get him out of my system. It's not easy because I really fell for him.* When I click to open the first letter I ever received from him, my heart starts to beat faster. *Why can't I let him go? He hurt me so badly. I need to learn how to live without this man before I go into a depression or something so I start to cry. Patrick, w/'.,m/nhe could have been so perfect together, I say, looking at his picture on my computer. Snap out of it, Melissa! Maybe it's time to give your husband a call and try to see if there's something there to salvage.*

CHAPTER 36

"This Is Awkward."

"So, Melissa, what are you doing today?" Kalin asks, while waiting for the girls to come downstairs.

"Who wants to know?" I ask.

"I want to know. I'm the one asking, ain't I?"

"Just wondering because I didn't think that what I was doing, where I'm going, or with whom I'm going with is any of *your* business", I tell him.

"Girl, come on! It ain't all that. I just don't want you here by yourself and I was just thinking that if you don't have anything to do, you can come shopping with me and the girls", he offers.

As much as I don't want to admit it, he just may have a point. When he and the girls leave, the house is going to be extremely quiet. Princess is out with some friends, so I just may go with them. The good thing about this is that I get to help the girls pick out clothes and not Kalin.

"Yes, Mommy!! That's a great idea!" Justice yells, coming down the stairs. She obviously heard Kalin ask me to join them.

"Okay! You twisted my arm. Let me change clothes. I guess I can go and hang out with my girls." Kalin smiles.

Putting on my day of comfort clothes, I finally make it back downstairs. We jump in Kalin's car and head down University, sure to avoid all the Saturday traffic. The girls are either extremely happy because they're going shopping *or* they're happy because we're together as a family *again*. We finally make it to the Mall and I'm not surprised at all when I see how full the parking lot is. Because the girls need winter coats, we end up at *Burlington Coat Factory*. From what I remember about the holidays in Alabama, I already know that they'll need these when they get there.

It feels kind of awkward riding in the car together with Kalin after all that's passed between us; but, I notice how he doesn't say much. I can tell that he's hoping I'll be moved by the sls because he lets the music speak for him. I'm sure he's hoping that I'm sitting over here reminiscing in my head the good times that we've shared. It's hard not to remember. It's a good thing that we're right around the corner from the house, so we can both stop feeling awkward.

"Ok, girls, wake up. We're home! Wake up! Let's get in here and eat so you can get ready for bed", I tell them.

"Let me help you get them in", Kalin offers.

"No. I got it. Thanks, though."

"Melissa, let me help you", he says, forcing himself out of the car.

After he helps us inside, he turns to me and asks, "Is there anything I can help *you* with?" He licks his mouth to indicate oral pleasure. As tempting as it is, I tell him to go home. After flirting for a few minutes, he finally gets the hint that I'm not interested in having sex with him. Looking back one last time, he walks through the door and leaves the house.

Just as he leaves, Justice runs to me and says, "Thank you, Mommy."

"Whoa! What are you thanking me for?" I ask her.

"For going shopping with us and being nice to daddy. It felt like old times."

"Justice, the old times are just that. That was our past with daddy. Your father and I are *not* getting back together or anything like that. We just went shopping, okay."

"I saw how you both looked at each other when we were driving. Why do you think me and Amber fell asleep?" she says, rushing off to wash her hands to eat dinner.

"Amber?" I say, but she rushes off with Justice.

Boy, these kids are something else! I understand why they do this, though. No child wants to see their parents get a divorce. I understand it, but my heart is no longer with Kalin and even if I try to put our marriage back together, it will still be hard because I don't think Kalin has changed or will ever change.

Me and the girls sit down and enjoy our greasy burgers and fries but say nothing more about Kalin. We have to get up early in the morning for church so we decide to call it a night.

The shower has rejuvenated me and I'm wide awake now. Since I have this burst of energy, I might as well check my emails and get on Facebook and see just how many requests I have today. Since I'm not ready to go to sleep now, I get on the computer and check my email messages, as well as my Facebook page to see if I have any new friend requests. What better way to connect to people from your past *and* meet new people? Right away in my email messages, I notice that I have an email titled *Anonymous.* Who sends an email and the subject line is Anonymous? How in the world would anyone know who it is from? Out of curiosity, I open the email and it says, *"I love you. I hope you had a good time."*

Now, who would send this? This seems like something that Kalin probably sent trying to be romantic. He is the only one who knows that I was out today. Delete!

I have a few more requests in Facebook and I accept them all. I don't know any of these people, but what's wrong with meeting people over the internet? What harm can it do? Now, this is a strange request; a guy from London. I *know* that he doesn't know me. How does he know me to friend request me? It doesn't matter. I'll accept it. No big deal. He *is* cute. This one could be interesting. Just seeing the word *London* takes me back to Patrick and I get sad all over again.

Let's see if there are any jobs that are waiting for me in my inbox. I have to find a job. I can't believe that my son wanted to give me money. That is a slap in the face when I should be receiving support from my husband. Now that I think about it, Kalin has never really come through financially for this family. I mean, he has worked a few jobs, but he always quits them and he never had a problem leaving me hanging to figure out how to pay for everything. I will be so glad when that day comes when I can know what it feels like to have a man satisfy me completely and not just in bed.

Sales jobs galore! I don't think I can do sales, but it looks like those kinds of jobs are plentiful, but if I'm going to go this route, I need to find one with a base pay at least. I just may have to apply to one of them and see what happens. Flipping through the sales positions that are available, I finally see something interesting. Headrest DVD Systems? I should be able to sell these. So, instead of pondering over it anymore, I send them my resume and cover letter. *Now, if it's for me, I'll get the job. This is all I can do.*

Dear God, thank you for this day. Thank you for walking with me step by step. Forgive me, Lord, when I do or say things that disappoint you. Teach me more and more of your ways. Lord, I ask you to forgive those who come against me. Protect me from my enemies Lord. Watch over this family. Watch over Darren and Kameron as they travel back to Philadelphia. Watch over Christy and Sharelle. Lord, you know and you see the immediate needs of this family. I need a job, Lord and I need it now! But, I trust you. I trust you to always give me what I need. These and other blessings we ask in thy son Jesus' name. Amen.

CHAPTER 37

"This Man Just Doesn't Quit."

"*D*id you get a job yet, Melissa?" Cynthia asks.

"Girl, it's rough out here. I've applied to so many property management jobs and nothing is coming through for me. I can't even get a job interview. This is what I've done for the last 10 years or so and *nobody* is calling me. I may have to settle for a sales job and I don't know how to sell anything. I just can't believe that it has come to this, Cyndi", I tell her.

"I'm shocked by that because you're really good at what you do", she says.

"Yeah, I know that and you know that, but these employers don't know it", I say, sounding defeated.

"But you can't give up, Melissa. You can't", she advises.

"Tell me about it. My funds are running low and I don't want to use my savings, but it's coming to that. And you know I can't depend on Kalin for anything. But, I have to give him a little credit because he *did* take the girls shopping the other day. And at least they'll get to be around family for the holidays. They're going to Alabama *with him* for Christmas", I tell her.

"Really? That's good. I can't believe you're allowing them to go with him for Christmas away from you", she comments.

"I know. I know. They want to go because they miss their grandmother and her good cooking. So, I guess I'll just hang around the house."

"You know that you are more than welcome to my house. You know that."

"I know. My sister, Diana, invited me over to her house. My family from Alabama is here and everybody's going to her house, so that's probably where I'll end up, but thanks dear."

"Okay. As long as you're not alone on Christmas, I am happy", she says.

"Well, I gotta go now. I'll talk to you later."

"Okay. Love you!", she tells me.

"Love you too."

Cynthia and I hang up and all of a sudden, I get this very uneasy feeling in my stomach and I don't know why. I don't recall her saying anything to make me feel like this. *Who knows? Maybe something is coming up that perhaps God needs me to see.*

"Mommy, my bag is ready for you to check it", Justice yells, coming downstairs with her suitcase.

"Ok, great. Let me check and see if you got enough outfits and underwear. You know my Mother always taught us to pack more than enough because you just never know what will happen", I tell her.

"Do you have our snacks ready yet?" she asks.

"Of course! Who's the best mommy in the world?" I ask her, jokingly. "I have everything that you'll need for snacks. There's enough for both you and Amber and I even packed enough for your father to have some if he wants", I tell her, opening up her suitcase. "It looks like you've done a good job of packing, but grab some more underwear."

Justice runs upstairs to grab more underwear and Amber is now heading downstairs with her suitcase. "Ready for me to check yours now?" I ask her.

"Yes, Mother. I'm ready. I know that I have everything!" she says confidently.

I check her suitcase and she's correct. She has done an excellent job of arranging her suitcase. The doorbell rings and Kalin is here. Amber lets him in.

"Good morning, girls. Are you ready to go?" he asks, shutting the door behind him.

"Almost! Almost! I need to grab a book to read", Amber says, disappearing upstairs.

"I've been meaning to ask you this, Melissa", Kalin says.

"What?"

"Would you like to spend Christmas with me and the girls?" he asks.

"Are you serious?"

"I'm dead serious. You're still my wife and I'm still your husband. We have two beautiful daughters together. You and I have a lot of history together and I want to spend the holiday with you", he explains.

"I can't do that, Kalin. You know that I can't go to Alabama with you and have everyone thinking that we're getting back together. It's just not going to happen and I ...", I begin to say but he interrupts me.

"Melissa, stop it! Why do you have to always go there with everything?" he says, sounding irritated with me.

"Because it is what it is, Kalin. It's over between us and I'm not going to go to Alabama and pretend that everything is fine between us. I want you to spend this holiday with your daughters. I think that it's a good way for them to get in some quality time with their father, especially since we *are* getting divorced", I tell him.

"Fine. I'm not going to beg you", he says, sounding angry. Both girls are coming downstairs now.

"Ok, looks like you're both packed and ready to go", I say to them, reaching out my arms for a hug.

"We love you Mommy. We wish you were coming to Alabama too", Amber says.

"Yeah, I tried to tell her the same thing, girls", Kalin says, sarcastically.

"No. Mommy has things to do herself. I'll be with Auntie Diana for Christmas. I'll be just fine. I want you both to enjoy spending time with your father and make sure you bring me some of grandma's good food back with you", I say, walking towards the front door.

"Kalin, take care of my children", I tell him.

"They're also *my children* or did you forget that?" he asks.

Kalin and the girls are all packed in. They all seem to fit comfortably. Both girls are in the backseat. I wave goodbye to them and watch them as they drive off of our street. Being outside in this beautiful Florida weather, just one week from Christmas, feels so good. Needless to say, we won't get any Christmas snow here any time soon. I'm actually standing here in shorts and flip-flops today. Some of my neighbors are working in their yard and this feels like a day to go hang out at the park.

Since I have some time on my hands, I might as well clean up a little. It's no surprise that the first place I land is my office. The mail is stacked so high that it's unbelievable. I haven't checked my mail in a few days and when I do, I have tons of junk mail, but the red envelope stands out. It's a letter from Stevie. I'm sure that it's probably just a Christmas card. No matter what goes on around us, Stevie has never missed sending me a card. *Happy Florida Holidays to a Hottie!* This is what the card reads. There's a picture of Stevie and his family inside. His wife is absolutely beautiful. Sharelle? He named his newest daughter, Sharelle. Unbelievable!!

Now what? What do I do with myself now? Princess will be gone for a few days, but will make it back here in time for Christmas. My Christmas tree is up and the house is empty. My heart feels so empty too. I think I'll just get back in bed.

It's so quiet in here. I'd probably be able to hear a pin drop. Music! That's always a good thing and there's nothing like listening to the Classics during this time of the year. It always gives me a good feeling. Grabbing a tangerine and candy peppermint, I turn on the computer to see if there's anyone out there who loves me. At first glance, I see that there are tons of junk emails in my inbox. They are immediately deleted. But, there is one from Anonymous again. *Why in the world won't Kalin stop sending me emails like I don't know it is him?* I open it up and it reads, *I love you and I miss you. I would love to be spending this holiday with you. I wish you were here with me."*

This man just doesn't quit, does he? He was just here. He must have sent this from his phone. There is no way in the world I would have gone to Alabama with him, only to have to answer tons of questions about me and him from his family. Or to sit and hear speeches about why God wants us to stay together. But, his family has no idea that Kalin has been abusive to me and has been throughout our marriage, but I covered it up until I finally got tired and started to realize that I deserve better.

I wonder what Patrick is doing right now. Is he thinking about me? Does he still love me? Does he feel bad at all for leaving me like this or did he plan this all along? I'm so lonely right now. I feel like just going to sleep and never waking up again. This pain in my heart hurts so much. I don't know if I can do this, Lord. I can't believe that you saved me for this. You should have just let me die when I wanted to die. Why does someone have to go through this all the time? I have gone through enough.

The tears are flowing down my face and before I know it, I'm on the floor beating my fist on the floor. I can cry out as loud as I need to because nobody is here but me. I've been waiting for weeks to be alone. I'm tired of having to hide and pretend that I'm happy when I'm *really* miserable. I was miserable in my marriage. I'm miserable about the relationship that I thought was going to be the one. I'm miserable that I can't find a job in property management and may have to settle for a sales job. I really thought that having my kids taken from me for almost two years would have been the worst pain possible, but this pain hurts in a way that I can't explain. I don't think I ever want to be in a relationship ever again. Now, I know I don't trust men. *Maybe I should just go out and meet a guy at random just to sleep with him and have no ties to him whatsoever and see if that will make me feel better.*

Wanting this pain to end, I go to the bathroom to see if I have any pain pills that can put me to sleep. I open the medicine cabinet, only to find some empty prescription bottles, but nothing more than that. I see an Excedrin bottle, but, immediately my mind takes me back several years when I wanted to kill myself and I took all those pills, which put me in the hospital's emergency room getting my stomach pumped. From that ordeal, I remember how I asked God to give me my life back and that if He did, I promised never to try this again. As if I just woke up from a nightmare, the pills end up flying across the room, leaving me crying out to God instead. *Dear God! Please Lord! Please take this pain away from me. It hurts! It hurts! I don't want to feel pain anymore. I just want to die. I can't go through this heartache. I didn't do anything wrong, Lord. Why do men always break my heart? I want to give them all of my love, but they keep taking me for granted and walking all over me. I need you to take this away from me, now! Now, Lord. Now! And now, I want to go to sleep and get some rest. Let me rest in Your arms, Lord. In Jesus' name. Amen.*

CHAPTER 38

"Who Is *Anonymous?*"

*P*atrick is starting to feel like he made a mistake by leaving Miami without the love of his life. His days are starting to run together and he realizes that this could all be better if he had brought his best friend along with him. Patrick can't stop thinking about the phone call he made to Melissa's house and the *man* answered. He's heartbroken that Melissa may have moved on without him. He's desperate to know if this is someone in Melissa's life and the one person who'll know the truth is her best friend, Cynthia.

"Hello, Cynthia. It's me, Patrick."

"Oh, hi, Patrick. How are you feeling?"

"I'm not doing that good, Cynthia. I'm about to start chemotherapy. May I ask you a question?" he asks.

"Sure, Patrick. Anything."

"Has Melissa moved on? Is she *already* seeing someone? I'm just wondering."

"She hasn't said anything to me about her having met anyone, Patrick. I know that if she had met someone, I'd be the first to know. Why would you ask that?"

"I've sent her a few messages, anonymously, and she hasn't....", he begins.

"That was you? Did you say it was from you?" Cynthia interrupts.

"No, of course not. I can't let her", he says, but Cynthia cuts him off.

"She thinks those emails are coming from Kalin. She told me about the emails that she's receiving from *Anonymous*. She's not responding to them because she thinks they're coming from Kalin. I will tell you this, though. She's starting to meet people on Facebook. If you want her, Patrick, you better speak up because a woman is going to wait around only so long on you. She loves you and the woman is really hurting. I think you're doing more harm to her by not speaking up and letting her know what happened. She is in so much pain over you, Patrick. And it doesn't help that she can't find a job and her finances are suffering."

"I want to help her. Can you give her some money for me?" Patrick asks.

"She won't take it. I've already tried that. She doesn't want hand-outs as she calls it. She can't see it that people who love her want to help. So, she won't take the help. Before he left town, Darren asked me to look out for her because he's worried. He said that when they were there with her for a week, she was always crying and she actually thought they didn't notice it. They're very upset at how you did their mother", I tell him.

"I bet they are. I'm not proud of this, but I did what I felt was the best thing to do. I felt that just walking away would be better than dragging her through this "thing" that I am going through. She would be worried all the time and she already has things that she's dealing with and …", he tries to explain, but Cynthia interrupts him.

"But what's wrong with you two going through things together like couples do? Melissa would never leave you hanging like that. She would go through the fire with you if she had to do so and you just bailed on her and you *still* refuse after all this time to let her know why you walked away. Doing something like this can kill someone like her because when she loves, she loves hard. And now, she hates men and she hates the idea of falling in love with a man because she has lost all trust in a man and I can't say that I blame her, Patrick", Cynthia explains.

"Strike up a conversation with her and tell her that you heard a rumor that I'm still alive, but had to leave town for an emergency", Patrick suggests.

"Okay, Patrick. I'll do that. I just want my friend to stop crying. I need her to snap out of this and start living again, but she's really going through hell right now. This whole thing of her not being able to find a job yet, really has her confused because she has never ever been without a job. I'm even starting to worry about her a little", Cynthia tells him.

"I don't like hearing this. With all I am dealing with here, it would have been hard for me to be there for her. I just hope she pulls it together. I know you all may be unhappy with me for hurting her, but I love Melissa so much. I really do love her and I did this to make things better for her, not worse", Patrick says, sounding like he is about to cry.

"I know you did, but she's miserable without you and I hope that you'll find it in your heart to change your mind and go back to her. She needs you. How are you doing, by the way?" Cynthia asks.

"I'm doing as well as can be expected, considering I'm starting chemotherapy next week. Now, you know your friend. What do you think she would do if she knew that I was having chemo? She would drop everything and worry herself to death. I just want to do this without her and when I'm better, I'll definitely find my way back to Melissa. She is my sweetheart and I love her so much", Patrick says.

"Ok, Patrick. Just don't take too long. She *is* a woman", Cynthia tells him.

Cynthia hangs up the phone, but gets a different vibe from Patrick this time, as if he may soon break from this separation from Melissa. It is such a shame because Melissa has no idea that it is really Patrick who is sending her the anonymous messages. Taking Patrick's advice, Cynthia decides to call Melissa.

"Hello", I say, answering the phone.

"What's up girl? How are you?" Cynthia asks.

"I'm doing okay today. How are you? What's going on?"

"Nothing much. Just thinking about my friend and thought I'd give you a call. You doing okay?"

"What do you think, Cynthia? How would *you* be doing if you were almost out of money and not getting any support from the father of your children?" I ask her.

"I can only imagine what you're going through. All I know is that you have to trust God, no matter what", she encourages me.

"And deep down inside, I know this. I know that you're telling me right. I do trust Him, but I don't understand. I don't understand why I have to keep struggling and suffering. I'm getting tired, Cynthia. I am. I really am", I tell her.

"Let's have lunch today, just you and me", Cynthia offers.

"I would love to, but I can't spare any money on this right now and I ...", I respond.

"I asked you to lunch, so obviously I'm paying, crazy girl", she says.

"See, you should have started with that. You're paying? I'm in! Where do you want to meet?"

"Let's meet at Crispers on University", she suggests.

"Sounds like a plan. Say around 1pm?"

"Yes. I 'll see you then."

Cynthia and I hang up the phone and although I'm happy to see her, I don't have the energy to get out of bed and get dressed. *Am I starting to feel depressed? No way! I can't be depressed! Black women don't go through this, do we? Isn't depression just a figment of my imagination?*

Checking my emails, I'm surprised to see an email from Kalin. He's asking me to join him and the kids in Alabama for Christmas that is just 2 days away. The email reads *Good morning beautiful. Me and the girls are here in the wintry Morganstown, AL missing you like crazy and we would be honored if you would agree to come to Alabama to spend Christmas with us. I will get you whatever you want if you come. And besides, nobody keeps me warm like you. Let me know asap so that I can book your flight before it gets too expensive. Tomorrow is Christmas Eve. Love, Kalin.*

If he's sending me an email from his own personal email, then *who is Anonymous?* I may be sad and lonely, but I am not *that* sad and lonely to settle being with the man on Christmas that I'm divorcing. I'll just have to be alone if that is what it means. I can't wait to tell Cynthia about this. I might as well respond to him now. *Good morning Kalin. I just received your invitation to come to Alabama for Christmas and I am going to have to decline on your offer. I just want you to enjoy this time with your daughters as they crave time with you. I just feel that it is better for everyone if I am not there.*

Not all bad news shows up in my emails. There's one here from Envision saying that I meet their criteria for their sales position. I don't necessarily like Sales Jobs, but I have to take it. Before getting up to get dressed, I fill out their application and submit it back to them. The job only pays half of what I'm used to per hour, but I have to take it. Feeling somewhat more hopeless, I get up to get dressed, but the doorbell rings. *Who can that be at my door? I am not expecting anyone.*

Putting on a tank top and shorts, I walk to the front of the house. It's the landlord and no doubt, he wants to discuss where his rent money is.

"Good morning, Robert" I say, opening the door and inviting him in.

"Did I catch you at a bad time?" he asks.

"No. I was just about to get in the shower, but it's okay. Listen, Robert, I know that I owe the rent for this month, but I ran into a little difficulty with the job. I'm actually running behind in everything, but I promise you that I will get it to you as soon as possible", I explain.

"Yeah, I figured it had to be something like that because you have never been late with your rent. Do you have any idea when you will have it so that I will know when to come back?" he asks.

"Honestly, I don't. I have to make a few phone calls to see if I can expedite it, but I will give you a call by the end of the week to let you know something. Is that okay?" I ask.

"Sure, Mrs. Thomas. Sure it is", he says, walking towards the front door. "Well, I am going to go so that you can get your shower", he says. "Goodbye."

This whole idea of the landlord having to come to my door to collect the rent just has me sick to my stomach. It makes me feel like a bum or something. I don't know if I want to go to lunch with Cynthia. I just want to crawl right back into bed, but I know that she will just come here if I don't show up. Let me just do what I gotta do to get through this lunch.

CHAPTER 39

"That's Not the Question!"

"So, where is your *wife*?" the woman just walking into Kalin's brother's house asks.

"I'm getting a divorce", Kalin tells her.

"Really? I can't believe that any woman in her right mind would let a good looking man like you get away", she says.

"So, what's your name?" Kalin asks, being as flirtatious as usual.

"Kesha", she says, looking Kalin up and down as if she's ready to take a bite out of him.

"That's a pretty name. My brother's wife's name is Kesha. So, do you live around here?" Kalin asks.

"Yes. I live about 5 blocks away. I've known your brother for a long time, so he invited me over and said that his twin brother was here visiting", she explains.

"Oh. I see. You know my brother."

"Yes, but I'd love to get to know *you* better", she says, moving in pretty quickly.

"I'm here with my daughters, Amber and Justice", he tells her.

"And their mother didn't want to come?" she asks.

"No. I told you. We're getting a divorce. I don't want her following me here", he says, inviting Kesha into the family room.

"So, what do you like to do? I want to make sure you have a good time before you leave", she says.

"I like doing things outdoors. But since it is like 30 degrees, I'm not that interested in doing anything outside", Kalin says. She moves in closer to him.

"You have the prettiest eyes I've ever seen", she says, with her lips not even an inch away from his. The girls walk into the room and Kalin quickly moves away from her.

"Hey daddy. We're ready to go to the park!" Justice says, running to Kalin and hugging him around his waist. Amber just stares at the strange woman, but quickly focuses her attention back to Kalin.

"Absolutely! Hey girls, this is Ms. Kesha. She's one of your uncle's friends and she stopped by to check on us. Well, Ms. Kesha, the girls and I are about to go over to the Park. Thanks so much for coming by", Kalin tells her. She catches on and stands up to leave.

"Well, you all have fun", she tells them. Kalin walks her outside to her car while the girls look on.

Kalin's brother, Greg, comes into the room and tells the girls to stop spying on their father and to close the blinds. "Why don't you all go ahead and get your coats so that you're ready to leave when your father gets back inside", he advises them.

Kalin walks back inside and announces, "So, who's ready to get some hot chocolate and go to the park?"

The girls rush out of the bedroom and run to him. "We are!"

On the way to the park, the girls are somewhat quiet and Kalin knows that there must be something wrong. "So, who's going to tell me what's wrong here?"

"Who was that woman who was all over you?" Amber asks. "We don't appreciate that."

"I told you. She's a friend of your uncle's and she just came over to meet us", Kalin explains.

"She likes you", Justice says. "I can tell that she likes you."

"Honey, I just met the woman. She doesn't like me, but was just being nice to me. That's all", Kalin explains.

"Do you still love Mommy?" Amber asks.

"Guys, you know that me and Mommy are getting a divorce", he responds.

"That's not the question, daddy! Do you still love her?"

"Come on now. That woman has been my wife for the last 15 years. Of course, I still love her. It doesn't just go away just like that, but listen you two, this trip right now is about us. Button up your coats and put on your hats and let's enjoy our time here at the park."

Kalin and the girls get out of the warm car and walk through the park enjoying the cold Alabama weather. Amber's eyes light up when the reindeer prance through the park past them. Hours pass by and it's finally dark outside. Kalin knows he needs to get the girls back, but this moment and time with them is priceless. After letting his phone vibrate for at least 5 minutes, Kalin finally checks to see who's blowing up his phone. When he flips the phone open, he can clearly see that this is just a long text message that reads, *I enjoyed meeting you today and I look forward to having some fun with you before you leave to go back to Florida. You are even better looking than the picture that I saw of you. You have my number so use it. I know you will want some private time so use my number whenever you want. I felt how hard you were when you hugged me goodbye. Waiting on you, Kesha.*

Kalin becomes so involved in reading his message that he doesn't notice that the girls are walking towards him.

"Is that Mommy?" Justice asks.

"Yes, it was. She said to tell you both that she loves you and misses you so much.

CHAPTER 40

"I've Been Thinking."

"I'm really starting to feel lonely, Cynthia", I tell her.

"What do you mean by that?" she asks.

"I'm thinking that just maybe I should give Kalin another chance to prove his love to me. He practically begged me to come to Alabama for Christmas. People can change, can't they?" I ask her. Cynthia doesn't look too happy to hear me say this. I can tell by the way she's looking away that she doesn't approve of the Kalin comment.

"Are you serious, Melissa? After all the tears you've cried, all the struggling you've done with this man, and the time you have taken to file a divorce and you want to now take him back?"

"I miss having a man next to me, Cynthia. I miss having someone to spend the holidays with and birthdays and any …", I begin before she interrupts me.

"I'm here for you. Your family is here for you. Why are you so willing to go backwards? Do you think this is what God wants for you? Have you prayed about this?" she asks.

"Actually, I have. I've prayed about this and I believe that God wants me to mend my marriage to my husband. Maybe that's why it didn't work out with Patrick. I mean, it's obvious that Patrick doesn't love me. Look how he left me. I hate him for playing with my heart like that and…", I say, but Cynthia interrupts me.

"About that", Cynthia mumbles.

"About what?" I ask.

"Patrick."

"What about Patrick? What have you heard, Cynthia? C'mon!! Tell me. What?" I demand.

"Don't scream when I say this, but I heard that he's alive, but that he's really sick and moved away or something like that", Cynthia lies.

"Really? That makes it even worse. He talked all this noise about how much he loved me, but he couldn't trust me to be there for him if he is sick. I don't need a man like that, who wants to stick around just when times are good", I say.

"Melissa, you know you love Patrick. You're only settling for Kalin because Patrick left", Cynthia says.

"Ok. Maybe you're right. I ended up getting hurt anyway so I might as well stay with my husband."

"Melissa, you know I love you unconditionally. But, this is one time when I know that you're making a big mistake. I know that Patrick loves you. I know what it may look like, but don't jump back into something that makes you unhappy. It's like you're going right back to the thing that broke you in the first place."

"That's just the thing. I'm unhappy *now*. At least, if I'm with Kalin, I have someone here to hold me. At the end of the day, I'll have arms around me wen I get into my bed. I just want your support, Cynthia", I say to her.

"I'm your friend and I love you, but I don't agree with this. Whatever you decide won't keep me from being your true friend. I love you, Melissa."

"I love you too. I think I'm going to call Kalin and tell him. Just be happy for me, please."

Cynthia and I finish our late lunch and say our goodbyes in the parking lot. Because it's New Year's Eve, the local grocery and liquor stores are packed. I don't want to wait to get home so I decide to give Kalin a call. He answers.

"Kalin, I have something to tell you and I just want you to listen", I tell him.

"What is it, Melissa?" he asks in somewhat of an annoyed tone.

"I know you're a little upset that I didn't accompany you and the girls for Christmas, but I've been thinking about the things you said and I need to tell you something", I say.

"Ok, what is it?"

"I want us to work on our marriage and see if we can salvage it."

"Are you serious?" he asks. "Don't play with me woman!" he yells.

"I wouldn't play about something like this. Of course, I want to take things slowly and see where it goes", I say.

"There's one problem."

"You've met someone else? Ok, never mind then. I didn't mean to...", I say, without giving him a chance to say anything.

"No, that's not it at all, Melissa. But, I have decided to move to Alabama for a while just to see if I can work here and make things better for my family. Greg's wife made a few phone calls and got me a job with her store. At least I can work and get some insurance so that they can at least have that", he says.

My heart drops. *No Patrick and it appears as if there will be no Kalin. I can't imagine not having anyone around. What should I do now? Do I really want to have a long distance relationship with my husband? The last time he visited Alabama, he became friends with a woman which led me to file for a divorce. Can I trust him?*

"Are you there, Melissa?" he asks.

"Yes, I am. I was just thinking about something."

"It doesn't matter that I'll be here. I just want to work long enough to see where it takes me. There's also a modeling agency here that I want to work with to see what I can do with the modeling career. I just feel that I'll have better chances here than in Florida", he explains.

"Do you really think we can do this?" I ask.

"I know that we can do this. I always knew you loved me, Melissa. You will always love me and nobody will be able to take my place or your place", he says.

"We'll tell the children together. Don't say anything to them now. Where are they, by the way?" I ask.

"They went to the store with my sister and her kids. I'll have them call you when they return. This is a really good decision for our family, Melissa", he adds.

"I need to be able to trust you again, Kalin. This is our chance to prove what we have had all these years. What do you think?" I ask.

"I think it's great. I never stopped loving you and I will never stop loving you. I want you to trust me too. I won't ever hurt you again", he promises.

"Let's just take one day at a time. Oh, I didn't notice. It's New Year's Eve and we're starting our year off together as a reunited couple. This is really great. Are you driving, Kalin?" I ask him.

"Yes. I was trying to tell you that a few minutes ago. Greg got these tickets to this Black and White Ball for tonight and I'm meeting them there and I just…", he begins to explain.

"So, when the New Year comes in, just call me", I tell him. "I want to be the person who brings in the New Year with you. Can you do that?" I ask him.

"Sure. I can do that. Be by the phone", he tells me and hangs up.

What have I done? Did I make a mistake by bringing Kalin back into our lives? Was Cynthia right about Kalin? Will I be able to trust him? Why couldn't he talk on the phone with me just now? Is it possible that he was about to pick someone up and he couldn't be on the phone with me while he was with her? Why did he have to get off the phone with me before making it to the place of the event? Just watch television, Melissa!

I'm so lonely in this house by myself. At the last minute, Princess decides to go out with her friends, leaving me home all alone. Cynthia invited me to church with her and her husband, but I want to make sure that I'm here when Kalin calls. This is not what I thought I would be doing on New Year's Eve. I just knew that I'd be out on some romantic date with Patrick and having the best time ever. But, now, all I have to look forward to is sitting by the phone and waiting on the call from Kalin. In my mind, I'm thinking of how it will be now. Kalin will call and we'll exchange all kinds of sweet and romantic over-the-phone conversation and at midnight, having a couple of sweet kisses over the phone. I had pictured tonight totally different than what I have gotten. I guess I will sit by the phone and watch the New Year's shows. The only one that is half way interesting is BET and it has all these young people on there playing music that I have never heard of before, but at least they're having a good time.

I'm starting to get sleepy, but it's close to midnight. Plenty of people will be calling soon, but I will have to ignore their calls because Kalin will be calling and I want to talk to him more than anyone. It's a minute away from midnight and he hasn't called yet.

He missed it! Kalin didn't call at midnight like he promised and I had to bring in the New Year all alone. My phone is ringing off the hook, but none of them are from Kalin. I'm too sad to speak to anyone right now. *He can't even do this one simple thing for me. This is why I had to break it off with him in the first place because he has never been a man of his word. Who did he bring in the New Year with? Who was giving him a hug or a kiss when the clock struck midnight? I am even sadder now than I was before.*

Flipping through the channels, I run across a station that has Babyface on and he's singing "Sorry for the Stupid Things" and I hear the words "*...sometimes a man is gon be a man, it's not an excuse, it's just how it is, sometimes a wrong don't know that they're wrong...*" and the tears are just falling down my face because all I can think about is that I may have made a mistake by bringing Kalin back into my life, but the truth is that I really do love him and it's almost as if I'm willing to accept that he may have another woman in Alabama with him right now, but I love him and I can't let go. Tomorrow is another day.

CHAPTER 41

"I Tried to Tell You."

"*I*t's not looking good, Patrick. We're doing all that we can for this rare form of cancer that you have, but we just have to keep trying and ...", Dr. Smith tells Patrick, until Patrick interrupts him.

"...and I'm not giving up either. I have a beautiful woman back home that I want to get home to who has no idea that I'm even here", Patrick confesses.

"If you don't mind my asking, why didn't you tell her?" Dr. Smith asks.

"I love her too much and I didn't want her to have to worry about me. She already has enough to deal with. She's going through a divorce and she has a daughter who had been giving her problems and I just didn't want to add to that", he confesses.

"So, what *did* you tell her?" he asks.

"Nothing. I was supposed to take her on a trip and I didn't show up because I was here. I'm not happy to say this, but I still haven't contacted her, but it's because I love her, but I have a strong feeling that I may have made a big mistake by doing it this way", Patrick admits.

"I think you may have made a mistake. If she is as wonderful to you as you project, you have to treat her like gold. I don't know much because I haven't been in a relationship for several years, but I know enough to know that a woman, a good woman, is a precious gift from God and when you're fortunate enough to find your match, you should cherish it", he tells Patrick.

"That's great advice, Doc. I don't want to lose her so I'm thinking that maybe I should make this right by first apologizing to her and begging her to come back to me because of how stupid I've been. And besides, she's the only woman who can make me laugh and forget about life's issues and honestly, I miss her", he admits.

"I wish you the best with that. I really do because I would give anything to have a woman who gives me love and attention", the doctor admits.

Patrick's therapy begins and after just 20 minutes into it, he's already throwing up his guts. The doctor warned him that this could be a side effect because the drugs being used are very potent. More than ever before, he's determined to finish therapy so that he can call Melissa. Talking with the doctor makes him realize that he has made a mistake by not reaching out to her before coming to Connecticut. He realizes that she's his partner and should go through this with him. He knows he can't get through it without her.

"I think I'm going to head back to London now. It looks like you're doing just fine and my angel misses me", Dr. Smith tells Patrick.

"Your lady friend, huh?" Patrick asks.

"No. My daughter, Anita. She's my only angel right now. I've been single for many years now, but I've prayed for God to send me a wife and I know he will. To tell you the truth, I'm looking for that special lady who can be my best friend and partner for life. But, only God knows what can happen in the future", he tells Patrick, standing up to walk towards the door.

"Hey, thanks for everything", Patrick says.

"Absolutely. I love what I do. Keep your head up and be patient. Things will work out just the way they should. You'll see."

He closes the door behind himself and Patrick continues to work with the trainer. On a scale of 1 – 10, his pain is about a 100. But, he realizes that without pain, there is no gain. He knows that at any moment, he could throw up his lunch, but before he can leave, he has to complete the therapy session. It doesn't look like the trainer is going to let him off the hook, either.

"How ya feeling, man?" the trainer asks Patrick.

"Like I'm going to pass out!" Patrick says. "This is so hard. Is my back supposed to feel like this?"

"Suck it up. We're almost done and then you can get your weekend started", the trainer tells him. "Does this hurt?"

He stretches Patrick's back muscles to ease his pain a little and it seems to be working. Irregardless of the pain he's in, Patrick seems pleased with the trainer's knowledge of muscle tissue. One thing's for sure, Patrick feels better than he did when they first got started. Just 10 more reps and he's off to his hotel room so that he can finally call Melissa and end his misery. It's funny how it took the advice from a foreigner to make him see the light.

Back at the hotel, the steam bath is giving Patrick just the relaxation that he needs to forget about the painful therapy training he just experienced. The hot water beads are trickling down his chest and he can't seem to get the memory of his hot water baths with Melissa out of his mind. No matter what he does, he still sees her face. Patrick calls for room service to bring his dinner. He feels like eating steak and potatoes. An expensive bottle of wine sounds good right about now. In his mind, he is gearing up for a celebration with the woman that he loves. In no way does he feel that what he's about to experience with Melissa will be easy because he knows that she must be upset, but in the back of his mind, he knows that she's worth it.

Patrick powers up his laptop and goes straight to his emails to see if he has received any correspondence from Melissa at all. Since he left Florida, he has received a total of 182 emails from Melissa, but he quickly notices that she has recently stopped sending them. His heart stops for a second and he's now wondering if she finally gave up on him. *Is there someone else? Did she go back to Kalin?*

He begins contemplating on whether he should make a call to Cynthia to see if she has any news. And now, Patrick's even more nervous to contact Melissa, but he knows that if he doesn't, he can lose her forever. Nervous as all outdoors, he dials Melissa's home number. After several rings, the voice messaging system picks up, but Patrick hangs up without leaving a message. His final option is to dial her cell phone. One ring, two rings, three rings, four rings and five rings. *You have just reached Melissa and I'm sorry that I am not available to take your call; however, if you leave your name, your number, and a very brief message, I will return your call as soon as possible. Have a great day.*

His mind is racing faster than he can think, so he calls his brother to hopefully get some kind of reassurance that there's still hope with Melissa. "Hey man, you got a minute to talk?" he asks his brother.

"Yeah, what's going on? How's therapy? You ok?"

"No. I'm not okay. I love her and I don't want to lose her, man. I didn't realize it until today. I need her. I didn't realize that she was the reason I was so happy. Please tell me that I can have her back. Please tell me that it's not too late for us", he pleads.

"I can't do that, man. I tried to tell you that you should have called her. That's a woman and they are super sensitive to stuff like this. All you can do is pray at this point."

"I will. I'll do just that. Thanks bro'!"

CHAPTER 42

"And You're Right About One Thing."

"Why didn't you call me?" Melissa asks Kalin when he finally calls the next day, several hours after he was supposed to call.

"Melissa, slow down. I wasn't able to call because it was really loud at the party and I couldn't hear anything. Why are you acting like this?"

"Why am I acting like this, Kalin? Why do you think?" I ask him, getting really annoyed.

"Look. It's a new year. Let's not start it this way. Let's start off the right way. Please", he comments.

"Okay."

"Listen. Since I'm staying in Alabama, I was wondering if you could meet me at the halfway mark to pick up the kids", he says.

"Sure. Isn't that going to be Tallahassee?" I ask.

"I think so. Do you think you can do this? We can stay overnight in Tallahassee, and of course, get adjoining rooms for the kids. I promised to take the girls shopping, so we can do that after breakfast the next morning. Does that sound like a plan?" he asks.

"That sounds fine, Kalin. What time are you leaving Alabama?" I ask.

"Say around 5pm Thursday evening. That'll put me making it to Tallahassee around 9 or 10. What will help is if you could go ahead and get the room and just call me and let me know where you are", he tells me.

"Ok. That's fine. I guess I can do that since you'll pay for breakfast and the girls' shopping spree", we agree. "Hey look, I'm getting another call. I'll talk to you all at some point on Thursday to let you know when I'm on my way", I tell him.

"I love you, Mrs. Thomas", he says before hanging up.

"I love you, too, Mr. Thomas. I'll talk to you later. Take care of my children", I say, then click over. *I don't recognize this number. It's probably some bill collector. It says it's coming from Connecticut. What bill collector could that be? Should I answer? It could be something important. I don't feel like talking to anyone right now. I have to get prepared for my trip to Tallahassee.*

So I can start packing for my trip, I decide to let voicemail pick up the call. It's time for me to go through some sexy lingerie for my husband to see what he's been missing. I won't anticipate sleeping with Kalin, but let's just see where it goes. It has been a while for me, but honestly, I don't know what Kalin has been doing. It's not like he's going to tell me the truth anyway. I need to talk to my girl. It's not too late. Cynthia should still be up.

She picks up on the first ring. "Hey girl! What are you doing up at this hour?" she asks, answering the phone.

"Guess who I just finished talking to?" I ask her.

"Patrick!"

"No! Patrick is gone, Cynthia. I am done with all of that. He left me and now, I am finally over it", I say.

"And since when did you get over Patrick? You are in love with him, Melissa, and you know it. Why are you playing games?" Cynthia asks.

"I'm not playing games. I'm all over him. Besides, I'm meeting *my husband* in Tallahassee on Thursday to pick up the children", I tell her, sounding proud.

"What! He can't bring them back. He took them out and now he can't.....", she begins, until I interrupt her.

"No, it's not like that. He went up there and made some contacts in the modeling industry. So now, he's going to stay in Alabama and see what he can make happen there and so....", I begin to explain.

"You remember what happened the last time he was in Alabama, right?" she asks.

"Well, if we're going to have a solid relationship, I have to forgive him for all of that; we have to both start with clean slates", I say.

"Ok. You're my friend and I support your decisions even if I don't agree with them. Me, personally, I believe you should wait for Patrick because I know that he's the man who truly has your heart, but you're a grown woman and I have to assume that you know what you're doing", she tells me. "Are you going to drive to Tallahassee by yourself?"

"Yes. We're staying overnight together. And can you believe that after all of these years, I'm actually *nervous* about possibly having sex with my *own husband?* If you could only see me now! I'm standing here in my bedroom going through all sorts of sexy lingerie like I'm getting ready to meet up with some old flame or something", I tell her, blushing in secret.

"Well, I can imagine that you're somewhat nervous about this overnight stay with him, even if he *is* your husband. Be yourself, Melissa, and enjoy yourself. And please, be careful on that road. I want you to call me as soon as you make it to Tallahassee", she says.

"I will do that. Thank you, friend, for being there whenever I have needed it. It means so much to me. I just want to be happy, Cynthia. That's all. And you're right about one thing. I do love Patrick."

CHAPTER 43

"My Gut Instinct Tells Me."

*M*any years ago, I never would have agreed to drive all the way to Tallahassee by myself. Anticipating mine and Kalin's reunion, I was able to get plenty of rest last night and now I'm wide awake. My *falling in love* CD's are all loaded, the tank is full, my snacks are in the front seat and I'm all ready to go. Because Kalin and I haven't slept in the same bed for several months, I have to admit that I'm somewhat nervous about sleeping in the same bed with him.

What is this Connecticut number that keeps calling me? I don't know anyone from there. These bill collectors are something else. I am not ever going to answer it, so they might as well stop calling me. I may have to eventually just block the number. Gheez!

I promised Kalin that I would give him a call when I am at least half way to Tallahassee. He picks up on the first ring. "Hello beautiful", he says, answering the phone.

"Hi there, sweetheart. How are you guys? Where are you?" I ask him.

"We've been driving for a couple of hours already. Where are you?"

"Same here. I should arrive in Tallahassee around 7pm or so. Do you have a preference for a hotel?"

"No. I don't. Whatever you pick for us is fine. Just make sure you get adjoining rooms for the girls. They'll probably fall right to sleep. These girls have had a busy day today. Their grandma sent them off with an awesome spaghetti dinner", he tells me.

"That sounds good. I'm glad that they enjoyed themselves. Thank you so much for taking such good care of them."

"They're *my* children, too", he says, laughing on the sly.

Kalin and I are both very leery about driving while talking on the phone, so we hang up and decide to share everything once we make it to the hotel. The drive continues to be pleasant for me. *The Best of Luther* CD is playing right now and is totally putting me in the mood. One of my favorite songs of all times is playing right now, "Endless Love" with Mariah Carey. Personally, I like how Lionel and Diana sang this song also. All I can think about are the good times that Kalin and I shared. There was a time when we were so in love and inseparable. Can't help but thinking how during our first few months together, we must have had sex at least 5 times per day. I never got tired of him and he was the same way. But throughout the years, things changed drastically and as a result, I have filed for a divorce, but the truth is that I still love him and I can't let go just yet.

The closer I get, the more excited I'm getting. The sign I just passed says that I'm only 32 miles from Tallahassee. Finally driving onto Capital Boulevard, I finally pull into Hampton Inn. Their rooms are usually very comfortable. Thank goodness for AAA and Sam's Club because it cuts down on the price of the room.

Now that I'm on my way up to the room, I decide to call Kalin and let him know where the hotel is. Amber answers the phone. "Hi mommy!"

"Hey Amber! How are you, sweetheart?" I ask her.

"I'm good. Daddy says that we're almost in Tallahassee. Where are you?"

"On my way to the room now. I made it here about 20 minutes ago. I'm calling to give ya'll the hotel information", I tell her. "So get a pen and write it down."

I read the address and room number to her and to confirm, she reads it back to me. "I got it Mommy", she tells me. "Do you need to speak to Daddy?"

"No, sweetheart. I'll talk to him when you all get here."

Kalin and the girls are not that far away, so I have to make this a quickie shower. As much as I'm enjoying this hot water beating down in my chest, I have to lotion up and put on my most comfortable lounging clothes. As soon as I finish putting on my clothes, I can hear the girls come through the door. "Mommy! You here?" they yell.

"I'm here! Look at ya'll. Seems like you have gotten so much bigger in 2 weeks", I tell them, giving them a big hug.

"Wow, Mommy! You look beautiful. Did you take a shower already?" Justice asks.

"As a matter of fact, I did. I needed to take one after that long drive", I say.

"Sure, Mommy. You're trying to get all pretty for daddy. I know!!!" Amber comments.

"NO! Mommy just really needed a shower. Let me show you where you two will be sleeping", I tell them, walking through the adjoining doors. The girls seem to be pleased with their sleeping quarters. Watching them jump up and down on their beds, I didn't hear Kalin walk in.

"Hey beautiful", he says, wrapping his arms around me. "You smell so good."

"Eeewwwwwwwwwwww, Mommy and Daddy", the girls say in unison.

"Ok. It's lights out for you two. You need to get your rest. Get in your pajamas and brush your teeth. Give me a kiss", I say to them both.

The girls run up to me and Kalin and give us our hugs and kisses before they dive into their suitcases to find their pajamas. Kalin shuts their door and we both go back to our side of the suite. Now that Kalin and I are alone, he walks up to me and kisses me like a man who misses his wife. "Do you have any idea how long I have waited to do that?" he says.

"No, why don't you show me?" I tell him, returning the passion even more.

"Let me take a shower, sweetheart. I have been driving for 4 ½ hours and I want to give you my best", he says.

"Okay. I'll be right here waiting", I tell him.

Kalin rushes into the bathroom to take a shower. As soon as he turns on the water, his cellphone rings. *I hate to be nosey, but I must see who is calling him. The caller ID says Kesha. Now, why in the world is Greg's wife calling Kalin? That's a little odd to me.*

I'm not going to let anything ruin mine and Kalin's night. When he gets out of the shower, I'll just let him know that his phone rang and I won't ask any questions because if we're going to have a successful relationship, I need to trust him. To make the time move along faster, I find the Tallahassee station playing the slow songs to set the mood just right. Out of the corner of my eye, I can see Kalin walking out of the shower and he's butt naked. I almost forgot just how sexy this man really is. He walks over to me and says, "Now, where were we?"

"Your phone rang while you were in the shower", I tell him.

"Ok. Hold on a minute. I know that Greg wanted me to let him know when I made it. Give me just a moment."

He walks over and picks up his phone and his face somewhat changes when he sees who called. He calls the number and after all the pleasantries, he finally says, "Yes, I made it just fine, but I can't talk right now." Kalin comes back to me and starts kissing me harder and harder and with more passion than before as if he's trying to prove something to me.

It's not long and Kalin is already starting to undress me. He picks me up and takes me over to the bed and makes passionate love to me. It wasn't as if we were strangers, but two lovers who crossed paths in the night and both had sexual needs. He fulfilled mine and I fulfilled his. We lay there in each other's arms reminiscing about the days when we were so much younger and having sex like rabbits. His phone rang again and I have to admit that I'm somewhat annoyed that he has enough energy to give attention to this distraction. "I told you that I can't talk right now. How are you?" he whispers to his caller. "I am sorry, too."

Kalin can tell I'm starting to get annoyed, but it doesn't matter because he stays on the phone. *Why won't he just hang up? And who can he be talking to anyway?* I finally get up and put my clothes on and stand over the bed and just look at him, like a kid needing some attention. He continues to talk on the phone, not sounding like he's getting off the phone anytime soon. I grab my keys and head for the door. And do you think this man is making any attempt to stop me? He lets me walk out the door.

When I get into my car, I look back to see if he's coming out of the room to try to stop me, but he isn't coming. I wait around on purpose, but he still doesn't come. *What in the hell is wrong with this picture? Why is the person he's talking to on the phone more important than him spending time with me? I can't believe that this is the type of relationship that I have settled for. What am I thinking? Do I need a man this badly?*

I start the engine, but have no idea where I'm going because I'm not familiar with Tallahassee at all. But from what just happened upstairs, I know I have to get out of here before I hurt this man. Honestly, I can't stand to look at him right now. Struggling with where to go, I head south down Capital Boulevard and end up at Krispy Kreme doughnuts. The girls will love me for bringing doughnuts back to the room, so I order a dozen for them. They smell so fresh and I can't wait to make it back to the hotel.

When I get back into the room, Kalin is sound asleep. Moments after I enter the room, he wakes up. "Honey, why did you leave like that?" he asks.

"It didn't seem to me that you would miss me at all. I mean, you were on the phone without any concern about me. It hurt my feelings deeply, Kalin. Here, we're supposed to be celebrating our getting back together and you're already making me cry.

"I didn't mean to do that, Melissa. Please forgive me for that. I was just talking to a friend and I didn't think you would have minded. I thought you were resting and I just...", he begins to explain.

"Right. You didn't think. I totally get that. Now, shut up and kiss me", I tell him.

He takes the doughnuts out of my hand and places them down on the table and leads me back to the bed, taking off my clothes. He pushes me backwards and begins to please me orally. I can't think of anyone who does this better. I have to admit it, but the argument that we had earlier is so far from my mind right now. We make love well into the morning. Surprisingly so, the girls have not disturbed us.

As much fun as we're having, we have to get up to shower because check out is at 10 and both of us really need to get on the road as soon as possible. By the time I get out of the shower, the girls are in our room munching on the doughnuts. So proud of them both because they've already taken their shower, dressed, and waiting on me and Dad. There's a Village Inn right across the street, so I think this is where we're going to eat our breakfast before we head for the Mall. Kalin keeps his word and pays for breakfast.

I'm starting to notice that even though Kalin and I shared a passionate night together, he seems somewhat distant with me, but I'm assuming that it's because he's just trying to spend as much time with the girls as he possibly can.

As soon as the girls see that we're finally pulling into the parking lot for the mall, they seem quite thrilled. I'm just glad that he kept his word. Three hours of going up and down this mall is enough for me. I'm almost ready for a nap, but we need to get on the road. Kalin takes me back to the hotel to pick up my car and surprises me when he tells me to follow him to the gas station. He fills up my tank, kisses the girls, kisses me, and we say our goodbyes.

"Mommy, look at the clothes we got!" Justice yells, taking all of her clothes out of the bag to display them for me.

"Wow! Daddy was good to ya'll, huh?"

"Yes, he was Ma!" Amber says.

"I'm so glad that ya'll got a chance to go to Alabama to spend time with your father and his family", I tell them.

"And Ma, you know grandma cooked good for us every day. That was the best part of the trip", Justice says. Amber smacks her. "Well it was!"

"I spent Christmas with Auntie Diana. Granny was here for Christmas this year, so you know the food was awesome", I say.

"Yaaaaayyyy! I'm so glad that you weren't alone. Daddy said he missed you and wished you would have come with us", Amber says.

"I know. I know. Maybe next time we go to Alabama, we will all be going as a family. How does that sound?" I ask them.

"That sounds great, Mommy!" Justice says. "What about that other lady?"

"What *other lady*?" I ask her.

"That lady that came over to Uncle Greg's house to see Daddy. She likes him, you know", Justice tells me.

"Amber, what is she talking about?" I ask, looking at them both through the rearview mirror.

"This lady who daddy says is his friend", Amber says.

"Just curious, but do you know what her name is?"

"Ms. Kesha. Daddy said they're just friends, but I didn't want to go with her after the first time", she says.

"What do you mean *go with her*?" I ask, starting to not like how the conversation is going.

"She took me and Justice shopping one day because Daddy had to work. He gave her his card, though. She took us to the museums downtown and then over to her house", Amber explains.

I am livid right now. If Kalin were standing in front of me, I could probably kill him with my bare hands. What in the hell is wrong with this man playing me like this and then involving my children? Kalin is not going to like me after I tell him what I have to tell him. Oh no! It makes sense now. That is the Kesha that called him last night at the hotel.

"And what else? Tell me!" I demand.

"She asked us if it was okay that she be daddy's girlfriend", Justice says. Amber agrees.

I'm too upset to drive right now. I need to pull this car over and call Kalin right now. He's on the phone, no doubt, talking to this Kesha person. I'm not moving this car until I have a word with him. After a few attempts, he finally answers the phone. "Honey, what's wrong? I see you've called a few times", he acknowledges.

"You're not going to believe what my children just told me", I tell him.

"What did they tell you, Melissa?"

"Well, let's see. Who is Kesha? And why is she asking my children if it is okay for her to be your girlfriend? And why is this Kesha person taking my children to the store to shop for clothes when it should have been you doing it? You can jump in at any time, Kalin!" I tell him.

"Will you please calm down? Let me explain. Kesha is just that, a friend. She's one of Gary's friends and she was doing me a favor taking them to the store because I had a meeting with the Modeling Agency. She was just being a friend, Melissa. And as far as her speaking to them about being in a relationship with me, I didn't know anything about that and I will speak to her about that."

Dead silence on the phone. He knows I'm pissed.

"Yeah, but what the hell have you been telling this woman? What makes her think that she can even have a relationship with you? And she's the one who called you last night, isn't she?" I ask him.

"She only called to make sure I made it to Tallahassee safe and sound. Melissa, please calm down. You have no reason to be upset like this. Are you driving?"

"No! I had to pull over on the side of the road to talk to you. I'm not going to put my life at risk. I'm so upset with you right now that I can just scream! Do you want this woman? Tell me now before we go any further!" I tell him.

"Melissa, no! You're my wife and I want *you*. I'm just friends with this woman. You have to trust me. Now, please get back on the road so that you and my daughters are not driving after dark. You know that you can't see all that good at night", he tells me.

"Ok. Fine. We'll talk about this later if need be, but you make sure you let your little friend know that she should never ever in her life address my children again and I mean that", I tell him.

"Melissa, that's not necessary. I got this. Call me when you make it home", he advises.

The girls and I get on the road again, but my heart and my mind are no longer at ease. My heart was so happy with the night that Kalin and I spent together, but now to find out what I have found out is starting to make me think that Kalin has not changed at all. Just because he's telling me that there's nothing going on with this woman doesn't mean that it's the truth. My gut instinct tells me that he's not telling me everything.

Unless the kids are talking to me, the ride back to Miami is a very quiet one. The girls are sitting in the back and so content just talking to each other, which is good for me right now because my mind is going a mile a minute. The sign I just passed says that we're only 35 miles from Miami. I can't wait to get home. *Who is calling my phone? I have no idea why this Connecticut number keeps showing up on my phone. I don't feel like talking to anyone right now, especially a bill collector.*

In Too Deep
Torn 2: Passion, Pain & Promise.

CHAPTER 44

"You Will Always Have a Place in my Heart."

*L*ord, thank you for this opportunity that you have afforded me to interview for a job. I know that Sales isn't something that I particularly wanted to do, but I am going to have to trust you because I have to do what I have to do. I ask that you be with me in this interview, help me to stay focused and not bring anything else with me in this interview. Watch over my children, watch over our household, watch over Kalin while he remains in Alabama, and watch over our marriage. These blessings I ask in Jesus' name, Amen.

The recruiter for Envision left a message for me while I was out of town and now, I'm on my way to meet with Mark Pritchett, the HR director. After so many interviews, you start to lose that nervousness. I just need to find a way to convince Mr. Pritchett that I can be successful at a sales job, even though I have not technically had any experience in sales. I'll use the property management to fit that somehow.

This place was not that hard to find because his directions were on point.

"Yes, I'm here to see Mr. Pritchett", I tell the receptionist. *I wonder who decorated this office. It must have been a woman. Very well put together. I love how the decorator used the red, black and white. If I had the money, I would definitely steal this idea.*

"Mrs. Thomas, Mr. Pritchett will see you now." Through a set of double doors and down a hallway, I finally end up at his door and in his office going on and on about how I can be an asset to his company. He must be totally convinced because he asks me to return on tomorrow to start working.

By the time the kids make it home from school, I already have dinner prepared and when we finally sit down to eat, I tell them the news that Mommy is going back to work. This seems to make their day. "Did Daddy call us Mommy?" Justice asks.

I could tell her the truth, but I won't. The last thing I want them to see is that their father is not a man of his word. "Of course he did, honey. He called while you were in school and said to tell his angels that he loves them and that he misses you already."

"That's so sweet of him to say. We love him, too. Can we call him, Mommy?"

"Maybe later. Let's get the kitchen cleaned first. Who wants dessert?"

"What's for dessert, Mommy?" Amber asks.

"Strawberry cake. Yummy, right?" I say.

"Yaaaaaayyyyyy!!"

While the girls are cleaning the kitchen, I decide to go into my office and check my messages. Subconsciously, I must be missing Patrick because I start looking at old emails from him. For some reason, he's on my mind tonight. I wonder what he's doing or *how* he's doing. I still can believe that he left me the way he did. Did he not think that I would be able to handle whatever issue came up? It's what you do when you love someone. And now, I feel as though I was forced back into a relationship with Kalin. I am going to send one final email to Patrick to basically tell him goodbye. My email reads, *Dearest Patrick, I hope this email finds you in the best of spirits and I just have to pray that you will receive it. I just want you to know that I have always cared for you since the very first day we met years ago. You came into my life at a time when I really needed it. Even though I tried everything I could to resist you, I ended up giving you my heart. And unfortunately, you broke it into tiny pieces without an explanation at all. Besides all of that, I still care for you and I hope that you are doing okay wherever you are. Whatever it is that you are dealing with, just look to God for help. Trust Him with all of your issues and He will certainly bring you through them. I am writing this letter to say goodbye to you because I have decided to mend my relationship with Kalin. I have discontinued the divorce so that we can work on our marriage. It is the best thing for the children and for me. I am sorry that things did not work out for us, and I won't throw blame in any direction for that. The truth is that you will always have a place in my heart, Patrick. Love Always, Melissa. Xoxoxoxoxoxo*

The tears are flowing down my face because I really loved this man. I am hurting to my soul because of how he treated me by leaving without saying one word to me. I am surprised that he did it, knowing everything I went through with Kalin. He left me with no choice.

Hitting the "send" button will end my relationship with Patrick officially. This hurts, but I have to do it. He's the reason I have to do this. There is no way I would have taken Kalin back if Patrick had remained in the picture.

Why hasn't Kalin called me today? What is he doing? Is he with this Kesha person? Am I being played by him or what? I need to know more about this woman. Who is she? Where did she come from? I have to know more and I will figure this out one way or the other.

Checking through my emails, I see that Kalin has sent a message about an hour ago and it reads, *Hello sweetheart. I'm sorry that I haven't called you today, but I had a meeting with the Modeling Agency and we have scheduled a photo shoot for me to get some pictures taken. I wanted to call, but I figured you would be having dinner at this time. I'll talk to you tomorrow. Love, Kalin.*

What kind of message is this and why can't he pick up the phone and call me? Is he that busy that he can't talk to me? I will give him the room he needs for his career. I will support him in every way that I can, without nagging him. But for now, I need to get some rest because my first day of work is tomorrow.

CHAPTER 45

"How Dare You!"

"*D*id you see the email I forwarded to you, bro?" Patrick asks his brother.

"I saw it, man. I read it. So what?"

"What does she mean, "Saying goodbye to me"?"

"Patrick, did you not read the same email I read? She was very clear in it. She has moved on and is back with her husband. You'll have to move on with your life as well. I guess it just wasn't meant to be. Did you try to call her like you said you would when we last talked?"

"I did, but she never answered. And I never left any messages, nor did I send an email."

"So, how do you expect to win her back if you can't even leave a voice message?"

"I'm afraid of rejection. I don't do well with it. I know she's angry and I just felt like leaving a message would have been the cowardly way of handling it", Patrick says.

"Man, look, just call her and see what happens. It can't get any worse. I mean, she's already said goodbye to you. Take a chance and if she rejects you, then she just rejects you. Move on. Find someone else", his brother advises.

Patrick knows that he has to make a move now because Melissa is no longer sitting around and waiting. He hangs up with his brother and dials her number.

"Hello."

"Melissa? Hi", Patrick says.

"Who is this?" I ask.

"It's Patrick. Please don't hang up", he says.

"Patrick! How are you? Are you okay?" I say. It feels like my heart just skipped a beat.

"Not really okay, but very happy to hear your voice", he comments.

"I'm glad to know that you're alive, Patrick. How dare you hurt me like this?" I ask.

"I know that I hurt you and I'm sorry, Melissa. It's just that...", he begins to explain.

"I don't want any excuses, Patrick. There is nothing in this world to make me understand why you cut me off like you did. We were supposed to be partners. We were supposed to be best friends. But you killed all of that, leaving me with no choice but to pick up the pieces with Kalin", I tell him.

"Melissa, you don't love him. You're just mad at me. Tell me you don't love me!"

"I can't say that, Patrick. People change. Kalin has changed and is ready to be a husband and ...", I begin to say until he interrupts me.

"Excuse me. Are we talking about the same man?" he asks.

"Listen, there's no need for you to insult him. He's trying to be a better husband. *Getting these words out of my mouth really hurt because I don't believe this for one minute.* I have to go, Patrick", I say.

"Melissa, why? Please don't do this? I have to tell you something", he pleads with me.

"I'm not interested in your excuses as to why you disappeared on me for 3 months without any type of hello. You didn't think about anybody but yourself. Do you have any idea what I have gone through not knowing if you were dead or alive and ...?" I say to him, now starting to cry.

"Baby, I'm so sorry that I hurt you, but please don't go back to this man just because you're angry with me, Melissa. Please! Hear me out!" he pleads.

"Maybe another time, Patrick, but I have to go right now. I can't do this right now. Please, maybe another time!" I say, before hanging up the phone.

Patrick is beside himself and has started crying way out of his control now. He feels even worse now than before regarding how he treated Melissa. He really thought he was doing the right thing and now, there's nothing he can do to get the love of his life to understand him and take his hand in this thing, but he honestly can't blame her for the way she has reacted.

For now, he has decided that he will continue his therapy and get through it the best way he can.

CHAPTER 46

"He's Still Not Answering."

"So, how was your trip to meet yo' husband?" Cynthia asks Melissa.

"It was fine at first and no, I don't want to talk about it!" Melissa states.

"Oh, no you didn't! How you gon' treat your best friend like that? What happened?" she asks.

"I think Kalin is cheating on me with another woman that he recently met in Alabama", I blurt out.

"What! But you two just got back together. Why do you believe that?" she asks.

"My children told me that his *friend* asked *them* how they felt about her dating their father", I explain. "I was livid!"

"I bet you were, Melissa. I don't understand how you can feel…", she begins, but I interrupt her.

"Hey, hold on. Somebody is at the door and ringing the doorbell like crazy, so that can't be but one person, Diana! Hold on", I tell her.

The closer I get to the door, I can see that it is Diana and she comes bearing gifts. "Hey sis, how are you?"

"I'm fine! I just came from one of your favorite stores and they had a huge sale today and since you're starting work next week, I thought you could use some more clothes", she tells me.

"That's so nice of you, girl! But hold on, let me say goodbye to Cynthia. I was on the phone with her."

"Cynthia, my darling, my sister has arrived. What are you doing tonight?" I ask her.

"Nothing, actually. My husband is hanging out with some of his buddies to watch the football game", she replies.

"Then, it's settled! Come on over. Me, you, and my sister can put some steaks on the grill, open up a bottle of wine and have a great dinner. What do you say?" I ask.

"Ok, sounds like fun. I'll be over in about an hour."

Diana seems anxious to tell me about the sale at the mall. The girl does have a good eye for shopping and picked out just the right things that I would picked out for myself. "I can't pay you for these items, Diana", I tell her.

"Did I ask you for any money? What's wrong with me doing something nice for my little sister? I just want you to look your best for your new job, that's all", she says.

"That's so nice of you, sis. Thanks so much. Now, let's get something to eat. I asked Cynthia to come over, so we can throw some steaks on the grill, pop open a bottle of wine and just relax. The girls are out with some of their friends, so they won't even be back tonight. And besides, this gives us a chance to really talk without having to be quiet", I tell her.

"Talk? About what? What's wrong, MeMe?" Diana asks, looking extremely concerned.

"It's Kalin, Diana. I don't know if I made the right decision. Guess who called me yesterday?" I ask.

"Who? Tell me."

"Patrick. He called and he was basically begging me to take him back. The man was being all apologetic and everything and ….", I begin but she interrupts me.

"Let me guess. You cut him off, didn't you? If I know my sister, you probably didn't let him even finish explaining what happened. Don't you want to know?" she asks, looking concerned.

"At one point, I wanted to know, but he messed up and put me in a position to think that, perhaps, I should be with my husband. So, what he went through or why he didn't call doesn't matter to me anymore", I say, looking away.

"And something tells me that it ain't going too good, either", she says, moving around in her seat to face me.

"Oh, God, sis, you have no idea!" I say.

"I'm here. Talk to me. Tell me what's wrong", Diana pleads with me.

"It's Kalin. I just don't know what….", I begin to explain.

"Already? You're having issues with him already? For crying out loud, what has he done now?" she asks, rolling her eyes.

"I think he's cheating with a lady he met in Alabama, one of his brother's friends."

"Wow! Are you sure?" Diana asks.

"Girl, she called him while we were at the hotel. And not only that, this heffa had the nerve to ask my kids what they think about her being with their dad", I explain.

"I know you checked him on that", she comments.

"Yes. I told him that he needs to let his friend know not to ever do that again. I am not playing with him about that. I think I may have made a mistake taking him back, D", I say.

"You think?" she says sarcastically.

"I'm serious! I thought I loved him and needed to be a Christian wife and mend our marriage. But, there's something wrong. I can just feel it!" I say.

That must be Cynthia ringing the doorbell. She's the only one I'm expecting. And just like she always does, she comes bearing gifts. "Hey sweetie! I picked up your favorite wine. They had a 2 for 1 sale at Publix on the Kendall Jackson Chardonnay wine", she tells me.

"Oh great!"

"What are ya'll talking about?" Cynthia asks.

"Men!" I answer.

"Hope you ain't mentioning Kalin's name!" Cynthia responds.

"Whewwwwwwwwww! That wasn't nice, Cynthia!" Diana says, then laughs.

"Now, ya'll wrong for that!" I comment.

The steaks are on the grill, the jazz music is our background noise, and the wine is chilling. Our Saturday afternoon is just as I expected it would be. We carry on into the night discussing our "men" issues. It seems so much easier when discussing these "issues" with other women. They understand where I'm coming from when I have my doubts that Kalin is working on this marriage as sincerely as I am. *I can only imagine what they would say if they knew that I had been trying to reach him all weekend and he isn't answering his phone. The conversation would then go an entirely different way. Where is he? And now, his phone is going straight to voicemail. His brother isn't answering his phone either. I can't believe this! The sad part about it is that I have to pretend like nothing is wrong.*

"Girl, these steaks are so good! What's your secret?" Cynthia asks.

"I let them marinate all night. They're good, aren't they?"

"Yes. This is so nice of you, Melissa", Diana comments.

"You have both been so supportive to me over the last months and I appreciate it. It's the least I can do", I say.

I can honestly say that I really needed this time with other women. So glad they took time to come over. Honestly, just having another adult to listen to the issues that I'm having with Kalin is rewarding enough. It feels differently when you speak it to someone else. Once I say goodnight to the girls and get ready for bed, I realize that I'm not quite ready to go to sleep. I continue calling Kalin and he's *still* not answering his phone and now it's off because it's going to voice mail. The clock says 1:30am and my husband is not answering his phone.

Dear God. Father of our Lord and Savior Jesus Christ. Thank you Lord for being you. Thank you for loving me when, at times, I don't know how to love myself. I ask that you please be with me right now and give me the peace that I know can only come from you. Lord, only you know what is going on right now with my husband. Only you know the truth and I pray that he is not dishonoring you or this marriage. Forgive him, Lord, if he is. And give me the strength to know how to deal with it if I should find out that he is being unfaithful to me. Bring us back to each other, Lord. Teach us how to love each other. In Jesus' name. Amen.

CHAPTER 47

"When Are You Coming Home?"

*T*oday is my first day at Envision and I'm not sure what to expect since I've never worked a sales job ever in my life, but as always, I welcome new challenges to become better.

"Good morning, Mrs. Thomas. Welcome to Envision. This is where you'll sit. This is your phone and the number. Here are the instructions for how to set it up. This is my extension if you should have any questions", the HR director tells me, leaving me at my new desk and with my new supervisor, Bobby.

"So, Melissa, no sales experience, huh?" Bobby asks.

"No sir."

"Nothing to fear. By the time you're done with this job, you will!" he says, laughing.

"I'm sure. I look forward to learning from all of you."

My first day is a success. This office seems to be pretty fast-paced and there are so many people who have gotten this thing down to a science. When you sell something, you get to hop up and put the sale on the board. This one guy, Brendan, is awesome. He's a top seller in the company. Rumor has it that he drives a free BMW because of all of his sales. The good news about this sales job is that they still give you base pay whether you sell or not.

The only bad part of this job is the time that I have to be at work. By the time I get off work, it's already the evening hour, so I have to prepare dinner for my girls before I leave home to come to work. But the good news is that I don't have to work on the weekends.

It's about time! Kalin is finally calling! I can't wait to see what lie he comes up with this time. "Hello", I say.

"Before you say anything, I know that you're mad at me and I just…", he begins, but I interrupt him.

"What? Apologize? Is that what you want to do?" I say angrily.

"Melissa, please listen. I'm sorry that I didn't speak with you over the weekend. I was out with Greg and we just turned off our phones and everything and I just…", he says before I interrupt him.

"Kalin, you think I'm a fool, don't you? And what's this number that you're calling me from?" I ask him.

"Melissa, I'm over to a friend's house right now and I know that I needed to call you before you start going crazy and stuff", he tells me.

"Ok, Kalin. Ok."

"How was your first day at work?" he asks.

"It was fine. I think I may be okay with this sales thing. It seems a little scary at first, but I'm sure that I'll get the swing of things in no time."

"I know you will too, Melissa. Just be yourself. Become very familiar with the product. If you think about it, being a property manager was like being in sales. And what was *Mary Kay Cosmetics*? Selling make-up. Girl, you'll be just fine", he comments.

"Thanks so much, Kalin. It means a lot to me that you believe in me."

"Of course, I believe in you", he tells me.

"Kalin, if we're going to have a successful marriage moving forward, you need to not ever do that again. How would you feel if I did that to you? And who is this friend's house that you're at?"

"Melissa, it's just a friend, okay. There's nothing for you to worry about. I'm faithful to you and I want our marriage to work as well. I should be getting another phone soon and I won't have to come to my friend's house to contact you and…", he begins to say, but the phone goes dead.

"Hello. Hello. Kalin, are you there?" I say, repeatedly.

For whatever reason, the phone disconnects. *Did the phone disconnect or did he disconnect the phone because someone was coming? Why am I being so skeptical and suspicious of everything? My gut instinct tells me that something isn't right. Something doesn't fit. I'm going to call this number, but I have to do it from a payphone.*

Just up a mile is a gas station with a payphone outside. I'll deal with the consequences later, but I need to do this. I have to stop there and call this number because I really need to know what's going on with my marriage. This is a good time to contact the attorney to move forward with the divorce if I need to do so. When I pull in, someone is already on the payphone, but I decide to wait because there's no guarantee that there'll be another one down the road.

My knees are starting to shake, now that I'm here and moments away from knowing the truth. Honestly, I'm somewhat relieved when I hear a male voice. "Yes, hello, this is Mrs. Thomas and I was just speaking with my husband, Kalin. He called me from this number. May I speak with him, please?" Right away, I can tell that my call may have caused a disturbance because the mouthpiece is covered and the voices in the background are muffled.

"Hello", Kalin says, coming onto the phone not sounding happy to hear from me.

"What happened that we got disconnected?" I ask.

"Why did you call here?" he asks. *The first thing that comes to mind is that this is a woman's house! What is wrong with me calling my husband if he is at a friend's house?*

"What is wrong with me calling there?" I ask.

"And then, you have to announce that you're my wife. What is wrong with you, Melissa? Why are you acting like this?" he asks, sounding annoyed. I can hear voices in the background.

"Acting like what?!! I am your wife!! What? Is this your girlfriend's house or something?" I say, almost in tears. I'm getting so upset that I can feel that my monthly is coming on before its time.

"If you want to talk, you gotta stop acting childish. I don't have time for this. Now, what do you want, Melissa?"

"Oh, I see. It's like that! What do I want? Hell, I thought we were still talking. Did you hang up the phone or were we disconnected?" I ask.

"Look. Let me go. I'm not going to do this with you right now", he says, as if I'm just *any woman* calling to bother him.

"I can't believe you're doing this to me!" I yell, immediately beginning to cry.

Oh God! Oh God! Why is he hurting me like this? Why, God? Why didn't I learn my lesson? He must be cheating on me, Lord. I can't take this pain in my heart right now. I just want to die. I just want to close my eyes and never wake up again. But my children need me. Oh no! The children! I have to get home now. Please give me strength to deal with this. Please, Lord.

I hope that the children got their food okay and have taken their baths and ready for bed by the time I get home. I need to wipe these tears away because the last thing I want them to know is that Mommy and Daddy are fighting. They would, somehow, think it's their fault and I can't have that. After almost an hour, I'm finally pulling into the driveway. For some reason, it looks more dark than usual and the front light isn't lit up. *What's wrong? The neighbors aren't having any issues with their lights. I'm not going to panic. The children are ok. The children are ok. Dear Lord, they are safe. I know it. They have always been protected.*

I put the key in the door and I can hear them crying. "Girls!" I shout. "Where are you?"

"Mommy, is that you?" they shout.

"Yes, where are you?" I yell in the dark.

"Over here! Over here in the family room!" Justice yells.

"Why? Why are ya'll sitting in the dark?" I ask. "Where is Princess?"

"We don't know, Mommy! We had just finished eating and all of a sudden, the lights went out and wouldn't come back on. Princess didn't come home yet. *Oh God, no! Oh God, no! I forgot to pay the electric bill. What was I thinking? This man has my mind going so bad that I forgot to pay the bill.*

"Girls, it's Mommy's fault. I forgot to pay the bill. I'm so sorry. Will you forgive me? I hope you weren't too scared", I tell them.

"Ugh, yes, Mommy. We were definitely scared", Amber responds sarcastically.

"I'm so sorry. This won't happen again. I'll get it taken care of first thing tomorrow morning", I tell them.

"Here's the mail, Mommy. I don't know if you can read it or not", she says, handing me a stack of mail.

"Junk mail, junk mail, bills, bills, but this letter is from the Department of Juvenile Justice. I rip open the letter and it reads,

Dear Mrs. Thomas,

It is with regret that we inform you that your daughter, Sharelle Williams, been discharged from our facility due to an altercation that she had with another inmate, in which the inmate suffered a broken nose. She is being transferred out of this program

immediately. Due to her behavior. She will now be placed in a
high risk facility, where she will be closely monitored.

Sincerely,
Denise Hall, Director
(386) 555-1285, ext. 653

"Mommy, what is it?" Justice asks.

"Your sister has gotten in trouble again", I tell her. "I just don't understand this. I just don't understand why this child won't just do like she's told and ….", I say, starting to cry.

"Mommy, don't cry. Me and Amber will talk to Sharelle and make sure she does what's right", she says, wiping my face.

"I appreciate that, sweetheart. Mommy also has some other things on her mind. You guys want some ice cream?" I ask them.

"Yaaaaaaayyyyyyyyyyyyy! That would be great, Mommy! Let's go!"

I am more than amazed at their attitude after having sat in the dark for hours. We jump in the car and head to Ben & Jerry's for ice cream, but on the way, I explain to them that I need to stop by the payphone to call their father. "Yaaay!" Justice yells. "I miss him, Mommy."

"Yeah, I am sure he'll be happy to hear from you too", I tell them.

My stomach is getting nervous about how Kalin is going to react when he hears his children on the phone. Knowing this plan could easily backfire on me, I drop the coins into the slot and wait for an answer on the other end. "Hello", Kalin says.

"Hey, it's me again, but before you say anything, I have your children here. They want to speak to you", I tell him, handing the phone to Justice first.

"Hey daddy! We miss you! When are you coming home?" she asks, not giving him a chance to answer. They exchange a few words and then she passes the phone to Amber, who gets on and tell him that she loves him. Their conversation is brief and she hands the phone back to me.

"Hello", I say.

"Yeah, honey, what kind of game are you playing? Is this how it's going to be?" he asks.

"What are you saying? If you have a problem with me and your children calling you, then maybe you are the one who needs to come clean because the day you're ashamed of us is the day I say goodbye to you forever, Negro!" I tell him.

"Melissa, what is it that you need, honey?" he asks.

"I thought I would say good night to my husband. I also wanted you to know that Sharelle got into a fight at the facility and is now being transported to a high risk facility. I'm worried sick about my child. It's not like I can just call her up and chat with her. I was hoping you would offer comfort to me. I need you, Kalin. When are you going to start being here for me? When, Kalin?" I say, starting to tear up.

"Melissa, I'm sorry about that. I really am. You need to stop babying those kids and let them grow up and maybe they'll change. Those folks don't have time for her mess. So, you act up, that's what you get!" he says, without a care in the world.

"Thank you, Kalin, for being the most insensitive jerk I know! You're right about one thing. I never should have bothered you. Go back to whatever it is that you were doing. I'll find comfort somewhere. Don't worry! Goodnight!" I say, hanging up the phone.

"Ok, girls, let's get our ice cream!"

CHAPTER 48

"What's the Password?"

"*A*nd our Rookie of the Month, Melissa Thomas!" the sales director announces. "Having only been in sales for 3 weeks now, this girl sold 18 kits in one week! I have heard her on the phone and let me tell you, she's good! She's got that silver tongue. Come on up, Melissa. Speech, speech!!" the crowd cheers.

Who would have thought that I would win this award without having any sales experience? From now on, my name will be on the wall of fame. This company really believes in giving good perks when you excel in sales. This is just the beginning as far as I'm concerned.

"Congratulations, Melissa!" says Arnie, the guy who sits in the cubicle next to me. "Let's get some lunch. How does Chic-Fil-A sound?"

"Sounds good!" With only an hour for lunch, we leave right away to avoid the busy lunch hour traffic. Upon our return, we approach our work area and I notice that my phone's red light is blinking. In a sales room, that's usually very good news because that means that one of the dealerships is either calling in for questions or calling for an order.

"Whew hoo, superstar! Looks like someone wants more kits!" Arnie says, as we approach our cubicles.

"Boy, you're crazy! But yes, I do love the blinking red light on my phone."

I hit the voicemail button and as I start listening to my message, my heart sinks. "Melissa, hey it's Diana! I tried to reach you on your cell phone", she begins. "Give me a call back. I have some news for you." I drop the phone.

"Melissa, what's wrong? Who was it?" Arnie asks. "Why are you looking like that?"

"That was my sister. Something's wrong. She asked me to call her back because she has to tell me something, but I don't want to. My heart is racing, Arnie."

"Melissa, hold on. Call her. That's the only way you'll know", he tells me.

Nervously, I dial Diana's number. She picks up the phone on the first ring. "D, what's up?" I say before she gets a chance to say hello.

"Melissa, I have some bad news", she says.

"Oh no! What's wrong?" I say, with my heart in my stomach.

"Melissa, I hate to tell you this. Larry died this morning. He had a massive heart attack at a hotel. He tried to call the....", Diana begins to explain.

"No! No! Oh God, no! Please don't tell me this! Oh God, no!" I yell, starting to cry.

"Melissa! Oh no! What's wrong?" Arnie says, grabbing my hand. I'm watching Arnie, but trying to pay attention to my sister at the same time.

"Melissa, calm down. Please don't get too upset, sis. I know that he was your favorite cousin, but at least it was quick. He was trying to call 9-1-1, but it was too late", Diana continues.

"I gotta go, D", I tell her. "I'll call you later", I say to her and hang up the phone.

"Melissa, you okay?" Arnie asks me.

"No, friend, I'm not okay. I need to get out of here for a moment. I'll be right back", I tell him.

"Ok, I'll let the supervisor know", he says, as I walk away.

Dear God. This pain in my heart is so painful right now. Why, Lord? Why take him away from his children, from his family? I don't understand this, Lord. I know you don't make mistakes and I'm trying my best not to question you, but I don't understand this one. For crying out loud, he was only 42 years old, just 3 years older than me. Lord, please help me to be there for my cousin's son. I think one reason I feel so horrible is because when I was in Alabama this past summer, I wanted to see him, but didn't get a chance to see him. Ok, Lord, this is obviously your Will, so I will just have to deal with it. In Jesus' name, Amen.

Winning Rookie of the Month doesn't quite mean the same to me anymore. It's hard to celebrate this victory because now, I will forever associate the day I won *Rookie of the Month* as the day my favorite cousin died. Due to the sudden death in my family, my supervisor gives me the option to go home, but I decline. Being alone right now will only make me feel worse.

After a while, I stop crying long enough to get some work done, knowing full well that it's taking everything in me to hold back the tears. It seems like it took forever, but the work day has come to an end and I'm finally on my way home. I really need to speak with Kalin right now, but when I call his phone, I get his voice mail, so I have to leave a message. It looks like I've actually missed quite a few phone calls today. My cousin is loved by so many people and I'm sure that people are calling to show their love and concern in this situation.

"Mommy, why are you crying?" Justice asks, when I come through the front door. She's sitting in the family room and sees me when I come in.

"Honey, help me with the bags, ok", I tell her instead.

"Mommy, but you're crying. Why?" she asks again.

"One of my cousins died today and it has me really sad. When we were growing up in Middleton, he and I would talk for hours on the phone. He played basketball and I was a cheerleader. He used to get cranky with me when I dated his basketball friends because he always said that I was a distraction", I tell her.

"That's so sad, Mommy. Isn't he in heaven with God?" she asks, wiping the tears away from my eyes.

"Yes, he sure is. He sure is", I say. "How was school?"

"School was fine."

"That's good. Where's Amber?" I ask.

"In her room doing her homework, of course", she responds. "Princess is in her room also."

"Wanna help Momma prepare dinner?"

"Sure. What are we having tonight?" she asks.

"Spaghetti. Just wanna cook something that won't take too long because I have plenty of calls to make and I also need to get some work done on the computer", I respond.

Justice and I prepare dinner in what seems like the most silent time I have ever spent with my daughter. She must be disappointed that I don't have much to say while we prepare dinner together. But, whether she likes it or not, she doesn't say anything at all. Princess and Amber come down to eat and over dinner, I hear about how their day was in school. As usual, both Amber and Justice are on a roll to complete this grading period with honor roll status.

"Girls, I really need to get upstairs and get on the computer and spend some time in my office. Will you be okay down here?" I ask them.

"Mommy, just do what you need to do. I got the girls. We'll go ahead and clean the kitchen and I'll make sure their homework is good", Princess tells me.

"Thank you so much. Mommy really appreciates that", I respond.

When I leave to go upstairs, the girls are already starting to clean the kitchen. They work so well together and I have to be the most blessed mother in the world. While the computer is powering up, I look around and notice that my mail has started piling up, forcing me to separate the junk mail from the others. The envelope from my divorce attorney sticks out like a sore thumb. The final papers are inside for me to review before they serve them to Kalin. *Should I move forward with this divorce or not? I still love him, Lord. I still love him. For some reason, I just can't let go of him. I am still in love with this man no matter how much he has hurt me and is still hurting me. I just really love him so much that I would probably die for him. But, is this my way out? Is this God's way of giving me the relief I have been praying for? Since the letter gives me 30 days to respond, I'll need all of this time to see what's really going on in my marriage.*

There are several messages in my inbox, some for myself and some for Kalin. We set up this account a couple of years ago just to keep things all out in the open. Are my eyes deceiving me? There's an email here that's addressed to Kalin and the subject line says *For Your Pleasure.* From Kesha McPherson! And there is a picture attached. At least I will get to see what she looks like. I click on the link for the picture. Nooooo! This woman has sent a picture of her vagina to my husband!! I am in total shock at this moment. With all that I'm going through right now, this is the last thing I want to deal with. This is bizarre! *How can Kalin do this to me now? How? Why does this woman feel this comfortable to send this type of photo to my husband?*

I can't dial Kalin's number fast enough. He doesn't answer his phone. He's probably at work. I call his job and they say he's already left for the evening. I call Greg's house and nobody picks up. The last call I make is to his sister who answers the phone.

"Hello, Monica", I say.

"Hey, Melissa. How are you?"

"Not good at all. Is your brother there?" I ask.

"No. He isn't. Is everything okay?" she asks.

"No, it's not, Monica. No, it's not. Tell your brother that I saw the picture. I saw it and he needs to contact me as soon as possible because I am tired of this mess. You tell him that, please."

My heart is breaking right at this moment because my husband has chosen to share in something with another woman that was once so special and unique to us. I was always sending nude pictures to my husband. She has sent this picture to at least two other emails and I suspect that one of the other emails is somehow connected to Kalin. I am so angry right now.'

There is only one other person that can be here for me right now and it's Patrick. I need to talk to someone who knows me and cares for me to help me get through the death of my cousin. I can't stop crying. This hurts so much. I slowly dial Patrick's number. He answers on the first ring. "Hello."

"Patrick, hey there", I say. "I need you."

"Baby, what's wrong? Did Kalin hurt you? Are you okay?" he asks.

"No. None of that. My favorite cousin in the world died today and I don't have anyone I feel comfortable enough to talk to about it", I begin to explain.

"Baby, I'm here for you. Give me just one moment and I'll be right back. I was right in the middle of something and I ...", he begins to say until I interrupt him.

"Oh, I'm sorry if I disturbed you. I didn't know if I ....", I apologize.

"Honey, don't worry about it. Just give me a moment", he says, coming back moments later.

After everything we've gone through, I can't believe that I still end up needing Patrick. He's a good friend and I appreciate him for being here for me right now. I need to be able to talk to someone to help me sort through my feelings and who better to do that with than the man who captured my heart when I really tried to resist him.

"Ok, I'm back. You have my undivided attention. Talk to me. What's wrong?"

"Patrick, my heart is ripped and torn today. My favorite cousin of all times died of a massive heart attack and he was only 3 years older than me. I can't begin to understand why this has happened and ..", I begin to explain.

"Oh my God, Melissa. I'm so sorry, honey. I'm so sorry. I wish I could be there to hold you right now and tell you that everything is going to be okay. I want you to cry if that's what you feel like doing. I'm here for you as long as you need me to be", he says.

"I appreciate you for being here, Patrick. It means a lot to me. It really does. You have always been a good friend. I'm sorry for being rude. How are you doing?"

"You're not being rude. It's okay. I'm doing fine. My therapy is starting to work and it looks like I may not have to be here too much longer and I'm really happy about that. I miss my house!" he tells me.

"Where are you, Patrick?" I ask him.

"In Connecticut."

"Why are you there? Is that where you've been all this time?" I ask him.

"Yes, it is, Melissa."

"Is there someone that you went to see there? Is there someone else in your life now?" I ask, not really wanting the answer to this question.

"No, there isn't, Melissa. I had to come here for business and my business is almost wrapped up now", he says, feeling as though this isn't the right time to talk about his health, especially knowing that her cousin just passed.

"So, it was you calling me from Connecticut? I remember getting a call from a Connecticut number", I tell him.

"Yes, that was me", he says, softly.

"Wow, and I thought it was a bill collector and that's why I didn't answer", I admit. "Hopefully, I'll get to see you when you get back to Florida. I've missed you, Patrick", I tell him.

"I've missed you, too, Melissa. Please tell me you feel better."

"I'm starting to feel better, but even though I'm trying to deal with my cousin's death, I'm also dealing with something else that has my heart in knots", I tell him.

"It's Kalin, isn't it?"

"Yes, it is. I just got my divorce papers in the mail. The attorney wants me to review them before they're sent to Kalin and ...", I begin.

"...and what's the problem? He's a loser, Melissa! Why are you thinking about it? What's there to think about?" He doesn't deserve to have a woman like you", Patrick says.

"I'm contemplating it because he *is* my husband and I was really trying to make the marriage work because I feel that it's what God wants me to do. Marriages are oftentimes challenged and we have to just forgive one another and work through it", I say, not totally believing what I just said myself.

"Melissa, that's beautiful and all, but does he feel the same way? Is he trying to make the marriage work? What's going on with him now? Why is it that you're *still* going through things with this man? What's the problem?"

"Patrick, I have a confession to make. Just before I called you, I saw an email in mine and Kalin's inbox that came from a woman in Alabama, who he claims is just a friend", I begin to explain.

"And what did the email say?"

"It didn't say much, but it was a picture of her vagina!" I blurt out.

"You're kidding, right? What kind of married man does this? And what did he have to say about it?" Patrick asks.

"I haven't talked to him about it just yet. Can't seem to get in touch with him, but I've left messages with his family to have him contact me."

This is really starting to get to me, but there's no way that I can let Patrick know I'm crying.

"You think he's sleeping around with this woman?" Kalin asks.

"I have no idea. I'm so upset about this! How could he do this to me? You know what else I saw?"

"What?"

"I noticed that she included an email address that looks like Kalin's, but I don't recognize the email. I don't know if this is his or not. I'm determined to get to the bottom of this", I tell him.

"What are you going to do?" he asks.

"Put in the user ID and guess the password and you know what, I'm going to do it right now", I say, going to the Hotmail website.

After typing in the user ID, I have no idea what his password could be. I try *Justice,* but that isn't it. I try *Amber* and that isn't it. I try *jesuscares* and that isn't it, so I decide to bring up the password question. *Where is your mother born?* is the password question.

"Are you having much luck?" Patrick asks, as he listen to me try to get into the account.

"I'm stuck! The password question is *Where is your mother born?* I know that he's told me, but I can't think right now. Hold on for a second, Patrick. I'm going to call his father from my cellphone and get the answer to this question.

I pick up the cellphone and call Kalin's father and find out where his mother was born and when I type in *South Carolina,* I'm in!

"I'm in!" I yell into the phone.

"He told you?" Patrick asks. "He actually told you, huh? That is so funny. I'm sure that you didn't tell him what you wanted it for", he comments.

"No! I told him that I was working on a birthday video surprise for Kalin and I needed to know where his mother was born and he gave it to me."

"Wow! You're sneaky, Melissa", he says.

"I don't believe this! Oh my God, Patrick! It's an email account that they have together with correspondence in here from the two of them only. There are tons of naked pictures in here of the both of them. There are E-cards in here! This is too painful to even look at! I can't believe this man is doing this to me! I can't believe this, Patrick!" I say, starting to cry even harder.

"Melissa, please don't cry, sweetheart. Please try to hold it together. He's an idiot! If he can't see the kind of woman that he has in you, then forget him! Forget him, baby. You're way too special of a woman to sit here and be disrespected and mistreated this way. I'm so sorry, Melissa", he says, trying to comfort me.

My eyes are full of tears and there's a frog in my throat. I can't speak right now. I don't know what to say. The emails in here are X-rated. It's definitely not conversation a married man should have with another woman.

"I can't take this anymore, Patrick. I've done nothing for this man to treat me this way. Nothing at all! And just when I need him the most, he's off doing God knows what with another woman. What is wrong with men these days? A woman gives a man her heart and that's still not enough for him. I don't get it, Patrick!" I cry out to him.

"Sweetheart, I'm so sorry for ever hurting you. I feel horrible because I hurt you too, but I promise you that if you give me another chance, I'll never hurt you, baby. I'll always be honest with you, Melissa. Kalin is a fool! He has such a beautiful woman in you and I don't know why he 's doing this, but he's definitely a fool!" Patrick says to me.

"I appreciate that, Patrick. I do. I want to see what happens with my marriage first. Can you respect this and be my friend for now?" I ask him.

"I will, Melissa. I'll be right here by your side for as long as you need me to be here for you", he says.

"And just when I need him to be here for me. He *still* hasn't called me back after I have left several messages for him to call me. I'm so upset about this picture that I saw and now, this secret email account with this woman. I feel so stupid for sending her an email because ….", I begin to say, but Patrick interrupted me.

"You sent the woman an email?" he asks.

"Yes. I sent her an email wanting to know why she would send a pic like that to *my* husband and I also told her to never, ever in her life speak to *my* children about her desire to have a relationship with their father. I told her that if he was interested in having a relationship with her, he would speak to them himself. I told her that when Kalin came to Tallahassee to drop off the girls that night that he slept with me and that he always will because I'm his wife. I went on to tell her that she needed to put herself in order because he wasn't even a man who took care of his kids. I mean I just went on and on and now I feel like a fool!" I say, starting to cry again.

"Please don't cry, Melissa. You're about to make me find this man and kick his behind. I don't want to hear you crying. Please don't", he pleads.

Oh God! Please give me strength. And I thought that I was done with crying so much. I thank God for this man for being here for me because there's just no telling how this would be going tonight if I didn't have Patrick to talk to. Listening to him makes me so angry that he ever hurt me because if he had never left, I would not have thought about trying to work on my marriage with Kalin. But I'm definitely glad that he's here. He's being so sweet and I want to give in to him, but I promised God I would give all to my marriage.

"I'll be okay, Patrick. Thank you for being here to listen to me and to help me get through this", I say.

"Of course."

Patrick and I continue discussing other emails in the account. I can only read the emails that are open because I don't want to alert either one of them that I'm watching. As painful as it is to see these emails and read them, this is how I've decided to monitor what's going on in Alabama with my husband.

The kids are calling me to come downstairs to watch a movie with them so I wrap up my conversation with Patrick. Before he hangs up, he tells me how much he loves and misses me. He constantly reminds me that he'll be back in Florida soon.

"Ok, I'm here! What are we watching?" I say, flopping down on the couch.

CHAPTER 49

"This Is All Your Fault."

"**M**rs. Thomas, what do you want me to do with these divorce papers? I sent them out to you at least two weeks ago and I haven't received a reply from you as of yet. What's going on?" Attorney Abney asks.

"Kalin and I are working on our marriage. It's a little rocky right now, but I just believe that it's what God wants me to do", I tell him.

"Are you serious? This doesn't sound like the woman who wanted better in life, who was tired of being abused, or who was disgusted with the way she was being cheated on", he begins to say.

"I know what I've said in the past, but, yes, I'm serious. I'm very serious. People change. I forgive him, Mr. Abney. People change, right? I mean, if they really want to change, they can", I say, sounding as if I'm trying to convince myself.

"If you say so. I'll keep the papers for another 2 weeks or so and then I'll close out this file, but if you ever change your mind, I'll be right here", he tells me.

"Thank you. I appreciate that."

What in the world did I just do? Kalin is acting a fool right now. Why didn't I just move forward with the divorce? Is it that I really love him or is it just about winning right now? I have to think about the answer to this question because I don't want to make the mistake of a lifetime by wanting to still be with my husband just to keep him from Kesha.

For the rest of the afternoon, my mind continues to replay my conversation with the attorney regarding the divorce. I don't think he agrees with me, but he also knows that it is *my* decision. Deep in thought, I almost don't hear my phone ringing. The caller ID alerts me that Kalin is calling. He's just the man I need to speak with right now.

Before I can say *hello,* Kalin says, "Melissa, I know you're upset and I'm going to get to the bottom of it."

"Honestly, there's nothing to get to the bottom of, Kalin. So strange to me that you insist on being friends with someone who's trying to destroy our marriage. This woman sent you a picture of her vagina!! That is completely disrespectful, Kalin. You're a married man! And you need to start acting like one!" I yell into the phone.

"Can you please calm down? We won't accomplish anything if we continue to speak at this tone, Melissa. I know you're upset and I have one question", he says. "Why in the world did you send an email to Kesha? I know you're upset, but if you and I are having any issues, you should address those issues with me and not someone else", he tells me.

"Whatever, Kalin! That was messed up! But, don't worry about it. I'm crying for you now, but you better believe one day I will stop crying, Kalin, and when I do, that's when you'll know that I'm over you", I say, starting to cry.

"Melissa, this woman said that she sent this to me by mistake. So, please calm down and stop letting this stuff come between us", he pleads with me.

"Come between us? Give me a break, Kalin! This is all your fault! You've made it very clear that you'll continue your friendship with this woman and it doesn't matter what I say or what I want, so there you go. *That* is our problem!" I tell him. "I'm going now, Kalin. I have things to do."

I don't want to hear anything else that he has to say so I hang up the phone without giving him a chance to give any further explanation. To further punish myself, I go to her and Kalin's email account just to see if there'a a response to the email that I sent to her. But there isn't. But what I do find is an email from her to him telling him how much she cares for him and wants to be with him. He hasn't responded to it yet.

CHAPTER 50

"It's Not Going Good at All."

"Did you see him yet?" Cynthia asks.

"See who?"

"Patrick. He's back in town. I ran into him at the grocery store. He was with his son. He said that he had just gotten into town", she tells me.

"No. I haven't seen him yet. I don't think I want to see him. As a matter of fact, it probably wouldn't be a good idea if Patrick and I see each other, especially since I'm trying to work things out with Kalin", I say.

"And how is that working out, Melissa?" she asks.

"It's not going good at all, Cynthia. I think that I love him way more than he loves me. His friendship with this woman, Kesha, is making our marriage more and more difficult. He refuses to discontinue his friendship with her, knowing that it's causing some serious issues in our relationship", I comment.

"Because he's a jerk and I don't know what it's gonna take for you to see that."

"So, how did he look?" I ask Cynthia, changing the subject.

"Who?"

"Patrick. How did he look?" I ask again.

"He looked good. He really did, girl", she answers. We both laugh.

"Then, I know I don't need to see him. You know what I mean?" I say, sarcastically.

"I spoke to him briefly, but he was with his son. He said that they were going to spend their afternoon grilling some steaks."

"That's nice", I respond.

"You know you want to call him, Melissa. So, why don't you? I'm sure that he would love to see you. That's the man you deserve, Melissa", Cynthia tells me.

"Come on, Cynthia. You know I'm trying to work on my marriage. Seeing Patrick would really mess things up and I really don't want Kalin to know that Patrick is back in town. God's desire is for me to make it work with my husband and I just have to pray that God will fix our issues", I say, trying to convince Cynthia.

"I think it's great to be a part of God's Will, but you are so unhappy. Have you seen yourself lately?" she asks.

"I know. I feel it. I do. But, I have to do this and I just need your support", I tell her.

"Of course you have my support. No matter what you choose, you have my support", Cynthia says, putting her arm on my shoulder. "But, Melissa, what about this secret email account? Doesn't it matter to you that *your husband* is having an affair with another woman? When are you going to confront him about what's going on?"

"I can't do that just yet. I need more time to see what happens", I tell her. "Look, I have to get out of here and get to work today. They've been laying people off and I don't want to give them any reason to let me go."

"Let's do dinner together tonight. It's on me. I'll be here around 7 or so", Cynthia suggests.

"Okay. That sounds good to me. I'm so glad that my hours changed so that I can do stuff like this. Enjoy your day and I'll see ya later tonight."

CHAPTER 51

"Why Are You Home?"

*T*hree weeks later.

"Melissa, the work you've given this company can never be matched. The problem is that we have to downsize and we can only keep one person in the accounting department and unfortunately, the Sales Manager has chosen Arnie to stay", the HR Manager explains. He seems to be very uncomfortable explaining this situation to me.

"I understand that it has to be done. I mean, we could see it coming. But, hey, I appreciate the time that I did have working here", I say, battling with the tears that are forming in the corners of my eyes. *My voice is about to go. I just need to get out of here before the tears come. I'm so glad that I brought my purse in this meeting with me so that I don't have to go back into the sales room. Im devastated right now. What are we going to do now? Now I understand why nobody was able to make eye contact with me today.*

Exiting out the back door, I make it to my car, where I finally release my tears and my anger. This feeling that I have right now is the same one I had when I was let go from the property management position. This hurts like you won't believe. It feels like God has abandoned me and is feeding me to the wolves. *Lord, why have you left me? I trusted you, Lord. I'm sitting here and unemployed again. Why does this keep happening to me? I'm an excellent employee and don't understand why I'm in this position again. My husband is not any help to me. He's too busy doing God knows what with his female friends. He doesn't care about me. I thought I heard from you that I should work on my marriage, but what has it brought me Lord? What?*

Half an hour has passed by before I realize that I haven't left the parking lot just yet. I need to start the engine and get home and figure this out. I just purchased this car and the payments are over $200 per month. The rent is $1500 per month and not to mention the grocery bill. They didn't offer any type of severance package. Without a job, I may lose everything!

Driving through Centennial to get home, I stop by the Park just to clear my head before I go home and share this news with the girls. It's such a sunny day outside. This Fall weather is the best in Florida. This is the one thing that relaxes me and makes my mind not wander so much. Let me make these ducks happy by feeding them some bread that I just remembered is still in my car from the other day.

Watching this elderly couple makes me wonder if Kalin and I will grow old together. Will we have grandkids together? Will we make it to that stage or will our love wither away like a high percentage of marriages have? If I must be honest, I have to admit that I'm actually in awe of them. I'm sure that this couple has had some disagreements from time to time, but they must have figured out how to handle their issues without offending the other person. In my heart I know I love Kalin but my instinct tells me that he's having an affair with this woman.

"Excuse me. May I speak with the two of you?" I politely ask as they walk past my bench.

"Sure", the woman responds.

"I'm married and have been with my husband quite a few years already, but we're having some difficulty now and I'm struggling with whether I should stay with him or not", I begin to explain. They seem to be interested in where I'm going, displaying a look of anticipation on their faces. "I think he's allowing a woman friend of his to destroy our marriage. What should I do? Does this sound like grounds of divorce?"

"Awwww baby. I'm so sorry to hear that you and yo' husband going through thangs", she begins to say. "But baby, you got to trust God in all thangs even yo' marriage. God is able, baby. Just trust Him. You and yo' husband need to sit down and pray 'bout yo' marriage and let God fix it. That's all you gotta do", she says, rubbing my forearm. She and her husband keep walking on by, hand in hand.

I hear what she's saying, but I know that it has to be both of us working to make the marriage work. I wonder if Kalin is going to step up to bat to do what needs to be done for our family right now. I wonder if I can convince him to come back to Florida now.

Traffic is moving at a comfortable pace, so I end up making it home before the girls do. Burgers and fries sound like the perfect meal right about now. And besides, they love my turkey burgers. Amber and Justice should be home soon and when they get here, I can then start cooking, but since I have a few minutes to spare, I might as well check my messages. They'll be surprised when they get in the house and find that I'm here. My stomach is always nervous when I know that I'm about the check the email account that Kalin has with his friend, Kesha. It is mind-boggling to me as to why I continue to punish myself in this matter by continuing to look at these emails without confronting him.

There are only a couple of new messages, but since none one of them has been opened, I can't open them first or he may start suspecting something. *I can't for the life of me understand why this man keeps telling me one thing but is living another thing. He makes it seem as though he is so in love with me. Other people really believe that we have the perfect marriage and that we make the perfect couple. Only a few friends of mine aren't so convinced of it because they are the ones whose shoulders I need when he breaks my heart.*

My aunt sends an email to me that Larry will be laid to rest this coming Saturday. I have to be there and since it's in Alabama, Kalin can come right over and be there for me at the funeral. Where he lives is only 45 minutes or so from Middleton. I'm really not loking forward to seeing my cousin in that casket. It's not how I want to remember him. Diana has agreed to ride to Alabama with me and since I'm not working, I can leave out on Thursday instead of waiting for the weekend. The girls are excited to go to Alabama because they'll get to see their father. I need to send Kalin a message and let him know.

"Mommy, are you here?" Justice yells. She just got home.

"Yes, honey. I'm here. I'm in my office!" I yell back.

She comes upstairs and looks at me with a sad face. "You lost your job *again?*" she asks.

"Yes, sweetheart. I did. They laid off our entire department. They have their own accounting department in New York, so that was that!" I tell her.

"Don't worry, Mommy. God will provide", Justice says, giving me a hug. Her words of encouragement are just what I need at this moment.

I'm so glad that she isn't complaining right now because I probably couldn't handle that right now.

"Thank you, precious. Thank you for saying that."

"It's true. God has always been there for us. He has never let us down. We just have to pray, Mommy", she says, leaning over to look on my computer. "Are you sending a message to Daddy?"

"As a matter of fact, I am. I'm letting him know that we'll be in Alabama for the funeral and hopefully, he'll come to Middleton to spend some time with us", I tell her.

The message is sent and Justice and I head downstairs. "Mommy, what are you cooking for dinner tonight?" Justice asks.

"Turkey burgers and fries."

"Yummy! Can I help you make the burgers?" she asks.

"Of course you can." By the time we make it into the kitchen, Amber comes into the kitchen and is surprised when she sees me.

"Mommy, why are you home this early? You're never here when I get home. What happened?" Amber asks, looking concerned.

"Mommy lost her job. They laid them all off", Justice tells her. Amber looks over at me and throws down her book bag.

"Why does this always happen to us? Why? It's not fair. This is getting so old!" she says, running upstairs.

"Mommy, she doesn't mean to be mean. She must have had a bad day or something. Let's finish cooking.

CHAPTER 52

"I'm Not Okay, Kalin!"

O ne hundred and 24 miles left to go before we arrive in Miami. "Why didn't Daddy come to Middleton to see us, Mommy?" Justice asks.

"I wish I knew the answer to that. He must have gotten busy or something. We'll call him later, okay", I tell them both.

I can't believe this man didn't make an attempt to contact his family. The girls were sitting around the entire weekend waiting on him to come. They were planning on asking him to come home to Florida with us, but when he didn't show up, that just crushed their hope and that makes me so angry. They don't know this, but I tried to call him quite a few times while we were in Alabama.

"Too busy for us? What could have possibly been more important than Daddy coming to Middleton to see his family? I'm starting to feel like he doesn't love us anymore. And why won't he come home with us, Mommy?" Justice asks.

"Sweetheart, your father loves you girls very much. I'm sure that he has a very good reason for not coming to the funeral and I wouldn't be …", I begin to say when my phone rings.

"Hello", I say into the phone without seeing the caller ID.

"So, how was your trip?" the person on the other end says.

"It was fine. I am on my way home now", I respond. I have no idea who this is, but I continue talking as if I do. I haven't caught the voice just yet.

"I thought of you the entire time and was hoping that you were feeling comforted. I know how much your cousin means to you", he says.

"Oh!!!! This is Patrick! Hey there. How are you? I'm sorry, Patrick. I just realized that it's you that I am talking to. I didn't catch your voice at first", I tell him.

"I see! You've forgotten about me already, huh?"

"No. It's not like that. You just sound a little different than before. That's all."

"How was your cousin's homegoing celebration?" he asks, sounding concerned.

"The service was beautiful. There were so many people who came out to say goodbye to my cousin. He was loved by so many. It was very touching. It was nice to see all of my friends from high school", I say.

"I'm glad. Sounds like everything went well", Patrick adds. "I just wanted you to know that I was thinking of you."

Can you believe this? Patrick took time to check on me and I still haven't heard from Kalin. The fact that Kalin didn't show up to Middleton has somehow changed my whole attitude towards him because this time, he not only disappointed me, but he disappointed his children.

"You have no idea how much I appreciate you for caring and calling, Patrick. It means a lot to me. Thank you so much", I comment.

"Thank me? You don't have to thank me. It's my pleasure to be here for you. I love you, Melissa. I don't expect you to tell me you love me. I know and I understand. I hurt you and it will take time for you to get over it, but I just hope that...", he begins to say until I interrupt him.

"I do too, Patrick. But you're right. You hurt me and honestly, it's gonna take some time to get over it. I have to go now. I'm getting another call", I tell him.

When his phone hangs up, my heart starts beating faster. This is not the right time to go into *our feelings* and everything because he'll surely suck me in if I'm not careful.

"Mommy, who was that?" Amber asks.

"Where? On the phone?"

"Yes. On the phone. Who was it?" she asks again.

"That was my friend, Patrick. He called to see how we were all doing because he remembered that the funeral was this weekend and he wanted to make sure I was okay", I answer.

We're finally pulling into the driveway after 12 long hours on the road. In my heart, I have to find a way to let Larry go. As hard as it'll be, I have to do it and I have to do it now. Justice grabs all the mail from the mailbox. Amber helps me to get everything out of the car. The first thing I notice when we get inside is the flashing red light indicating that there are messages on the answering machine.

"Girls, let's get everything out of the car first and then we can start putting things away", I tell them.

"Mommy! The mail!" Justice shouts, handing all of the mail to me.

Quickly, I thumb through it and there's nothing here but bills, bills, and more bills. The financing company for the car is looking for their payment. The landlord is looking for his money. The insurance on the vehicle needs to be paid and I have no clue how I'm going to pay all of this without a job and without any savings. There are several messages, but one in particular quickly grabs our attention. When the girls hear their father's voice, their face lightens up.

"Hey guys. It's me, Daddy. I am so sorry that I didn't make it to Middleton while you were here in Alabama. Daddy was very busy at work and I also had a photo shoot that I had to attend. I feel so bad that my wife and kids were this close to me and I missed ya'll. Call me when you get in and we can talk about Daddy coming back to Florida. I love all of you. Bye!

My heart is beating even faster now. This is good news that Kalin wants to come home. He can transfer his job here and we can possibly get out of this financial mess that we're in. This is great news. *So maybe, just maybe, he really does love us. Maybe my husband is growing up and our marriage may have a chance after all. He's ready to come back to us. Thank you Jesus!*

"Did you guys hear your father's message?" I ask them.

"Yes!!!! Yes!!!!! Daddy's coming home. I'm so happy!" Justice says. "Can we call him? Please, Mommy, please!"

After a few attempts, the girls finally get him on the phone. It's amazing to me how kids quickly forget it when they've been hurt. It doesn't seem to bother them that he didn't show up in Middleton like he said he would. They're just happy to have him now. Listening to them talk reminds me that Kalin and I have a matter that we have not discussed just yet. We still need to address this *secret email account* and the contents in it.

"Mommy, Dadddy needs to speak with you", Amber says, handing me the phone. I decide to walk upstairs to talk to him in my office.

"Hello."

"Hey baby. I'm so sorry that I didn't make it to the funeral. You okay?"

"No. I'm not okay, Kalin. We just buried my favorite cousin who didn't really get a chance to live his life and whose children won't see their father anymore. I am sad and I really needed you to be there for me", I explain.

"I'm sorry, baby. I really am sorry. I wanted to…", he says before I cut him off.

"What happened to your phone? You couldn't call. You called here and left a message and I know that you saw all the calls I placed to you. I know you have several missed calls. You just didn't want to be there for some reason, but it's fine. I'm aldredy over it. I can't seem to depend on you for anything, but it's funny how every single time you need me, I'm there for you", I say, not apologizing for my anger.

"What's *your* problem? It's not like you talked to him *every day*. You're trying to live in the past and the truth is that you had lost touch with him, Melissa. So, I don't understand why or how this can hurt you so much", he says, sounding mean.

"You're such a jerk! What happened to the sensitive man I married? Where did he go? That's the man I want back. I don't know who *you* are", I tell him.

"Baby, I'm sorry. I should not have said that. This long distance relationship gets to me sometimes because I love you and the girls and it's just hard, Melissa", he explains.

"It's even harder for me. I'm the one who is here with our children, trying to make all of this work. Kalin, I have to tell you something."

"What is it?" he asks.

"I lost my job. They laid off our entire department except one person. We had no warning or anything. They didn't offer a severance package and there is nothing left in the bank", I tell him. The phone goes silent for a few seconds.

"What!!! Are you serious?" he asks.

"Why would I lie about something like this? But I'm sure I'll find something else. I have a good reference from the company, so we should be just fine", I tell him.

"I hope so. I really do hope so."

"So, it looks like you have made two young ladies very happy that you're coming home", I comment.

"I was hoping to make *three* girls happy that I'm coming home", he says.

"Of course, Kalin. Of course", I respond.

Because it'll be another 3 months before he can make his transition back to Florida, we plan a trip to Alabama for the Fourth of July weekend to spend it with Kalin's family. There's going to be a big picnic at Greg's house. In the meantime, I need to find a job. I have put in applications everywhere. But this time, I hook up with agencies that specialize in finding accounting jobs for you.

Going through the mail, I notice that there's a letter from the Academy in Stuartville. It looks like they're seeking my approval to Sharelle specific types of medicine that they believe will help her cope better during the time that she is there. I have to admit it, but I don't recognize any of these, nor am I familiar with what they do for you. *I think I need to call them because I am certainly not going to sign off on this without knowing anything about these meds.*

"Good morning, it's Felicia with Mart Girls Academy. How may I help you?"

"Yes, good morning. This is Melissa Thomas and I'm Sharelle Williams' mother. I just received a letter in the mail asking for my permission for you to give her these medications, but I need more information about them. I'm not familiar with them at all. Is there a doctor or a nurse there that I can speak to?

"Sure. Hold on, ma'am. I'll get the doctor for you."

Moments later, the doctor comes on the phone. "Yes, Mrs. Thomas. Hi, this is Dr. Randall and I understand that you have questions about the medications prescribed for your daughter."

"I just have questions about them. What are they for?" I ask.

"All of these medications prescribed are to make her calm down. Your daughter has gotten irate on more than a few occasions and we can't have that in here. She's a danger to the other kids if we're not able to control her", he explains.

"I see. I had no idea that it had gotten that bad with her", I say.

"Yes, because if we have another incident like she had at the prior center, she'll definitely be terminated from the program and could possibly do her time in county jail. So, to prevent that from happening, we had to find a better way to control her", he further explains.

"But, if the meds are to control her, why are there *three* different types; what are the others good for?" I ask.

There is complete silence on the phone. The phones have somehow become disconnected. *Did he hang up on me or did I somehow disconnect the phone by mistake?* I decide to dial him again.

The nurse answers the phone and transfers the call again. The doctor picks up. "Sir, I'm not sure if it was my phone or yours, but the question I was asking...", I begin to say, but he interrupts me.

"Ma'am, I have explained it thoroughly to you and I'm sorry if you *still* don't understand, but I'm certainly not going through it again. We know what's best for her", he tells me, much more stern than before.

"Understand this, sir. This is *my child* that we are talking about and you can't possibly love her like I love her. Let's get that straight. So, if I ask you questions about my child, it is my right because she is *my child*.

The Doctor hangs up the phone *again* without warning. I'm in total shock at the lack of professionalism with the people who represent this state run facility. After this conversation, I feel like I have no choice but to sign the paperwork authorizing them to give her these prescribed medications and hope for the best. I need to make sure to attend their *Family and Friends Day* next month so that I can get a better look at this facility.

But for now, back to the Jobs Search.

Dear Lord, I thank you so much for your love. I don't know what I would do without it. I know that I disappoint you sometimes, but I love you. I love you, Lord, with everything I have. You are the only one who still believes in me and I can feel your love. Lord, please watch over me and these kids. Lord, you know that there are times when I don't have a clue how I will feed them or clothe them, but you always seem to make a way out of no way. I am here, again, in need of your help to find a job. I need you to watch over Kalin and his job. Protect this family. Please forgive Kalin for his indiscretions that he may or may not have with other women. Please give me strength to forgive him, and a loving heart when I deliver my knowledge of them. In Jesus' name, Amen.

CHAPTER 53

"Would You Like to Come Over?"

"*M*ommy, there's a note on the door", Justice yells, walking into the house with the paper in her hand. "Oh no! Oh God, no! It's a letter of eviction from the Landlord. He's giving us 3 days to bring the balance due to current and she will go to the courts to remove us from the home. The balance due on the rent up until this point is $3,000 and that doesn't include the late penalties. *Where in the world am I going to get this kind of money without having a job? Oh God! I feel like you have totally abandoned me and these kids. Where are you? Where is my miracle? I know it can't be your will for us to live on the streets. Please Lord, you gotta help us!*

"Mommy, please don't cry", Justice says.

It's too late. This letter brought me to my knees and I cry out to the Lord. Justice feels helpless as she stands by and watches me fall to my knees and cry out to God. God bless her heart because she's doing her best to console me, but it's not working. I think that these tears are a combination of everything going on in my life right now. I'm thinking about this letter of eviction, not having a job, not having any money, and all the things I've learned about my husband since he has been away.

After a few minutes of crying, I finally realize that crying won't change this. I get up off my knees in peace, not afraid to lose this home, if it boils down to it. I need to listen to my gospel music right now to settle my mind. It's the only thing that can wipe these tears away. Listening to Yolanda Adams telling me to *Never Give Up* seems to work. Her voice has always soothed my broken heart. *This Battle Belongs to the Lord* is another one that makes me feel comforted in the midst of my troubles. One thing I have learned is that talking to friends does me no good. I need to hear God's voice.

"I'm okay, baby. Why don't you go to your room? I don't want you to worry about this. This is Mommy and Daddy's problem. I'll be just fine. I promise you, okay."

Later in the evening, I tell Kalin about this letter and he agrees that he should return now, so that we can work this out as a family. In my mind, I want to go to Patrick for help, but I know that Kalin would not like it at all if I go to my ex-boyfriend for help, but we have nowhere else to go. I really don't know what else to do at this point, but pray and trust God to work it out.

In two weeks, the girls and I are going to Alabama to pick Kalin up and bring him back home. He's putting money in the account to cover the gas for the trip. And hopefully when he gets here, we'll be able to come up with *something* to save our home.

Kalin had to get off the phone because he claims he's about to go somewhere with his brother. Since I'm not quite ready to go to bed yet, I decide to check my messages first and then venture over to Kalin's secret email account to see if there are any new messages between him and Kesha. My messages are nothing compared to what I find in Kalin's account. Kesha sent him a thank you e-card for a special evening. A special evening? *I wonder what that's all about. What kind of special evening? This is crazy. I think it's time for me to confront him with what I know about this account. It's finally time! I have had enough of his lies and deceit. I deserve better than this. If I have to walk away from him at this point, I'll do it because I'm not happy and God knows, I'm ready to be happy and Kalin is not doing it for me. I'm tired.*

Instead of calling Kalin to confront him, I dial Patrick's number instead. "Were you asleep?" I ask him when he answers the phone.

"No. I wasn't asleep, Melissa. Are you okay?" he asks.

"I'm not okay, Patrick. I'm so freaking confused right now. I really am. I know that I set out to ultimately work things out with Kalin, but he's been cheating on me, Patrick. I just checked that account again and Kesha sent him a message thanking him for a great evening. That can only mean one thing. He spent the evening with her. Now it makes sense to me why he doesn't want me to call him after he leaves work. He's been using me, Patrick. For what? I don't know why. Why did he do this to me? How could he do this to me? All I have ever done is love him", I begin, starting to cry now.

"Melissa, please don't cry, baby. He's *not* worth the tears. I told you that he was probably cheating with this woman. I mean for crying out loud, he didn't want to end his friendship with her, even after the two of you agreed to work on your marriage. I would have cut all my ties with her to save my marriage if I *really* wanted to save my marriage. I'm here for you. Would you like to come over? Let me cook dinner for you tomorrow evening. No strings attached. What do you say?" he asks.

"I think it's a great idea. Where? At the condo or your home?" I ask.

"Which makes you most comfortable?" he asks.

"The condo."

I can't believe that I just made plans to have dinner with Patrick on tomorrow evening. But the truth of the matter is that I miss him. I miss his touch. He always knows how to make me feel better about everything and right about now, I need that. So, whatever happens tomorrow night will just happen and I won't hold back either. Kalin has made a very conscious effort to ruin this marriage with his lies and deception and now, we may not have anywhere to live. I need to get a little bit of happiness myself. Kalin doesn't seem to be having a problem getting his.

"Well, tomorrow night it is", Patrick confirms.

"Ok. I'll meet you there by 6. I really am looking forward to spending time with you tomorrow night", I say.

CHAPTER 54

"Deny It!"

"You look beautiful, Melissa!" Patrick says, when I walk through the door at the condo. The aroma coming from the kitchen is delightful. He remembered that I love his famous pasta dish. Patrick walks towards me with his arms opened wide

"How did you know that I needed a hug?" I ask him, falling into his arms.

"I've always known what you needed, Melissa. I love you, woman. I really do. Let me make you feel better", he says.

"It's so good to see you again after all this time apart, Patrick. You still look good", I tell him, looking him up and down. His arms, chiseled, complimented well with the olive colored shirt against his olive skin. The black slacks fitting his body just right.

"Come here, Melissa. Give me a kiss. I have dreamt of this moment for months", he says, placing his hands around my waist.

I give in to his kiss. His lips are so sweet and his embrace is so inviting that we just stand there holding each other for several minutes. No doubt he's reminiscing just like I am. We had some very special times at this condo. There are no words spoken but many that are just plain understood between the two of us. Our body language is doing the talking. The longer we hug, the closer he pulls me in. The warmth of his body soothes me and brings calmness to my mind.

"You feel so good, Patrick", I finally say.

"You do too, baby, and you smell so sweet. Would I be wrong if I told you that I wanted to taste you again?" he comments.

"No. No, you wouldn't. I need you to taste me."

I lead him to the bedroom, but on the way, he turns the stove off and grabs the bottle of wine and two glasses. His remote turns on the music and our night has just begun. Patrick grabs my face and gives me a sweet kiss. His tongue is lost in my mouth. The warmth of his mouth on my neck drives me insane. He turns me around and unzips my dress and plants small kisses on the back of my neck and down the center of my back. He unhooks my bra and it all falls to the floor. He slips off my thong and I begin to undress him. We're both standing naked before each other and the passion between the two of us takes over. We make love over and over as if we are two love-strucked teenagers.

"Baby, you feel so good. I've truly missed making love to you", Patrick says.

"And you feel good to me, too, baby. I can tell you were pretty hungry for me", I say, laughing.

"You know I was. Aaahhhh yes! Girl, you wore me out!" he says, laughing. Patrick pours a glass of wine for me and then himself. We make a toast to "reuniting".

"I have a confession to make, Patrick. I only felt the need to work things out with Kalin because I became extremely lonely over the holidays. When you left me the way you did, I took that as a sign from God that you weren't the man for me and that I should have been working things out with my husband all along. And since I have made that decision, I have cried more than I did when he was living in the house with me. It has been a nightmare!" I confess.

"And it's my fault, Melissa. If I had not left you the way I did, you never would have gone back to him. I just know it. But, baby, please hear me and look at me when I say this. I did it to protect you. I didn't want you to go through that situation with me. I didn't think that it was fair to you to watch me like I was and I....", he begins to explain.

"Are you serious with me right now? When you're in love, you'll go through anything together. I don't care how ugly or painful it is, you go through it together. I would have been right by your side every step of the way and you know it; but, no, you decided for us that it was better to leave me out of it. Do you have any idea what you did to me by leaving me like that?" I ask him.

"I'm sure that it devastated you, baby. I know now. I hurt you and I'm so sorry. If there was anything I could take back, that would be it. Please tell me that you forgive me. Please, baby, please", he begs.

"Of course, I forgive you", I say, with tears in my eyes. He kisses my eyes and then my lips.

"Melissa, I want to love your pain away. I want to love you and never hurt you again and I want….", he begins to say before I interrupt him.

"Wait a minute, Patrick. Our having sex has nothing to do with us getting back together. I still have unfinished business with Kalin. I'm still working on my marriage. I hope you didn't get the wrong impression of tonight and that it meant that we were…you know…", I say.

"You *still* want that man after all he has done to you and still doing to you. What is it going to take for you to wake up, Melissa? The man is playing you. You deserve better than that. I just don't want to see you get hurt because that's definitely where this is headed."

"Can you just be my friend through this? Hold my hand when I cry? Walk with me through it? And then, who knows? And who knows? If our love is stronger, we'll eventually be together anyway", I say.

"Ok, baby. I'll be here for you whenever you need me", he says, holding me in his arms.

"You never told me", I say.

"Told you what, honey?" he asks.

"You never told me what it was that you were going through that you couldn't discuss with your woman at the time. I was your girl, Patrick, and you went off and did this all on your own thinking that is, somehow, what I would have wanted. So, what was it?"

"I was in Connecticut and was going through some serious therapy for my sickness. Because my situation was getting worse and worse, my doctor had to bring in a friend of his from London, who specializes in rare diseases. I swear this man must have had healing hands or something because right after he left, my condition got so much better", he explains.

"Really? From London? What a coincidence!" I say. "Wait a minute! You told me that your situation was getting better when you were seen by the doctor here. You lied to me, Patrick?" I ask, putting down my wine glass.

"Baby, yes, I lied", he says, grabbing me and looking into my eyes.

"How could you do that? We were supposed to be best friends, Patrick. How could you do that?"

"I thought I was protecting you. I realize now that I should not have done that, Melissa."

"So, the guy from London was that good, huh?"

"Yeah, he was good. He really knew what he was talking about."

"Just out of curiosity, did you send me some emails while you were away?" I ask him.

"Yes, I did. They were from "Anonymous", he tells me.

"And all this time, I thought those emails were coming from Kalin", I respond.

"Come here, Melissa. Kiss me. Give yourself totally to me. I don't want you to think about anything outside this room right now", he says, rubbing his fingers through my hair. "We're in a world right now and it's just me and you. Relax and let me make love to you before you have to leave. I want to give you something to think about all day", he says, spreading my legs and climbing on top of me. The candles are still burning from the night before and surprisingly, they last throughout our lovemaking. We spent the night together and I'm sure Diana is wondering when I'll be home.

This time spent with Patrick has made all the difference. What Kalin is doing or not doing doesn't seem to matter as much to me at this point.

"Baby, I have to go now. I've had a wonderful time. Dinner was delicious and so were you", I say, turning on the shower. Patrick decides to join me. He washes my back and I wash his.

"When will I see you again?" Patrick asks, when I walk towards the door.

"Not sure, Patrick. Kalin will be here in a few days and we have quite a bit of things to discuss, so I would appreciate it if you wouldn't contact me so that I can work things out with him and if I see that it can't be worked out, then you may hear from me a lot sooner", I tell him.

"Oh, and what if you *do* work things out with him? Does that mean that it's over between us, Melissa?" he asks, sounding somewhat upset.

"I have to go, Patrick. Don't do this *now*", I tell him. He's just standing here looking away from me. I try to turn his face towards me, but he refuses to look at me, but says "Goodbye, Melissa."

Leaving out of the condo this time is nothing like any other time. He's clearly hurt because of what I just said. I walk away from Patrick with a hole in my heart. I know that Patrick cares for me and for last night and this morning, he gave me just what I came looking for, but the truth is that I really want my marriage to work.

On the way home, the guilt is starting to set in on my heart. I know that I needed a man to love me, but it was supposed to be my husband doing that. Kalin is supposed to be here to take care of my sexual desires, but instead, he seems to be playing "house" with another woman. What does he expect?

Dear God. I know what I just did was wrong. I knew it was wrong as I was doing it, but I felt so strongly that I needed to do it. Please forgive me, Lord, for what I have done. I sinned with another man who was not my husband. I fornicated with him and I know that you won't bless that. I fell into the temptation of needing to feel loved. And I also know that I can't base my decision to be unfaithful just because my husband is being unfaithful. That is not Your Will and I am sorry. I am very sorry, Lord, and I need your forgiveness. Please give me strength to only keep the love for my husband. In Jesus' name, Amen.

By the time I pull into my driveway, Diana is walking outside with a piece of paper in her hand. She makes it to my car window and says, "Melissa, what is this all about? Are you about to be evicted?" she asks, looking me straight in my face.

"Diana, don't concern yourself with this. Kalin and I will figure this out when he gets here in a few days", I tell her, putting the car in park.

"Kalin? You can't be serious, Melissa! He didn't do anything when he was here and you honestly think he is going to come here and fix this. That is one man you can't depend on and in your heart, you already know that!" she exclaims.

"Not now, Diana. Please, not now. I've had a long night and I just want to get in my bed right now", I tell her.

"So, how was Patrick?" she asks, smiling and looking me up and down.

"What makes you think I was with Patrick?" I ask her.

"Melissa, come on! I am your sister and I know you, okay. Nobody puts a smile on your face like *that* man. So, how was he?"

"He was fine, okay. You happy now?" I say, jokingly hitting her and laughing. She lets me get out of the car and we head straight for the kitchen.

"Ok. Let's have a cup of coffee before I leave. It's time for us to play catch up. I haven't seen nor talked to you in a while and I want to know why. So, sit down and let me fix you a cup of coffee. You still like a pound of sugar in your coffee?" she asks.

"You're so funny. Just 3 scoops."

"So, what's going on with you and Kalin, sis? Before you say anything, it can't be too good because you spent the night with Patrick. So, now tell me", she insists.

"Things are very rocky with Kalin. I thought that taking him back was the best decision, but the truth is that it has been a total nightmare since the day I decided to work on our marriage. It has been one-sided and the stuff I have learned about him should make me run, not walk, but run to the divorce attorney and continue the divorce, but I really want to do what God expects of me and…", I begin to explain.

"What has he done, Melissa? Stop beating around the bush. Tell me!"

"He's having an affair with a woman in Alabama and they have a secret email account together and…", I begin to tell her, but she is already furious.

"What!!!! That no good son of a ------. Low down dirty dog. He ain't even worth it, girl! You can do so much better than him. I don't know why you stick around and put up with his mess. Ain't no way in hell I could do that. No way, Melissa! You are better than me. There's no way!" she says, jumping up and down.

"And I plan to confront him about it when he gets here. I'm curious to see how he'll respond when I let him know that I know about it", I say.

"You mean to tell me that even knowing all of this, you want this sorry behind man back in your life?" she asks.

"He just so happens to be Amber and Justice's father, Diana. I'm trying to make this work out for everybody. I have to be able to forgive, D. I mean, look at what I did last night. God had to forgive me for what I did. No matter how I may feel justified in sleeping with Patrick, it was wrong in God's sight and he forgave me, so I have to forgive Kalin."

"Ok. Whatever, Melissa. You always seem to find just the right excuse for that sorry behind man. And you know what? You're going to see the *real* Kalin real soon. I just know it!" she warns me.

"Yes, and even if all of this blows up in my face, I expect you to be right there for me. Will you be there, Diana?" I ask her.

"You know I will. I just want better for my sister. That's all", she says, giving me a hug. "And how did you get access to the account anyway?"

"Come on! You know I'm good like that!" I say.

"True. True. You are", she tells me.

This morning, I've shared all of mine and Kalin's secrets with my closest sister, and it's no doubt in my mind that Diana hates him now more than ever. As much as she tries, she doesn't do a good job of hiding it. But, I know it's because she wants the best for me. I want the best for me, but I feel that this is what God wants.

When Diana leaves the house, I go upstairs and right away, I check my messages and there's one from Patrick telling me how much he loves me and how he enjoyed last night. I don't reply to his message this time. There are no new messages from Kalin at all. So, I log out of myYahoo account and go over to his Hotmail account that he has with Kesha to see if there are any new messages opened up that I can read. I see that there are a few unread messages. I click on the first one that says "I love you" as the subject. The email is from her to him. It reads,

> "Kalin, I love you. I know that you're leaving to go back to Florida to be with your family and although I'll miss you terribly, I hope that the memories that we share will stay with you forever and when you get lonely, it will be me that you're thinking of. Love and kisses, Kesha. xoxoxoxo"

...and further down the emails are at least three more sexy pics of her that she wants him to look at when he gets lonely. How inappropriate is this! I should have responded to Patrick. I should drop everything and run right back into his arms, but I can't keep sinning knowingly, but it is so hard not to when you see that your husband is having an affair on you. But, I get through these moments by reminding myself that he'll be here in a few days and I'll finally get my chance to address all of this. I want to see his face when he tries to lie about not having an affair with this woman.

One right behind the next, the tears are rolling down my face. I can't stop them. I feel like I just want to die! I'd rather die than feel this pain right now. This is so intense that it's beyond a description. To be honest, I wouldn't wish this hurt, pain, and betrayal upon anyone, not even my enemies. It's beyond me to understand why *my husband* would put me through this much agony. He fought for a friendship with this woman just so he could have an affair with her. Now, I see why he doesn't have time for his own kids, but can find the time and the money to give to this woman to help her take care of her kids. He forgets that I have access to the bank account and can see how and where the money is going.

He forgets that I have access to his phone records and can see who he is talking to every minute of the day.

Dialing his number, my heart is racing, which is my confirmation that I should confront him right now about this affair. I can't wait for him to get here. I need to do it right now. One ring, two rings, three rings, four rings, and now his voicemail. I'm not leaving a message, but decide to dial his number again. One ring, two rings, and he picks up! "Melissa, what's wrong? Why are you dialing my number like this? I'm busy right now. Are the kids okay?" he asks.

"Yes, the kids are just fine, but we aren't. We aren't fine, Kalin!" I say to him, crying and yelling.

"Will you please calm down, Melissa! What's wrong with you?"

"Now, you want to know what's wrong with me! Kesha is what's wrong with me, Kalin! Now, deny it! Deny that you've been having an affair with her! You are such a jerk! I can hardly stand you!" I yell into the phone. He hangs up on me. The phone goes dead. I call for his name and he doesn't answer.

I'm crying so hard that my head feels like it's going to pop out of my head. It's obvious to me that this man doesn't care for me. He couldn't even stay on the phone to make sure I was okay. It's painfully obvious that all these months of agony have eventually led to this moment. He really *is* having an affair. I mean, how can he deny it anyway? I just want to sleep and never wake up again. Nobody cares anyway; at least, this is what I'm hearing in my head right now. In the back of my mind, I start to remember the promise I made to God about taking my life. I want to keep this promise, but I'm starting to convince myself to go into the bathroom and go to the medicine cabinet. The force that's driving me to do it is much stronger than I am. I can't stop. My feet won't stop moving in that direction. And before I know it, I'm holding a bottle of Excedrin in my hand. I take all of them, but before I fall asleep, I dial Kalin's number and it goes straight to voicemail. Without thinking, I put my phone on silent so that when he calls he won't be able to get me either.

CHAPTER 55

"Keep an Eye Out!"

"I think Sharelle meets all the qualifications to be released. By December, I'm thinking", the Academy Director Nelson tells the counselor.

"It seems that way, but I want to make sure. Let me spend some time with her this week. We'll need to get a letter out to her parents informing them of our decision. We'll also need to get their input. I know we always talk to the mother, but is there a father in this picture?" the Counselor states.

"No. But there's a stepfather in the picture. Based on the notes that I'm looking at here, she doesn't have a good relationship with him and because of that, she has no interest in going back to live in her mother's home if he's there", the Director mentions.

"I see. Well, I want to explore that in more detail with her and in the meantime, we need to contact the mother to see if there's anyone else who can take her into their home if the need arises", Counselor Angela states. "Is it okay if I meet with Sharelle today before I leave?" she asks Director Nelson.

"I don't see why not. There's no time like the present. This should be dealt with as soon as possible."

The Counselor reviews the file while the Director calls for Sharelle to come into the conference room. Within 15 minutes she's walking into the conference room, with her usual happy and cheerful attitude.

"Hey Ms. Angela", Sharelle says, walking in and giving Angela a hug.

"And why are you so happy, Sharelle?" she asks her. "You would think you won the lottery or something!"

"No. I just talked to my mother and everything is going good at home, so that makes me happy to know that she's doing okay. My sisters are also doing well in school and my older sister, Princess, is getting ready to go to college. So, all is well with my family and that makes all things be well with me", she answers.

"Well, I want to talk to you about going home and how….", she says, but Sharelle interrupts her with yelling and screaming.

"Girl, you're gonna get us both in trouble", Angela tells her.

"That's excellent news. Just so happy!! Sorry", Sharelle says.

"In your file, I reviewed your counseling session when you first came in and you mentioned in that session that you weren't too fond of the stepfather. You wanna talk about that?" Angela asks.

"I hate him. It's really just that simple. I hate him for hurting my mother. She doesn't deserve it. She works and takes care of everybody and he never does anything to help her. He would just sit and watch her go out every day and struggle to make sure we ate and to make sure we had clothes on our backs. He didn't help much", she tells them.

"Let me ask you a question. Will you go back into the home if he's there?" she asks Sharelle.

"No. Absolutely not! I don't ever want to live in that house with that man ever again. Not only is he useless, but he's abusive."

"How do you mean? Is he verbally abusive or physically abusive?" Angela asks.

"I know he's verbally abusive to my mother, but I've never actually seen him hit her, but I would hear them arguing all the time and I would hear a thump and …", she begins to say.

"But you never actually saw him hit her?" Angela asks.

"No. I never did", Sharelle admits.

"Ok. This has been helpful. We're extremely proud of you for almost completing the program. According to the records here, you're doing well in your classes and you basically have the recommendation of everyone to get out by December. Who knows? Maybe you'll get to go home before Christmas. I'm sure your mother would love that", she says, putting her file back together.

"Yaaay! I'm super excited now. Thank you so much Ms. Angela!" Sharelle tells her, giving her a hug and then leaving the room.

Angela stops by the Director's office before leaving and says, "Yeah, she hates the stepfather. We may have some abuse issues going on in the home. We'll need to keep an eye out on this one. I may have to contact CCF if I feel that it's warranted", Angela states.

"Ok, sounds good. Just keep me in the loop", the Director comments.

CHAPTER 56

"What Did You Say?"

" Have you spoken to Melissa today?" Cynthia calls and asks Diana.

"Sure, I was over there earlier today. I stayed with the kids last night and I was there when she came home this morning. We sat down and had coffee together. She was fine when I left. Why? What's wrong?" Diana asks.

"I don't know yet. I just got a call from her neighbor and she said that she *thinks* she saw Melissa leave the house in a police car. She couldn't tell because it all happened so fast. She's not sure if the police car was parked in front of Melissa's house or the lady on the other side. Are you close by there to be able to check on her?" Cynthia asks.

"I'm at an appointment right now, but as soon as I'm done, I'll go over there. Let me call her and see", Diana begins.

"Yeah. Her phone is going straight to voicemail. Please just go over there and call me as soon as you're with her so I can cuss her out for making me worry like this", Cynthia says, sounding very concerned.

"You bet I will."

Diana hangs up the phone and goes into her appointment, but is side tracked now after this phone call from Cynthia. She's starting to wonder what could have happened because when she left the house, Diana was fine *or was she?*

Cynthia decides to dial another number. She calls Patrick. He answers right away. "Hi, Cynthia. Everything ok?" Patrick asks.

"It's Melissa. Have you spoken to her today?" she asks.

"Yes. I don't know if she shared this with her girls, but we spent the night together last night. She left here this morning. Said she needed to get home because Diana was there with the kids. Is there something wrong? You're scaring me. Please tell me, Cynthia!" he demands.

"Melissa's neighbor just called me and said that she *thinks* she saw Melissa get into the back of a police car a little while ago. She couldn't get a good look because it was so fast, so it *could* have been the lady who lives on the other side of Melissa. She wasn't sure", Cynthia explains to Patrick.

"Oh God, no! What could have happened? She was fine when she left here. We had a good night together, but oh…oh God, no! I didn't mean to…", Patrick says, but Cynthia interrupts.

"What! What happened? What did you say? Did you say something to upset her that you can remember?" Cynthia asks.

"At the end of the night, she tried to get me to face her and I refused to do it because she had just told me that she was still going to try to make things work with her husband even after all we shared. I was somewhat hurt by that comment. But, I didn't mean to make her upset. I'm so sick now. If that caused her to lose it or something, I'll never forgive myself!" Patrick states.

"Calm down, Patrick. I'm sure that this most likely has *something* to do with Kalin. She really loves you. As her friend, I know that better than anyone. We just need to wait. Her sister is going over there to let me know what's going on and when she does, I'll make sure to let you know. Just pray, Patrick. If you love her, just pray for her right now", Cynthia encourages him.

"Please let me know something. I love her and if he did anything to hurt her, I'm telling you right now that I'll find this man and he does NOT want to be found by me. I mean it, Cynthia!" he tells her.

"Me and you both!"

Cynthia tries Melissa's number again and it goes straight to voicemail. Her first thought is to contact Kalin. Maybe he'll know something. He may have been the last one to make contact with her. She dials Kalin's number and he answers right away. "Hello."

"Kalin, how are you? This is Cynthia. I'm worried about Melissa. Have you spoken with her today?" she asks.

"Yeah, I did. She called me and was acting crazy. I wasn't trying to hear all of that noise she was talking, so I hung up on her. Your girl has issues sometimes and believes all of her lies, so I just….", he begins but Cynthia interrupts her.

"You're such a jerk, Kalin! Do you have any idea what this woman is going through being here trying to make it on her own, still trying to make her marriage work and you got the nerve to be so arrogant! Whatever! I am sorry to have bothered you. I guess you have more important things to do than to be concerned about your wife. Thanks, but no thanks! Diana is going over there to check on her shortly", Cynthia tells him, then hangs up the phone.

He tries to call back, but Cynthia is already on another call. She's not interested in hearing anything that Kalin has to say. He leaves a message, but when Cynthia gets off the phone, she doesn't check the message, but continues with her month end reports.

CHAPTER 57

"Tell Me What Happened."

"*M*elissa, if you don't answer this phone, I'm going to call 9-1-1. I just listened to your message about wanting to kill yourself. Have you lost your mind? Call me now!! Where are you and why are you doing this? Please call me", Kalin says on Melissa's voicemail.

He waits for several minutes and calls back. This time, Melissa answers the phone with a very groggy "Hello."

"Melissa, why didn't you answer the phone all those other times when I called you? You had me worried sick about you! What's going on? And what's this about you wanting to kill yourself? Why would you say something like that?" Kalin asks, sounding as though he's about to cry.

"Well, you didn't have time for me, Kalin. But I bet you had time for Kesha, didn't you? She's the woman you want so why do you keep playing these games with me? I'm over it already. I don't want you to love me anymore and I just…", I say, before he interrupts me.

"Check this out. When you didn't answer the phone, I called 9-1-1 and they should be at your door any minute now", he says.

"And what did you tell them?" I ask him.

"I told them what you said to me and that they needed to get over there to check on you", he explains.

"Oh my God! Oh my God! No you didn't. I can't believe ….oh no!" I say, walking towards the door. "They're here already."

"I told you. You should have answered the phone."

"It was on silent! Oh God, no! I gotta go, Kalin."

As soon as I open the door, I see two uniformed officers standing in front of me, looking at me as if they're convinced that something is wrong. It could very well be the way I'm dressed or the way that my hair looks. I don't look tidy at all right now, so I'm sure that this doesn't help my case.

"Ma'am, you ok?" one of the officers asks.

"Yes sir. I'm ok. There's clearly been a misunderstanding here today", I tell

"Is there someone else in the house?" he asks, following me back upstairs.

"No sir. It's just me. The kids are all gone to school", I tell him.

"What's going on here? Why is your husband worried that he can't get in touch with you?" the female officer asks.

"My phone was on silent and that's why I didn't hear the phone ring, ma'am. That's all this is about", I try to explain.

"What did you take?" she asks, walking into my bathroom.

"Excedrin. That's it. Here's the bottle", I say, going into the trash to show her the empty bottle.

In the corner of my eyes, I can see that the EMT's have just walked into my bedroom with their medic bag. "Ma'am, do you want to go to the hospital?" the young medic asks.

"No sir. There's no need for me to go to the hospital. I only took 3 Excedrins. I was *not* trying to kill myself. I just wanted my husband to think that I was. This is a huge misunderstanding", I try to explain.

"Ma'am, we're going to do this either voluntarily or involuntarily. It's up to you which one", the police officer says.

"Ok, so I don't want to go", I say to him.

"That's not what I'm talking about. We'll either cuff you or we'll let you walk out of here, but either way, you're leaving this house today. We don't take it lightly and it had to be serious enough for your husband to call us. Maybe you can work this out at the Center, but because we received a call, we have to take you with us", he explains.

"Are you serious? This is crazy! I don't need to go to anybody's Center! Oh my God! I can't believe this is happening to me right now", I say, rubbing my hand through my hair. "What can I do to just make this all go away?"

"Unfortunately, there's nothing you can do", the female officer tells me.

"Ok, well, I guess I'll have to do this then. But, I'll need to change my clothes, please", I tell the officer.

"You may, but you have to leave the door open, ma'am. We can't leave you unattended", she tells me.

"Ok. Fine! Can you at least turn around while I change my clothes?"

And just like that. The police are walking me outside and against my will, I'm getting into the back of the police car and hopefully, no one sees me. During my ride to the Center, the police officer engaged in a conversation with me and we talked about our children and our lives. After hearing all of that, he's even more shocked that I allowed myself to get into this position. When we make it to the Center, he lets me out the backseat and walks me in to be processed. We are at a Parkview Behavioral Center. When I walk into the lobby, there's another woman waiting to be processed. We make eye contact, but never actually speak to one another. The police officer waves goodbye and leaves me sitting there.

"Ma'am, I'll be with you shortly", the lady behind the desk says to me.

Sitting here, I begin to reflect on the chain of events that led me to this place. The last concrete thing I remember is reading Kesha's email to Kalin and the pain I felt after reading it is coming back to me now. None of these things matter. It doesn't change the fact that my husband had an affair with another woman. He didn't even care enough about me to *talk* about it. I don't know if I want to still be with Kalin when I leave this Center.

"Ma'am, you're next. Come on up", the woman behind the counter tells me.

I walk to the desk and take a seat. We go through all the particulars. She instructs me to hand over the shoelaces in my shoes, the hair piece in my hair, and my glasses.

"Ma'am, why am I having to give you all of these items?" I ask her.

"You're being booked into our facility and these are health hazards and can't be on your person", she explains.

"Wait a minute! We don't get to discuss this. This was a big misunderstanding. Please talk to my husband. Talk to him and he'll tell you!" I say to her, getting a little excited now.

"What's his phone number? We definitely want to speak with him to get a better understanding of this, but first I have a few more questions to ask you", she responds.

"Ok. Fine. What else?" I ask her.

"What did you take and how many?" she asks.

"Ma'am, first of all, I didn't try to kill myself. I took 3 Excedrins and that was it! This is a big misunderstanding", I say again.

"Did you go to the hospital?" she asks.

"No. I didn't. I refused treatment."

"You refused treatment? It doesn't work like that. You don't get to refuse treatment. We're going to have to send you across the street to be checked out", she explains.

"I didn't need it and they asked me. So, yes, I refused it", I tell her, matter-of-factly.

The interview agent gets on the phone with her superior and they send for the ambulance to pick me up to transport me next door. After 2 ½ hours, the results come back proving that there are NOT elevated amounts of Tylenol in my system just as I told them earlier. The last test to pass is to be approved for dismissal by the Psychologist. They call in Dr. Bishop to get his recommendation after speaking with me. While waiting on him to arrive at the hospital, a nurse comes in to sit with me to monitor my activity.

"Hey young lady. You're so beautiful and I can't imagine what would make you want to kill yourself", she comments, not knowing any of the facts, but assuming that I did.

"Ma'am, I didn't try to kill myself. This was a big misunderstanding. I only took 3 Excedrins, but where I messed up is that I made my husband believe that I took more than that and now, I am stuck here going through all of this for nothing. They said that if the psychologist comes in and recommends that I be released, I won't have to go back to the Center and they'll let me leave from here", I tell her.

"Oh, that would be wonderful. Just remember when you speak with him, be honest, look him in the eyes when you talk and answer only the questions that he asks you and then if….", the nurse begins to explain. Another nurse taps on the door and she has the doctor with her. The sit-in nurse leaves and Dr. Bishop takes a seat. "So, good afternoon Mrs. Thomas, tell me what happened this morning that made your husband feel like you wanted to kill yourself", he begins.

CHAPTER 58

"She Still Chose You."

"*D*iana, did you go over to Melissa's yet?" Cynthia asks. "On my way there now. My meeting lasted a little longer than I expected it would, but I should be there within the next 10 minutes. I have a key to the house and can let myself in and I'll be sure to call you as soon as I find out what's going on", Diana tells her.

Diana's mind is racing and she just starts to pray out loud. She has no idea what she will find when she gets to the house, but she just hopes that Melissa hasn't done anything too crazy. In the back of her mind, she feels like this has *something* to do with Kalin. She was fine when she left the house earlier. So, something had to happen after she left Melissa this morning.

At first glance of the house, nothing appears to be wrong or out of place. Diana rings the doorbell and after a couple of minutes when there is no answer, she lets herself in and immediately yells for Melissa. Still, no answer. She opens the entrance to the garage and Melissa's car is still here. So, at this point, she knows that Melissa's either upstairs or she left with someone else, which may explain the neighbor seeing her get into a police car.

"Melissa! You here? Yell back at me if you're upstairs! You're scaring me! Where are you?" she yells out. There's a still silence in the air. Not a clock is ticking or an alarm or music or anything. Diana walks upstairs. The girls' bedrooms are intact. Nobody is in either of the bathrooms. The laundry room is clear. Diana continues to call out to Melissa. She's now standing at the entrance of Melissa's bedroom. She silently prays to God and hopes that Melissa is *not* in this room and that she *really did* get in the back of a police car.

Diana slowly opens the door and calls out to Melissa. The bed is not made so she knows something is wrong. Melissa would never leave home without making her bed. "Melissa, you in here? Melissa! Melissa!"

She's not in the bathroom, or the closet. She's not here! Thank God that she isn't, but now, Diana needs to find out *why* she allegedly got into the back of a police car. What happened here, she wonders.

Diana flops down on the bed just to clear her head and to look around to see if there are any clues. There's a piece of paper that looks like it's out of place. It's sticking out from underneath the bed. She picks it up and it's a letter and it reads,

> ***To whoever finds this note***...My name is Melissa Thomas and if you're reading this, it means that I am already dead. I didn't want to leave this world without someone knowing what it was that would make me want to be dead. I fell in love with the wrong man and for the life of me, I was not able to let him go and it eventually killed me. Today, I wanted to speak with my husband about the affair he was having with another woman and he didn't have time for me and I couldn't handle that. Over the last several months, I have been monitoring a secret email account that he has had with this woman and today, she sent an email to him telling him to think of her when she gets lonely and sent some sexy photos to go with it and he responded to her and said that he often thinks of her and how sexy she looks when she works out and how he has even thought of her when he makes love to me. I don't need to tell you that this brings indescribable pain to a woman and I can't take his lies anymore. I want my sister, Diana, to please take care of my children. There is good life insurance so there won't be a need to struggle to care for my children. And to my children. I am so sorry that your mother wasn't strong enough to fight anymore. I really tried. I tried with all that I have. And to my best friend, Cynthia...I love you. And to one last person, Patrick...I really loved you and thank you for being a real man and making me feel like a real woman. Too bad that it was just too late! To all of you. Please don't cry for me. I lived a good life. Goodbye to all of my family..............Love, Melissa.

"I don't believe this!" Melissa shouts. Even though nobody can hear her, she says it again. "I don't believe this! This jerk had my sister wanting to kill herself. It makes sense now. That's why she left with the police. I need his phone number!!!!!" she yells as if someone can hear her.

Melissa is so devastated after reading this letter that she falls to the floor beside Melissa's bed and begins to cry. She's crying out of control, but don't have the first clue as to where she should start looking for Melissa, so she calls Cynthia.

"Did you find her, Diana?" Cynthia asks without saying hello. "Why are you crying? Please tell me that my friend is okay, D!! Oh God, no!!"

"She's not here, Cynthia. The neighbor was probably right that she got in the car with the police officer and it's....", she begins to explain.

"Well, if she's not there, why are you crying?" Cynthia asks.

"She left a suicide note. She tried to kill herself, but something alerted the police and it saved her. I just finished reading the note. Diana reads it word for word to Cynthia. They're both crying now.

"What's wrong with her? Ain't no man worth dying over! That asshole! And I called him to see what went on and he told me that she called and was being irate and he didn't want to hear it. She was confronting him about the affair. And that bastard didn't have time to talk to her and it set her off, but how did the police know to come to the house?" Cynthia comments.

"I don't know, but I'm getting ready to call him and cuss his behind out right now and I don't give a care about his feelings. This man is about to kill my sister. Hell no, Diana! It ain't going down like this. Ain't no way in hell!" Diana says, and hangs the phone up immediately.

She dials Kalin's number and he answers on the first ring. "Hello."

"What did you do to my sister?" she asks angrily.

"What do you mean? I didn't do anything to Melissa. She did this to herself", he responds in a matter of fact manner.

"I read the note! She tried to call you and talk about the affair and you didn't want to talk to her and you hung up the phone on her. That was low as hell! It's bad enough you were having an affair, but then when she catches yo' dog behind, you ain't even man enough to talk to her about it and I don't know why she still puts up with you, Kalin!" Diana tells him.

"Look. I have NOT been having an affair on her. This woman is losing her mind. She comes up with all this crazy behind stuff and believes it too and I can't...", he begins to say, but Melissa cuts him off entirely.

"Stop telling yo' lies! Stop! She knows! She was going to tell you this, but she has been monitoring your email account with this woman for several months. Now, sit there and lie to me, you jerk! Tell me you didn't have an email account with that woman Kesha. I looked at it. Melissa left it up on the screen, which means she was looking at this when she tried to kill herself. I am looking at it right now!! How could you do this to the mother of your children, your wife? You are a low behind man to do something like this and I hope she divorces yo' raggedy behind and take everything she can!!" Diana tells him.

"She did what?" he asks.

"That's right dumb son of a -----!! My sister got into the email account and she has all the proof she needs for the divorce. She forwarded all the emails between the two of you to her attorney already. I see it! I'm looking at it right now. What the hell! Why are you sitting around with pictures of another woman with her ugly body? At least do better than my sister Loser!" Diana yells at Kalin.

"That woman is crazy for real! That's not even my account. That's my brother's account. She has no right breaking into other people's property like that."

"You still gon' sit up here and lie to me! The woman specifically called yo' name, Kalin, so try that with somebody else. I thought you really loved her", Diana says, starting to cry.

"I do love her, Diana. None of us are perfect. I'm the one who called the police", he explains.

"You? You called the police?"

"That's right. When she left a message for me that she took some pills and she wanted to die, I tried calling her and when I didn't get a response, I called 9-1-1 and explained what happened and they went over to the house and took her in", he explains.

"I guess I *can* say thank you for that, but you are the son of a ----- who made her want to die in the first place. I wish she never would have taken you back. She really believed that God wanted her to work on her marriage. No, you know who really loves her? Patrick *really* loves her. You know when yo' sorry behind couldn't take care of her, that man was the one making sure ya'll ate. That man was the one making sure she got a ride to and from work. And yo' dumb behind thought she was getting bonuses. Come on Kalin! She did that so you wouldn't feel less than a man. That's how much she loved you. But even after all that man did for her, she still chose yo' sorry behind!" Diana tells him and hangs up the phone.

Diana immediately calls the local police sheriff to see if they can give her any information about Melissa, but it ends up being a dead end. Just like she figured, they refused to give her any information over the phone. It doesn't matter much to them when she explains that she's Melissa's sister. As much as Diana hates Kalin, she knows that because he's the husband, they'll be in contact with him. She needs Kalin to find out where Melissa is. Instead of being his enemy right now, she realizes that she needs to be his friend if she's going to get any information on Melissa's whereabouts.

"Hello", Kalin says, sounding surprised to hear from Diana again.

"Kalin, look, this is me again. I'm sorry about yelling at you. I'm just so upset about my sister and you already know how I feel about her. I'm sorry. Please accept my apology", she tells him.

"Of course, I accept your apology. We're all worried about her, D."

"Great. So, will you please call me when she or the doctor contacts you?" she asks.

"Of course, I will. Of course."

CHAPTER 59

"This Is Not the Way!"

"Doc, this was all a big misunderstanding", Melissa begins to explain to the psychologist.

"Really? How is that?" he asks.

"My husband and I have been on shaky ground and just recently, I found out that he's been having an affair with another woman through an email account that he and her share together. And I know it makes no sense, but I have been torturing myself for several months over it by checking the emails, but I never confronted him about it. I wanted to see how far it would go and you know, just see how deep they were into it", I continue.

"Go on", he tells her.

"So, this morning, I finally had enough of it. I confronted him on the phone about the affair and he hung up on me and when I called back, I kept getting his voicemail. All I could think about is that he doesn't have time for me because of *her*. In my head, all I felt was that he's choosing her as a priority over me. And for a minute there, I lost my mind and...", I say, but he interrupts.

"...and that's when you took the pills?" he asks.

"No sir. It wasn't like that at all. This is how it went down. When he hung up, I kept trying to call him back and kept getting his voicemail. So, the last time I called, I figured the best way to get him to call me back was to act like I wanted to kill myself, so, as crazy as it sounds, I left a message saying I was going to take some pills to end my life since he felt the need to ignore me. I didn't have but 3 pills, sir. I had a headache. But I wanted him to think I took more and that I took them to kill myself", I further explain.

"Oh. I see", the Doc comments. "So, how did you get here?"

"That's where the confusion comes into place. When my husband wasn't able to reach me after receiving that message, he called the police. But right before the police arrived, I answered his call and that's when he told me the police would be coming for me shortly because he was worried about me, but by that time, it was already too late."

"Now, it all makes sense. You were upset, no doubt. But you wanted your husband to feel bad for having an affair on you. You wanted to scare him into coming back?" he says, looking at me with no smile on his face.

"I don't like to think of it this way, but if you give it enough thought, I guess you may be correct", I admit.

"Well, I do want to contact your husband just to confirm your story and then I will come back with my decision", he says, getting up to leave the room.

The sit-in nurse returns. "So, how did it go?" she asks.

"I think it went just fine. I feel like he's going to let me go. I really do. I think he knows that I'm telling the truth, considering the fact that I didn't have high levels of Tylenol in my system", I answer.

"Well, we'll just have to wait and see", she comments.

"Does it take a while for them to decide? I need this whole mess to just go away because I need to be there when my children get home from school", I say.

"You have children? How many?" the nurse asks.

"Yes I do. I have 6 children", I tell her.

"Wow! You don't look like it. You look like a baby yourself", she tells me.

"Thank you, ma'am. Thank you", I say.

Dr. Bishop walks back into the room and once again, the nurse excuses herself. "Mrs. Thomas, I spoke with your husband and he clarified everything and his story was very similar to yours, so I'm going to recommend that they release you from here and get you back to your family", he explains. "I do believe that this was a misunderstanding. What I am recommending for you is that you and your husband get some counseling if you wish to remain together. It seems as though the bonds of trust are certainly broken in this relationship", he suggests.

"I agree, sir. Thanks so much", I say, relieved to be going home.

The sit-in nurse returns and we celebrate for a few minutes until Dr. Bishop returns, but with a look on his face that's not sitting too good with me right now.

"Mrs. Thomas. There seems to be a problem. When I gave the Center my recommendation, they overrode my decision and…", he says until I interrupt him.

"Oh no! Why? Why did they? This isn't fair!" I yell.

"Calm down dear. They're telling me that they, too, spoke with your husband and, unfortunately for you, at the time they spoke with him, he gave a different response. So, for safety reasons, they're going to keep you overnight for observations. Looks like they're going to admit you into the Center", he explains.

My whole world is spinning around me and I almost lose my balance. Did he just say that I'm going to have to stay here tonight? I can't stay here! I've only seen places like this in the movies, but I never thought I would end up in one. I'm scared. I need you, Lord! You have truly abandoned me this time. I can't do this. I just can't.

"What?!!! I can't stay here, Doc! I need to get home to be with my children. This is a big misunderstanding", I tell him. He's shaking his head.

"Melissa, I was not aware that they had already spoken to your husband. It's their decision at this point. There's nothing I can do for you. Just be admitted and tomorrow, you'll meet with their psychologist and hope for the best. Try to get some rest tonight, okay", he says, leaving the room.

I'm left sitting on the table with my mouth wide open. The nurse comes back in. "What happened?" she asks.

"I can't go home. I have to be admitted", I tell her. "I can't do this. What am I going to do with my children? I don't want anyone to know that I'm in a mental facility. My family won't understand this. Oh God! What am I going to do?"

"You really do need to contact a family member. Don't risk it by leaving your children at home alone. If CCF finds out they're alone, they will definitely go to the house and pick them up. It is unfortunate, but you need some help now", she advises.

There is only one person I can call to help me out with this. My sister, Diana. I will tell her that I had an appointment at the hospital for some tests or something and they need to keep me overnight to complete them and pray she buys it. I don't know anyone else to call.

"Yes ma'am. I guess I do", I say, starting to cry.

"Don't cry baby. God gon' fix all this. It's gon' be alright. Just trust Him. Okay. Gone and cry if you need to, but handle yo' business. I'll step aside to give you a minute to get yo'self together", she says, leaving the room.

Dear God. What mess have I gotten myself into this time!! Oh God! Please help me out of this mess, Lord. I truly let other stuff get the best of me that I should not have. I obviously stopped trusting you. I tried to handle it my way and this is the result. This is the result of my not trusting you. Lord, if you get me out of this mess, I will never play with my life again like I did this morning. All I can think about is what if there had been more pills in that bottle? I may not even be here to pray to you. Forgive me for that. I don't know what I am doing here. I need you, Lord. I am going to have to give up on doing things Melissa's way. I give myself to you to do whatever you need to do with and for my life. I give it all to you and I will just have to accept whatever Your Way is.

Right here in the hospital, I lift my hands to God and a tear falls from my eyes. I can feel peace coming over me that even I can't understand. It's almost as if someone else is in the room sitting next to me, rubbing my back helping me to relax. The tears falling aren't making me sad, but making me happy. I can't explain it. It's almost as if I'm happy about something God has already done that I don't know about.

The nurse lets me use her phone and I dial Diana's number. She answers the phone sounding unsure. "Hello."

"Diana, it's me. It's Melissa. I'm using the nurse's phone to call you so I know you don't recognize the phone number, but I....", I say, but she interrupts.

"Are you okay, sis? I've been worried all day about you. I found....", she says, but I interrupt before she finishes her sentence.

"Listen. I had an appointment and they have to keep me longer, so I really need for you to go over to the house *again* to be with the girls and tell them not to worry. I'll be home as soon as I can", I tell her.

"Melissa, stop. It's time to face the truths in your life, sis. I know that you're not at an appointment. I'm at your house right now and I just finished reading your little suicide note. Little sis, what were you thinking? Did you really try to kill yourself over this man?" she asks, sounding like she had been crying.

"I didn't, D. It's not as bad as it looks. I only took 3 Excedrins, which is certainly not enough to kill you. I just wanted Kalin to think I took more. I just wanted my husband's attention", I tell her.

"Honey, this is *not* the way to get your man's attention. You go to the negligee store or something, but not this way", she says, humorously.

"I know, D. I have to go now, but thanks for always being there", I tell her.

"Where are you? Are they keeping you overnight?" she asks.

"Yes, they are. It's a place called Parkview Behavioral Center and why they're keeping me overnight is a long story. I was almost out of here, but I'll tell you all about it when I get out of here tomorrow", I say.

"And you're pretty sure you'll get out tomorrow?" she asks.

"I have to. I have to. I can't stay here another night. I can't!" I exclaim.

"Sis, I know you're probably scared. You're not familiar with these kinds of places. Can I come there? What can I do? Oh God!! Don't be afraid, okay. God is always with you through stuff. I have seen it and I don't see where He'll leave you now. Trust Him, sis", she encourages me. "It's so funny that you're the one in that place and I'm the one worrying. You seem way too calm."

"I do trust Him. I'm not afraid, D. I know He's with me. I feel Him. I feel His presence right here with me right now. I'm at peace and you know what else? I don't even hate Kalin. I don't hate him", I say. "Good night, sis."

The nurse returns to let me know that the Ambulance is ready to take me back to the Center.

CHAPTER 60

"They Kept Her Overnight."

"*M*ommy, there's a letter in the box and I think it's about Sharelle", Justice screams running into the house. She's startled when she sees Diana instead of her mother. "Where's Mommy?"

"Your Mother had an appointment today and they have to keep her longer than she thought so she asked me to come over and look after you two until she returns on tomorrow."

"She didn't tell us about her appointment. Can I call her and tell her goodnight?" Justice asks.

"I just spoke to her and she was getting ready right then to go upstairs for X-rays", Diana tells her.

"What are X-rays?" Justice asks.

"It's like a picture they take of her to see what's going on inside her body", Diana explains. Justice seems to understand, but whether she does or not, she runs off to the family room to watch television.

Diana decides to take the girls out for dinner instead of cooking. She has had a long day and has no interest in standing over a stove. As soon as Amber gets in, they leave the house. Because it's Family Night at TGIF's, Diana doesn't have to wonder for long about where they'll go.

It's amazing how resilient the girls are. Diana can't imagine these girls in this world without MeMe. They love their mother and to think that a man could have taken that away from them just angers her. She's sitting in this restaurant, but her mind is miles away from this place. *Is that Patrick's voice? she wonders. That voice sounds just like him. Which way is it coming from?*

The closer the voice and the person gets, Diana can see that this is Patrick and he's not alone. He's with a woman. She's very beautiful. Her heart sinks. She can only imagine what Melissa would feel if she saw him with another woman. But the truth of the matter is that Patrick gave Melissa a fair chance and she chose her husband. So, the man has the right to move on with his life.

"Auntie, do you know that guy?" Amber asks.

"Yes. I do. I was just making sure it was him", she says, grabbing the menu.

"Well, he's coming this way, Tee Tee", Amber tells her.

Before Diana can think of her next words, Patrick is standing right next to her, but his dinner accomplice just walked out of the restaurant. So, it was most likely a business dinner.

"Hi everyone", Patrick says. "May I take your Auntie away for a second?" he asks.

"I'll be right back, girls. Look over the menu and decide what you want", she says, walking off to the side to speak with Patrick.

"I've been worried sick all afternoon about Melissa. Is she okay?" he asks.

"Yes, she is, Patrick. She left a suicide note. I found it. Kalin made her upset and she wanted to make him think she took several pills to kill herself but she really just took 3. He got worried when she didn't answer the phone and called 9-1-1. They came over and picked her up and she's spending the night at Parkview Behavioral Center", Diana explains.

"That bastard hurt her? What did he do? What did he say?" Patrick asks, looking concerned.

"Melissa confronted him about the affair and he didn't have time to speak with her and she lost it, Patrick", Diana explains.

"I love that woman so much. I wish she would just leave him already and let me love her and care for her, but she said that God wants her to work on her marriage, so there's nothing I can do about that", he says.

"I know. I understand your position, Patrick. I'm just glad that you were a friend to her when she needed it the most. God knows I'm praying for my sister! I'm mostly praying that she'll wake up and leave that no good husband of hers. And you know what's sad?" Diana asks him.

"What's that?" Patrick asks.

"When it's all said and done, she'll walk out of that place and right into his arms. I don't understand the hold that he has on her. And that suicide note? It had me so upset with him that I could have killed the man with my bare hands", she tells him.

"Did you call him?" he asks.

"You bet I did. I cussed him out, too, but I ended up calling him back because everyone knows that if you don't get along with Kalin, you might not ever talk to Melissa again. So, I knew what I had to do", she tells him.

"And what was that?" he asks.

"I had to call back and apologize to that jerk. Honestly, I'll do whatever it takes to get along with him just to keep my sister in my life", Diana admits.

"You have my number. Call me if you need anything", he says, giving Diana a hug and then walking away.

Diana walks over to the table and the waitress is already there taking their order. The rest of the evening goes without any drama. Over dinner, the girls tell their Auntie about their days at school and the clubs they're in and what's coming up. Diana's mind is on her sister and what she must be going through at that Center. The kids have no idea what their mother is dealing with at this hour, nor should they know.

Finally arriving back home, the girls are getting their showers. Diana calls Cynthia with the updates and she answers on the first ring.

"Hello", Cynthia says, anxious to hear the entire story.

"Hey, Cynthia. It's D. Thought I would give you a call and give you the 4-1-1 on Melissa and what's going on around here. You got a minute?" Diana asks her.

"Of course I do. Talk to me", she says, sighing into the phone.

"When I got off the phone with you, I called Kalin. Can you believe he tried to deny the affair to me? He actually sat there on the phone and lied to me and told me that my sister is basically crazy and believes her own lies. So, I had to do it, Cynthia", Diana tells her.

"You had to do what?" she asks.

"I had to tell him how MeMe found out about the affair. I told him about the email account!" Diana exclaims.

"Oh no you didn't!" Cynthia shouts.

"Yes the hell I did! I sure did and he was shocked like crazy. He tried to deny it. That fool had enough nerve to sit there and tell me that it was his brother's account; that his brother wanted him to set up that account so that *his wife* wouldn't be suspicious. Ain't that some bull? This punk really thinks I'm crazy! I hope Melissa doesn't fall for that garbage!" Diana explains.

"I hope she doesn't, but you and I both know that MeMe is most likely going to take this fool back and let him come home. She really wants it to work. She's a better woman than me 'cause that brotha would be sitting in divorce court if it were up to me", Cynthia comments. "So, where is MeMe now?"

"They had to keep her overnight at Parkview Behavioral Center. She sounded scared. I could hear it in her voice, so, please pray for her. There's no telling what she's dealing with tonight at that place. I've heard people say that when you go there, it's the drugs that make people crazy and end up having to stay longer. If I know Melissa like I think I do, she won't take any medications from them. She's pretty stubborn when she wants to be, except when it comes to that jerk of a husband of hers", Diana mentions. They both laugh.

"Can we go see her?" Cynthia asks.

"No. It's strict. Very strict. Melissa really believes she'll come home tomorrow. So, let's see what happens", Diana tells her.

The evening comes to an end and the girls are all snuggled in their beds. A letter came in the mail from Princess. No doubt she's enjoying her first days of college. Melissa will be thrilled to come home to this letter. The Guidance Counselor from Sharelle's facility sent a letter in the mail for Cynthia as well. She'll have to deal with all of this when she gets out of there, along with this eviction and the people who are looking for a couple of car payments. Diana goes to bed feeling extremely sad for her sister. One thing's for sure and it's that the only way Melissa will get out of this mess is through God.

CHAPTER 61

"This Isn't Camp."

"*M*a'am, have a seat right here and we'll have the night counselor come in and get you admitted. Do you need anything to drink?" the attendant asks.

"No, but thank you", I say to him.

Am I really here? Did I end up at a mental facility today? I would love to wake up from this bad dream and be home in my warm bed. Just this morning, I was having a cup of coffee with my sister. Just last evening, I was having a great time with Patrick. And all of this because of my husband who doesn't really love me in the first place. If he did, I wouldn't be here. If he loved me, he never would have started an affair with another woman. Look at me. I look a mess. I look like a crack head or something. I know that I am better than this. I know it, Lord.

Dear God. Please, Lord, forgive me for all that I have done to disappoint you. Forgive me for going against your Word. But, Lord, if I have ever needed you, I need you right now. There is only one way out of this mess and it's through YOU. I need favor, Lord. I need favor from these people to let me go. Watch over my children as they sleep. Watch over my sister, Lord. She is so sad. I keep making her life stressful with all of my problems. But, I thank you for her and Cynthia. They really love me and I need to survive this, but like I told you earlier, I am now ready to give myself away for you to use me however you need to use me. I don't know what I'm doing anymore.

"They're ready for you now. Right this way", he says, directing me past the double doors.

"Have a seat right here. My name is Trey. What's yours?" the night attendant says.

"Melissa", I mumble, looking away.

"Ok, Melissa. We have quite a few papers to sign. I know you're tired and ready for bed, so we'll get through this as quickly as possible", he comments.

"Good", I say, scanning over the papers sitting in front of me.

"These first pages are just basic questions. Fill out both sides, front and back", he tells me. I fill them out, one by one, and he moves on to the next pages.

"And what is this page for? Medications?" I ask.

"Yes, that gives us permission to give you medications", he answers.

He looks at me strangely when I put an X through the entire page and sign my name in the center of the X.

"Why did you do that?" he asks.

"Because I refuse any and all medications and I need to make sure that nobody can come after I'm gone and write in here what they want", I say, not looking up at all and speaking matter of factly.

"Ma'am, what if you get a headache or a stomach ache or something? You're not thinking about all that, but this is really to help you", he explains further.

"I'll get over it. I'm refusing *all* medications. Are you telling me that it's not my right?" I ask, starting to get upset.

"No. Fine. It's your right to refuse the meds if you really don't want them", he says.

"Ok. Thank you, sir", I tell him.

Trey glances over and notices that I'm not just going through the pages signing them, but I'm actually taking the time to read everything. For some reason, this seems to annoy him. This tells me that most people probably just go through the pages and sign them, without knowing what it is that they're reading. "Just sign each page and date it 11:00", he tells me.

"First of all, Trey. I never just sign paperwork without reading it first. And second of all, it's not 11:00, but it's now 11:28 and that's what I'm going to put on this paper", I tell him. He scratches his head and when I look up, another gentleman and a woman are walking into the office.

"Ma'am, is everything okay?" the stranger asks, looking at me out of the corner of his glasses.

"Yes sir. Everything is fine here. What did he call you for? The only issue I'm having here is that I refused your medications and that seems to be a problem for your counselor here, which *I* know is my right to do. And then he's instructing me to put a different time of signing these papers than when I am *really* signing these papers, which is unethical. So, I don't think I'm the one with the issues in this room", I say, boldly.

"Ma'am, you have every right to refuse medications, but what we're simply saying is that you will relax better and this process will go a lot smoother if you took something to help you sleep", he explains.

"I appreciate your concern, but reading will do that just fine", I tell him.

"We'll have to take your glasses", he tells me.

"Sir, I can't see at all without them", I say, holding onto my glasses.

"Ok, let's take the eye exam and see what you can see without them." He pulls the eye chart out and points to the top letter and asks me what it says.

"Sir, I can close my eyes and tell you what that top letter is. I have taken so many eye exams to know that one. It's an "E", I tell him.

"Can you read anything else?" he asks.

"No. Nothing. Nothing at all", I tell him.

"Yeah, you're pretty blind", he says, jokingly.

"Ok. Now that all the papers are signed, let's see which room we'll assign you to. Looks like 13B is where I can put you. Here's a bag with items that you'll need; your toothbrush, comb, and soap. And the nightgown for you to change into is inside", he explains.

"Thanks, but I'd like to read when I get in the room. Don't think I'll be able to sleep. Do you have any books I can read?" I ask.

"Ma'am. It's lights out! I don't know where you think you are, but this isn't Camp. When you get in the room, take a shower, put on your gown and go to bed", he directs.

"Ok. Sorry, sir", I say, unaware of their rules and regulations.

The attendant walks me to my room and as soon as I enter, I can see that my roommate is already sound asleep. He shows me where everything is and I know he's telling me that I have to get a shower, but I refuse to get into this public shower. So, when he leaves, I turn on the water and let it run for a few minutes just in case they're listening. It's been running long enough so I turn it off and slide into the bed. I would give anything to be back home and resting in the comfort of my own bed.

Pulling the thin sheets over me, I start to realize that this is where I'm going to be for the night so I might as well try to get some sleep, but it's not long after I get in bed that my roommate starts tugging at my sheet trying to get in bed with me. Immediately, I jump up and push her away. And then, she starts to run into the walls in a zombie-like manner, which is really scaring me right now. I can't get out of this room fast enough so I run to the end of the hall to inform the attendant.

"Go to bed and mind your own business!" he yells at me.

I'm not believing this right now. Mind your business! This woman is a little crazy and they expect me to go back in there like nothing is going on. I have to get out of here!

This is so creepy and I don't understand why he won't help this woman. When I get back in the room, she's still running into the walls, so I lead her to the bed so that she won't hurt herself. I must have finally dozed off because I'm awakened when I hear the attendant knocking on everyone's doors to get up and come to the Lobby for breakfast. My roommate and I are outside joining the others within a few minutes.

"Today, we're having group therapy and it's important that everyone joins in. Your breakfast is being handed out to you now. Eat up! Meds will be ready in the next 15 minutes or so!" the attendant announces.

I can't believe how many people are running to the desk to get their meds. They're all standing around like the second coming is expected or something. This sight amazes me, but the truth of the matter is that I'm here just like they are and right now, I'm sitting in my little corner trying to hold down this atrocious breakfast we just received. Growing up in Middleton when our Mom would give us food we didn't like, we would spread the food all over the plate and that's exactly what I just did. This makes it look like I ate some of it. I don't have a problem drinking my apple juice, though.

Sitting here and going through this therapy is a joke! The leader tells us that we have to affirm something positive that we want to accomplish today to help us get to our desired goal. *Did I just hear my roommate tell the group that she's going to Italy today?* I know I shouldn't laugh, but I can't hold this one in. The affirmations coming from this group are starting to blow my mind.

"After therapy is done, the Review Board will take each one of you to monitor your progress and see if you're eligible to be released. We'll call your name twice; once to sit in the chair next to the conference room and second for you to go inside because the Board is ready for you. Any questions?" the attendant asks.

Nobody responds. I know that I can do this. I know that I can walk in there and convince these people that I am not "crazy", with God's help of course. What will my family think if I end up having to stay in here another night? This just can't go down like this. I don't accept it.

I know that counselors are standing by and watching to see who seems to have their stuff together, so I need to interact with some of the residents. By now, this is somewhat of a challenge because they're all very medicated. There is one young lady in particular who stayed close by me and seemed to really enjoy conversing with me. We started talking about her family and she went on and on about her children and how much they mean to her. "What got you in here?" she asks me.

"A big misunderstanding!" I tell her. "I'm not supposed to be in here and God willing, I will walk in there and these people will see that. I have to get out of here. You know what hurts me more than anything?" I ask her.

"What's that?" she asks.

"I let my kids down. I'm all they have and I let them down. And not only them, but one of my best buddies is burying her 17-year old son today and I am here and *she* was depending on me to be there. *She* needs me to be there and I am letting her down, too. I need to be there for her. I don't understand this", I say, tearing up and looking above to Heaven.

"What's your name again?" she asks.

"Melissa."

"Melissa, God has a plan for every single one of us. We may not understand it sometimes, but He knows what He's doing. He doesn't make mistakes and you have to trust Him in all situations, even one as embarrassing as this. Do you mind if we pray together?" she asks.

"Of course not. I would actually love that", I say.

"Hold my hand and close your eyes", she instructs. *"Dear Lord, we come to you, today, on Melissa's behalf, asking you to watch over her as she goes into this Boardroom. Go before her, Lord, and make the way that only you can make. Put the right words in her mouth and show her tremendous favor with this Board. Watch over her family and give them a peace of mind that passes understanding. And Lord, when you bless her, she will be very careful to give you all the thanks and the praise. In Jesus' name, Amen.*

"Thank you so much. I didn't catch your name", I tell her.

"Linda. It's Linda", she answers.

In the distance, I can hear the attendant call my name for the first time. This is my cue that it's time to move to the chair next to the board room. Waving goodbye to Linda while heading towards the boardroom, I know that I need God to work this out for me. I need Him to already be in this boardroom. I can't do it without God.

CHAPTER 62

"I'm Coming Home."

"*I* need to go home now. My wife needs me. I know that I planned to leave next week, but I need to go now", Kalin says to Kesha.

"So, it's true? You love her, right?" she asks. "And you're just gonna get up and leave me just like that, right?"

"Girl, what are you saying? You knew that I was leaving. I have never told you that I would ever leave my wife. I have never denied my love for her. My kids mean everything to me and keeping *them* happy is the most important thing to me. Family emergency going on and plans need to change", he explains. Kesha seems upset and walks to the other side of the room.

"You led me to believe that it would be us together, Kalin. Where was your wife over these last few months? I'm the one who's been here for you. So now, she tries to kill herself and you have to run off and save the day, right? That's not our problem that this crazy woman will do anything to keep you!" she yells angrily.

"You're right about one thing. It's not *our problem* at all. It's *my problem*. I haven't been there for her the way I should have been. I've been here doing God knows what and I'm ashamed of it. She didn't deserve this. I want things to work out with my wife and that's just how it has to be. I'm sorry if you feel that I led you on, but I never asked for your hand in a relationship. But, if I did anything to make you think that I was going to leave Melissa, I'm sorry. I won't ever leave that woman. She's the mother of my children and we'll always have that bond together", he goes on to say. "So, let's not let this be ugly. Give me a hug, Kesha."

Kesha starts crying. With tears falling down her face, one after the next, Kalin gives her a friendly hug and walks out the door.

As soon as he's out the door, she rushes to the computer because at this point, she needs revenge on Kalin and wants him to feel the pain as deeply as she feels it right now. The plan is to send the emails, e-cards, and everything to Melissa so that she can see what Kalin has been up to; but much to her surprise, all the emails are gone. She's furious at Kalin that he deleted the entire inbox. But she immediately sees an email that she's not familiar with; it's an email from Melissa and it reads:

> *Kesha, all this time you thought you and Kalin were hiding, but God saw it all! And so did I. I have known about this secret email account ever since you sent the photo of your private parts to my husband through our email account. These last few months probably felt good to you, but you had to know that it wouldn't last. He's a married man and his heart belongs to the woman of his youth and that is me and it will always be me. If you haven't learned anything from him, you should have found out that his children mean more to him than anything in the world and certainly more than free love. Next time, think! I have been in this account from the beginning and I am the one who deleted all of these disgusting emails. Have some pride about yourself than to throw yourself on a married man.*
>
> *Mrs. Melissa Thomas*

Kesha's mouth drops wide open. She's in total shock that it all went down like this. Her heart is broken because she thought that giving Kalin what he wanted would make him want her more. After receiving this email, she's now wondering whether to respond to Melissa or whether to just let it go. She decides on the latter, deletes Melissa's email and permanently closes the account.

Hoping to catch him before he leaves town, Kesha dials Kalin's number, but it goes straight to his voicemail. At this point, she figures that leaving a message is pointless. All she can do now is just sit and wonder how her dreams of marrying Kalin have all gone down the drain.

Kalin finally makes it to his sister's house, where they're just sitting down for his mom's fried cabbages and homemade cornbread.

"What's going on with Melissa, Kalin", his sister, Monique asks.

"Why do you ask that?" Kalin asks.

"Somebody from a Behavioral Center or something like that called here today looking for you saying that it was very important that they speak with you concerning your wife. What is wrong with her? Are the kids okay?"

"She's going to be just fine. We're working everything out. That's why I'm going home on the next bus going to Miami. Think you can take me to the bus station?" he asks.

"Yes, I can do that. Just go online and reserve your ticket and we can be ready to leave here within the hour", she tells him.

"But first, let me return the call to the people who called", Kalin says. He dials back to the Behavioral Center and speaks with Mr. Cunningham, the Head of Directors.

"Sir, we're getting ready to meet with your wife and need to hear what it is that you have to say about your wife being here in the facility. We've read the report and now understand that you're the one who called the police in the first place", he says.

"Yes sir. That's correct. Melissa and I are temporarily separated right now and she has been caring for the children by herself and just basically dealing with everything. She called to speak with me yesterday morning about a personal matter, but because I was busy, she took it the wrong way. And when she left a message to me that she was taking pills and then going to sleep, *I* took *that* the wrong way. I called back and couldn't get her and I panicked and assumed that she had hurt herself and...", Kalin explains.

"But, she *did* say that she took pills, making you believe she was going to hurt herself?" he asks.

"Yes....yes....she did, but by the time I got her on the phone, it was too late because the police arrived. They actually arrived while we were on the phone together", he adds.

"Ok, sir. That's enough. If we need to call you, will you be at this number?" he asks.

"Yes, I will be here for at least another hour or so. I was scheduled to be in Florida in two weeks, but I'm leaving today instead. I need to be there for her and our children", Kalin tells him.

"Have a safe trip, sir", he says, getting off the phone with an idea of an appropriate resolution.

Kalin goes online to check out the itinerary for the Greyhound Buslines and decides on the 9pm bus leaving Alabama to arrive in Miami by 12 Noon on tomorrow. His father agrees to pick him up. He still has some time before the bus will leave so he takes a nap to mentally prepare himself to face his wife.

CHAPTER 63

"It's Not Funny!"

"**M**rs. Thomas, we're ready to see you now", one of the ladies from the Board says, opening the door slightly. When I walk in, I notice right away that there are several men and women seated around a large conference room table. My first impression is to be intimidated because it feels like they're all staring and looking their noses down at me.

"So, we reviewed your file and this doesn't look too good to us. You wanted to kill yourself on yesterday", the man seated in what appears as the Director's chair says.

"No sir. This has truly been a big misunderstanding", I say, smiling.

"What do you have to smile about? Do you think this is a laughing matter? It's not funny, ma'am", the Director says immediately.

"No sir. I don't think this is funny at all, sir. I promise you that I'm not taking this lightly. I realize what this must look like, but I can assure you that I'm driven to succeed, I'm a good mother and friend, and I do value my life very much so", I explain, making eye contact with several of the board members.

"That's all well and good, but the fact still remains that you did *something* on yesterday that scared your husband enough for him to contact the police in fear for your life", he tells me. "Was he wrong for calling the authorities?"

"Like I said, it was a misunderstanding and my husband…", I say, but he interrupts me.

"Your husband loved you enough to call 9-1-1. That sounds to me like someone who really cares about you.

"I tell you what we'll do, ma'am. We'll monitor your progress over the next 24 hours and when you speak with us after that, we'll see about letting you go home", he says, closing my folder.

"With all due respect sir, I can't spend another night in this place. I really need to go home to be with my children, sir. I just can't be here and go through this again. I'm begging you for mercy to help me get back home and ....", I plead with the Director.

"Why should we give you that chance?" he asks.

"I'll do better sir, please. I will. I promise. I just need to get out of here so I can get my life together", I tell him.

"Well, I'm gonna give you the benefit of the doubt, Mrs. Thomas. Just for you and just this one time, I'll break my own rule and speak with your husband and see what he thinks. I need his version of what really took place on yesterday and what he thinks about you going home", he explains. "That's all I can give you at this moment."

"That's good enough for me. At least you're willing to give me a try. I appreciate it so much. Thank you! Thank you!" I say, standing up to leave the room.

As I'm walking outside, the lady in the seat tells me that she'll call me back up when they have reached their decision. While waiting, I decide to go back to my room just to have a few moments alone to reflect on what just took place.

Before I can make it to my room, the tears have already started to fall. *What if I don't get out of this God-forsaken place and end up being stuck here? What's gonna happen to my children? Would anyone ever visit me here? I am sure Kalin wouldn't wait around for me if I end up stuck in a place like this. I feel sorry for the people in here who have been here so long and can't get out of this cycle. This just can't be what God intends for my life.*

A knock at my door startles me. It's the lady from the conference room. They say they're ready to see you", she says, speaking through the door.

"I'll be right there", I tell her.

Wiping the tears away from my eyes, I fix my hair and walk down the hall to the conference room that I just visited half an hour earlier. As soon as I walk into the room, I make eye contact with the Director. He clears his throat. "Ma'am, I just spoke with your husband again and he filled me in on more of the details of this morning and it all begins to make sense to me now", he begins to explain.

My mind is going in so many directions right now. It sounds like he just may let me out of here. Did God come through for me? My heart is beating so quickly right now.

"Yes sir", I mumble.

"I'm going to let you leave here today, but under one condition", he says.

"Yes! Yes! Thank you Jesus! What is it?" I ask.

"I want to see you in my office next week to follow up and make sure all is still well with you", he comments.

"Anything! I will do that, sir. I'll do that. Thank you so much for going the extra mile to seek the real truth. I'm extremely grateful to you, sir. Extremely grateful!" I tell him.

The entire group is smiling. They seem to be happy for me. Getting up from my chair, I realize that I never want to be in a room like this or a situation like this ever again. Happy to be going home, I don't stick around to wait for my free bus ticket, but instead, I leave the Center walking. It isn't long before I run into a pay phone that I use to call a cab. The friendly cabdriver picks me up and drives me all the way to my house. This can just go down as one of those experiences that I never want to experience again.

Melissa's World Goes Dark
Torn 2: Passion, Pain & Promise.

CHAPTER 64

"Did You Enjoy That?"

"Mommy's home!" Justice shouts when she hears my key turning in the front door.

As long as I have my children around me, I never have to worry about getting enough love or hugs. Immediately, as I walk through the door, both of the girls run to me and give me hugs. Diana walks out of the kitchen when she hears all the commotion.

"You could have called, honey. I would have picked you up", Diana tells me, walking towards me.

"I know you would have, but I really needed that time alone. Thank you so much, D! I appreciate you for everything. I mean that more than you know. Thank you!" I say, giving her a big hug.

"You are more than welcome. Me and the girls had a blast! Since you're home, I'm going to get out of here, unless, of course, you need me. I'm supposed to meet a friend later for drinks", she announces.

"No, I'm good, dear. Get out of here! Go and have some fun", I tell her.

"Please call me if you need me", she says, grabbing her things to leave.

We all walk her to the door. Once her car is out of sight, we go back inside. "Mommy, do you feel better now?" Justice asks.

"Yes, sweetheart. I do. Much better", I say, trying to change the subject. "So, tell me. How was your time with Auntie D? What did ya'll end up doing last night?"

"We went out to dinner. Tee Tee didn't feel like cooking", Amber comments.

"That's Tee Tee for ya!" I say, jokingly.

We all laugh.

"Girls, I really want to get a shower and get into some more comfortable clothes. Do you mind?" I ask them.

"Of course not, Mommy! We'll be right here watching our favorite movie, "New Moon". Auntie D bought it for us."

Being home after what I just went through is truly a blessing. My room is just as I left it on yesterday. Within minutes, I'm standing in my very own shower, lifting my hands to God as the hot water runs over my body. I'm at peace and realize that it's by God's grace, His mercy and favor that I'm standing here right now. Tears of joy begin to flow down my face and my reality starts being "real" to me. Kalin's affair with this woman almost killed me.

Dear God. Thank you for always being there for me. Thank you for not leaving me alone in this World. I don't know where I would be if it weren't for you. Forgive me, Lord, when I disappoint you. Forgive me for anything I may have done to contribute to the demise of mine and Kalin's relationship. We didn't always do things your way Lord, and for that I am sorry. But Lord, I really need you to help me deal with this huge hole that is in my heart. I don't know what to do. Is it Your Will for me to continue working on my marriage or walk away? I want to do Your Will. And Lord, you know the situation we are in regarding this house. I am not going to even pretend to know what to do. We need you, Lord. Please don't turn your back on us. I am trusting that You will work this out. In Jesus' Name, Amen.

It's not until this moment that I realize how much I appreciate a nice hot shower, but there was no way I was going to shower in that place. I don't ever want to end up in that situation again. Telling that lie to Kalin about taking several pills to kill myself was not worth this headache and aggravation. Knowing what I know about him and Kesha makes me sick to my stomach. Neither of them are worth me putting my children through the heartache of losing their mother. But, I have to admit that being in the Behavioral Center has humbled me a great deal. I was so close to being lost in this system forever.

Was that the doorbell? Who could be coming here at this time? I know that I'm not expecting anyone. I hear screams coming from downstairs. Sounds like those are screams coming from Amber and Justice. Are they into that movie that much?

Next thing I know, the door to my bedroom is opening and I'm quite shocked when I see Kalin walk through the door. "Baby, I'm home!" he yells. The girls are clinging on to him for dear life.

"Mommy, daddy's here! Isn't this wonderful? Now, we can be one big happy family all over again. Yeah, daddy!" Jusice shouts.

I'm totally speechless right now. I didn't expect this right now. *Why didn't he call me and let me know that he was coming?* And honestly, I'm not sure how I really feel at this point to see him after all that's happened. If he had not had an affair with Kesha, this would have been the most beautiful moment. It would make this reunion so much more special to me. I finally manage to get some words to come out. "How was your trip, Kalin?" I ask him.

"My trip was fine. I sat next to this woman and her crying baby for the majority of the trip, but other than that, it was okay. I've missed you, baby", he says. The girls get a kick out of hearing him say this and follow up with oohs and aahs. But, this time, his sweetness doesn't impress me.

"Oh, I see. Girls, can you please excuse me and your father for a little while?" I ask Amber and Justice.

"Sure, Mommy. We knowwwwwww...Mommy and Daddy stuff", Justice comments, sarcastically. Both girls run back downstairs.

"So, you changed your plans to get here early, huh?" I ask, drying off.

"Yes, I did. I love you, baby. I know that I haven't been here for you in the way a husband should and I'm so sorry for that. This nightmare of you wanting or not wanting to kill yourself opened my eyes and it placed everything out in the open and very clear to me. It has placed perspective on my marriage. I've been hurting you and I....", he begins to explain, but I rudely interrupt him.

"Bullshit, Kalin! You had an affair with another woman and you didn't think about me or your kids. We were supposed to be working on our marriage and you just messed all of that up because you can't control yourself. I don't deserve that at all!" I say, starting to cry.

"I want to explain about Kesha. Please hear me out, baby", he says, trying to give me a hug.

"What can you possibly tell me about Kesha that I don't already know? Huh? You have no idea the pain you've caused", I tell him, starting to cry.

"Melissa, I didn't have an affair with this woman. The email account that you were following was not mine and hers, but it was hers and Greg's. The account was set up with my name just in case Greg's wife found it and ...", he begins to explain.

"Oh, but you didn't care whether *your* wife found out or not, right? Do you honestly think I believe that those responses were Greg's and not yours? Ok, Kalin. Then tell me this. Why were there racy photos of you sent to this email account taken from *her* cell phone? Now I know who you were with on New Year's Eve. You are such a liar and honestly, I hate that I ever tried to work on this marriage. I should have just let the divorce go through and it would have been final by now and ...", I say, starting to cry harder.

He walks over to me and takes me into his arms and we stand there crying together. I can't control my tears. Kalin takes the towel away from me and drops it to the floor. He kisses me passionately and whispers, "I need to make love to my wife. I have missed you so much. I need you, baby."

As much as I want to resist him, the truth is that I need him too. His touch is so familiar to me and I crave his body right now, despite everything that has happened in the last 24 hours. So, I grab him and pull him in even closer and whisper in his ear, "Make love to me. I need to feel you inside of me."

Kalin gets undressed, but quickly jumps in the shower, only to be out in seconds to keep from ruining the moment. He walks over to me, kisses me, wipes the tears away from my eyes and plants a small kiss on each eye. Kalin takes his time kissing every part of my body and loving on it as if it is the last time he'll ever make love to a woman. I'm enjoying all of this attention. It feels like he's saying "sorry" with every kiss and every touch. He parts my legs, kisses my calves, my inner thighs and then the most intimate part of my body. Kalin takes his time making sure I feel him and desire him more and more. And I do! We make love for the rest of the afternoon, giving ourselves one to the other. We manage to forget about his infidelity, the situation with this house, any anything on the outside. For the first time in a long time, it felt like my husband wanted to make love to *me* and only thought of *me.*

"Did you enjoy that, baby?" Kalin asks.

"What do you think? Did I act like I was enjoying you?" I ask him.

"Yes, you did, actually", he responds, laughing. "You really missed 'big daddy', didn't you?"

"I think we should get up and spend time with the girls before they run upstairs. Start the shower", I tell him.

Kalin and I take a quick shower together and head downstairs to join the girls in the family room. They're both so attentive to the television that they almost didn't notice us standing in the doorway.

"So, what were you two doing?" Amber asks, sarcastically.

"Minding grown folks' business. You guys wanna go to the park?" I ask them.

"Sure! Let's make it a picnic", Justice suggests.

"I think it's a fantastic idea!"

We pack the picnic box with all of our favorite goodies and decide to spend the day at the park with the kids. Kalin and I still have plenty to discuss about this marriage and our financial status as it relates to the house and its requirements. I have no idea where everything will end up, but for right now, I'm enjoying this moment.

CHAPTER 65

"You Mean My Kids, Right?"

"Sharelle is 60 days away from being released and we need to decide where she'll go upon her release", the Director tells Angela, the Counselor.

"I'll make a call to the Aunt who called our office just 3 days ago inquiring about Sharelle. According to her, Sharelle *wants* to live with her instead of going home to live with her mom and Kalin. She said that they don't get along and she can't live in the same house with him", Angela says.

"Really? How does Sharelle know what's going on with her mom?" the Counselor asks.

"The Aunt has told her. So, amongst the two of them, they've agreed that Sharelle will go to live with he r, but we both know that Mom has to approve of this first. I'm going to call her today and I'll let you know what she says", Angela confirms.

"Ok. That sounds like a plan. Let me know because I want things to be in order by the time she's discharged from the Facility", the Director comments.

Angela pulls the records from Sharelle's teachers, the psychiatrist, and the medical nurse to see what her progress has been like throughout her time here. Scanning through the notes, Angela can't deny Sharelle's improvement since she began the Program. She runs across Melissa's number and decides to call.

"Hello", I say into the phone, not recognizing the number on the caller id.

"Hello. May I speak with Melissa Thomas, please?" says the person on the other end of the phone.

"This is Mrs.Thomas. How may I help you?" I answer, still not so sure who this is.

"Mrs. Thomas, this is Angela Spivey from Mart Girls Academy. I'm your daughter's counselor and first, I want to say what a pleasure it has been for me to work with your daughter. She's such a joy to have here and is such an inspiration to the other girls", she begins to explain.

"Thank you for saying that. How is she doing? Is everything okay?" I ask.

"Oh yes ma'am. Everything is fine, but it's almost time for her completion of the program and a certain issue has arisen. It appears that Sharelle has issues with your husband, her stepfather", she says.

"Really? I wasn't aware of that. I mean, I knew that right before she left, she wasn't all that happy with him, but I never really knew why", I tell her.

"Your sister, Diana, has agreed that she can live with her when she's released; but, because you are her legal parent, we have to get permission from you to allow this", she says.

"I haven't even had the chance to speak with my sister about this", I say.

"We spoke with her a couple of days ago", Angela admits.

"A couple of days ago, really?" I ask. *Why didn't Diana tell me about this? I guess it's because of my being in the Center and all. It must have slipped her mind. This really does hurt. My own daughter wants to live with her aunt instead of me, her mother. This devastates me. Why does she hate Kalin so much? Maybe Diana knows.*

"Ok, ma'am. Give me time to speak with my sister about this and I'll call you back by the end of the week", I tell her.

"That's fine, Mrs. Thomas. I'm really sorry that you had to hear this from me like this. But, it's all for the better of Sharelle. We just want her to leave here and begin again in the environment of which she feels most comfortable", she explans.

"Of course. We all want that for her. I'll be in touch", I tell her before hanging up the phone.

Before I call Diana, I need to get a cup of coffee for me and Kalin. He has been so sweet and attentive these last couple of days since he returned. And to be honest, we've talked more over the past week or so than we've talked in years. It took a minute for me to calm down after he told me he quit his job instead of transferring it to Florida. So now, we're both sitting here without employment. I have at least applied for unemployment, but Kalin has no income coming into the household at all.

"So, who was that?" he asks, walking into the kitchen.

"Who was what?" I ask, shocked that he overheard me on the phone from the other room.

"Come on, Melissa. On the phone? Who was it?" he asks.

"Oh! That was Angela from Mart Girls Academy, Sharelle's counselor. She's about to get out and they're trying to decide whether to send her home or to Diana's. Apparently, Sharelle would rather live with Diana than to live here because of the issues that she has with her stepfather. What issues, Kalin?" I ask.

"What you asking me for? You should be asking her!" he yells, getting defensive.

"Why are you getting so defensive?" I ask.

"Why do you think, Melissa? I'm so tired of these kids and their attitudes", he comments.

"You mean *my kids,* right?" I say with an attitude.

"Well, yeah, if you wanna put it like that. I'm tired of it! Just tired! If she wants to go and live with Diana, let her go! Let her deal with the headache if she wants to", Kalin says, walking away, leaving me in the kitchen alone.

I can't believe I just had this conversation with a man who claims he loves me. How could he be so insensitive to this situation? And so insensitive to my daughter and what's going on with her. How is that I believed he ever loved me or my kids for that matter? What really happened between him and Sharelle? I need to hear Diana's position on this.

"Hello", Diana says, answering on the first ring.

"Hey, sis. I just hung up with Angela, Sharelle's counselor", I begin.

"Yeah?" she asks.

"So, what's this about Sharelle coming to live with you when she's released in December?" I ask.

"Listen, Melissa. That lady called *me* and asked about whether Sharelle can come here. I thought that you already knew about it. It isn't my intention to intrude and you know that", she says.

"I know, D. I'm just trippin' off Kalin. He's such an a—hole!"

"What did he do *now?*" she asks.

"When I went to him about Sharelle coming to live with you, he acted as if he could care less whether she did or not. That bothers me. And why is it that those two hate each other now?" she asks.

"Who knows? Forget him, Melissa. Take care of yourself and your kids. Kalin don't care 'bout nobody but Kalin", she says.

"Ok. So, words of advice for you about Sharelle. You know she's a con artist, right?" I ask her.

"Girl, you crazy! No she ain't!" Diana shouts.

"Yes, she is. So, watch yourself. Don't just let her tell you anything. She's definitely going to try", I tell her.

"I'm sure! I got this, lil' sis. I got lil' Miss Sharelle", Diana says.

For some reason, I get this eerie feeling deep down in my gut that this may not turn out to be positive in the end, but I have to trust God that things will fall in line. While the phone is ringing to the Academy, it feels like I'm about to abandon my child and send her off.

"Hello", the lady on the other end of the phone says.

"Angela?" I ask.

"Yes. This is she. How may I help you?" she asks.

"This is Melissa Thomas, Sharelle's mother. How are you?"

"Oh, I'm fine, Mrs. Thomas. Did you get a chance to speak with your sister?" she asks.

"Yes. I did. And after talking with my sister and going over everything in my head, I do give Sharelle permission to leave the facility to live with my sister, Diana", I tell her.

"Ok. Good. I know it's hard for you, but it's better for Sharelle. And when things cool out at your house, I'm sure Sharelle will then want to spend time with you and her sisters", she explains.

"Yes. I'm sure. So, what's the exact date of her release?" I ask.

"December 11th", she answers.

"Great. Thanks. She'll be home just in time for Christmas. We're excited about that!" I say, cheerfully.

"Absolutely. Will you pick her up or will your sister?" she asks.

"No. I'll pick her up myself", I say.

"Wonderful. Well, I'll send more detailed information to your email at least a week before she's to be released", she tells me.

In two weeks when Sharelle is released from the facility, she'll go live with my sister, Diana, but I'm not sure how I really feel about it. *Will this make a difference? Will Sharelle be better off being raised by her Aunt than her mother? Why does it feel like I'm choosing Kalin over my daughter, again?*

CHAPTER 66

"Where Do We Go From Here?"

"Honey, did you see the paper delivered to the door today?" Kalin asks, coming into the kitchen.

"No, I didn't. What does it say?" I ask him, not looking up from cooking my dinner.

"It says that we have two weeks to respond to this eviction. What are we going to do, honey?"

"Why are you asking me? Aren't you the head of this household? Why is it that every time something like this comes up, you always look to me for the answer? For just once, I would love to look to you sometimes, Kalin", I say. I can tell that he didn't like this response because he stares at me as if he wants to hit me.

"How the hell do you think I know, Melissa? I don't have any money. If you would have made better decisions, we wouldn't be in this position", he charges.

"Did you just say what I thought you said? Listen Negro. I was the only one working up in here for a long time. You take your behind to Alabama, had a job while you were there, helping *another* woman, but then when you bring your behind back to Florida, you quit the job. And you got the nerve to come in here and blame *me* for this. You know where you can go with that, right?" I tell him, starting to get upset.

"And I'm tired of you and your family making me feel like I don't contribute anything to this household. Just 'cause I don't bring in any money right now, ya'll think I don't do anything and I ain't 'bout nothing. I'm tired of this!" he yells, slamming down his book.

"Don't raise yo' voice in this house! You ain't coming up in here with this yelling and stuff!" I say loudly.

Kalin and I walk away so that we can both calm down before the children hear us arguing. Tensions are high right now and I no longer have an appetite. My mind is now focused on what it is that we can do to avoid this eviction. *How in the world are we going to come up with all of the money that this Notice says that we need to stop this eviction? Kalin is absolutely no help at all! Why am I married to this man? This is a time when I wish I had a real man to deliver me from this wrath. Kalin doesn't really seem to care. It's almost as if he is looking to me to figure this out just like everything else.*

"I'm sorry. I'm sorry. It's just that this has come at a very bad time. Neither of us are employed and as the head of this household, this doesn't make me feel too good knowing that my family may end up on the streets if we can't come up with this money", he explains.

"You don't think it bothers me, too? I honestly have no idea how to fix this one", I tell him. "I usually have a solution, but not this time and I'm scared, Kalin."

"We just have to trust God. That's all I can say. We just have to trust God", he says.

"But, in the meantime, we need to start writing our response and as soon as your unemployment check comes in, we need to put as much money as we can with this response", I say.

Blocking everything out, I start writing the response letter, citing Florida Statutes along the way. Kalin leaves me alone to write the letter, but for some reason, I have no motivation to do it. Once Kalin is done fixing the lunch, he calls for the girls to come down to eat. When they're done eating, they clean the kitchen and watch a movie in the family room together.

"Melissa, would you like to join us?" he asks.

"No, thanks, Kalin. I really need to get this done, but you guys should enjoy yourselves", I tell him.

My heart is beating fast and my thoughts are going in so many directions right now. I am in the middle of a divorce, my house is up for an eviction, and to top it all off, Kalin came back to me but without a job, so neither one of us are working. I don't know how it can get any worse than this. Maybe I should just make love to him to make me feel better right now. Maybe this will take my mind off our problems. But, I have to admit that I am actually thinking about Patrick at this moment and wondering what he's doing.

"What are you thinking about?" Kalin asks, noticing that I'm pre-occupied in my thoughts.

"Nothing. Just thinking about where we go from here", I answer.

"Do you mean about where we'll live or about this marriage?" he asks, looking away.

"Both, Kalin. You have to admit that things haven't been all that great between us since you've returned. And now, we're at this point where we may end up on the streets with our children. This has never happened to me and I don't know what to do. I may have to end up moving in with my sister or something and honestly, she won't allow you to come along with us. I'm not happy about this, but my family is not that fond of you right now", I begin to explain.

"Your family hates me that much that they don't have a problem seeing me on the street. I'm not that bad of a person, MeMe", he says.

"When they think of you, they think of you as the man who would have been responsible for my death. I just got out of a mental facility because of my issues with you. That's why they don't have much love for you right now", I explain to him.

"Wow. I had no idea that it was like that. Listen. I'm truly sorry that I failed you and our kids", Kalin says, walking away. He sits in the chair next to my office desk and drops his head in his hands. "If I have to go back to Alabama, I will."

CHAPTER 67

"Don't Worry, I'll Figure it Out!"

"I'm here to pick up Sharelle Williams", I say to the receptionist after arriving at the facility on December 11th. The receptionist looks through the computer, clicks on something then looks up at me.

"Yes. She's with the counselor now and they're completing her paperwork. Ms. Angela will call down when they're done. In the meantime, I need to go over the medications' list with you", she announces.

"Ok. No problem", I tell her, putting down my purse and keys.

Linda reads the list of medications to me that Sharelle is leaving with, but the one that I don't recognize from previous calls with the nurse is the birth control pill. I had no idea that Sharelle was on the birth control pill. "How is it that Sharelle was prescribed the birth control pill without my knowledge?" I ask.

"Ma'am, I have nothing to do with that. You'll need to take that up with the doctor or the nurse. My job is to just go over this with you", she explains.

"I see", I tell her, shocked that I knew nothing of this.

Before long, Angela comes from behind the double doors, with Sharelle walking right next to her. She looks surprised when she sees me in the lobby.

"Hey Mommy!" Sharelle yells, running towards me. She looks amazing! Sharelle catches up to me and gives me a hug. "I'm so glad to finally be out of here!"

Angela laughs and looks at Sharelle. "You're ready to leave me?" she asks.

"Oh yeah, I love you, Ms. Angela, but I'm very glad to be leaving this place!" Sharelle tells her.

"Well, all your Mom has to do is sign in a few more places and you're free to go", she tells Sharelle, looking over at me.

Within 30 minutes or so, my car is packed with all of Sharelle's belongings and we're finally on our way to Miami, where Amber and Justice are home, busy making *Welcome Home* signs for Sharelle's return.

"So, Mom, how are things with you and *him*?" Sharelle asks, as we begin our trip.

"It's okay", I lied.

"Really? Well, it's about time. I sure am glad that it's better for you 'round the house. Personally, I don't see how you put up with him", she comments.

I really do wish I could tell my daughter the truth about what's going on between me and Kalin, but I need her to have the respect that a daughter should have for her father. It would be nice to know why she has so much resentment for him. I wonder if she will tell me if I ask her. As much as I want and need to know, I won't bother her with this today because I don't want anything to set her back. I just hope that our afternoon is drama free.

The radio stations aren't playing anything interesting, so we both agree to put in Yolanda Adams and listen to her. We both like to sing, so we start singing *More Than a Melody* right along with Yolanda Adams. In between songs, I ask, "So, how was your time in the facility? Did you really learn your lesson from being in this place?"

"Oh, yes ma'am. But, it wasn't all that bad for me because I got to do whatever I wanted", she admits.

"How is that?" I ask.

"I just did. The Staff loved me, Mommy!" she admits.

We've been driving for at least an hour or so and Sharelle is starting to get restless, so she falls asleep. Reflecting over everything, I listen to the music and relax while she sleeps.

Dear Lord, thank you for delivering my daughter back to me. I ask that you please watch over her as she returns back into society where all of the temptations still exist. Keep her mind at peace, Lord. Be with her at every stage of her new life. In Jesus' Name, Amen.

After 2 ½ hours, we're finally pulling into the driveway and Sharelle is ecstatic when she sees the homemade signs in front of the house welcoming her home. Her favorite meal is being prepared inside and then later this evening, she has to report to Diana's house, as per the orders from the Juvenile Center.

"Welcome home, Sharelle!", Justice yells, when Sharelle walks through the front door, looking around as if this a strange place to her.

"Thank you, little sister! This is so sweet of ya'll", Sharelle says to her, putting down her bags.

Sharelle isn't in the house 10 minutes before she recognizes the sweet aroma coming from the kitchen. "Are those collard greens that I smell?" Sharelle asks.

Kalin pops from around the corner and yells, "It sure is! That's what my daughter wanted and that's what she gets!" he says. Sharelle doesn't seem to care at all about his statement and completely ignores him. She does; however, speak to Diana. "Hey Auntie D! I'm so glad to see you here and the food smells really good!" Sharelle says. Kalin just turns around and goes back into the kitchen.

"Well, looks like we'll be ready to eat shortly", I say, trying to lighten the mood.

"So, how was it, sis?" Amber asks. "How long will it be before you go back to that place?" she asks, jokingly.

"Never! That was *not* for me! I think I'm done with all of that. I'm focused and know what I need to do", she tells Amber, looking around at all of us.

"I really do hope so, Sharelle. Those folks said that if you don't do like you need to do, you'll go back to court to face the charges that landed you in that facility. The choice is all yours", I tell her. "But, who's ready to eat?"

After a long day, we all sit down to eat collard greens, cornbread, fried chicken and potato salad. The meal is delicious. Kalin did an excellent job preparing it, but it's now time for Sharelle and Diana to leave because Sharelle has to check in with the officer by 7pm.

Sharelle's clothes are already in Diana's car, but before they leave, she gives her sisters and me a big hug, but shows absolutely no love for Kalin at all. I feel bad for him, but whatever is going on between the two of them, he created it. My guess is that it has something to do with his affair with Wendy that has her so upset with him. I just have to pray that she somehow finds a forgiving heart to deal with this matter.

"Ok, sis. We're outta here! Sharelle and I have to get her registered for school so I'll be calling you for stuff", she says, walking towards the front door.

Our dinner party is over and the girls retire to their bedrooms while Kalin and I take care of cleaning the kitchen. "Why does our daughter hate me so much?" Kalin asks.

"I don't know, Kalin. She'll eventually come around. You know how teenagers can be. I guess she needs time to see if you're going to do right by us this time around", I tell him.

"You act like I messed this up all by myself", he says.

"Well, you kinda did and...", I say, before he interrupts me.

"I'm real tired of you *and* yo' family always treating me like the bad guy. It's starting to get old and I'm just...", he begins to say, but I cut him off.

"Look. Right now, the most important thing for us is to figure out what to do about this eviction and coming up with the money to save us in this house. Now, do you have any ideas?" I ask him.

"Who, me? Why are you asking me? I haven't been here. You were the one who was here. So, you need to figure this out. I ain't even got no job so I don't know what you expect me to do", he states.

What do I expect him to do? How about, man up? This man has gotten to be the laziest man alive! He acts like we're not his family and that he shouldn't feel just as responsible as I do about our family about to be on the streets. Why am I with this man? He is never around when we really need him and when he is around, he can never help us and God knows, I am so tired of this. I really hate to call Patrick for help. I shouldn't have to call him; he's not my husband.

"Don't you feel responsible for making sure your children are safe and with a roof over their heads?" I ask, starting to get frustrated.

"I still don't know what I'm supposed to do if I don't have anything to help with", he stated again.

"Don't worry about it, Kalin. I'll figure this out just like I have to figure out everything else when it comes to our family. I don't know what you think, but I didn't marry you to have to figure everything out. Honestly, I could have stayed single if I was going to live like this", I say, walking away from him. Saying this to him usually sparks a serious argument, so we may be in for a long night.

"Really? So, I guess you would have been better off with that white boy, huh? Is that what you want? You think *he* would go through all the trouble for your ungrateful behind kids. No! He wouldn't!! You think he would put up with your nosy family the way I have? No! He wouldn't!! So, I'm a little sick and tired of hearing this mess from you, okay?" he yells.

As much as I want to keep this argument going, the truth is that it does no good because none of what we're saying to each other right now is going to fix the problem that we're having trying to avoid this eviction.

Who does he think was taking care of us when his sorry behind wasn't working? And he really thought I was getting all those extra bonuses from work that helped pay our bills. It would totally crush his manhood if he knew that those were fake checks I created on the computer because I didn't want him to feel bad for not working. I'm just ready to go to bed now because I have to get up bright and early tomorrow to draft this letter and get it to the attorney to see if this situation can be saved.

CHAPTER 68

"Right On Time."

"Florida Manag2ement versus Kalin and Melissa Thomas", the judge announces.

This is the moment that we've been waiting for. The letter that I wrote only bought us a few weeks, but it all boils down to this judge's decision. I know that God has heard our prayers and in my heart, I know that it *can't* be God's will for us to be on the streets with our children. At this point, I hope that the money that we put with the letter is enough for the Judge to at least work with us. Kalin and I look at each other, but exchange no words. There is nothing that can be said at this point.

The attorney for Florida Management opens up the argument and presents a pretty solid case to the Judge, citing Florida Statute under Landlord/Tenant. Having been in the industry, I am very familiar with the statutes. Due to our inability to afford an attorney, Kalin and I opted to represent ourselves. As best as we can, we begin to explain our side of the story.

When it's all said and done, Judge Kathy Brown agrees with Florida Management by giving them possession of their home and it certainly didn't help when Kalin told the Judge that we didn't have money and didn't know *when* we could pay the Landlord. When he said that, I knew that it was over at that point.

"What are we going to do, Kalin?" I ask him, starting to cry.

"What are you crying for? You had to know that there was a possibility that this could happen. Ain't no sense in crying", he states, walking past me to push "elevator down".

"This has never happened to me before!! I have managed properties for several years and never thought in a million years that I would ever see this day", I say, wiping the tears away to keep Kalin from becoming even more angry. For me, I'm really starting to get angry because for the first time ever in my life, my family is evicted and I don't have a clue where my family will live and I have never felt more alone and abandoned in my life.

The drive home is an extremely quiet one. It seems as though Kalin is starting to get even more agitated when he hears me sniffle from crying.

All I can think about is who I can call that will let me, Kalin, and the girls come and live with them until we can figure this out. I know that my sister would take me and the girls, but certainly not Kalin. I have to look out for all of us and not just me and the girls. I can't think of anyone. My family is completely out of the question because neither of them have any respect for Kalin whatsoever. How am I going to go home and tell Justice and Amber that our life will have to be uprooted and they may have to withdraw from their schools and from their friends? And just when they're starting to get comfortable with everyone.

"Ok, we're almost home. And when we get there and have to explain this to the children, please don't cry. If they see you cry, then they're gonna panic and that's not what we're trying to do. Remain calm so they will remain calm", Kalin advises.

"Oh yeah? Calm? I am not calm right now! What in the world is my family going to do? Dear God, please help us!!!" I scream.

Kalin is finally pulling into the driveway and the kids see us and come outside to meet us. "Mommy, how did it go?" she asks. She can already tell that it's not good news just by the look on my face. "We have to move, right?" she asks.

"Yeah, baby. We do. We gotta move on, but God always has our back, right?" I ask her.

"Yes. He does. But where will we go, Ma?" Justice asks me.

"I don't know, sweetheart. I don't know. I know that whatever we have to do, we have to trust God and know that He has us covered", I tell her.

Justice runs back into the house and Kalin looks at me and shakes his head. He seems to be annoyed with this whole situation, but not half as annoyed as I am. I specifically remember all the conversations and arguments that we've had about him finding employment instead of just sitting here every day. And now, not only are we evicted from our home, but we have nowhere to go. I know that Diana is waiting on me to call her, but I don't think I'll be able to get the words out of my mouth. She'll hear the crying in my voice and I'd much rather not have any drama with her and Kalin today. Instead, I think I'll have a glass of wine to clear my head.

"I think I could use one too", a woman voice says, coming through my backyard fence. "Hello, nice to finally meet you. I'm Audrey's mom, April", she announces.

"Well hello, April. It's so nice to finally meet you. My daughter is at your house all the time and I just haven't had a chance to meet you face to face, so I'm glad you came over", I tell her.

"Thank you! Justice is welcome in our home anytime. She's a good girl, which brings me to why I'm here. Audrey came to me in tears and told me that Justice doesn't have anywhere to live and will be leaving. Audrey was crying so hard, she could hardly tell it to me", she admits.

"Oh goodness! I'm so sorry that Justice bothered you with this. Please forgive her. She gets so….", I begin to say. Audrey interrupts me.

"Listen, we have two empty rooms in our home that are yours for as long as you need it. It would be our pleasure to have you in our home. Please! It's okay. It's why God blesses us. He expects us to be a blessing one to another. I am sure that if this were reversed, you would do the same thing for me and…", she continues.

"Oh my goodness! I can't be a bother to you", I respond.

"You're not a bother. Please, take it!" she insists.

"I don't know what to say, Audrey. Thank you! Thank you so much!"

God has worked it out again for us. This woman, whom I have never met until today, walks in here and lets God use her to bless us with a roof over our heads for as long as we need it. Again, God has proven himself to us. As she is leaving, Kalin comes down the stairs. "What's all the yelling and praising God about?" he asks.

"Look at how good God is!! Just an hour or so ago, we had no idea where we would go and God stepped in on time and made a way! It may not be the solution I would have wanted, but at least me and my family don't have to live on the streets!" I tell him, shouting even more.

"That's great! So now, we just need to figure out where to keep all of our stuff", Kalin comments.

"I'll get the Yellow Pages and start looking for affordable storage units", I say.

Kalin and I finish boxing up all of our items and begin to prepare ourselves to be guests in someone else's home. The good news is that we are only moving a few houses over. By the time the Sheriff comes to put us out, we will be long gone.

CHAPTER 69

"We'll See!"

"Sharelle, what are you in there getting all dressed up for?" Diana asks Sharelle.

"It *is* the first day of school for me, isn't it?" she asks.

"Well, excuse me! You're such a beautiful girl and Tee-Tee wants you to remember that, okay?" she tells her.

"Yes ma'am. I'll do that. I'm really happy you let me stay with you", she comments.

"It's no problem. I'll do anything to help my sister, but I tell ya one thing. I'll be so glad when she leaves that no good man of hers", Diana tells Sharelle. They high five each other in agreement.

"You ain't neva lied", Sharelle says. "I can't stand him now!"

"I can't believe that because you used to be his biggest fan. What happened that made you hate him so much?" Diana asks.

"First of all, I don't like how all that stuff went down with Christy and that accusation and everything. I'm starting to think that there's something to it. I *know* he's a dog and Momma deserves better. He's abusive and we didn't realize it 'cuz we were little kids, but I see it now and I hate him for what he put our family through. And now, they over there and having to live with somebody else 'cuz his sorry behind can't get a job. Please! My momma shoulda stayed with the white man!" Sharelle says, grabbing a soda out of the refrigerator.

"And you know what? I think you're right. Patrick was a lot nicer to my sister. Kalin knows I can't stand his ugly behind and Melissa knows it, too, but I love my sister and I just pray to God that one day she wakes up and realizes that she is better off without Kalin", Diana comments. "Would you go back home with your mom if he didn't live there?" Diana probes.

"I would. I love my momma. I just don't like him", Sharelle admits. "So, what happened with Patrick? Why did my mom leave him alone? Anybody is better than *her husband*. She should have stayed with him", she comments.

"Your mom felt as if God wanted her to work it out with her husband. She may have finally blown it with Patrick because I saw him the other night with another woman. Melissa doesn't know about that. I just didn't have the heart to tell her. She's probably regretting her decision to stay with Kalin", she tells Sharelle.

"I hate him, Auntie! I absolutely hate him!" she tells Diana.

"Don't hate him, Sharelle! God doesn't like that. You have to find a way to forgive him in your heart so that you don't suffer. Let it go and realize that your mom was just doing what she thought was the right thing to do", Diana advises.

"Whateva! I ain't tryin to hear all that forgiveness stuff. Ain't nobody trying to go through that junk again. One time was enough for me. You need to talk to yo' sister and make her wake up!" she tells Diana.

"You don't think I've tried. He has some kind of a hold on her something serious. She's not trying to hear it. She's in love with this man and nothing we say is gonna change it. She can't see the real him because of what she feels in her heart. And just between me and you, I really don't think this was the man that God intended for her because from day one in their relationship, it has been a struggle to be together. And the Bible says that when God gives you something, He doesn't add any sorrow with it."

"That is so true!" Sharelle says.

Diana, knowing way more than Sharelle, isn't happy with the recent circumstances of Melissa's eviction and having to live with someone else, but at least they're not homeless. Tomorrow is the first day of school for Sharelle and everyone is crossing their fingers and hoping she'll start and finish the school year on a positive note.

Diana uses the documents that were already given to her to enroll Sharelle in school and it it's almost too good to be true that Sharelle has been in school for two weeks now and no incidents whatsoever. Time is passing and Sharelle seems to be happy with this change from my house to her auntie's house. Maybe this *is* the change she needed.

Two Weeks Later.

Since Sharelle started school, Diana hasn't heard any negative reports from the teachers at the school. Maybe this was just the thing that

Sharelle needed get her on the right track. She seems to be coping pretty well with this change. Little did Diana know, but this is all about to change. "Tee-Tee, where are you?" Sharelle yells running into the kitchen.

"I'm in here, Sharelle! What's going on?" I yell out to her.

"I got suspended from school for fighting! I'm so sorry, but she asked for it. She had no business calling me a name!!" Sharelle yells, putting down her bookbag.

"Hold up! What do you mean, Sharelle? And I guess you couldn't walk away, right?" Diana asks.

"No. I couldn't. They said that because of the severity of the fight, you have to come to the school and have a meeting with the principal to see about trying to clear this up", Sharelle explains. "And can we please *not* tell my mother? You know how she gets!" Sharelle pleads.

"I'll go down there and see what I can do, but if your mother has to get involved, then you'll have to suffer her consequences", Diana explains to her. "Why, Sharelle? And you were doing so good, too!"

As the days passes by, Diana mentally prepares herself for this meeting with the School Board. Enough time has passed, and unfortunately for Sharelle, they're not interested in giving her a second chance. When there's a fight that breaks out and the police are involved, the school takes immediate notice that this is a problem beyond the school's repair. Sharelle has to enroll in Virtual School to complete the school term.

Diana decides that it's time to get me involved because she's been trying to do things her way, but it's not working out so well. She's starting to see a behavior pattern in Sharelle that she was clearly warned about. Oftentimes without her permission, Sharelle gets on the phone with boys that she has met in the neighborhood. Diana grows extremely concerned when Sharelle starts seeing one guy, who's over 18 years old, according to Sharelle's own admission. For whatever reason, she's being very secretive, but Diana is so annoyed by her behavior that she doesn't pry too much.

"I have plans in about two weeks, Auntie. A friend of mine from the Program is coming to visit me. It won't be a problem. I promise you. Okay?" she asks.

Diana doesn't know enough information to agree to this, so she says, "We'll see, Sharelle!"

CHAPTER 70

"I Don't Know You Anymore!"

"*M*elissa, there's mail for you!" April yells from the kitchen.

This must be my check from the attorney for the settlement of the accident. I was wondering when that would get here. This means that I will be able to give the landlord down the street the first and last month's rent for the house that has become available and we can move out of here. Nothing against this family, but there is nothing like living in your own place.

"I'm coming!" I yell back to her.

By the time I make it into the kitchen, April has placed the Fedex envelope on the countertop. "Thanks! What are you cooking? It smells good", I comment to her, grabbing the envelope and walking away.

"I hope you guys are good and hungry! It's curry chicken", she says.

I make it back to the room and Kalin is just getting out of the shower. "Did it come?" he asks.

"Yes it did. Thank God! Thank you Jesus! And now, we can move and get back on track. And haven't we agreed that we should both work this time?" I say, trying to be humorous by kissing him on the lips.

"Don't start with me, Melissa! Since when does a woman tell a man what to do in his own house? You always know how to get me upset", he comments, walking back into the bathroom to dry himself.

Now, what did I say? Does he think that I want to go back to the way things were just 30 days ago when we were facing an eviction? I'm tired of struggling with this man. He doesn't seem to get it. Does he think that I want to take care of him or the rest of his life or what?

Three Weeks Later.

The paint is dry, the move-in fees are paid, and we are finally moving into the house at the end of the street. Having lived with April and Ricky for the past 30 days has not been all bad, but it feels good to be in my private space again. Although we got into this house without having jobs, it is imperative that Kalin and I both seek and secure employment so that we don't end up in this position again.

After approximately 3 weeks, my Employment Agency is on the phone telling me that they have a job for me. Of course, this is the best news right now because Christmas is right around the corner and a job coming through at this time would mean that our children can finally get some joy without all the holiday stress.

"So, what did they say?" Kalin asks as soon as I get off the phone.

"They have a job for me that should start next week or so", I tell him, taking out the chicken to prepare for dinner. Kalin and I haven't been talking much these days because every time we start communicating, we seem to end up talking about *him* and why he hasn't been physically looking for employment.

"That's good. We really need that and I just hope….", he begins to say, but I interrupt him.

"But nothing. You need to get a job too. I'm tired of having to do it all on my own. I need your help, Kalin. This is crazy. I'm tired just like you're tired and I just…", I say, but he stops me from saying anything further when he slams the phone to the floor.

"I'm so tired of you telling me what to do! What? You think you have a penis or something? What in the hell do you want me to do? I can't make people hire me! You want me to force somebody to hire me? I'm so tired of you and your mouth!" he shouts and before I know it, he has put his fist into my left side of my temple. I can't describe the pain that I feel right now. I can feel this all down my back. *Why does he have to hit me like this? This man is going to kill me. He knows that my neck and back are injured from the car accidents. Does he just not love me anymore? He can't possibly love me anymore. If I could dig a hole and crawl into it for the rest of my life, that would be just fine with me.*

"I hope you're proud of yourself! Does that make you feel like a man? Does it?!!?" I yell at him, running upstairs. He makes no attempt whatsoever to soothe me or to apologize. *What have I done here by accepting this monster back into my life? I have to find a way to get out! I can't tell anyone my secret or there will be a riot in this city. I never thought that he could be so violent! Is it my fault that I make him so angry and lash out at me all the time? What is it about me that make this man so angry? Is it that he just doesn't like me? I can't tell anyone, at least not just yet. I feel trapped inside my own home. I wish that there was someone I could tell. For now, I will have to just tell my God.*

"Melissa, the telephone is for you!" Kalin yells from downstairs.

"Ok. Coming!"

By the time I make it back downstairs, Kalin is preparing a bowl of ice cream for me. *Does he think this is an apology for what he has done? Does this man not know that what he has done to my spirit is far worse than anything he could have ever done to my body? He just doesn't get it. This is one of those moments that I wish I were in Patrick's arms.*

"Hello", I say, grabbing the phone from Kalin. He tries to kiss me, but I pull back from him.

"Melissa, there has been an accident", the caller says.

"Who is this?" I ask.

"This is Jamice, your niece. I'm here at the hospital with Diana. Sharelle tried to kill herself. She took all these pills, but the police found her in time", she explains.

"What!!!!! Oh my God!!! No!!!!!! Is she okay?" I yell into the phone.

"Auntie Melissa, I can't tell you anything more than that. They aren't saying anything! The doors are closed and they aren't saying anything. Diana is back there, but she's not in there with her. I'll call you as soon as I know something!" she tells me.

"Where are ya'll? I'm coming over!" I yell.

"We are way on the other side of Miami. You might as well wait, Melissa. They ain't gon' let you back there. Just sit by the phone and I'll call you or I'll have Diana call you back as soon as they tell us something. Calm down, Auntie. God is in control!" she says, trying to comfort me. "Just pray", she advises.

"Oh my God! I can't believe this!" I shout, beginning to cry.

I hang up the phone with Jamice and fall to my knees. Kalin comes over and tries to comfort me, but I push him away and begin to cry. The girls hear my cries and run downstairs. "Mommy, what's wrong?" Amber asks, starting to cry.

"Your sister's in the hospital!" I yell. "I should have been there! I should have been there! Oh God, please help us! Please help us! Please,

Lord! I am so sorry for anything I have ever done that was not pleasing to you, but, Lord, please don't take my daughter! Please, Lord!" I yell, crying and rocking back and forth on the floor.

"Mommy, what's wrong with Sharelle?" Justice asks.

"She's in the hospital, girls. Let's pray. Come here. Pray with Mommy."

Amber and Justice grab my hands and we begin to pray. Kalin walks away and goes upstairs. He doesn't see the need to comfort his wife and right now, I could care less. By the time we're done praying, the phone rings again and this time, it's Diana. Right away, I can tell that she's crying. "Melissa, I am so sorry!" she says, sobbing into the phone. "I had.....", she begins, but I interrupt her.

"Please, don't tell me my daughter is gone. I won't hear of it.....I just won't!" I yell.

"No! She's not dead, but I need to explain to you what happened. First of all, I had no idea what she was doing! Oh God!! I am so sorry!" she says, sobbing heavily.

"Diana, is she really okay? Please tell me that my child is okay!" I yell.

"She's going to be okay, but she's definitely going to sleep for at least 2 days", Diana says, sounding a little clearer.

"What happened? Oh my God!! What happened that made her do this?" I ask, holding my breath.

Diana is crying and can hardly get her words out enough to speak to me and tell me what happened. She finally stops crying long enough to say, "It was that man!"

"What man?" I ask. "What are you talking about, Diana?"

"In that place that she was at, Melissa. Sharelle has been talking to one of the security officers in that place. That grown behind man has been talking to her and he was going to come here to take her shopping and.....", she begins to explain.

"Wait a minute, wait a minute. Are you saying what I think you're saying? Are you telling me that there was a security guard at that facility that's been an adult man talking to my 15-year old daughter in that way? Is that what you're telling me?" I ask, taking a seat in my family room.

"That's exactly it! I got a chance to speak to him briefly and asked him how old he was", she says, sniffling. "And then, I told him I wanted to see his ID when he got here and I guess that scared him off and when he told Sharelle that he wasn't coming, I guess that's when she freaked out and took all those pills", Diana says. Diana can't control her tears now. She starts crying even harder and is obviously too upset to speak with me right now.

"Diana, listen, this is *not* your fault. I don't blame you at all. I know that you have done your best with her. She's just a disturbed child with a mind of her own and it didn't matter whether she was here or with you, she would have done this. Ok, so please stop crying. This is *not* your fault", I reassure her.

"You sent her to be with me and I didn't do a good job at all. And I'm so sorry, Melissa", she says, apologetically.

"I just need you to calm down a little and tell me exactly what happened", I tell her. "You know me and you know how I operate, so you know I'm gonna say something to the powers that be, so please try to remember all that was said."

"I was about to go to bed when I walked past Sharelle, who was already on the phone and I overheard her say, "when you get here". I thought to myself that there shouldn't be anyone on their way to the house to see her. So, I was like, what?" Diana explains.

"I see."

"She knew that she wasn't supposed to invite anyone over to the house without my permission", Diana adds.

"Exactly. And then what happened?" I ask.

"When she got off the phone, I asked her what *that* was all about and that's when she said that a friend was coming over to take her Christmas shopping. She told me he was one of the officers at her program and I thought I was going to lose my mind. Now, I knew he had to at least be 18 years of age to work in that place, but I was shocked when the real truth came out", she explains.

"Which was what?" I ask.

"That the man was actually 32 years old with 2 children", Diana blurts out.

"Ohhhhhh my Godddd!" I say, putting my hand over my face. "I'm in total shock that this is happening. She went in there to get help and they messed her up even worse."

"I know. I feel the same way, Melissa. His name is Jeremy Stevens. I checked the phone and I can get his phone number and everything. He was the last person who talked to her and…", she goes on to say.

"And then, what happened?" I ask.

"So, I told her that I wanted to see his ID and that I was gon' tell him, but after I got done talking to him, I went back in my room. Melissa, I never should have left her. And you know with my sickness, I fell asleep and next thing I know, the police were banging on the door!" Diana explains.

"Oh Jesus! I bet that was scary for you. I know it had to be scary!"

"So, I get up and go to the door and the officer was like, "Ma'am, we received a call from this address of an attempted suicide and I had no idea what he was talking about", Diana says, sounding like she's about to cry again.

"It's okay, D. Just tell me what happened", I tell her, trying to keep her calm.

"So, I was like, 'no, ain't nobody here but me and my niece and she's in the room' and before I know it, the officer rushes past me and went straight for the back room. Little did I know, but both of the doors to the bedroom were locked. He had to break the lock. And sis, when he opened that door, she was.....", Diana tries her best to explain before she starts crying.

"Oh no, Diana! It's okay, sis. It's okay!" I tell her.

"She was passed out on the floor! I couldn't believe it! Oh God, I started screaming!" Diana says.

"I can imagine how hard this is for you and I'm so sorry that you had to go through this. I am so sorry!" I say, trying to comfort her.

"They rolled her out of here and into the ambulance. They got to her in enough time and was able to pump all the pills out of her system. One thing's for sure; she'll sleep for a couple of days, though", Diana tells me.

"It's been a long night. Right now, all I can say is 'Thank you, Jesus!' I say, wiping the tears away from my eyes.

Justice and Amber are standing next to me and anxiously wanting to know what is going on with Sharelle. "Girls, don't worry; she's gonna be okay. She just needs to get some rest. So, we should all head upstairs and get some rest so that we will be there for her when she wakes up", I tell them.

"Is she going to die, Mommy?" Justice asks, with tears in her eyes.

"No, sweetheart. She isn't. She isn't. It's okay. I know I may have scared you guys, but you have to understand that you all are the most important people in my world and when one of you are sick or hurting, it hurts me just as much. That's why I was crying like I was crying. I didn't know what was going on with Sharelle and it made me sad for a moment. God's got her in His hands", I say, making it to Amber's room first. After tucking them both in bed, I head towards my bedroom. Because of the altercation that happened earlier between me and Kalin, I dread walking into this room, not knowing what type of mood he's in at this point.

Hoping to find him fast asleep, I walk past the bed into the bathroom and his movement startles me. "So, how is she?" he asks.

"She's fine", I say. He can sense that I'm just not in the mood to have a conversation with him. As a matter of fact, my face is *still* stinging from where his open hand met the side of my face sending me into the cabinet.

"So, what? You mad at me now? What do you want to do, Melissa? You want to leave me, now? Is that what you want?" he asks, standing and walking towards me.

"I don't know who you are anymore. The man I fell in love with would have never put his hands on me. When we first got together, Kalin, you never spoke a harsh word to me. I wish I knew what happened so that we could fix it and be happy again. You have to know that I am not happy in this marriage and I....", I begin to say, when he puts his finger over my mouth to keep me from completing my sentence.

"Don't say it, baby. I was wrong. I never should have put my hands on you. You're my wife and I should treat you better than this. For what it's worth to you, I'm sorry. I'm truly sorry for how I have hurt you and not just tonight, but all of the other times, as well. I'm sorry", he says, wrapping his arms around me and pulling me closer to him.

This is starting to get old. He punches me and then thinks that he can excuse it all away just because he flashes his gorgeous smile and holds me tight and does the one thing that he knows I love in the bedroom. But not this time. Not this time. I am done and I'm not interested in his apologies. He treats me like a 3-year old and I am worth so much more and he is going to be in trouble when I remember who I am and whose I am.

"Ok, Kalin. Whatever. You say it every time. Don't you think it's getting a little old now? You don't even act like I'm your wife and you sure as hell don't have any respect for me. And one day, I'm gonna get tired of it and you'll lose me forever. I promise you that", I tell him, pulling away from him and going into the bathroom.

"Melissa, I'm sorry. I'm sorry", he says. I have shut the bathroom door and can't hear him anymore.

I lock the door behind me and fall to the floor. Tears are flowing heavily from my face. Marital problems, coupled with the issues surrounding Sharelle's attempted suicide, has my mind going around in circles. I'm surprised that I haven't lost my mind. The pain that I feel at this very moment takes my breath away. My daughter was near death and I wasn't there when it happened. But, now that I have this news of inappropriate conduct from the facility, I have to address this matter and I have to address it immediately.

CHAPTER 71

"Ready to End This Chapter of My Life."

"**M**elissa, what do you plan on doing?" Diana asks me, opening the door for me. She goes right back to cooking.

"Something smells good. What are you making?" I ask her.

"It's salmon. Want some?" she says.

"You know I do. You got some salad?" I ask her, peeping underneath the lid to get a better sniff.

"Check the refrigerator. I just bought some. Did you do your complaint letter, yet, to the Department of Juvenile Justice?" Diana asks, looking up to see my reaction. "I know that you must be working on something. It's not like you to do nothing."

"I did. Yes, I did. What I did first was call to see who I should send my letter to. You think I'm playing? I'm not playing about this. I mean business about this. These people may have caused more damage to my daughter than what she had *already* experienced out on the streets. I can't let it go", I explain to Diana.

"I hear ya, Melissa. If you say something, that guy may lose his job", she says.

"So be it, then. This grown behind man had no business messing with my child and besides, he may be doing this to someone else's child too. He needs to be stopped!" I respond to her. "I'll get to the bottom of it. You can believe that!" Diana shakes her head. "But, what I need from you is to sit down and write your version of what happened so that we're better prepared when they start investigating", I tell her.

"Ok. No problem. We can do that. Let's just get something to eat first and then we can do that."

Diana and I sit at her dining room table and eat our salads. We catch up on all the latest news going on in our family. The family reunion is coming up soon and neither of us plans to be there.

"I went to see Sharelle today. It was so good to see her laughing and being herself again. The doctor says that she's getting better and better every day. They plan to set her up with counseling when she's released from the hospital."

"Really? That's good to know. Did they say when she can be released?" Diana asks.

"Physically, she's ready to go, but they're extremely concerned about why she wanted to end her life over this man", I tell her.

"Yeah. That's the question on everyone's mind. All I know is that he was the last person who spoke to her that and I just can't see how....", she begins to say.

"Listen. There was nothing you could do. Sharelle has a mind of her own and she would have figured out how to make it work. So, no need in beating yourself up over this. She's alive and didn't die. So, for that, I'm grateful", I say, walking to the computer.

"Are you ready to get started?" Diana asks.

"Yes. I am. I want to go ahead and get this done because I have some things to do at home that need my attention", I tell her.

Diana and I sit down to her computer and finish the package that has to go to the Complaint Department at Juvenile Justice. After spell checking and making sure all the names are correct, I hit the "send" button and my complaint letter is now in Tallahassee.

"Well, we did it!" Diana says.

"Yes, we did. Now, we just have to let the chips fall where they fall", I say, putting all my things back into my briefcase. "That should do it, D. I'm sure somebody will be calling soon."

Before I can make it to the door to leave, my phone rings and it's Kalin. I answer immediately. "Yes, Kalin." I'm sure that he can tell how *unhappy* I am to hear his voice.

"When will you get back?" he asks.

"I'm walking to the door now to leave", I tell him.

"Okay. Great. I was hoping we could have some quiet time tonight, just me and you. What do you think?" he asks.

"I don't know. 'We'll see when I get there", I tell him.

"Listen, Melissa. You have every right not to want to listen to me or hear anything I have to say. I've hurt you and I admit it. But, I'm truly sorry. You're my wife and I shouldn't behave the way I've been behaving", he says, sounding sincere.

"Ok. I appreciate that, Kalin. I really do appreciate that and I hope that you truly mean it this time. So, I'll see you when I get there." I hang up the phone and Diana is standing there tapping her feet with a look on her face that I have seen so many times before.

"So, what did *your husband* have to say *this* time? I don't know why you keep putting up with that…", she says, shaking her head.

"Don't say it!" I say, turning the knob on the kitchen door to leave. "I'll be in touch!"

The weather is beautiful today and I can appreciate this quiet time by myself. On days like this, it seems that my mind is clearer and things seem to make more sense to me. I have been so busy these days that I haven't had time to speak to Kalin about the receipt I found in his pants the other day and as much as I need to talk to somebody about it, I am just so tired. He will have an excuse about it. My feelings for him are beginning to change. The romance that I once felt when we first met is dwindling away and I am scared that without divine intervention, we aren't going to make it to our 20th year anniversary. This is one of those times where talking to friends is not going to do it for me. I need to talk to God because He's the only one who can fix me and Kalin.

Lord, I need you. I know that you know my heart and you know that I love my husband, but I'm not in love with him anymore. I don't want to cheat on him, but I really needed him to be a husband. I needed him to love me the way you love me. He puts others before me and I can't force him to remember what we once had. I know he's trying, but it may be too late. I know that it's not your Will for me to meet someone else and fall in love. I know that it's your Will for me to make it work with my husband, but so much damage has happened to this marriage and I don't trust him anymore and I don't know if I will ever be able to trust him again. I just feel in my heart that he has feelings for that woman in Alabama that he became friends with. He had the nerve to tell me that no matter what, he would continue to have a relationship with her. And what's funny is that he doesn't understand why I feel so hurt these days. Lord, please forgive me, but I think that it is time to tell my husband that I want to end our marriage. I deserve better and so do our children, but I need your blessing on it. I need to know that you forgive me, Lord. Please forgive me!

Pulling into my driveway has me somewhat anxious and nervous all at the same time. I know that when I get in here, Kalin is going to put all the moves on me, but it may be too late for all of that. It's time to confront him about this receipt that I found in his pants for a hotel and it just so happen to be the night when I couldn't reach him on his cell phone and then when he did pick up the phone, he said that he couldn't talk. He's coming towards the car.

"You gon' sit there all night or what?" he says, coming towards the driver's side of the car. "Let me help you with your things."

"No, I'm coming. I'm okay, really", I tell him.

"I hope you're ready for your massage", he says. "My beautiful wife has had a long day. You look tired, honey. Let me get these things for you."

Kalin grabs everything and I walk inside without having to grab anything. He's also prepared dinner. "The children have already eaten. Get ready for dinner and we'll sit right out here", he says, pointing and opening the sliding glass door to the back patio.

"Aaaah, that's nice, Kalin. Thanks. Thank you so much!!"

"You're definitely worth it. I know that I haven't been the best husband to you and I'm sorry. I want to do better by you, Melissa. God knows that we've been through so much over the years. Our children deserve to have this marriage work out. They deserve a happy family and I want to do whatever is necessary to make this work and I know that...", he begins, but I have to stop him at this point.

"Kalin, I want a divorce", I blurt out. "I'm sorry. I'm so sorry."

"What!!" he yells. "You want a divorce? Where the hell is that coming from?"

"Kalin, please stop yelling before you wake up the children!" I tell him. "We can talk about this like adults. I can't take this marriage anymore. It's draining me and it's starting to affect my health."

"Melissa, what happened? Is there someone else? Who is he? I know that you probably met someone else. I know you, Melissa. And you can't be with him because of me, right?" he asks without stopping to breathe in between.

"Why do you automatically assume that there has to be someone else? You messed this up, Kalin! You're so changed, right? Well, what the hell is this? Why did I find a receipt to a hotel room in your pants pocket? Huh, what is this all about?" I ask, standing up from the makeshift dinner table on the patio and walking back into the kitchen to dump my plate.

"Melissa, please let me explain!" he yells. "You're looking at this all wrong. It's not like that! Please listen to me, Melissa", he pleads.

"I have heard all the explanations I want to hear from you. You, obviously, want to be with someone else, so please go and be with her. Don't let me stop you, Kalin. Get your happiness because I'm gon' get mine. I just know that it was not God's plan for me to have to struggle like this in my marriage. I just don't believe it was part of the plan. I promise to be fair in this divorce as it relates to our children. But, you and I both know that there is really no need to share anything between the two of us because you haven't really invested much into this marriage financially. So, you should be fair, as well", I explain, while he sits there looking off into space.

I finally said it! I can't believe I found the courage to tell him how I feel. And I feel so much better for it. I'm tired of crying myself to sleep wondering when and if he will find someone else and come home one day to me and the girls to tell us that it's over. I know it hurts now, but I would rather hurt now than to hurt for the rest of my life.

Kalin is crying out of control. He is grabbing me and trying to kiss me and undress me. "Kalin, please stop! That's not the answer to everything. Sex can't fix our problems. I don't trust you anymore! I'm not in love with you anymore!" His eyes tell it all. He seems surprised by this comment and lets me go. Our eyes meet one last time before he runs upstairs.

I don't know what just happened here. Kalin and I have been together for so many years, but I don't think I have ever seen him respond like this. The look he just gave me says a lot. The night has suddenly come to a close and I think I should sleep in the office. I don't feel like we should share our bed tonight. It's time for me to start thinking separation. I just hate that he spent his afternoon preparing this meal for us and in just a matter of seconds, it is destroyed.

The house is quiet as a mouse. You can literally hear a pin drop. Not wanting to watch television, I turn off the lights and go upstairs to the office. The computer is already on and it looks like Kalin was on the recipe website, most likely to get a recipe for the dinner I just scraped into the disposal. It looks like he was also in his Yahoo account. After logging into my Yahoo, I see almost immediately that I have an email from Patrick. It's been awhile since I last spoke with Patrick. His email couldn't have come at a better time.

> *"Hey stranger. It's been a long time, hasn't it? I saw you today when you were driving down Dolphin Parkway. You still look good to me. Good enough to eat, actually. :--) Just wanted to say hello and to let you know that I was thinking of you. I love you, baby. Xoxoxoxooxxoxoxo......Love, Patrick.*

Patrick must have forgotten the memo that I was married and working on my marriage. He doesn't seem to be bothered by it at all, but since I'm not working on my marriage anymore, maybe I should call him up and offer to take him to dinner, but, then, maybe that's not the best way either.

It looks like I got a friend request from a Morgan Shem Smith. He's certainly a looker, but I wonder if this is really his picture or not. London? He's from London. I had no idea that there were people on Facebook from other countries. He's my first! This should be interesting.

After deleting all the junk mail, I'm definitely ready for bed. This has been a long day, but something tells me that tomorrow will be even longer. I don't hear Kalin stirring around in the bedroom. I wonder what he's doing. Not once has he come out to see if I'm ok or not. Tonight, I'll have to grab my pillow and blankets and sleep right here in the office. My heart can't take another conversation with him about his infidelity. Finding that receipt and watching how he treats other people and other women so much better than me has finally done it for me. I'm no longer interested in being Mrs. Melissa Thomas. It's safe to say that I'm more than ready to end this chapter of my life.

CHAPTER 72

"Are You Seeing Someone?"

Christmas seems to come and go this year. We aren't in our usual holiday spirit and the girls can certainly tell that there's something going on with me and their father. "Ma, why do you sleep on the couch?" Justice asks, while putting away the dinner dishes.

"Why do you ask so many questions, child?" I ask her.

"Are ya'll getting a divorce?" she asks.

"Why do you say that?" I ask her, shocked that she's become so candid.

"One of my friends from school said that when parents stop sleeping in the same room together, it usually means that they're going to get a divorce. Is that what's going on with you and daddy? Tell the truth, Ma!" she demands.

"Ok. We should talk about this later. Me and Daddy should talk ....", I begin to say, but she interrupts me.

"No! We just want to talk with you about this because Daddy gets way too loud when you try to talk to him. So, Ma, just tell me the truth", she asks again.

"Yes, Justice. Your father and I are divorcing. People grow apart sometimes and can't seem to find their way back to each other. But, please know that this has *nothing* to do with you and Amber. You two will still be in his life. That won't ever change, okay?" I explain to her. She seems to be okay with it so far.

Kalin and JT are in the living room watching football. Sharelle and Diana have already gone back to Diana's house. Amber is upstairs in her room trying to figure out how to work her new Ipod that she got for Christmas. Painfully, we have made it through the holidays pretending to be a happy family. Kalin's father came over for Christmas Eve to spend time with Amber and Justice. I know that he can tell that something is not quite right here, but he won't dare ask.

"Well, Pops, my wife doesn't love me anymore", Kalin tells his father when I walk into the room to get the remote for the TV.

"Is that right?" Pops asks, sounding as if he doesn't want to get into this right now.

"Yeah, she wants to leave me. Can you believe that? After all these years, she wants to leave me and let some other nigga get what's mine", he comments, taking a sip out of his wine glass.

"Son, I think that this is something that you should talk to your wife about", he says, getting up to leave the room.

"What is wrong with you?" I ask Kalin, sounding extremely annoyed.

"Oh, snap! You talking to me? I didn't think you could talk", he says, with a smirk on his face. "Hey, why don't you follow me upstairs and let me taste you."

"Kalin, please go to bed! You're drunk! And there's no way I want to have sex with you. I don't know why you have this thing where you think sex fixes everything. I am not...", I say before he interrupts me.

"Maybe it can fix my broken heart, Melissa. You broke my heart, girlie. But, I tell you one thing. I don't care who you go and be with, I will always love you, Melissa. In my eyes, you will *always* be my wife. I put your name on my body, for crying out loud! Look at that!" he yells, pointing to his groin area, where his tattoo is.

The girls come into the room and their presence certainly lightens the mood when they share the things they're learning about their Christmas gifts. I hope that he never loses the relationship that he has with Amber and Justice because they will need it on those days when things are tough and they need their father.

Leaving them alone, I decide to go into the office to see if I have any new mail before flipping on the television to watch Lifetime for the rest of the evening. I have new mail from Morgan.

"Hello beautiful. How are you today? Are you married?

He doesn't waste any time, does he? How can that be the first thing he wants to know? Is this how the men in London handle their business? I wonder why he's asking.

I respond to his question, *"Thanks for the compliment, Morgan. I am doing just fine. To answer your question, I am married, but going through a divorce right now from my husband."*

It looks like he is online because he responds right away. He responds, *"You're quite welcome. Sorry to hear that. Well, not really. I'm sorry for him. I would love to get to know you better."*

I respond, *"I bet you're sorry. You're funny. I see you live in London so I guess we'll be internet friends."*

He replies, *"No, I'll come to wherever you are. I really do want to get to know you better."*

Then, I ask him, *"How do you know you want to get to know me better?"*

He answers, *'I've been watching you. I checked out your profile already. I like how you respond to people. I like you. Is that really your picture on the profile?"* he asks.

"Of course, it is", I tell him.

Morgan and I continue late into the night talking about how things are there versus how things are here in the United States. He has a 9-year old daughter, Anita. He tells me about his brother and how his brother is married to a black woman. He tells me about his mother. He seems to be really close to her because they talk every single day.

I have to admit that I've found myself getting lost in our conversation tonight. He has a totally different attitude than the men I'm used to speaking with in my life. I'm already starting to like him. We agree to speak again tomorrow, but say our goodbyes first.

I'm so caught up into my conversation with Morgan that I don't notice that Kalin just walked into the room. "So, who is responsible for that big smile on your face? He must have been talking some good stuff to you", Kalin says, walking towards me.

"Please don't do that. You and I are over, Kalin. As soon as I can, I'm filing the divorce. So, you might want to figure out where you're going to live. I think it's only fair that me and your children remain in the house. You're not working, so ....", I begin to say. He interrupts me.

"You're such a bitch, you know that? I mean, really you are and I am so glad....", he tells me, starting to get angry. "You ain't working either!!"

"Yes, I'm glad, too. I won't be *your* problem anymore. You can stop blaming everything on me now. Now, you can get out there in the world and experience what it's like to struggle and how to make ends meet.

You'll see that it's not as easy as what you think", I say, shutting down my computer.

"Are you seeing someone else, Melissa?" he blurts out.

"Really, Kalin? Really? I don't even have time to think about that. My priority right now is getting a job to keep this roof over me and my kids' heads because, honestly, I can't depend on you for anything. I've never been able to depend on you and I just feel that if I'm going to struggle *anyway*, why in the world do I want to be responsible for my children *and* a grown man? I married you to be *your* help, but instead, I just got another child to be responsible for. I hate to put it this way, but this is how I truly feel, Kalin.

He storms out of the room, even angrier than I've ever seen him before. I hope that the children aren't affected by this divorce. I think it may be a better idea if one of us moves out of the bedroom so that we can keep the peace without making this a nightmare for everyone. I think it's time for me to call my sister and let her know what's *really* going on around here.

CHAPTER 73

"Lights Out!"

"Why don't you call Patrick and ask him for help, Melissa?" Cynthia asks.

"I can't do that. I haven't been with him after all this time and all of a sudden, I'm going to call him and ask for some money. How does that make me look?" I ask, finding us a table. *Crispers* is especially crowded today. Although this is a busy time at work, Cynthia agrees to lunch with me to discuss my crisis.

"He's your friend, isn't he?" she asks.

"Yes, he's my friend, but I just don't feel right to do that. The last conversation we had was when I was telling him that I wanted to make my marriage work and now….", I say, looking away.

"Melissa, he's your friend and I'm sure he won't mind helping you if he knew that your lights would be turned off if you don't make this payment to the electric company. He understands what it was that you were trying to do", Cynthia explains.

"I still can't do it. I just care about people too much to do that to him. I'll figure something out. It will be alright. That's enough about me and my problems. How are you, my friend?"

"I'm doing just fine. I got a promotion! Sharon gave me another property to manage when they sat down with me on my evaluation. She went on and on about my progress and how I manage, but I made sure that she knew that you were the one who taught me everything I know", Cynthia says, rubbing my hand.

"Aaaah, you're so sweet, Cynthia. You didn't have to say that", I tell her.

"Why not? It's the truth. I learned a lot from you, Melissa. The company is not the same without you. So many of the residents have asked about you. They all want to know when Melissa's coming back", she tells me.

"Send my love to them, will ya? How sweet! Well, I'm gonna actually do it this time", I say, with such confidence.

"Do what? The divorce?" she asks.

"Yeah. Yes. I'm ready this time", I tell her.

"Really? So, why now? What's different this time?" she asks, looking concerned.

"I'm no longer in love with him. I no longer have a desire to make love to him or have him touch me. I find myself thinking about what it would be like to be with someone else. You're not gonna believe this, but I met this guy on Facebook that I really like, Cynthia. I know it seems sudden, but there's something so different about him that I have never had in my life and I just...", I begin to explain.

"Oh, now, Melissa! You haven't even gotten divorced yet and you're already moving on to someone else. Are you sure that this is what you want to do? Why don't you give yourself time to heal from Kalin and then slowly start seeing other people? Girl, you are something else! What's his name?" Cynthia asks.

"Morgan. Morgan Smith", I tell her.

"That sounds like a white boy's name", she says, laughing and friendly patting me on the hand.

"Yes. He is. He's from London", I say, as a matter of fact.

"London! Girl, have you lost your mind?" she asks.

"Maybe. Maybe I have. Only God knows and only time will tell", I say.

"You are always so full of surprises. Melissa, be careful. There are crazy people on the internet. You don't know this man and you don't know what he's up to, so just be careful and ....", she advises.

"I know, Cynthia. But, he makes me feel like a real woman. It's not sexual or perverted or anything of the sort. Our conversations are so pure. He wants to know about me, the real me. He doesn't care what I've done before. He makes me want more out of life. I'm just having a good time right now having someone to talk to. That's all", I say, finally.

"As long as that's all you're doing. Girl, keep it here in the States. Men from the other countries are crazy", she comments.

"Well, it can't get any crazier than that man that I am married to because he's truly a monster in green eyes", I tell her. We both laugh.

Cynthia and I continue to catch up until it's time for her to return to work. I need to get some applications out there myself because this temporary assignment is almost over and I'll need to secure employment as soon as possible to avoid another eviction.

Driving back home today seems so much harder than any other day because I have to go home to a dark house. I didn't have the confidence to tell Cynthia the truth about my situation at home. The lights are *already* turned off. The light company turned them off this morning while I was getting dressed to meet her for lunch. Kalin has moved upstairs into one of the empty bedrooms and I decided to stay in my bedroom. We hardly talk or see each other. Amber stays upstairs with him mostly. Sharelle is out of the home still at my sister's house. And because Justice has a hard time being in the house with no lights, another family has agreed to take her in to give me time to get this together.

Up to this point, Kalin hasn't offered any financial assistance and I'm just too embarrassed to go to Patrick or anyone else for that matter. Without having a job, it's hard to get any type of assistance. The good news is that I have a job that will start in a couple of weeks. The job is slated to only be for 3 months, but you never know. Maybe, just maybe, it will last longer. In the meantime, I'm going to have to do something that I know I shouldn't do, but I don't see another way out of this.

Dear Lord, I am so lost now. I don't know what to do or where to go. I have never felt so lost or alone in my life. Where are you? Why have you abandoned me? Why have you allowed me to be with this type of man? I thought I was doing the right thing to work on my marriage? But, that is so far from what I believe your plan is now. Why did I allow him to come back into our lives? If this is how it was going to end, I should have given this up a long time ago. Lord, help us! Lord, please forgive me. I don't feel good about what I have to do to keep a roof over our heads. I don't have a support system here at all, Lord. Please forgive me.

The tears roll down my cheeks one after the other because I feel as though I have run out of options. People are tired of me coming to them for help. They have told me this on numerous occasions. I have gone to so many people for assistance in the past and I can't do it anymore. I can't stand to hear another person remind me that I'm married and how disgraceful it is to get help when I have "a man right next to me in bed". I feel that I am left with no options.

As usual, I sit in my car in the garage to get warm and to listen to my gospel CDs. To make time pass quickly, I go to FB on my phone and communicate with people. Nobody has any idea that I'm sitting in my garage right now. The temperature is dropping outside. Although it's cold, I can't run this car too long for the risk that I may fall asleep while it's running and never wake up again.

Dear Lord. I am here and I know what I have to do. I have to just give this thing to you. I don't know what to do. It seems like my options are few. I'm trying to pray, but where are you. I am sitting here in my garage just to get warm. My marriage is over. My husband is in the house and he's upstairs. We don't talk anymore. And when we do, it's always an argument. There was a time that I really loved him, but I don't anymore. He drained it out of me, from the physical abuse right down to the mental abuse. I don't know who I am anymore, but I do know that I am your child, Lord. You created me. You are my Lord and I give up doing things Melissa's way. I give myself to you to do what is necessary. I trust you. You're the only one I trust, Lord. I forgive Kalin, Lord. I forgive him for hurting me. I forgive him.

The tears are falling down my face and they're unstoppable. My heart is broken into many pieces. I don't remember ever feeling like a failure like I do right now. Does it get any worse than this? I don't have time to worry about what Kalin is or isn't doing. I have to maintain this house for me and the girls. So, if I have to choose which bill to pay, it won't be to let the rent go, so if I have to stay longer in the dark, I will. It's getting late and I need to close my eyes and get some rest as best I can so that I am at my best on my first day at the new job. This should be over soon. By the time I save a few checks, it should be enough to get the lights back on. I'll have to wait to get a new bill to see what amount I need to come up with to restore the services.

CHAPTER 74

"Lights Off!"

---

*I*t's been five months and the lights are still off. The new bill came and it's $1,100 and because something keeps coming up, I have not come up with all of the money. I had no idea that we were using that much electricity. But now that I think about it, I can certainly see how the bill ran as high as it did. With Kalin being home all day, running both of the AC units, I can see why. During the time when things were good, I bought a Lexus and now, the upkeep of the vehicle and the gas and the tolls take everything. So, with all this responsibility, it's very difficult to save this much for the electricity at one time. Over the last few months, the car dealership threatened to take my car. I've been in 2 car accidents and now, going to therapy has become my new best thing.

Kalin and Amber hardly speak to me. It's almost as if he has turned her against me. I don't want to go to church. I feel like I'm just going through the motions. It's almost as if I'm having an out of body experience. I can't feel anymore. This hurts so much that I can't cry anymore. I don't know what to say to God. I don't know how to pray. I don't even feel worthy to go to God in prayer. Nobody has a clue that I'm living like this except my sister. Diana has been trying to get me to come to her house, but I can't do it. I don't want people to feel sorry for me. This is the most embarrassing thing I have ever had to live through. A couple of nights here and there with the lights being off, but never five months of bathing in cold water, getting dressed in the bathrooms in local restaurants and going to a job pretending as if everything is just fine. Through it all, I have to give God the praise because my performance is stellar on the job. Amber is performing exceptionally well in all of her classes. As a matter of fact, she's consistently on the High Honor Roll at school, in spite of all that we are going through in this house. I went online to check on Justice's grades and she's also on the A & B Honor roll. I'm very proud of them. Sharelle is not doing as well as she should be doing in school. My sister is having major problems with getting her to do as she should, so she has told me that I'm going to have to get her back. *What am I going to do with a child who is 8 months pregnant?*

Sharelle went out and got herself pregnant. When I first learned of it, I was devastated, but I'm finally starting to come around. I guess I might as well. How ironic it is that the baby's due date is on my birthday. What I hear is that it's a boy. Sharelle says that she will name him Isaiah. That's really a nice name.

This load is getting heavier and heavier every day. But, there is some light at the end of the tunnel. My income tax check is coming and that $3,000 will be just enough to get the lights taken care of and get some other bills paid. So, it looks like we should be out of this real soon.

I've always heard the older women in the church say that sometimes when you don't know how to pray or what to say, just moan. Tonight when I close my eyes to go before the Lord, I have no words, so I find myself just moaning and crying. I have to let the Holy Spirit speak to God on my behalf. The car is warm enough so it's time to turn off the radio and go to bed.

Later in the night, I am awakened out of my sleep for no reason at all, but when I sit up, in front of me is a tall dark shadow. *Someone's in here! Oh God! Someone has sneaked in here and they're probably looking to hurt me or something.* Afraid, I lock the doors to my car and flip on the car lights to get a better look. "Who's there?" I yell, hoping *not* to see anyone. "Is there anyone there?"

Although there isn't anyone in the garage that I can see, it feels like someone is here with me and all I can do is say, *"Protect me, Lord. Watch over me as I sleep and protect me from all evil that tries to come against me. I am your child. Please allow nothing to come against me. Give me peace as I sleep. Amen."*

The Next Morning.

"Ma, you're not gonna believe what happened last night", Sharelle tells me the next morning when she wobbles into the garage.

"How did you sleep? Was it warm enough for you with all the blankets?" I ask her first. "What happened last night?"

"I was sleep, right? And I heard a noise and when I woke up and looked up, there was this tall shadow standing in front of me", she explains. The entire time she's talking, my mouth is wide open, knowing what also happened to me in the garage last night.

"Ma, why are you looking like that?" she asks.

"Sharelle, you're not going to believe this, but I had a very similar experience in the garage. I woke up and a tall shadow was standing there in front of the car, but when I turned on the car lights, it went away", I tell her.

"Oh my God! Oh my God, Ma!! Were you scared?" she asks.

"Yeah, a little. It felt like someone was in here with me, but I just couldn't see them. So, all I did was just start praying", I say.

"I know what's going on", Sharelle says.

"What do you think is going on?" I ask her.

"The devil's giving up, Ma. Think about it. You've been in this situation for almost 6 months and you haven't given up yet. You keep giving God the praise. You still go to work and help people and the devil can't understand why you haven't quit by now", she says.

"You know, Sharelle; that sounds about right. Where did you get that from?" I ask her.

"It's the only thing that makes sense. We're almost out of this. It's almost over. We just gotta hang in here and not let the devil win. Your grandson will be here soon", she tells me, putting a smile on my face.

"Sharelle, we really need to do something about you being here like this. I want you to hear me out. I need you to…", I begin to say, but she interrupts me.

"I'm not leaving you, Ma. So, don't even think about that. We're in this together", she tells me, looking away.

"But, watching you live under these conditions like this and you're pregnant makes me…", I say, starting to cry.

"Ma, please don't cry. I'm okay. Don't worry about me. We'll get the income tax check and this is over! It's finally over!" she tells me, giving me a hug and a kiss on the cheek.

Although it's cold, I have to fill the sink with water to bathe myself before going to work. The check should be in the mail any day now and I'll feel so much better about bringing Justice back home and making it comfortable for my pregnant daughter. She decides to freshen up before we leave the house. Going to work today feels so much better knowing that after all this time living in a house without lights, heat, and warm water, it will be over soon.

Collections are going good at work today. It feels like I'm going through the accounts with a breeze. The attorneys are cooperating as they should and it feels good right now. The Controller over our department is very excited today and takes us out to lunch at Houlihan's. The food is just as delicious as I remember.

Now heading back to the office, I realize that I missed a call from Amber. It looks like she called several times. *I wonder what the emergency is. Oh God, please let this be something good. I don't know if I can deal with anymore bad news.*

"Melissa, you okay? Sounds like you're thinking?" asks Jason, my supervisor.

"Oh. No. I'm fine. Just thinking about something back at the house. That's all", I tell him.

"Anything I can help with?" he asks.

"No. Everything is okay", I tell him, anxious to check my messages.

"You know, Melissa. I have to tell you. I'm very happy that I picked you out of the 3 other people to come with me to this assignment. You're truly one of the best I've ever seen to get on the phone and collect money and to get it from attorneys. That takes great skill", he compliments.

"Thank you, Jason. I appreciate that. I give God all the glory because I couldn't do it without Him. He gives me the skill to get it done", I respond.

"Well, it earned you the top award with the highest collections in one week at this company. Do you understand that you have exceeded the totals for *their* collections team? I'm so honored to work with you. I don't know what your motivation is, but whatever it is, it's working for you, so keep up the good work", he says, pulling into the parking lot.

Now that we're back at work, I decide to go to the restroom first before calling Amber. Seconds after dialing her number, she picks up the phone right away. "Hi, Mommy", she says.

"Hi, honey. What's the problem? You've called several times. What's the problem?" I ask her.

"Mommy. Bad news. When I got home, there was a sticker on the door and it says that we can't go back into the house", she tells me.

My heart drops. My mouth drops. It feels like I just got punched in the face. I can't breathe right now.

"Mommy, are you there?" Amber asks.

"Yes. I'm here. What does the sticker say, exactly?" I ask her.

"It reads, 'Miami-Dade County Code Enforcement is placing this sticker due to a violation of code enforcement. Entering will lead to a violation of trespassing. To avoid any further penalties, please contact Aila Brunson at 305-555-1279', she reads.

"Oh my God! Code Enforcement? Where is your father, Amber? What is he doing?" I ask her.

"In the house. He saw the sticker and went inside the house anyway. He didn't say anything", she tells me.

"Did he try to call them?" I ask her.

"No ma'am, he didn't", she responds.

Why am I not surprised? Of course, he's leaving it for me to do. So, now, here I am, at work, to have to figure out what to do about this. Seriously, what do I need this man for? I know now that I'm definitely making the best decision to remove him from my life. This man offers me nothing and from the looks of it, he offers nothing to his kids either. Just one more thing!

Of course, I get the voicemail and have to leave a message. Now, when I get home, I have to figure something else out as far as our sleeping arrangements. In the meantime, I have quite a few attorneys that I still need to contact before my job is done here today. I have to keep telling myself that all of this will be over as soon as I get that income tax check. Although it's easy for me to put things in the back of my mind, this feels quite difficult today. I want to cry and hide my face from the world, but I have a job to do.

Exceeding the expectations of the company is what I set out to do and we did that today. If only I can be as successful in my personal life, life would be so much better. I have no problem coming here or to any job and exceeding, but my personal life is not exactly where I would like it to be, but I have to keep telling myself that it's God's Will. It's not always easy to see it this way.

The ride home today is bittersweet. I just got a text from Amber that a letter from IRS came in the mail. That has to be the check! Thank you God! I'm so happy that we'll finally be out of this and back living normal, but Kalin has to go. If we're getting divorced, he needs to move on and let me be happy. I need to rebuild and I don't want to do it with him around.

Pulling into the driveway, I have a much better attitude today. But, it looks like the car that was parked is now following behind me. *What now? Oh God, who can this be?*

He gets out of the car, but because it's dark, I can't tell who it is until he's standing right in front of me. I can't believe my eyes… It's Derek, the CCF social worker, who was here six months ago. *I thought we had settled everything. Why is he here now?*

"Mrs. Thomas, hi there. How's it going?" he asks, when I open the car door. *I just remembered that there are no lights in the house and he's going to see it. I'll be exposed tonight.*

"I'm good. What brings you here tonight?" I ask him.

"I got a call saying that the children are living in unsafe conditions. So, I told them that I would not mind checking it out", he explains.

"I'm going to be honest with you, Derek. We don't have lights. I've been trying to save up to get them back on, but it's going to cost over $1,000 to get them back on. We are 2 months behind and I'll have to do a new deposit", I begin to explain.

"Let's go inside", he suggests.

I haven't had a chance to warn the girls that I'm coming in with a CCF representative, so I hope the house is presentable. As soon as the front door is open, I can smell the horrible scent and I know, immediately, that it's from the fish that we ate last night. *What was I thinking? I know better than to have left the leftovers in the garbage inside the house. I know I should have put it in the outside garbage.*

Before another word is spoken, I apologize for the smell. The fortunate thing here is that Derek came around during a time when things were much better, so he uses that as his confirmation that we aren't pigs.

"Mrs. Thomas, I know that you're an excellent mother to your children, but we have to fix this. We have to get these lights back on, so the children can have clean water to drink. You need to make it warm in here, too, especially for your daughter who's pregnant", he goes on to say.

"That goes without saying, Derek. You don't have to tell me. Do you have any idea how hard it is for me to go to work and continue doing a good job knowing that my person life is in shambles? All I was waiting on was the check from IRS and that came today, so we should be just fine. I haven't opened it yet, but Amber sent me a message today to let me know the letter from the IRS came. Just give me at least a few days and this will be just fine and you can go back to whomever called and turned me in to let them know that we are just fine. It still amazes me that people couldn't just come to me and talk to me, but they had to call you instead", I tell him, making sure to shield him away from the bright orange sticker on the front door, warning us about entering the home.

"I know you will, Mrs. Thomas. Don't cry. I trust you. I have all the faith in you that you will do the right thing", he says, comforting me. Derek is on his way to his car without removing either of the children and that in itself is a reason to shout, "Hallelujah!!" I am very well aware that he could have taken the girls. He would have been well within his rights to do so.

"Mommy, here's the mail", Sharelle says, handing it all to me.

The only piece of mail I care about is the mail from the IRS. When I first glance at the piece of mail, I know right away that this is NOT a check. *Oh God, no!! Oh no!* I open up the letter and my heart is beating faster than ever before. The letter explains that they're taking the entire check because of a student loan that I owe.

"Oh God!! Oh God!! Why, Lord? Why does this keep happening to me? Why!!!!!!" I shout, without thinking of anyone watching. I fall to my knees and cry out to God in a way that I have never done before.

"Mommy! What's wrong?!!" Amber asks, starting to cry with me. She falls on her knees to join me on the floor. "Mommy, don't cry! God will provide. We'll figure it out", she says, wiping the tears away from my face.

Sharelle looks on, but leaves the room. Kalin comes to the edge of the stairs and looks down upon us and shakes his head. It sounds like he mumbles something, but I'm not interested in what he has to say right now. All I know is that I am going to work every day to come up with this money to get the lights back on, but the harder I try, the more problems I run into.

"Ok, guys, we have to all get out of this house. I have a bad feeling that someone will come here with that sticker on the door. I just really have this bad feeling", I tell everybody.

"Where will we go? We don't have anywhere to go", Amber asks, as she turns to go upstairs. Kalin has called for her. She runs to him in a flash, afraid of what he will do if she doesn't.

"I'm gonna have a neighbor take you girls and I'll just sleep in the car", I say, but before I can say another word, Sharelle comes around the corner and interrupts, "Mommy, I'm not leaving you! Wherever you go, that's where I'm going! I told you that, Ma. We're in this together, no matter what", she tells me. "Let me grab some blankets just in case we have to sleep in the car."

I wake up and see Kalin and Amber walking downstairs with overnight bags hanging over their shoulders. "Where are you going?" I say, looking at Amber. She doesn't answer, but point to her father.

"What difference does it make to you?" he asks, continuing to walk.

"Where you go *really doesn't* matter to me, but you're taking my daughter with you", I say, following behind him. "I asked you a question. Where are you going with my daughter?" I ask him again.

"Melissa, let's not do this. I don't owe you an explanation when it comes to my child. But, if you must know, we're going down the street with April's family. I've already called them and they're expecting us. I guess you can call them to see if it's okay for you and ....", he begins to say, but I interrupt him.

"No thanks. I'll find my own way, even if I have to sleep in my car", I say, finding my way into the bedroom to grab more blankets.

"Suit yourself!" he says, walking out the front door. Amber runs back to give me a kiss goodnight. I'm trying to hide my feelings from the girls, but what I really want to do is just run away, crawl into a deep hole and die just to escape all of this. As much as I want to quit, I can't appear weak to the girls because my being strong keeps them strong.

"Hurry up, Sharelle!" I yell. "I'm gonna go ahead and get in the car, okay", I say, walking out the front door to the car.

Lord, God, please!! What's going on? What have I done so wrong that's causing me to go through this? Forgive me, Lord, for whatever I've done to anger you. I can't do this anymore. I've been strong, Lord. I've been patient. I've believed you, but now this. God, you know that this check is what we needed to get us where we needed to be with the lights situation and now this happens. I finally give up, Lord. I give up!

With each word I say, I start feeling a bad taste in my mouth. It doesn't feel right coming out of my mouth to say such things to God, but something else takes over and I really do want to quit. I want to die. This hurts like nothing I've ever felt before. I am in so much pain and agony right now that I can't cry. I'm numb. Sharelle will be out here in a little bit and I certainly don't want her to see me breaking down like this. I'm supposed to be stronger than this to be an example to my girls, but I can't control it anymore.

"Mommy, you okay?" Sharelle asks, sneaking up on me without my realizing she was coming towards the car.

"Yes, sweetheart. Mommy will be just fine. This is just one more thing, that's all. We'll make it through this….", I say, before I begin to burst out in tears without any warning. Sharelle seems shocked because she has never seen me break down in this manner ever before. I bury my face in my hands and begin to sob heavily.

"I can't take this, Ma. I have to go back inside. I'll be back", she says, walking back into the house.

This moment feels like death, final death at that. This feels like an impossible battle to overcome. How could I have failed my children the way I have. They deserve better. I have to do something and I have to do something now. Sharelle doesn't deserve to be out here like this. She is pregnant and needs to be in a warm place and in a comfortable bed. I know that if my sister knew that I was going through this, she would have kept Sharelle at her house, but I don't want anyone to know. It's embarrassing enough that the neighbors know. And why couldn't they have come to me first instead of calling CCF? I thought this was all behind me. And if that check would have come today, all of this would have been a bad dream.

After praying, my heart feels less troubled, but because I don't get paid until midnight, I have no gas to move the car. It looks like Sharelle and I will have to fall asleep right here in the car in our driveway. *Lord, please watch over us and protect us this night. Allow no harm to come to us. In Jesus' name. Amen.*

"Everything's gonna work out, Mommy. You know that, right?" she comments, piling all the blankets on top of her.

"I know, Sharelle. I know it will. It just hurts right now, not knowing how to get this done. I feel like I have failed you girls horribly and I am so sorry for ….", I begin to say, but she interrupts me.

"Mommy, are you kidding? You have been the best Mother any child could possibly have. You never turned your back on me no matter how much trouble I put you through. You have had to take care of us by yourself all these years without any support from *your husband*. So, don't worry about it. Something has to come through. It just has to come through for us. I know it can't be God's will for us to live like this. I just know it, Mommy. So, get some rest. But first, can you please turn on the heat for a second?" she asks.

At her request, I turn on the heat and turn down the radio so she can sleep. Sitting here and watching her sleep, I know that I have to do whatever I have to do to get her to safety, even if I have to give up my rights as her parent to get her the help she needs. It's hard for me to close my eyes knowing that we're outside the garage sleeping in the car. It was so much better when we slept inside the garage, but since that orange sticker is on the front door, we can't trespass. My eyes are getting a little tired. That's actually a good thing because I do have to go to work in the morning. Is that my phone beeping? There's a message…and it's from Morgan. It reads, *"Good night, beautiful. I have thought of you often today and I hope that all is well with you. Love and kisses…Morgan."*

CHAPTER 75

"It's the Police!"

"Mommy, wake up!" Sharelle says. At first, I think I'm dreaming, but she continues to say it, "Mommy, wake up!"

"What is it, dear?" I ask, waking out of my sleep.

"Look, there! The police! They're shining their lights into the car. Why are they doing that, Mommy?" she asks sounding frightened.

"I don't know, sweetheart. But I'm sure I'll find out in a few minutes", I tell her.

I let down my windows and look into the eyes of Miami's finest. "Yes sir, what's wrong?" I ask.

"Why are you sitting here in this car outside this residence?" he asks, shining his light into the back seat as well.

"I live here, sir. Here's a copy of my lease agreement", I tell him, taking it out of the glove compartment and handing it to him. He looks it over, but continues to shine the lights into the car as if we're criminals or something. I'm starting to get offended by this attitude that he's taking towards us. I feel as though he doesn't believe that we could live in this community.

"Ma'am, I got a complaint from the neighbors that someone was sitting out here in front of the driveway, so we thought we'd check it out and ….", he begins to explain.

"Really? These people recognize my car and know that I live here. I have lived here for awhile now. And, all of a sudden, they don't know who I am anymore. Well, isn't that something?" I ask him.

"Well, let me check this out. I'll be right back', he says, walking back to his patrol car.

Sharelle has fear all over her face. "Mommy, why are they doing this to us?" she asks.

"Because of the sticker on the front door. Can you imagine how ugly this could have been if we had been inside the house when they came? That's why I believe it was God that showed me that we needed to get out of there", I tell her. "Don't worry, honey. We haven't done anything wrong. We have the right to be in the driveway. This will be okay", I say. No sooner than I say this, the police officer appears again at my door.

"Ma'am, is there anyone in the house?" he asks.

"No sir. There's nobody inside the house", I respond.

"Ok. I'm going to check it out. I'll be back in a few minutes." He leaves us there, while the other officer follows him inside. Within minutes, the officer comes through the garage door and motions for me to come inside. Immediately, I look at Sharelle and mumble, "Anything wrong in there?"

"No ma'am", she says. I get out of the car and follow the officer inside the house. He takes me to my bedroom, located on the first floor, and points out the candle left burning on the nightstand next to my bed. He shines the light on the candle and says, "Right there, ma'am. That is enough to take you to jail. That tells me that you've been living in this house and..", he begins to say.

"Ok. Sir, I'm not going to lie to you. My daughter comes in here to wait for me when she gets out of school and then when I get here, we leave and either go to my sister's or we get a room and I just...", I say, shrugging my shoulders and looking down, feeling as if the whole world is on my shoulder. *Mentally, I am drained right now and don't really care whether I go to jail or not.*

"You seem like a nice lady, but you can't be here in this house. It's not safe for you and your family. And with your daughter in the condition she's in, you really need to figure something out", he tells me. *This man has no idea what I have just been through over the last hour, trying to get this collections company to see my situation and somehow return my income tax to me. All they could say was, "ma'am, we're sorry but there's nothing we can do".*

"Sir, do you not think that I know that? Do you have any idea how hard it is for me to watch my daughter live like this? I'm doing everything I can. Everything! I thought I had it all figured out, but just found out that the money I was waiting on from the IRS was intercepted and we're not getting it now and …", I tell him, starting to tear up.

"I know it's hard out here, even more than before. You seem like a Christian lady and I'm sure that things will work out for you. Just keep trying, but please, find somewhere else to go because *this* is not safe", he instructs.

"Well, is it okay for me to grab some clothes?" I ask him.

"Not a problem. I'll shine the light for you."

The officer walks through the house with me, allowing me the opportunity to get some clothes for me and Sharelle. Amber already got hers earlier and Justice has enough with her. By the time I make it back to the car, I notice that the second officer is already in his car. "Sharelle, we have to leave this spot", I tell her.

"But, Mommy, my phone is on the side of the house being charged", she tells me.

"Honey, they're watching! I can't do anything. I have to leave and we certainly can't get out of here and go pull a phone that's charging from somebody else's house. I'll surely go to jail then. We'll have to figure something else out. We gotta go!" I tell her. She looks so disappointed, but what else can I tell her? What else can I do?

Against my better wishes, I drive away from the house knowing that the car will most likely give out of gas at any moment, but I don't really have a choice. I don't have time to stop by the neighbor and tell Amber goodbye because the police are making sure I leave the community. With the angels of grace and mercy blowing fumes into the gas tank, we finally make it to McDonald's just down the street. We wait here until just after midnight when the funds hit my bank account. This serves our immediate need, but the bottom line is still that I need to get my daughter to a safe, warm bed. She calls her friend, Shayla, and after speaking to Shayla's mom, they both agree that Sharelle can come live in their home until things get better for us.

Driving to their place now, my mind is completely pre-occupied with so many thoughts. Although I'm finally glad to get Sharelle to a warm place, my mind can't erase the fact that my final destination will still be this car. But, my mind is finally at ease knowing that once I drop Sharelle off, my children are all safe and warm. We finally make it to Timberlake Apartments. The community appears to be very safe and clean.

"But, Mommy, if I stay here, where will you go?" Sharelle asks, getting out of the car.

"Sharelle, I'll be fine. I'll go to Aunt D's house. I'm just so glad that we found a place for you to go to be warm. That baby needs to be comfortable tonight", I tell her.

"You know I'm concerned about you, Ma", she tells me.

"I know, sweetheart. I'll be just fine."

Shayla and her mom, Shanice, are just as cute as can be. Both of them are so warm and so inviting. "Come in!" she says, opening the door.

"Thank you so much for taking my daughter into your home", I say, walking through the front door. *What a lovely and cozy home! Sharelle will be just fine here. Thank you Jesus!* I have to admit that it feels good to be in a warm place, where the lights work and there's real heat coming out of the vents.

"It's no problem. Listen, honey, we've all been there. You just don't know! So, trust me, when I say, I understand. So, go and take care of whatever you need to do to get yourself together. I got Sharelle", she tells me. She seems so sincere. It almost feels as if God, himself, answered the door and welcomed us into this home.

"Sharelle, I think you will be just fine here and just…you know what to do", I begin to say, but before I finish speaking, my daughter wraps her arms around me and says, "I love you, Mommy!"

My mind suddenly takes me to all the nights we've shared in my car, sleeping and talking, and getting closer each day, and now Sharelle is moving in with this family. Justice and Amber are both with separate families. Everyone is finally safe. This is an unusually cold winter in Florida and God has prepared a place for each of them. Darren and Kameron keep calling me, but I can't allow my children to take care of me. This is just something that I have to go through.

"Mommy, where will you go?" Sharelle asks. "Are you going to go to Auntie D's house?"

"Yes. I'll be just fine, sweetheart. Don't worry about me. You concentrate on getting some rest because in a little bit, we're going to have a beautiful baby boy in our lives", I tell her.

Giving Ms. Shanice a hug and not letting go tells her everything that I can't. I want God to give this woman everything that she asks for because of her unselfish act of love taking in my pregnant daughter. I know that I will never forget this woman, nor this moment that we share together for as long as I live. After freshening up in the bathroom, I leave this comfortable apartment to face a cold, wintry night alone, with nothing but gratefulness in my heart. I am tired and I know that there is absolutely no way I feel like going to Diana's house tonight. It looks like I'll have to sleep in my car tonight, so I might as well get comfortable. Walmart is open 24 hours, so I decide to go inside and get some hygiene products before closing my eyes.

Back in the car, one flick of the A/C button and my car is immediately warm. 94.5FM is playing all the romantic songs and listening to this right now reminds me of what I have lost in my marriage to Kalin. Being in love with a man who is in love with me is all I've ever wanted, but can't seem to find, but thank God I haven't lost hope that it can happen for me. In my heart, I know that deciding to stay with Patrick means that I am settling for less than God's best. I don't want to make the same mistake I made with Kalin.

Dear God. Thank you so much for being with me through this storm. Forgive me for wanting to give up so easily just because I thought this would end a certain way. In my heart, I know that you haven't forgotten me, but this is hard, Lord. Hallelujah anyhow!! I know you're with me. I ask that you watch over me as I sleep tonight. Protect this car from any danger. Send your angels to surround this car. Thank you, Lord, for all the people who have contributed to our family to make sure they are safe. I give you all the praise and glory and Honor that's due. In Jesus' name. Amen.

CHAPTER 76

"Love From London?"

I never thought I would wake up with the McDonald's arch shining through my window, but this morning I did. The fact that it's so bright is an indication that it's time for me to go inside to freshen up for work. My clothes are neatly stretched across the backseat so I take them in my hand, along with the bag I packed with personal hygiene items, and walk inside to prepare myself for work. I know I should feel somewhat embarrassed that the people behind the counter watch me walk in with my clothes, but I don't have time to feel embarrassed. I won't be productive at work if my mind is centered around the fact that I slept in my car last night.

Getting dressed as I would if I were in my home, I leave the parking lot heading to work with a song of praise in my heart and thanking God that He has provided shelter for my children. Kalin is no longer my concern. The last I heard, he went to Orlando to hang out with some of his family. It doesn't surprise me that he has left without making peace with his children. As important as even this is, I can't afford to lose my focus right now.

Driving the interstate, I notice the roads are somewhat wet, but I have driven on this interstate hundreds of times. As crazy as it sounds, I actually feel well rested this morning. Although I slept in my car last night, I am at peace with myself and with God.

Traffic is bumper to bumper this morning. The roads are filled with big trucks, little trucks, big cars, and little cars. My sister is on the phone with me wondering what happened to me last night and why I didn't come over to her place. Trying to reassure her that I'm okay, the truck in front of me is braking so I need to do the same, but when I hit my brakes, my car doesn't come to a stop. "Oh my goodness! My brakes aren't working", I mumble to my sister.

"What do you mean they're not working? Girl, you need to be careful out there", she says. Without telling her, I start to panic a little, but when I hit the brakes again, my car still doesn't stop and now, I'm extremely close to the black Ford truck in front of me. Before I know it, I've lost complete control of my Lexus and it's doing what it wants to do right now. It's spinning out of control and I see my children flash before me. My phone flies out of my hand. *Is this it? Is this how my life will end? Am I really going to die here today and like this? This can't be what God intends for my life. I can't believe that the plan is for me to die here like this today.*

Before I know it, my car is facing the oncoming traffic and something else has taken over. It's almost as if God is moving everything out of my way. I can't explain it at all. But, in one instant, it's almost as if the angels move my car out of danger and onto the shoulder of the road. I am visibly shaking out of control. A man is standing on the other side of the street waiting for traffic to move to get to me to see if I am okay. He finally makes it over to me. "Ma'am, are you okay?" he asks.

"I think so! I think so! Oh God! What just happened? Oh my God!" I shout, not stopping for air.

"It's okay. You're okay. You're going to be okay. Nobody hit you", he says, while trying to calm me down. I start looking around frantic that I was hit. In the middle of this bumper to bumper traffic, not one single car hit me! *How can this be? This is nothing short of a miracle. God is with me even in a car accident!*

"You're the guy in the black truck, aren't you? I hit you, didn't I?" I ask.

"Listen, I could care less about the truck. I'm just glad you're okay. That truck can be fixed. No big deal!" he tells me. He helps me out of the car and we stand there until the police come. Within fifteen minutes or so, the police arrive and take our insurance information and we're both on our way, except I drive away from this accident scene in a car that's not so safe anymore. I have some decisions to make. The money that I need to turn the lights on will now have to be used to repair the brakes and I will have to trust God to provide for us like He's been doing.

I don't think I ever remember a time being so afraid to drive my car. Finally making it to work safely, I decide to have a car repair shop pick it up. All I can think about is how different this could have been if I had

Sharelle with me. This could have easily aggravated her pregnancy. I dread thinking of what could have happened.

My phone rings and it's Cynthia on the other end. "Girl, are you okay? You scare me, Melissa. Every time I turn around, you're getting into an accident or something", she tells me.

"I know, right? But at least I'm okay every time. The devil is really trying to take me out of here, but he can't. Believe me when I tell you that if he could have, he certainly would have taken me out by now. But, look at God. He was right there. Oh my God! He placed me safely on the side of the road and I know it was nobody but God that protected me."

"Wow! Well, thank God! Do you need me to pick you up or anything?" she asks.

"No. I'll be okay and I …", I begin to say.

"This is not the time to be proud, Melissa. Let me help you. Why don't you just come to my house? It's okay. You're not putting me out. How long have we been friends?" she asks.

"I know all of that. I just can't right now. I just can't. Please let me do what I gotta do, Cynthia. I just need this time alone. If it gets too rough, I'll let you know", I tell her before hanging up. *I know she wants to help, but this is a time when I feel that I need to be alone. The divorce, the financial problems, and the loneliness at times gets to me and I don't want anyone around while I'm going through this. Honestly, right now, I just want to hear God's voice. I need to hear God's voice for my life. This is so hard and I don't think that friends will be able to get through to me at this point.*

I stop for gas, but before I drive off, I need to take a moment just to think about my next move. In the middle of my thought, I'm somewhat distracted because just across the street from where I'm sitting right now is a hotel. *Where did it come from? It sure looks tempting right now.* It's not that far away from the job and I can get a good night's rest. I decide to stop in and see how much a room is, but it doesn't really matter because it's going to be one of the coldest nights in Florida and I need to be warm. The hotel is pleasant and for the first time in several months, I get to have a good night's rest. My computer is beeping at me, so before going to bed, I decide to check my messages. It seems as if I have received quite a few messages from Morgan. What an awesome way to end my day. I begin reading at the beginning and by the time I am done with his messages, my eyes are full of tears. *He wants to visit me. Really? Why? What is it about me that interests this man? If he only knew how raggedy my life is right now!*

CHAPTER 77

"People Make Mistakes."

"God bless you and your family, Ms. Melissa. The checks are approved and you can pick them up now. I'm just so glad that we were able to help you and your family. There comes a time when we all need help like this. Do you think you can make it to the Agency by 2? They close early on Fridays", he tells me.

"I'm so grateful, Derek. How is it that you were able to get this approved?" I ask him.

"You must have been praying because we never assist with payment over $150. They just don't do it, Melissa. But, when I went to my supervisor, he said that he would make an exception in your case. So, you should definitely be thanking God right about now", he tells me.

"Oh, I most certainly am, Derek. But, I really do appreciate you. You have gone over and beyond the call of duty to help us and I won't ever forget this. Thank you, thank you, thank you", I tell him over and over again.

"You're very welcome. You're a great mother to your children and I have no doubt that the girls are safe with you, but, in the future, if you should ever get into this situation again, please reach out to CCF and they'll be able to help you", he encourages.

I can't help but think that this is also the same agency that put me through hell for so many years. I was angry that the neighbors called CCF and they ended up being the solution to a problem that I have had for months. Go figure!!

"Okay. I will make sure to do that", I tell him.

Our numbers look good at work, so my supervisor approves my request to leave work early today to go and take care of the requirements needed to get the lights back on. Because of God's mercy and favor, my family can finally move back into our home and be together again. The girls are all so excited. For this special occasion, I decide to pick up dinner for us at Boston Market. Justice's friends decide to come home with us to help clean the house. *So, this is what it feels like to win!*

Suddenly, the night is interrupted when the phone rings and it's Kalin wanting to come back home. What shocks everyone is that my heart turns to compassion and tells him that he can come back to live in the house. My intention is not to get back together, even though I know it's what he wants to do. He wants to salvage our marriage, but he's still not willing to do what is necessary for the family. For whatever reason, Kalin is having a hard time understanding that one of his duties as the head of the household is to provide for his family. Unbelievably so, he has gone to great depths to show me in the Bible that it's *not* his responsibility to have to work and provide for his family.

I'm not surprised when my phone rings and the caller ID says "Diana".

"You're going to do what?!!!!" Without my knowing it, Sharelle has called my sister, Diana, and told her of my plans. She is livid, to say the least.

"Diana, I can't just leave this man hanging like this. He doesn't have anywhere to go and I just can't do that", I tell her.

"Melissa, this man did nothing to help you and the kids get back in this house. He left ya'll to figure everything out. He didn't care whether you lived or died and now that everything is better, he wants to come back. You're crazy! You're such a sucker for this man. You really are and I don't know why. Is the sex *that* good?" she asks.

"It's not that at all. I just feel bad knowing that he doesn't have anywhere to go and is living from pillar to post. I mean he *is* Amber and Justice's father. It's just until he gets himself together. I'm not trying to be with him. As a husband, I have no desire to be with Kalin. That's done, but my heart still cares for people. That's all there is to it", I explain to her.

"Sure, Melissa. You have this thing for this man and I know it. Your children would be so much happier with him gone. Didn't you tell me that he even called his daughters the "b" word? I mean, come on now!" she says, sounding frustrated.

"People make mistakes, D", I tell her.

"Whatever, MeMe. Everyone knows that you're going to do whatever you want to do, whether it makes sense or not", she says. "You like this vicious cycle of dealing with Kalin's crazy behavior. I see that you're just not tired of losing. What's it going to take for you to realize that this man is just not the man for you?"

"Ok, sis. I gotta go now. Kalin's bus arrives around 6 tomorrow and I need to get some things done first", I tell her. "I don't want to arrive late picking him up from the station."

Diana and I hang up the phone and as much as I hate to admit it, she's correct about what she's saying. It really is time for Kalin to start being accountable for all the things that he needs to do in his life. We are currently in a divorce right now and it doesn't get any more real than that. I know his intentions are to try to change my mind, but I'm just not in love with him anymore. With all that's happened between us, there's no way I am remotely interested in continuing in a marriage with him.

When I tell the girls that Kalin will be in town tomorrow, they seem to be somewhat excited. I have to admit that I'm a little shocked with Amber and Justice who don't seem as thrilled to have him come home. Sharelle doesn't waste any time expressing her opinion of the situation. She's totally against Kalin coming back into the home. She feels that it makes sense that we be separated from one another now that we are going through a divorce.

It's been a long day and it's time for bed.

Dear Lord. Thank you. Thank you. Thank you. I am so grateful to you Father for what you have done for my family. We praise you and honor you Lord. Bless my family. Build us up where we're weak and make us stronger day after day. Give us a spirit of forgiveness for anyone who may have wronged us. Teach us how to love your way, Lord. These and other blessings we ask in your son Jesus' name. Amen.

CHAPTER 78

"It's a New Day!"

"*I* can't do it, Kalin!" I shout at him.

"Woman, you done lost yo'mind! You better start this car up and let's go home!" Kalin yells even louder.

"I can't do this to my children, nor can I do this to me. We have been through enough and I'm not about to put them through anything else. For the last couple of months, things have been so much more peaceful and I ....", I begin to say, but he interrupts me.

"You screwing around with that white boy again, ain't you?" he asks. "When are you going to learn that he's going to stick by his kind? That man is not going to be with you, Melissa. You've got to be out of your rabbit behind mind. What's wrong with you?" he shouts.

"That's none of your business! Who I decide to be with is no longer your concern. You had your chance to be concerned and that's gone now. If I want to be with Patrick, that is my choice. He's more of a man than you'll ever be, Kalin. So, you need to stop calling him 'white boy'. That's played!" I tell him.

"Whatever you say, Melissa Thomas. You are ...", he begins, before I interrupt him.

"And stop calling me that. To you, I'm no longer Melissa Thomas. I'm divorcing you and will bring back my maiden name, one that I respect", I say.

"Oh, it's like that, Melissa Thomas. I need for you to get this straight. You are still my wife. Do you understand that?" he asks.

"I'm only your wife on paper, Kalin. You have chosen to disrespect this marriage and let's say, I'm tired of it. I know in my heart that I deserve better than this. I can't be the woman that God has called me to be if I continue to accept less. I can't do it anymore. I can't do you anymore. This is the end of the road for us, Kalin, and I …", I explain to him.

Kalin and I go back and forth for at least 20 minutes until he finally removes his luggage from the trunk. He realizes that I'm not playing this time, so after getting his luggage, he walks around to my side of the door and looks at me strangely and calls me the "b" word. *At least he's consistent!*

"Please understand that I have to finally live for me and for my children. We have suffered long enough! I just can't live with you anymore, Kalin. You have hurt me over and over and you don't get to do it anymore! I'm done with you and I….", I shout, forgetting about everyone around me. *Oh no! Amber is with me and I can only imagine what she is thinking. Does she feel like running after her father or what?*

"You b****!" Kalin shouts. "You a trip!" he says, charging towards my car. "If you don't get your black a** back here. How dare you leave me out here! Where am I going to go, Melissa?" he shouts.

"It's time for you to start figuring everything out for yourself, Kalin. I'm not your mother. It's not my job to take care of you. We were supposed to take care of each other and you never got that! Let someone else do it for you. I tried. I can't do it anymore. If I stay with you any longer, I'll be dead", I say to him, starting to cry.

"Dead? You selfish b****!" he yells. "I've never seen anyone as selfish as you. All of these years that I sacrificed for you and your ungrateful kids. I took them in and ….", he says, getting louder.

"Took us in? Pleaseee! We took you in! You moved into my home. You drove my cars. You lived in houses that I paid for. What are you talking about? We took you in, Kalin!" I say to him.

'I oughta knock the …", he says, picking up a rock from the ground.

"Please do it! Please do it, Negro!" I shout boldly. I notice the guy seated nearby rises to his feet.

Kalin notices it and says, "Oh, I see! So you wanna call the police, right? That's what you wanna do!" he says, walking away from my car.

"If I have to. Yes, I will! Please do me that favor and hit me!" I tell him.

"I don't have time for this bull***! Good riddance, Melissa!" he says, walking away.

Kalin has no idea that my sister is being entertained with his drama. She has been on the phone the entire time listening to him go on and on about how he feels about me. I'm sure that she's shocked to hear Kalin speak to me this way because of how often he has declared his love for me in the past to her and my entire family. Now, everyone will see that we don't have the perfect marriage after all.

"Mommy, can we just go?" Amber says quietly. "I've never seen Daddy this angry. Why does he call you that ugly name? I thought we weren't supposed to talk like that?' she asks.

"Oh honey. Don't worry about that. It doesn't matter what people call you. Don't ever get moved by that. Don't ever let someone else's opinion of you shape the way you think or speak. I don't care what he says anymore. His words can no longer hurt Mommy. We're going to move forward from this and have a much happier life", I tell her. "I have to do what's best for my children and right now, this is unhealthy for any of us.

"I feel sorry for Daddy. I can't believe this, Mommy", she says, sounding sad.

"Sweetheart, I'm so sorry that you had to witness all of this. Our fights were only getting worse and worse. This is no way for anyone to live. You all don't deserve this and neither do I. We'll be okay. Your father will be okay. He's hurt right now, but he'll find his way. He has to find his way. It's not my responsibility to worry about where he'll land. Do you understand sweetheart?" I ask her.

"Kinda Mommy. I'll miss him", she admits.

"Of course you will, but I promise you that I'll never keep you and Justice from being a part of your father's life. If he ever chooses another woman, you and your sister will offer her the respect that she deserves. You got that?" I ask her.

"Yes ma'am. I got it."

"Great! Let's go home, sweetheart. Think your sisters would like for us to bring home some ice cream?" I ask her.

"I'm sure they'd love that", she answers.

Kalin has taken his luggage and is now out of sight. I don't know where he went. For one brief moment, my heart stops. I've never stood up to Kalin before and never have I said "no" to him in this way.

"Ma, where will daddy go tonight? He doesn't have anywhere else to go", Amber says, observing Kalin walk out of our sight.

I know, honey. He'll find his way, but I can't allow him or anyone else to disrupt our home ever again", I say to her, looking through the rearview mirror. She looks like she doesn't understand what just happened, so I feel it's best to turn off the car and give Amber my full attention.

I can't help but notice the sadness in her eyes. "Mommy, did we cause this?" she asks.

"Honey, of course not! Why would you say that? Your father and I will always love you and Justice. We're your parents, but it has come to that point when Mommy and Daddy will never live together again and I need you to be okay with it", I tell her.

"I see it now, Mommy. We understand. Let's just go home", she tells me.

Amber and I leave the train station knowing that our life will never be the same again. Tonight begins a new chapter in our lives. When we finally make it back home, Justice runs out to the car thinking that her father is inside, but instead, it's just me and Amber. Our silence says it all. The new chapter begins.

Does Melissa's pain gain her anything?
Torn 2: Passion, Pain & Promise.

CHAPTER 79

"I Give You My Word."

"*M*ommy, wake up! Somebody's trying to send you a message!" Justice shouts. "Your computer has been beeping for like the last 3 minutes or so."

It's such a beautiful day outside and as much I want to stay in bed, I need to get up before I allow myself to get depressed. Thinking about what happened 2 months ago when we left Kalin at the train station still haunts me sometimes. I often wonder if I should blame myself for him getting sick and having to be hospitalized. Knowing that he will soon bounce back and meet someone else gives me hope for his future. I can't think about meeting anyone right now. I get this feeling deep down inside that my troubles aren't over and if the dream I had last night is any indication of the trouble before me, I need to stay prayed up.

"Mommy, it's still doing it!" Justice yells from the front room.

"I'm coming! I'm getting up now!" *This is probably Kalin. He's been stalking us ever since that night. I was hoping that he would have moved on by now.*

I finally make it to my office and to my surprise, it's actually the London cutie. It's Morgan Smith. His last words are that he's waiting. *Should I let this go or should I engage him in conversation? Do I have anything to lose at this point? Maybe he can cheer me up.*

Melissa: "*Hello, Morgan. How are you? So nice to hear from you.*"

Morgan: "*Hi beautiful. I am doing fine. Just thinking about you.*"

Melissa: "Really. What were you thinking?"

Morgan: "How I'd like to get to know more about you."

Melissa: "Really, what do you want to know?"

Morgan: "If I can be your man."

I have to admit that I don't ever remember a man being this upfront about what he wants. During our conversation, he explains that it's just part of their culture to let a woman know what his intentions are for her so that there aren't any misunderstandings. Morgan doesn't waste any time in letting me know that I am the woman he chooses, not only for himself, but for his daughter, Anita.

We continue to talk well into the night and surprisingly so, he's able to keep my attention. His conversation is so intellectually revigorating that I forget all about the time or any plans that I *may* have had today. I almost didn't notice that Amber just strolled into my office, strolling around as if she's looking for something.

"Mommy, you've been on that computer all day!" she finally says.

"I know, honey. Mommy is talking to some friends from Alabama", I lie.

"I'm just glad to see you smiling. They must be saying something pretty funny!" she jokes.

"Yeah, yeah, they are", I tell her, jumping back into my conversation with Morgan.

He finally tells me that someone really special wants to speak to me.

Little Girl: *"Hello."*

Melissa: *"Hi there. How are you? Who's this?"*

Little Girl: *"This is Anita. My dad has told me all about you."*

Melissa: *"Really? What did he tell you?"*

Anita: *"He said that you may be my new mummy."*

Melissa: "He did? Wow! How do you feel about that?"

Anita: "I have never seen my daddy so happy!"

Melissa: "Is that right? Does it bother you that I'm black?"

Anita: "No, it doesn't. My Uncle Reo is married to a black."

Melissa: "Is that right? You and I will get along just fine."

After talking for awhile, Anita and I connect on so many levels that it's hard to explain. I can tell that she's somewhat sad about the loss of her mother, who she never got a chance to meet. I have a feeling that I'll be in this child's life for quite some time. Her mother died giving birth to her ten years ago and since then, it's just been her and her father. She's messaging me a final message to let me know that her father wants his chance to speak to me now.

Morgan and I talk for a little while longer until we both realize how long we've been talking and mutually agree that our children probably need us at this point. In London, it's bedtime, but here it's dinnertime. He has to tuck Anita in to bed and it's time for me to cook dinner for my girls. When I walk in the kitchen, the girls are busy rummaging through the freezer looking for a snack before dinner and as much as I can, I try to avoid any questions about the mystery person on the computer.

"Ma, who have you been talking to all day?" Justice asks when she finally notices that I'm in the kitchen.

"A friend, sweetheart. Just a friend", I tell her.

"A friend, huh? So, what are we having for dinner?" she asks.

"What would you *like* for dinner? Feel like some chicken and potatoes?" I ask her.

"That sounds good, Mommy!" she says, prancing off. She seems to be happy with this choice.

After tonight, Morgan and I continue to have these same types of conversations. We spend more and more time chatting and sending pics back and forth. I have to admit that I'm really starting to enjoy this attention that this Brit is givng me. I've never experienced anything like it. He seems to be very attentive to things that interest me.

Just as planned, he comes online at the time we previously agreed. Once we move past all of the normal conversation beginners, he asks me whether we attend church or not.

I have never met a man who was so concerned about whether I was going to church or not and this is his third time asking me.

"Why is it so important to you that I go to church?" I ask him, almost defensively.

"You always talk about God, but you never talk about worship. I'm just curious as to why that is", he states.

"I just don't go, Morgan. Is that a *problem*?" I ask.

"I want my woman to worship at church on Sundays just like I do. Promise me that you'll find a church and go this Sunday", he insists.

"Ok, sweetheart. I give you my word that I'll do that", I tell him.

CHAPTER 80

"There Has to be Something Else."

"So, what do you want to do, Mrs. Thomas?" Mr. Abney asks, tapping the top of the desk.

"I've had plenty of time to think about this. Let's go for it. I want full custody of the children, I want spousal support, child support, and alimony. I want him to take part in the responsibilities of what's still due from the house", I finally say, all in one breath.

"Wow! What a change of heart! A few months ago, I couldn't get you to return my calls", Mr. Abney tells me. "And now, you want it all!"

"People change. Circumstances change. Kalin has moved on with his life and so have I, but it doesn't mean that he won't fulfill his responsibilities to his children and to me", I say, with more confidence than ever before.

"That a girl!" Mr Abney says, giving me a high five. "If you don't mind me asking, what caused this change of heart? Why didn't you see this before?"

"I was blind. I was settling. I was ill-informed. I thought that this is what God wanted me to do. I thought that it was my responsibility to be his wife for life even if I had to die to do it. I gave him another chance and he hurt me again. His words just don't mean the same anymore. The butterflies that were once in my stomach are all gone. I have to live for Melissa now. I know it may be a little difficult to get used to being alone, but I was already alone anyway. He didn't support me like a husband should. He didn't treat me like a husband should treat his wife. Let's just say I had a moment", I explain.

We sit for a couple of hours filling out the proper paperwork for court. We have to expedite the divorce hearing because word has it that

Kalin met someone on Facebook and is getting ready to leave town. I don't want anything to prolong this divorce hearing.

"I think that's everything, Mrs. Thomas", he says after I sign the final document.

"You won't be saying Mrs. Thomas too much longer. I'm glad that the law allows for me to get my maiden name back. I never thought I'd call myself Melissa Williams again. It'll take some getting used to, but I think I need a new start. Get away from the Thomas name and start over", I tell him.

"Are you sure this time?" he asks.

"Yes. I'm 100% sure this time. I've found my peace with this divorce. I feel as though Kalin and I have done all we can do in the marriage. We've grown apart and now I can finally talk about it. I really do wish him the best and pray that he finds the happiness that he's looking for in a woman", I say proudly.

"I'm proud of you, Melissa. I know this can't be easy. Gotta give it to you, though. You gave him a chance to prove his love to you", he tells me.

"Yeah. But, I know that God must have a better plan for me. I have faith in that. I really do. In the meantime, I'll just keep working this job until He gives me another plan", I say, not knowing how we'll make the ends meet.

Mr. Abney and I finish up for the day. He says he'll give me a call in a few days with the court date. If all goes as planned, this will be the last day I'll be married to the man I thought I would be with for the rest of my life. It's the last day I'll be Mrs. Melissa Thomas. But now, every time I look at Amber and Justice, I'll see a tiny portion of the man I once loved. And over time, I'll learn how to deal with this loss. In the meantime, I'll get to know who I am and allow God to heal me so that I never have to be bitter and harbor hard feelings towards Kalin or an innocent man when the time comes.

Driving by all the tall buildings in downtown Miami, I can't help but remember the day that Kalin and I drove to the City Hall to get married. We were so in love and nothing could stop us from getting hitched at the altar. I remember having a stomach ache on that morning, but I realize that it was just my nerves. Nobody knew that we were doing this. Nothing mattered more to me on that day than being his wife for life. I remember just how inseparable we were. We'd make love at the drop of a dime. But somewhere along the way, we became different people. I have accepted the fact that it's all over now and I have to find a way to move on, knowing that God has a much better plan for my life.

Dear God. Thank you. Thank you, Lord, for the wonderful years that I experienced real love with Kalin Thomas. I don't hate him, Lord. Please help me to keep the hatred out of my heart. I pray for him, his safety, his dreams, and his life. Be with him, Lord, in all that his heart desires. I pray that he will be a good father to Amber and Justice. I pray that they don't have to suffer as a result of what is to come with me and their father. Forgive me, Lord, where I've fallen short in this marriage. Teach me better ways so that I can be the kind of woman, the kind of wife that you would have me to be. In Jesus' name, Amen.

CHAPTER 81

"Do You Need Time to Cool Off?"

"**D**idn't I tell you, D?" I tell Diana, after reading the letter from the Department of Juvenile Justice.

"Tell me what? What did you tell me?" she asks me.

"I told you that those folks were wrong for what they did to my daughter and the STATE of FLORIDA agrees with me. This letter right here proves it", I say, jumping up and down with the letter in my hand.

Diana grabs the letter from my hand and reads it for herself. "You did it, Melissa!"

"*We* did it, girl! That's what I'm talking about. Like I always say, it ain't nothing wrong for standing up for what's right. Do you know what this means?"

"Yeah. It means we should sue them for what they allowed to happen to Sharelle. She was just a child", Diana says, shaking her head.

"That's right, sis! I can't wait to tell Sharelle about this", I say, not realizing that she is actually walking through the door.

"Tell me what, Ma?" she asks.

"About this letter that just came in the mail from the STATE of FLORIDA and….", I begin to say, but she interrupts me.

"About the Facility and what happened?" Sharelle asks.

"Yes, dear. Of course."

"I won't help you do anything with that. Isn't it bad enough the man lost his job? Why can't you just let it rest? You always trying to sue somebody!" she yells, storming out of the room.

"What's wrong with *her*?" I ask Diana, now shaking my head.

"Just let her be for now. She'll eventually come around", Diana tells me.

Instead of running behind Sharelle, we decide to sit down and enjoy our dinner. I didn't know how much I needed my sister until I realized that today would have been my 18th year wedding anniversary with Kalin. I can't help but think about him today. It's not that I want him back, but a little part of me wonders how he's doing these days. My thoughts are quickly interrupted by Diana.

"So, tell me what's going on with Patrick these days?" she asks. "I don't hear you talk about him at all anymore."

"Because there's nothing to tell. After the divorce, I spent a few nights with him, but it just wasn't the same anymore. His busy lifestyle is just too much for me. Don't get me wrong; we're still friends, but I'm no longer interested in having anything serious with him."

"I can't believe what I'm hearing. You're not interested in having a relationship with Patrick? He must be seeing someone else" she comments.

"I don't really know, D. He said that he's married to his work right now. That's all I needed to hear. I'll just take it slow from now on because….", I say, but Diana interrupts me.

"Slow? Come on, Melissa! You know who I am? That's right! Your sister. You don't know what it means to go slow and you and I both know it", Diana says, laughing before she completes the sentence.

"True!"

"So, tell me about this Brit", she demands.

"What do you want me to tell you? I ask her.

"How is that going?" she asks. "Are they different from American men?"

"We're getting along better than okay. He's a sweetheart, D, and I think I'm falling for him", I answer.

"Hahahaha…what happened to *taking it slow*?" she asks, laughing harder and harder.

"I know what I said, but there's something about him, D. It's something that I've never connected with before, not even with Patrick", I explain.

"Go for it, sis. If he makes you happy, go for it", she advises me.

It's been several weeks since Morgan and I first started talking and honestly, we've talked about everything and I've made sure to tell him the good *and* the bad, but he doesn't seem to mind the faults that I have. In so many ways, I think it's cute when he acts a little jealous. From our conversations, I can tell that he takes a personal interest in anyone who befriends me on Facebook by the questions he asks when I get a new "friend".

Sharelle just walked back in the house without so much as saying one word to me. I guess this is where I allow her *time to cool off.* I honestly thought I did a good thing by making a complaint against the Academy and getting the state of Florida to agree that they were inappropriate in their behavior in how they dealt with a minor, but it's obvious that she has a totally different agenda than I do. It gets more and more difficult to understand these teenagers and what's going on in their minds.

"Sis, what are you thinking about?" Diana asks.

"Sharelle. What has gotten into her? I thought she would be happy that we can get some justice behind this mess and ..", I begin to say, but Diana interrupts me.

"That's what YOU thought! Do you know what she wants out of it, if anything at all? Have you stopped to think that just maybe some of this hurts her, MeMe?" she asks me. "You should really try talking to your daughter before you just fly off the handle witht this", she advises me.

"You're right. I assumed that she would want to ....", I begin to say.

"And therein lies the problem", she says, tapping me on the shoulder.

CHAPTER 82

"Let Me Pray For You."

"*D*, did I ever tell you what it is that I really want to do with my life?"

"No. You don't talk much about doing anything other than what you do. I'd love to know all about it. Tell me!" she insists.

"You know I went to college for Communications, right?" I tell her.

"Yes. I knew that. And?" she asks. "What is it?"

"While all of my other friends were pursuing teaching degrees, I wanted to be a broadcaster", I admit to her.

"I can see you doing that. Why did you stop? Why'd you give it up?" she asks me.

"C'mon! You know why!!" I say.

"Kalin. Did he *really* hinder you from completing school?" she asks.

"He really did. He didn't see why it was so important to me. He thought I should have just been happy to have a job at all", I tell her.

"I knew he was selfish, but that just tops the cake. I really don't see how you stayed with this man as long as you did", I tell her. "He didn't do anything to support you. So, what are you wanting to do now?" she asks.

"I'm thinking about going to that Broadcasting school I auditioned for several years ago", I tell her, anxiously awaiting her response.

"I think it's a fantastic idea! Seriously, I think you should go for it. These are the things you always wanted to do, but Kalin didn't let you", she reminds me. "Don't let him win, sweetie."

"So true! And now that he's not around to stop me from doing things that are dear to my heart, I think it's time for me to do something for Melissa", I say, agreeing with her.

On my way to work, I call to get the number to the Connecticut School of Broadcasting. Favor is on my side today because unlike several years ago, they now have a program for me to be able to get in and pay as a self-pay, without having to deal with the high interest student loans. Not having to audition again also means that I'm set to start the class right on schedule.

Now that I'm talking to Morgan, going to work, attending church regularly and going to my broadcasting class, it means that I'm finally experiencing the "happy" that I've been missing for years. And on the plus side, being *this* busy doesn't give me much time to think about the divorce hearing that's coming up in two weeks. Things are finally going like I want them for once. Having the support of the man in my life is totally different than what I'm used to having. Morgan supports me going back to school and oftentimes gives me his feedback on the assignments that I prepare for class. I feel so comfortable sharing my dreams with him. He's so positive and it makes me strive for even more.

By the time I make it to class, Morgan and I finish our conversation. My classmates notice that I have a different kind of energy tonight, but they have no idea why. We have to do a "pretend" news broadcast and the teacher picked me to be one of the anchors. After a long night, I drive off away from the parking lot, saying goodnight to my classmates. Driving home, I notice right away that something isn't right with my car. It almost feels like it wants to stop. I know it's not the gas because I filled the tank on my way to class. *What can this be? Oh God no! Please Lord don't tell me it's the tire. This can't be happening, not here and certainly not now. I already have the spare tire on the car and nothing's open at this hour to get a tire.*

Slowing down on I-95, I pull onto the shoulder of the road and get out to see what's going on with my car. Almost immediately, I see that it's my tire. It's as flat as a pancake. Because of the traffic going back and forth, I decide that it's safer for me to get back into the car and hope that someone will stop and help me to get home. Several cars stop to help, but realize that it's impossible to get my car off this road tonight because I need a new tire. I have two choices. I will have to either catch one of these rides home and leave my car on the interstate, risking it to be towed, or I can just stay with my car and first thing tomorrow, get someone to take me to get a tire. I realize now that I need to use what little life on my phone batter y I have just to call the kids.

"Hello, Mommy. Where are you?" Justice asks.

"I'm stranded on the side of the road, but I'll be fine. Looks like I'm gonna have to spend the night in my car tonight", I tell her.

"But, why Mommy?" she asks.

"I have a flat tire and the spare tire that I would normally use for this type of an emergency is already on my car. Make sure the doors are locked and set your alarms to get up on time for school. Mommy will be just fine", I tell her.

"Mommy, why don't you just get Auntie to come get you?" she asks.

"I can't leave my car. If I leave it here, it'll get towed and I can't afford that again. I just spent over $200 last week on tow charges. So, please, sweetheart, do what Mommy needs you to do", I say.

"Okay, Mama, just be safe", she tells me.

I have no doubt that the girls will be safe. Oh no! I just remembered that Morgan is expecting me to come online when I get home. It doesn't look like I'll be going home anytime soon, so I might as well message him now and let him know.

> Melissa: "Hello Morgan. Are you there?"

> Morgan: "I am, my Queen. How are you?"

> Melissa: "I am well. Thanks for asking."

> Morgan: "Is everything okay?"

> Melissa: "No. I'm stranded on the highway and won't be home tonight."

> Morgan: "You won't! That sounds dangerous. Why can't you get some help?"

> Melissa: "I will, but not until tomorrow morning."

> Morgan: "Where will you sleep?"

> Melissa: "I'm going to sleep right here in my car."

Morgan seems to be very concerned that I may have to sleep in my car tonight. I try to make him feel at ease about the situation, but it doesn't necessarily work. He's convinced that I should just leave the car and go home. He's mentioned all that could go wrong if I choose to sleep in the car.

Morgan: Sweetheart, let me pray for you, ok.

Melissa: Certainly. I'd appreciate that.

Realizing that there isn't anything he can say or do to change this situation, Morgan begins to pray and I immediately feel at peace. All the stress that I was feeling before has somehow disseminated. It's not as important to me as it was before. Morgan's voice alone is enough to make me feel like I'm floating on a cloud. His British accent is so soothing to me and to hear him praying for me makes me feel so safe. I don't know when the last time I've felt this way. Kalin hasn't prayed for me since we've been married. I don't know where this will go, but this moment earns Morgan quite a few brownie points in my eyes.

CHAPTER 83

"It's Finished!"

"*A*re you ready for this, Melissa?" my sister asks while I'm getting dressed.

"I'm as ready as I'll ever be", I tell her.

Today is the day that I'll say goodbye forever to Kalin as his wife. It's finally here and I don't know how I feel. Did I do the right thing? Was he the man that God gave me? I wonder what's going on in his head. Is he thinking about me today? How will I react when the Judge announces that we are divorced?

"I just want you to know that I'm extremely proud of you, sis. And don't you worry, I know that God will bring a man into your life who will treat you the way you truly deserve to be treated", she says, comforting me.

"I know that, D. I really do know that, but can I be honest?" I say to her.

"Please do. What's up?" she comments.

"I never thought it would have come to this with Kalin. We were so much in love at one time. When he got out of jail, he was never the same. The man I married didn't come out of that jail cell, but someone else did", I tell her.

"People change, Melissa. Kalin probably didn't understand what was going on with him. I might as well tell you now, Melissa", Diana says, walking towards the front door.

"What is it?" I ask her, looking quite concerned.

"I spoke to Kalin on yesterday. He actually called me to apologize for hurting you", she tells me.

"What!!! You have got to be kidding!" I say, surprised.

"Yes. But, he also said something else, Melissa", she says, opening the car door.

"What did he say?" I ask her.

"He admitted to me that he has moved on with someone else and that she's going to be in the courtroom with him today. He said that he just didn't want to catch you off guard and look as if he was trying to be disrespectful", Diana explains.

"Cool", I say.

"How does that make you feel, Melissa?" she asks.

"I'm fine. Really. I'm fine", I tell her.

"I know that look, Melissa. And it's okay if that saddens you a little. It means that you have a soul", she tells me.

"No. I'm fine. I knew he would. I didn't know that he would so quickly, but I knew he would. He can't be by himself for long", I say, getting into the car.

The ride to the courthouse is a quiet one. When we arrive, Diana finds a parking spot closest to the front. At this time of the day, most of the cases have already been heard, so it's no wonder we're getting a close parking spot. I look around, but I don't see Kalin's car at all. It could be that he's in the car with his new woman.

The divorce hearings are held on the 5th floor and within seconds, we're getting off the elevator. I'm so glad that we didn't run into Kalin on the elevator because that would have been a little awkward. *I don't know what I'm supposed to feel when I see Kalin. Will I look sad or confident? I'm aiming for the confidence option. I don't want him to ever think he's getting to me because the truth of the matter is that I wanted the divorce in the first place.*

"He's here, Melissa. Don't look now", she warns me.

I slowly look up and our eyes lock, but immediately, I see the woman that's holding onto him so closely. She's not letting go. I don't know if she's doing that because that's what she does or if she's doing that to prove a point to me. In some ways, I feel sorry for Kalin because she's acting a bit childish.

There's a slight smile between the two of us, but we eventually find our seats and wait to be called. Diana is keeping me engaged in conversation, which takes my mind away from every thing, even though deep down inside, my heart is breaking that it had to come to this. Mr. Abney just arrived, with his briefcase in his hand, ready for battle if the need arises. "How's our girl?" Mr. Abney asks, sitting in the chair next to me.

"Our girl is good", I say to him.

"She's doing fabulous, sir", Diana chimes in.

"Well, the good thing here today is that I spoke with Kalin's attorney and I made sure he was aware that the most important thing for you today is to get custody of your girls, but you better believe I let him know what I'm working with if he tries to fight me", Mr. Abney tells me.

"And, what did he say?" I ask.

"Based on his attorney, he said that all will be okay", he answers.

The bailiff walks out to the waiting area and announces for the "Thomas" family to proceed to Courtroom C. Kalin's friend and Diana aren't allowed in the courtroom. Kalin, the attorneys, and me all get up and head towards the courtroom, making limited eye contact. This feels so awkward. I've had two children with this man, but yet, I find it difficult to look at him today. We're finally seated inside the courtroom and the proceedings get under way. I can tell that Kalin is just as uncomfortable as I am.

"Are you both sure that this can't be worked out?" the Judge asks, looking over his glasses, like my Mother does when someone is about to get into trouble.

"Yes, we're sure, Sir", I say, and Kalin nods in agreement.

"Very well, then, let's proceed", he announces.

"If it's okay with both attorneys, I would like to speak directly to both Mr. and Mrs. Thomas", the Judge announces.

Both attorneys are in agreement.

"Mrs. Thomas, it appears as though you petitioned the court to dissolve this marriage of what, 18 years", he states. "And it's marked here as irreconcilable differences."

"That's correct, Sir", I mumble.

Out of my peripheral vision, I can tell that Kalin is staring at me and I'm guessing that he's looking this way to get some kind of reaction from me. *I came here today to be divorced and that's what I want, so it's imperative that I remain focused.*

"And, sir, how do you feel about this? Do you object?" he asks, directing his question at Kalin.

"If this is what she wants, then it's what it will be. I won't beg her to stay if she wants to leave. I always told her that whenever she's ready to go, she can do just that", he says, matter of factly.

"I can see here that you didn't sign the papers initially, but later agreed to do so", he comments.

"Yes, I realized how unhappy she was in the marriage", Kalin says.

"And just how unhappy were you, Mrs. Thomas?" he asks, looking my way.

"Very, your Honor", I say, looking away. "The man sitting here today is not the man I married. I don't know who this man is. Jail changed him and turned him into a bitter and angry person that I could no longer live with and ....", I begin to say.

Kalin interrupts me and says, "Yeah, and I guess that white man was better for you. That's who she wanted, Sir. When he came into the picture, it changed everything. She was sneaking around with him and leaving my kids at home by themselves and ...", he says, not taking a breath in between.

My mouth is wide open. I can't believe he's turning things around in here to make it seem as if it's my fault. God knows I don't want to bring out all the dirt in here today. I don't know why he can't just let this be a simple divorce and let us get out of here and call it a day.

"Sir, Kalin is turning this thing around to make it seem as if my responses to what he brought into the marriage are the source of this divorce today. Kalin abused me on our wedding night, your Honor. For 18 years, I have lived with that secret. He bashed my head into the headboard in our room. He abused my children and I can't say that I was much help for my children because in so many ways, I allowed him to do it. I allowed him to separate me and my children for years. This man sitting right here got another woman pregnant while he was married to me. She aborted the baby when he wouldn't leave me. This man had another extramarital affair, which sent me to a mental hospital for 24 hours. His abuse continued and I hid it for years. The kids didn't know, my family didn't know, and in some ways, I believe I forgot and looked over so many things with Kalin and I just want out", I say, starting to cry.

The bailiff hands me a tissue. My emotions have gotten the best of me. I guess I needed to get all of these feelings out so that I can deal with them once and for all.

"I'm so sorry, Melissa. I never knew that I hurt you this much. I'm ashamed of myself for what I did to you", he says, starting to cry.

This court hearing has everyone standing around in tears, with this sight of another marriage that failed. It's a sad thing when families are torn apart through divorce. Everything and everyone is affected by it. This failed marriage is no exception.

Knowin that he would do it eventually, the Judge brings the business side of it back when he says, "So, Mrs. Thomas, you're asking for the court to grant you full custody of the children", he announces. "Mr. Thomas, do you object to this?"

I hope Kalin doesn't contest this part because I'm prepared to discuss more details of the sexual allegation charges that were filed against him. I hope his lawyer was smart enough to tell him to bow down and give me my children.

"No, Sir, I don't object to this. She's a very capable mother for our children. I have no doubt that they will be well taken care of with Melissa", he says.

"Okay. She's also asking for support of the children and herself. Do you object?"

"No, Sir. I don't object."

Kalin and I sit in silence as we watch the Judge sign paper after paper, looking up every now and then. He doesn't say a word, but continues flipping through the papers. He finally speaks.

"I don't know what really went wrong here in this marriage. I'm assuming that there had to be *some* good times between the two of you. I'm not happy to hear that there were some abusive times, extramarital affairs, and those kinds of things going on. You two have children that are affected by all of this madness. Mrs. Thomas, you need to rebuild those relationships with your children and that's why I'm awarding you sole custody of the two children you have together, Amber Thomas and Justice Thomas. In regards to child support, Mr. Thomas, you will pay $90 per week for them and you will pay Mrs. Thomas $150 per month for alimony support.

Kalin is gasping at this point. He can't stand the thought of having to pay me one dime and deep down inside, I already know that he probably won't pay this anyway. Kalin has never been that responsible when it comes to his family.

"And, Mrs. Thomas, you may now regain the use of your maiden name, Williams", he announces. "Copies of this entire file can be found on the third floor. If nothing else, you may be adjourned", he says, standing up from his chair.

It's over and I don't know how I feel. I thought this moment would feel a little differently. I feel like I failed miserably at something and that's never a good feeling. But, for the first time in my life, I feel free. I feel like I can breathe. Did Kalin really have me imprisoned for all these years? I never felt free to think for myself or do things the way I really wanted to do them.

I walk out of the courtroom and my sister is standing right there waiting on me. She reaches out and gives me a much needed hug.

"So, how did it go?" she asks. "You okay?"

I can't speak right now because if I do, I may start crying and there's no way I want to cry here because Kalin may start to think that I'm crying over him and the ending of our marriage", I admit.

"Ok, sis. Let's get out of here. Want some lunch?" she asks.

"Yes. That sounds good. Let's go to Maggiano's. I feel like some Italian food. Does that work for you?" I ask her.

"Sounds good to me."

Diana and I leave the courtroom and I feel like I have just left all my heartache, all my worries, right here at the Miami-Dade County courthouse. I feel free to roam, as they say on the airplane after they give you the okay to take off the seatbelts.

"What's on your mind, sis?" Diana asks.

"Oh, nothing, sis. I'm just thinking about how many divorces actually go on in this country and why. Like, why do people promise God to love one another forever and then we don't?" I ask her.

"People change. It's just that simple. Kalin changed. You changed. Things happen. You're not starting to feel guilty, are you?" she asks.

"I'm just as responsible as he is. Right now, I'm thinking what I could have done better at to have been a better wife. Perhaps, I should have cooked more, or not work so hard, or...", I begin to say.

"No, ma'am. It's not about to go down like this. You're not about to sit here and do this. No way, Melissa! You and Kalin started out with the right intentions. It's not your fault he didn't want to work. He made you think that he had all these dreams and you thought you were marrying a man who wanted to go somewhere. But, it turned out that all he wanted to do was have you take care of him. There is so much better out here for you. You'll see. You're gonna be okay. I know it's new, but you'll get used to it. And look at you. You're *already* starting to talk to someone else who makes you feel like a woman. The way Morgan makes you feel is how a woman is supposed to feel. Take your time and enjoy it", she encourages.

"You know, sis? I think you're right. As of matter of fact, I know you're right. This is it. I've shed the last tear I will ever shed over Kalin. It's finished. Right here and right now", I say, wiping the tears away.

It's really over! I am divorced! I don't feel any differently than I did months ago. Or for that matter, years ago! There has been a disconnection between me and Kalin for a long time now. This pain that I feel in my heart is not something I ever want to experience in my life ever again. I wouldn't wish this pain on my worst enemy, but I know that with God all things are possible. With God, I will be able to deal with this pain and move on with my life, successfully.

CHAPTER 84

"Starting to Fall."

"*M*elissa, you got the internship!" Laura tells me through the phone.

"You've got to be kidding!" I shout.

"No, I'm not kidding! They loved you and want you to come to Orientation next week", she tells me. "Melissa, do you know that we have never had a graduate make it to WELS? You're the first!"

As excited as I am, I don't know what to do here. This is the moment I've been waiting on my entire life and now that it's here, I don't know what to say. I don't have a job right now and as much as I need to need to work to keep the roof over our heads and food in our bellies, I need to do this internship for me. I'm going to have to trust God because internships aren't paid. God said that He would supply all of my needs, so I'm going to have to put that to the test. God will provide a way. I just know He will because deep down in our hearts, we already know that we'll never see that money from Kalin.

Well, I do have that money I just got from the last car accident I had. It wasn't but $16,000, but it should be enough to keep us afloat just until this internship is over. I have to go for it here. I have to!

"Tell her I'll be there!" I respond.

"You will? You sure, Melissa? Don't make a fool out of me. My name is on the line and if you don't show up, it's gonna make me look bad, as well as this school. Do you need more time to think about this?" she asks me.

"No! I'll be there. This is my dream. This is something I've wanted my entire life and I'm not about to let it slip me by, even if I have to live off beanie weanies", I say. We both laugh.

It's official. In two weeks, I'll start working as an Intern at WELS, the #2 news station network in Miami. And my assignment? The newsroom. I'll get the opportunity to work alongside the top news anchors, creating stories, writing, and going out on news outings. This is the chance of a lifetime and I'll certainly make CSB proud.

A real job just came in, but I have turned it down just to complete this internship. I think it's high time I trust God for the things that I really want. When I was the wife of Kalin Thomas, going back to school was a no-no. Kalin didn't believe that it was necessary. I couldn't discuss a possible internship with him because Kalin would remind me of all the reasons I need to be the one working. But, the good news is that I get to make my own decisions now because Kalin is no longer here to control them.

Diana is ecstatic when I give her the news. She's always supported me in everything I've ever done. She seems to think that God will open up doors for me now that Kalin is out of the way. On more than one occasion, she's told me that she feels as if Kalin is the reason that some of my blessings have been held back.

"Girl, watch and see how God's gonna bless you now. You remember that dream you had about the snake that was on your neck? Remember what I told you?" she asks.

"Yes, I do remember. You said that it was someone close to me that's not in my corner", I say.

"That's right. The man you were sleeping with was your enemy. I believe that with all of my heart. He was keeping you from pursuing your dreams and going any farther than he wanted you to go. But thank God, he's gone now and God has opened this door for you to gain more knowledge and insight into the TV News World."

"Wow! You really think so?" I ask her.

"Yes. I do. But, what happened with Kalin is behind you now. Go for it, sis! God will make a way", she encourages.

Two Weeks Later.

The Orientation goes over very smoothly and from the first day, I can tell that I have just entered into a totally different level than ever before. I feel at peace with the decision I just made because the Bible says that when we delight ourselves in the Lord, He will give us the desires of our heart and I just have to completely trust Him now. I believe that everything I have gone through has led me to this very moment.

Oh no! Is that Martha Sakowitz over there? Say it isn't so! She's even more beautiful in person. And Tony Minnows, the weather guy. Wow! *Am I dreaming or what? There is no way this could have been possible except God bring it. Thank you Jesus!*

After several weeks of writing, practicing, and planning, I'm finally ready to do my broadcasting demo and by the graciousness of God, one of the cameramen has offered to put it together for me. We meet at the station on a day that he's not scheduled to work and after just a couple of hours, I am leaving the television station with my very own broadcasting demo to showcase to the world what type of reporter I can be.

I can't wait to get home to send it to YouTube, Facebook, and Twitter. Hopefully, I will get some type of feedback on it and just maybe, this will produce some positive results for me.

Walking in the door, I just know there will be fires to put out because Kalin called the girls today and upset them with his news. I don't know why he would ever discuss his sickness with Amber and Justice. He knows how they feel about him. Whether our marriage worked out or not, he is still their father and they love him like there is no love.

"Mommy, why did you make Daddy leave? That's probably why he's sick", Justice says, as soon as I walk into the kitchen.

"Sweetheart, what are you talking about?" I ask her.

"That's what Daddy said! He said that if we had still been a family, he would not be living on the street and he wouldn't be sick and ...", she continues.

"Justice!! Stop it!! Those things that your father is saying are simply not true. Don't listen to it, sweetheart!" I say, putting down my laptop bag.

"But, it's what he said, Mommy. Didn't he say it, Amber?" she asks, looking around for confirmation.

"I don't care what he said. It's not my fault that your father is living in the shelter. That's a choice he made and we won't discuss it anymore", I say, angry at this point.

"Sorry, Mommy. We didn't mean to upset you. It's just that when he called, he was crying", Justice tells me.

"I know, sweetheart. It's not your fault. I'll call and talk to your father. Does that make you feel better?" I ask her.

"Yes, Mommy. It does."

After putting the girls to bed, I decide that it's time for me and Kalin to have our conversation about the divorce and why he would call here today to upset our daughters. I want this conversation to go quickly because I'm not that interested in speaking with him for a long period of time, but there has to be boundaries.

"So, what do I owe this pleasure?" he says, after picking up the phone.

"What makes you think this is a pleasurable call?" I ask him.

"Just hoping", he mumbles. "You know you miss me girl."

"Listen. I don't want to take up too much of your time, but the girls told me that you called the house today and…", I begin to say, but he interrupts me.

"Yeah, and I know that they were a little…", he begins to explain.

"Upset…Yeah! They were a little upset because of what you told them. I'm really sorry that you're living in a shelter and all, but that is not their problem. You're a grown man and you need to handle your business, but don't ever call my house and upset my children again. Not cool, Kalin!" I tell him.

"I didn't mean to do that. I'm sorry. How are they doing? How are you doing, Melissa?" he asks, changing the subject.

"They're doing fine and so am I, Kalin. Thanks for asking. And what about you? How are you really doing?"

"Honestly. I'm not doing well at all, Melissa. I found out that I have diabetes."

Silence immediately comes over the phone line. Neither one of us says a word. I don't know what to say. In a way, I almost feel responsible. *Could this be because I put him out forcing him to live in shelters? What happened to his friend? Where is she?*

"I don't think I've ever known you to be this quiet", he tells me.

"This is horrible, Kalin. I'm so sorry", I say.

"Melissa, I didn't realize just how good I had it", he tells me. "I took you for granted all those years and I just…" he begins to say.

"Kalin, don't worry about it. It's the past and I've forgiven you and myself for all of it. Instead of being lovers, now, we are just parents for Amber and Justice", I say.

"Ok. That sounds like a plan!"

Kalin and I talk for at least another 30 mintues or so until I realize that my computer is beeping at me. Morgan is online and is ready to chat with me.

"Well, I have to go now, Kalin, but it has been wonderful to speak with you. Please take care of yourself. We'll talk again soon", I say, just before hanging up and clicking over to Morgan.

>   Morgan: *How is the most beautiful woman on earth?*

>   Melissa: *You're so kind. I am fine. How are you?*

>   Morgan: *Missing you. That's how I'm doing.*

>   Melissa: *Aaaah. How sweet! But guess what?*

>   Morgan: *Tell me.*

>   Melissa: *I 'm coming to London. Because of my internship at the TV station, I get a chance to visit BBC and where is BBC?*

>   Morgan: *It's here, honey! You're coming to London? Oh God! Wonderful!*

Morgan and I continue to talk about spending time together in London and all the places he wants to take me while I'm there. He sounds like he really wants to spend the rest of his life with me. We've talked about everything over the last few months. I still have to pinch myself because he, so boldly, is starting to tell people that we're in a relationship. Now that the divorce is final, Morgan and I have listed our relationship status as being "in a relationship" on Facebook. It was all his idea. It proves to me that he's not embarrassed or ashamed of our relationship. People are starting to wonder if this is real or not. I'm still getting used to the idea.

"Melissa, I love you", he says, totally taking me by surprise.

"Morgan, I love you too", I say, without thinking about it.

There's a sudden silence that comes over the phone between us two. I know that he's thinking about the comment that we both just made to one another.

"There's no turning back, Melissa. I want you. I know that I've made the right decision to choose you as my woman and mother for my daughter", he tells me.

"How can you be so sure?" I ask.

"God answered my prayer", he tells me.

This man prayed to God to see if I am the one? Wow! I didn't think people did that. I think I'm really falling for him.

CHAPTER 85

"What a Coincidence!"

"Ma, telephone!!" Justice yells, from the family room.

"I got it!" I say, picking up the phone. "Hello."

"So, what does it take for a man to get a phone call these days from an old friend?" the person on the phone asks.

Is this Patrick? It can't be. But, it is!

"Hi, Patrick", I say, sounding a little reserved.

"How have you been, beautiful?" he asks.

"I've been just fine, Patrick. How are you? How's your health?" I ask him.

"That's why I'm calling you. I'm so excited and I wanted to share my news with you first. I'm completely fine now, Melissa. The treatments that I got when I was in Connecticut worked! There's no sign of cancer at all!!" he says, sounding excited.

"Oh God, Patrick! That's excellent news! I am sooooo happy for you! I know that you must be....", I begin to say, but he interrupts me.

"Yes, I'm grateful to you, Melissa", he tells me. "You have been a good friend to me during the roughest time in my life. You loved me even when I didn't love myself and you were always there to give me support", he goes on to say.

"That's nice of you to say, Patrick. But, why such a turn around now?" I ask him.

"When I was in Connecticut, the doctor that I had there helped me see things more clearly", he says.

"Really? What did he help you see more clearly?" I ask him.

"That when you really love a woman, you should tell her, you should appreciate her and cherish her", he answers.

"Wow, what a special doctor you had? Where did this guy come from?" I ask him.

"London. They called in a specialist from London who was more familiar with my sickness and he was certainly no ordinary doctor. There was something different about him. He seems to really care about his patients and I don't think I'll ever forget him", he tells me.

"But, what does this have to do with me, Patrick? I haven't talked to you in months", I tell him.

"I love you, Melissa, and I want you to give me a chance to prove it to you. I want to mak e room in my life so that we can start working on us. I've had time to think about this and after talking to the doctor I met in Connecticut, he helped me see what's most important and I had to call you. You came to mind and I ....", he continues, but I stop him.

"Patrick, I've met someone. His name is Morgan and we have gotten to know each other over the last several months and I really care for him", I begin to share. "We're pursuing a more solid relationship and I just....", I say, noticing the silence over the phone.

"Morgan? That's funny. That's the name of the doctor that I met in Connecticut. What a coincidence!! This just can't be the same person because this guy I'm talking about is from London", he tells me.

"Patrick, the guy I'm talking about *is* from London. We met on Facebook. But, can this be, can this be the same person? There's no way!" I say, surprised.

"I'm sure it's not the same guy. This guy has a little girl that he calls his little Angel", Patrick adds.

"Don't tell me her name is Anita or I'm going to scream!" I tell him.

"Her name is Anita! Yes, that's her name, Melissa. So, are you telling me then that the man who helped me heal is the man who now has your heart?" he asks.

"It sounds like it. Everything seems to point to the fact this this man is the man I've been talking to for months", I respond.

"Oh my God, this can't be true!" he says, with more intensity. "I can't believe this!"

"I can't believe this either. What a coincidence!" I tell him, shocked.

"I'm starting to feel that for my healing, I had to lose something", he tells me. "If I had only done the right thing, this man would have never had a chance to speak with her.

"I really don't know what to say. I'm just as surprised as you are, Patrick. I can't believe this! Wow! Wow!" I tell him.

Patrick doesn't seem too interested in the conversation anymore. He has become extremely quiet now. All I can think about is that Morgan never told me what his occupation was. We never talked about it. I guess there was no reason to discuss it just yet.

"So, are you serious about this guy, Melissa? He lives in London. What kind of relationship are you having with a man who doesn't even live in the United States? What kind of life is that for you?" he asks. "I'm right here, ready to love you the way that you deserve to be loved", he says.

"We had our chance, Patrick. Did we not?" I ask him.

"Melissa Williams, I love you. I will always love you, sweetheart. Nobody deserves to be happy like you do and if he makes you happy, then go for it. But, answer my question, please."

"What question, Patrick?" I ask.

"What kind of relationship is this if you're living here and he's living there?" he asks again. "I want you, woman!"

"Patrick, please don't do this to me. I waited for months for you. It was a decision that you made to shut me out the way you did. I cried, I prayed, and I couldn't go on for months because of what you did to me. You didn't even stop to think of what it was doing to me that you left the way you did", I begin to explain.

"Baby, I was wrong for that. I never should have done that", he says, beginning to cry.

"Please don't, Patrick. You're going to make me cry", I tell him.

Before I know it, we're both sitting on the phone crying over our failed relationship. I'm sure that he's thinking of all the good times we've shared with one another. It's so unfortunate because Patrick was the best man I've ever loved, until now. Morgan fills me up with everything I need and I have to admit that I'm looking forward to seeing what else he can do. Our living arrangements are no issue at this point, even though we have already discussed that I would move to London to be with him.

"I don't want to lose you, Melissa. I need you in my life, baby. Please don't leave me now that we can be together. Your divorce is final and I'm no longer sick. I am the man for you. Nobody will love you the way I do, baby. Please don't leave me, Melissa", he begs.

"You're only saying this now. You have no idea how much I've cried over you. And now that you realize that you've made a mistake, now that you realize what you've lost, you want me to drop everything and run into your arms. Baby, it's too late! I've met someone else and I really like him. He was right there with me through the divorce and was a good friend to me. He's an amazing man! I can't begin to tell you how awesome he is and I ....", I say, but Patrick interrupts me.

"I have to agree with you, Melissa. He really is a nice man. I've met him and I think you'll be happy with him. I'm hurt because I really care for you, but I wish you the best in all you do because if there is ever a woman who deserves to be happy, it's you", he tells me.

"It means a lot to me to hear you say that, Patrick. Thank you so much for saying it", I tell him.

Patrick and I talk for a while longer, but he and I both know that there will never be a me and him ever again. There was a time when Patrick had my heart, but he lost it. He didn't take care of me like he promised he would and now, I have to go for something better, something that completes me, something that keeps me from twisting and turning all night.

After all of that, we finally say our goodbyes and thankfully so, it doesn't feel weird, but it feels peaceful. I'm at peace knowing that I did everything I could do to make it work with Patrick, but he decided to grow up and fly right just a little too late. It surprises me how men don't realize what they have until they see them with someone else.

"Take care of yourself, Melissa. I'm always here if you ever need me. You don't have to be a stranger", he tells me.

"How's your son? How's he doing these days?" I ask him.

"He's doing just fine. He's in Spain for the summer with his mother, but I'll tell him that you asked about him."

"You do that. Well, I have to go now because I'm leaving for London in a couple of days and I need to pack and make sure I have everything", I say.

"You're going to London to meet him?" he asks.

"Yes, I am, Patrick. I actually became an intern at WELS and part of the program is for us to visit BBC, which is headquartered there in London and I'll get to see him while I'm there. He's going to show me around the city and we'll get to spend more time together", I explain.

"Being from Scotland, I can tell you that you're going to love it there. We were supposed to go to London, Melissa. Remember?" he asks.

"How can I not remember? That was the day that my heart was shattered into tiny pieces", I tell him, sounding a little sarcastic.

"I'm so sorry about that, baby. So, I guess that's it, then", he says. "I guess this is the end of me and you. It's over between us, right?"

"Patrick. Baby", I say, wiping the tears away.

"Well, I guess I'll have to let you go then. My heart is broken. I won't ever forget you", he says.

"I won't ever forget you, either, Patrick", I tell him.

"Goodbye, Melissa."

"Goodbye, Patrick."

Once his phone clicks and I hear the dial tone, my heart sinks. I know that deep down in my heart, the feelings that I have for Patrick will never go away. He made a very strong impact in my life. He's the first man who has ever made me feel like a real woman. He was there for me when I was going through the worst time of my life with Kalin. His support got me through all of that. For that reason alone, I won't ever forget him. We shared the most special intimate moments that I've ever had in my life. The way he kissed me, touched me, and made love to me is like none other. I'm almost tempted to call him back and tell him that we can work it out, but Morgan is not dong a bad job of making me feel special and wanted. *Am I taking a chance with Morgan? Do I know if his feelings for me are real or not?*

Hearing Patrick tell me the things that he did about Morgan makes a huge difference in how I view Morgan now. Knowing that he's a real person is half the battle. What's baffling is how Patrick has met him before I have. *I can't believe Morgan is a doctor. No wonder he didn't tell me. I guess he just wants me to love him for who he is and not for anything else. He just doesn't know. I could care less that he's a doctor. I just really care about him and that's all. I'm looking forward to spending time with him alone in London. It's funny how London is where I was supposed to go in the first place, but with Patrick. It's funny how things come around like they do.*

CHAPTER 86

"Who's That on the Phone?"

"*M*elissa, do you have everything?" Diana asks, walking through the house one last time.

"Yes! Yes, I do, big sister. You know you act more and more like momma everyday" I say.

"Yeah, well, we have to be like that with you because you know you'll lose your head if it wasn't attached to your body", she comments.

Diana and I walk though my bedroom one last time just to make sure I haven't forgotten anything. I can't help but remember a few months ago when Diana was here doing the same thing when I was scheduled for my trip to London with Patrick. Scouring the room, it looks like I did a good job of packing. During this time of year, the weather is very cold in London, so I've packed for the weather. I'll finally get a chance to wear some of the boots that I don't get to wear here in sunny Florida. I can tell that the kids are excited for me. They have always just wanted me to be happy. Surprisingly, they help take my luggage out to the car.

"Mommy, please don't forget to bring us something back", Justice says, with Amber close by chiming in. "That's right, Momma!"

"Girls, now you know I won't forget! When have I ever gone out of town and didn't bring you something back?" I ask them.

"Ok, girls, give yo' momma a hug because we need to get on the interstate. It's usually crowded during this time of the day and we don't need anything to hold up this trip", she says, playfully hitting me in the side, as if she knows I have another agenda for this trip.

Amber, Sharelle, and Justice watch me and Diana drive down the driveway. They're standing in the front window waving goodbye until we're completely out of sight. Within 15 minutes, we're on I-95 heading for the Miami International Airport. Traffic is cooperating well with us and based on the traffic report, we shouldn't run into any delays.

"And you're sure you want to do this, Melissa? This is a big step, girl", Diana tells me after moments of silence in the car.

"Yes, sis, I'm sure. I've had more than enough time to think about this. He makes me happy and I make him happy and we're good together. He's who I want, Diana. Honestly, I can't wait to get off the plane and run into his arms", I tell her.

"Well, we're here. And on schedule, I might add."

Diana and I park the car in the '1hour parking' section. People are rushing back and forth getting luggage out of their cars. Children have this look of expectancy and excitement on their faces. The airport staff is busy checking people in. I realize that I need to put my phone on "silent" and as soon as I do, I get a text message that changes everything. The wind is knocked out of me. I can't help but gasp after reading this message. Diana notices me right away.

"Melissa, what is it?" she asks. "You look as if you've seen a ghost", she comments.

"I can't speak right now. I just can't....", I say, but she interrupts me.

"What is it? Who is that on the phone?" she asks, looking worried and scared.

"Diana, why? When will I ever be happy, sis?" I ask her.

"MeMe, you're scaring me. Who is it and what did they tell you?" she asks, reaching for the phone.

Diana grabs the phone away from me and immediately covers her mouth with her hand.

TO BE CONTINUED.

"People don't care how much you know, until they know how much you care."

-*Theodore Roosevelt*

ABOUT THE AUTHOR

*E*lla Johnson, native of Monroeville, AL, has acquired a great passion for writing, one that has moved millions of people across the world. Her passion for inspiring others is birthed from the burdens she's had to carry in her own life. Being the owner of both Mahogany Motivations LLC and Women at Work, Ella still finds time to participate in activities that meets the needs of those less fortunate.

At the tender age of eight years old, Ella began public speaking, which has graduated into motivational speaking. Ella's talents for broadcasting are also displayed on her Blog Talk Radio Show, The Mahogany Bronze Hour. Her most meaningful contribution in society is through her nonprofit company, Women at Work, where they have become known for Feeding 100 Families in her hometown of Monroeville, AL.

To purchase the entire Torn Series, go to www.torn-the series.com. If you would like to receive regular updates about appearances, book signings, or any motivational speaking engagements, please follow us at www.facebook.com/torntheseries.

Printed in the United States
By Bookmasters